A Lifetime of Terror

A McKinney Brothers Novel

P. J. Grondin

Loconeal Publishing
Amherst, OH

Originally published by P.D. House Holdings in 2011.

Loconeal books can be ordered through booksellers,
Handcar Press Distribution, or at
www.loconeal.com
216-772-8380

ISBN 978-1-940466-08-8

First Loconeal Publishing Edition: 2014

McKinney Brothers Mystery Suspense Novels

A Lifetime of Vengeance
A Lifetime of Deception
A Lifetime of Exposure
A Lifetime of Terror
A Lifetime of Betrayal

Dedication

This book is dedicated to the men and women who work in the nuclear power industry. They work tirelessly to deliver safe, clean, and affordable energy in an ever changing regulatory environment. The constant scrutiny by agencies of the federal, state and local levels of government, and by the industry's own internal oversight organizations places never-ending pressure on every nuclear worker to perform their jobs without error. It is a thankless job, but one that the American Nuclear Worker takes seriously and performs exceptionally well.

Acknowledgements

My dear wife, Debbie, and our children deserve medals for their patience and their feedback as the story was taking shape, then being reshaped, then reshaped again. Thanks also to my niece, Victoria, for allowing me to use her name in the story. Her suggestion for the role of that character helped direct the storyline for the refinery scenes. Heartfelt thanks go to my brother. Patrick, for his critical review of the manuscript. His suggestions for changes to key areas of the manuscript were invaluable in improving the flow of the story.

PROLOGUE

June 1967

Heat radiated from the desert floor in all directions as the sun beat down on the parched earth. The approaching aircraft rose out of the valley from the west towards the Golan Heights. As they passed overhead, the ground to the north of the Sea of Galilee shook. The roar of the jet engines caused the young Syrian to cover his ears. The formation was so close to the ground that he felt the heat from the engines' exhaust, the fumes filling his lungs, the whirlwind of sand stinging his skin. He followed the jets heading east into Syrian territory, his family's territory. He saw the missiles hanging under each wing. It had begun.

Just the week before, when his parents thought they were alone, he heard his father say quietly to his mother, "We cannot match the military might of the Jews. They will come with great force. Their American-made jets and weapons are superior to the Russian MiGs. I pray to Allah that we will put aside our hatred for the sake of our children."

His mother had said nothing in reply, but her eyes filled with the sadness of generations of Syrians. She'd begged her husband to move the family to Damascus, away from the border with Israel. Away from the hatred, the fighting, the oppression. But her words fell on deaf ears.

"This is our home. We will stay."

So they stayed. The day that she and her husband feared came upon them like a sandstorm and the young man was witness to his father's prophecy.

Those fateful words now echoed in his ears along with the thunder of the jets passing to the east. Moments later, the fifteen-year old heard the high pitched scream of the missiles as they darted from the attacking jets. The exploding fuel tanks of the Syrian MiG fighters, as they sat motionless on the ground, sent shock waves along the earth's surface. Shielding his eyes from the low morning sun, he saw the black plumes of smoke moments before he heard the muffled explosions. After another moment, the ground trembled again under his feet. He imagined the screams of men as their lives were snuffed out in an instant, either from the shock waves of a bomb blast or from the incinerating heat of a fireball.

From his position near the highest point in the Golan Heights, he looked to the northeast out over the lowlands towards Damascus. Then he looked to the southeast and the smaller cities as more explosions erupted at his homeland's air force bases. The complete annihilation of the Syrian Air Force was happening before his eyes. He slipped into a trance as another vision of his father came to mind. *We're not ready to defend our families. Our planes have no spare parts. Our pilots do not have the experience needed to survive real combat missions. They will be slaughtered.*

And his father would know. He was a jet mechanic at the military air base west of Damascus, north of Al Kiswah. He was trained by Soviet mechanics, the experts who knew the MiG jets inside and out.

With the early morning sun low over the horizon, the fifteen-year old placed a hand over his forehead to shield his eyes. He watched the area near the base where his father worked, and saw the plume of black smoke rising into the sky, casting a shadow over a large area west of the great capital. He feared the worst; that his father's visions of his own death had come to pass right before his eyes. He cursed the Jewish pilots and their American made weapons. He felt like crying, but tears would not flow. He was a man, after all.

Only hours later, his fears would be realized, as news of the attack on the air base filtered back to his hometown of Al Qunaytirah. Their small home was filled with his mother's shrieks of anguish. For hours, her sobs consumed her and her family.

But what he thought were his worst fears only proved to be the beginning of his real-life nightmares. Just days later, while sitting in the same spot overlooking the valley to the east and Al Qunaytirah to the north, Israeli tanks thundered into town, destroying everything in their path. The mighty Syrian Army retreated, leaving the city and its civilian population defenseless. A blast from an Israeli tank obliterated his family's home, killing his mother and two sisters as they hid, praying for Allah to deliver them from their enemies.

He knew what he had to do. The words of his mother came back to him. "*Move to Damascus, away from the border, away from the hate.*"

It was too late for his family, but not for him. He fled his hometown. He could move away from the border, but hatred was embedded in his being. As he walked along the road towards the great city, the hatred was displaced by a hunger, not for food, but for the blood of his enemies.

On the road to Damascus he met two people who would change his life. Salma Nidal, his future wife, would become his guidepost. Imam Khidir Khadduri, would become his mentor and financier.

July 1982

It had been a good day for Javier Lopez. It was late in the afternoon and not quite as hot in the South Texas desert as it had been earlier. He intended to go straight home and avoid the bars that would siphon his money away. He always managed to keep the majority of his pay from his job tending horses at the Double T Ranch, east of Del Rio. His mother and sister depended on him for support back in La Purisima, Mexico. Javier worked for an American ranch owner who empathized with the Mexicans who risked their lives crossing the Mexican-U.S. border to find work and support their families. The rancher knew he was taking a risk. If he were caught, he would be prosecuted. It would surely cost him a pretty penny, but he might also get jail time if some judge decided it was time to make an example of someone. But it was possible that most judges had illegals employed as well. It was all a game of chance.

Javier was a hard worker. He spent over sixty hours laboring each week, even though he was only being paid minimum wage for forty hours. He wanted his employer to know that he could depend on him. His mother needed him to survive ever since his father had died in a bar fight in Del Rio. That was another reason Javier steered clear of the local bars. He feared he would end up dead, like his father. Javier didn't want to die at such a young age. After all, at sixteen, he'd barely experienced life. All he knew was hard work and the church. When he wasn't working, his mother insisted he attend church services or help the young priest by working around the rectory.

Javier got a ride to within a mile of the border fence then walked the remaining distance in a dry wash. The area was low and hidden from most anyone's view. He was able to make good time while staying out of sight of the local population. Most folks in the area were tolerant of the Mexicans passing north by morning and south by evening. They understood they were working, doing the jobs that most U.S. citizens wouldn't do. The work was either too hard or didn't pay enough, or both. Either way, it was beneath them.

But the Mexicans would do it. They weren't happy doing the work, but they were happy to get the pay. Even at minimum wage, they could make more in one day in the United States than they could get in nearly a week in Mexico. That was if they could find work at all.

Javier Lopez was one of the lucky ones. He was tired after his long day, but he had his day's pay in his pocket, and he was headed home. Up ahead he saw the ten-foot high fence that had been built years ago on the banks of the Rio Grande. The rust had overtaken the barrier so much it was hardly a fence at all. The reddish-brown, jagged, chain-linked fence was nearly on the ground in places. Years of men, women, and children climbing over the fence had bent the posts over, even snapping them off in some stretches.

At his favorite crossing point it was still upright, but a large hole had been cut, the links pulled so far apart that several people could walk through it side-by-side. Once through the fence, he had to cross the river then walk another mile and he'd be home. He smiled thinking about a cool bath and a beer. Then he would ask about his mother's day and whether his little sister had studied like she promised.

His sister was really only a half-sister, but he adored her. She was beautiful. And she was smart, very smart. She could read, was good at math, and could already speak both Spanish and English fluently. He told her, *Stay in school, learn something new every day, and move to the United States. There is great opportunity for smart, beautiful women.* She would flash that radiant smile when he said that to her. Even at eight-years old, she was gaining confidence. Javier feared that if he didn't push her, she would never leave this pitiful little town. He'd made it his mission in life to free her from the daily rut of life in poverty.

Still walking along in the dry wash, he was now within fifty feet of the fence. He looked left. *Clear*. He looked right. *Clear*. He looked left again and started towards the fence, walking quickly.

He heard a voice yell in a loud, Texas drawl, "Hey, you! Hold it right there!"

He turned to see a large man in a tan cowboy hat, light green shirt, blue jeans, and boots heading in his direction. The man was about thirty feet away. Javier thought about running, but it was just one man. He was big and probably couldn't run fast. So he decided to wait. But by the time Javier heard the ATVs' motors, it was too late to make a run for it.

Two more men pulled up on ATVs, one blocking his path to the fence, the other blocking his path back to the wash. They were young, probably in their late teens, tanned, like ranch hands. They were also lean and strong.

The big man walked up to Javier, standing very close. He was nearly a head taller than the young Mexican. His face was hard and wrinkled, like he'd spent his whole life in the sun. His mustache was mostly gray with some black mixed in. He had a scar nearly three inches long just below his left eye, which was nearly shut. The closed eye had a nervous twitch.

For a long moment, nobody said a word. Then the big man rubbed his right hand over his mustache as he looked at the horizon where the sun was making its run for cover. In a gravelly voice he asked no one in particular, "What do we have here?"

No answer.

The man looked at one of the ATV riders then asked, "What does it look like to you, Jeb?"

"Looks like we got us a wetback, Daddy."

"It sure does. A dirty wetback. Takin' our jobs. Stealing our cattle. Gettin' free food. Who knows what else? Probably kidnappin' our women."

The man was so close that Javier could smell the alcohol on the big man's breath. He didn't know what to do. If he tried to make a run for the fence, he'd never make it. What if the man hit him? Should he dare to fight back? He knew he couldn't fight all three men and win. He wasn't a fighter anyway. *Try to reason with them. Try to keep calm.*

* * *

Across the river, his little sister waited. She'd come to greet her brother and walk with him the rest of the way home. She had good news to tell him about her day. Her lesson today was about how Mexico used to extend well into what is now the United States. It bothered her that her country had lost the land. But that was history. Maybe someday they would get their land back.

Then she saw her brother standing beyond the fence, surrounded by three men. This confused her. Why was he talking to them? Then she saw the big man point his finger at her brother's chest. Javier didn't raise a hand. Then one of the other men pushed him towards the bigger man. What was happening? She sensed that her brother was in trouble.

One of the men slapped Javier on the back of the head. He raised his hand to rub the spot as he turned to see which one of the men hit him. When he did, one of the other men punched him hard, sending him into the arms of the big man. Javier tried to stay against the man, but he was pushed back to the middle of the circle of angry men. She watched as the men took turns punching her brother until he could no longer stand. She wanted to yell to him to run, to get away from the bad men.

He fell to the ground. She hoped they would leave him alone now that he was defenseless. Then she saw the first kick from a pointed boot. It hit his right kidney with such force that he arched his back. More kicks followed to his head, stomach, and back. The men continued to kick him long after he lost consciousness.

She screamed Javier's name. She screamed at the men to stop hurting him. They laughed at her.

In those few short minutes, her world shattered as her older brother was beaten to death, his body tossed into the murky waters of the Rio Grande.

Chapter 1

May 28, 1998

Pat McKinney shifted his five-foot seven-inch, one hundred seventy-five pound frame to get more comfortable in the driver's seat. He glanced out the driver's side window of his light green Ford Explorer. The hills of southern Kentucky on either side of Interstate 75 were beautiful in late May, the trees now fully canopied with dark green leaves. The early morning sun angled in from the east, the hilltops casting shadows across long stretches of the four lane highway. Nearly a dozen vultures circled high in the blue sky, searching for that early snack of furry road kill. The few clouds were mere wisps of white, captured in the wide area of high pressure that kept the air in the Midwest warm, dry, and clear.

Pat smiled, thinking he'd come a long way from the hell he'd faced just eight months before. Nightmares had invaded his mind, making sleep difficult; his nights interrupted by frightening scenes conjured up from the depths of his mind. They were always different in some way, but the theme was the same. A former friend, turned business partner, turned enemy popped into his dreams to antagonize him from the grave. Even as Pat saw himself pulling the trigger of a high powered sniper's rifle, the face always laughed at him. Pat thought he'd get the last laugh, but he was wrong. He had tried to shake the dreams on his own, but they worsened. Finally, he succumbed to the realization that he needed help.

He first turned to his wife, Diane. She understood because she knew a little bit about his background. But what she knew was only a small part of the whole story. He would take the rest to his grave. Only three living people knew the whole story, and they each knew their own version. Pat was the only person alive who could understand the hell he faced each unbearable night. The dreams threatened to destroy his life. As he drove north on the interstate, he wondered if he would be able to continue to overcome the mental assault on his psyche.

Over the past eight years he'd faced a number of wicked people, many hell-bent on killing him and harming his family. But he'd faced them all and come out alive. Pat smiled at the thought. There was one very close call, one he would never forget. He still had the remnants of a bruise in the center of his chest that, were it not for a Kevlar vest, would have certainly ended his life.

Without thinking, he lifted his left hand to the scar on the left side of his chin, and began slowly rubbing it with his middle finger. The scar was from a nail that had ricocheted into his chin while building a greenhouse for a former employer. He'd missed hitting the large nail squarely with a hammer. The nail embedded itself over half an inch into his chin. There was no permanent damage except the white scar. If his brother Joe was in the car, he would have slapped Pat's hand away from the scar and told him to stop with the Obsessive Compulsive Disorder. He thought Pat's subconscious was hopelessly drawn to the scar. Pat thought it was merely a bad habit.

But it was just Pat and his wife, Diane, on this trip. They'd been on the road for less than two hours, having spent the night north of Knoxville, Tennessee, and Diane was already asleep in the passenger seat. He glanced at his wife, smiled, then looked back at the road. They were climbing higher for the next few miles. They wound up behind a pair of tractor-trailers chugging along, side-by-side, at fifty miles per hour, slowing traffic in both lanes. Normally, this would bother Pat. He wasn't a patient driver, but this trip was different. They were in no hurry. Their plans were to make a stop in New Bremen, Ohio to visit a friend. They then planned to stop in Port Clinton, Ohio, where Pat and Joe were born, and finally, take a grand tour around Lake Superior.

Pat had wanted to drive around the greatest of the Great Lakes since he was a kid. The specter of the Mackinac Bridge, the wonder of the Sioux Locks, and the beauty of the shore of Lake Superior had always fascinated him. He was surprised when Diane agreed it would be a nice vacation and a great way for Pat to relax.

Pat's brother, Joe, and his fiancé Lisa, were back in Dunnellon, Florida watching their children. It was Joe and Lisa's anniversary gift to the couple. They all knew Pat needed the time away from any excitement. He was doing well in his therapy. His doctor agreed that a trip away would be perfect, "Just what the doctor ordered" were his words, a lame attempt at humor.

Lisa and Joe had been more than happy to watch the kids. They said it was their warm-up session for the real thing. Lisa was moving slowly, her belly protruding. Their unborn baby girl was safe inside, only about a month away from joining her parents. Their plans were to marry after the baby was born and after Lisa had sufficient time to recover from her pregnancy. Lisa suggested a two month wait. Joe recommended three but wasn't putting up much of a fight. He would go along with whatever Lisa decided. He was as anxious as she was to be married. They'd already bought a house together in Winter Garden, Florida. Besides, they'd lived together for the better part of a year. They figured it was the next logical step. Joe's mother wanted them to marry before their child was born. Lisa's mother figured they were committed to each other and wasn't concerned either way. She felt her daughter had done well in her choice of a lifetime companion.

As Pat's thoughts drifted, he came closer and closer to the tanker truck in front of them. He wasn't dangerously close but when Diane stirred and opened her eyes, she thought they were going to hit the truck. She shouted, "Pat!"

Startled, he jerked his head towards her, took his foot off the accelerator and shouted back, "What? What did I do?" On an uphill angle, the Explorer slowed quickly. Pat had to hit the accelerator again to keep from disrupting the flow of traffic behind them.

"Damn, Honey. You scared the hell out of me." He no longer rubbed his scar, both hands were now firmly on the steering wheel. He was watching straight ahead at the back of the tanker truck, but made quick glances at Diane, who was now wide awake.

"I scared you? I nearly had a heart attack. I thought we were going to latch onto the back of that truck you were so close."

Pat thought that was a bit of an exaggeration. He waited a moment to calm his voice and let his heartbeat slow. "We really weren't that close."

All was quiet in the Ford for several minutes then Pat said, "I was just thinking about Joe and Lisa, and Mom."

"You probably should have been thinking about that truck in front of us," came the reply filled with sarcasm.

They remained silent for several more minutes while Diane looked around at the mountains. She enjoyed the scenery in this part of the country. The beauty of the hills was refreshing, a contrast to the flat, sandy ground found throughout central Florida. The predominant trees around their home in Dunnellon were pines. Palmetto bushes grew wild in most areas that weren't developed. The landscape was far from the majestic beauty of maples, birches, and oak trees that stood before her now. The foliage, intermingled with the rocky formations visible from the highway, enhanced the pleasant scenery.

Diane stretched and twisted, shaking the sleep from her mind. The sleek form of her body didn't go unnoticed by Pat who glanced over at his wife while still trying to concentrate on the traffic ahead. The truck in the passing lane in front of them finally moved into the right lane ahead of the other truck. Pat hit the accelerator, the Explorer's speedometer hitting the seventy-five mile per hour mark. The grade of the road switched from uphill to down. As Pat eased to the right lane in front of the tanker truck, the line of traffic that once trailed them began passing them in rapid succession.

"How far to New Bremen?" Diane was looking at Pat, thinking he had this all calculated out in his mind.

Pat hesitated. "We're about a half hour into Kentucky. It takes about three hours to get through the state and New Bremen's about ten miles off the interstate at exit 102. So I'd say about four hours of actual road time. But we do have to eat somewhere in there."

"Any idea where we might stop? I thought we might get a bite at that coffee shop you talked about."

Pat thought for a minute then suggested, "How about this? Let's get a snack in the next town we come to and we can do a little window shopping. That way we can get into New Bremen about dinner time."

"Amazing. You're not in a hurry to get there and get out? Who are you, and what have you done with my husband?"

Pat smiled. "Hey, this vacation is supposed to be relaxing. There's no reason to hurry. We don't have reservations at any hotels so we can stop when and where we want. The only thing is, I told Frank we'd get to New Bremen sometime this afternoon. He's not expecting us at any certain time, so we can take our time."

Diane looked at Pat and smiled. He really appeared to be relaxed. There was no tension on his face. She was cautiously optimistic he might actually be getting over his nightmares. She reached over with her left hand and stroked his right arm.

It gave Pat goosebumps.

* * *

Lisa sat on the floor of the living room in her and Joe's new house. She was playing dolls with Anna McKinney, Pat and Diane's three year old daughter. Anna was a happy little girl with dark brown hair and her mother's dark green eyes. She loved playing dolls with anyone who would join her. Lisa was enjoying the experience with the exception of the discomfort that came with being eight months pregnant. She hoped the baby would be full term. Though Pat and Diane were only supposed to be gone for about two to three weeks, she feared an early delivery might interrupt their trip. It wouldn't be good to go into labor while she and Joe had the responsibility of watching Sean and Anna. The grandmothers, Emma McKinney and Ann Goddard, had already promised they would step in if needed, but Lisa hoped it wouldn't be necessary.

Joe was in the backyard with Sean playing catch with a real baseball. Sean was serious for a kid nearly seven years old. He acted more like an adult than a kid who shouldn't have a worry in the world. The more he learned, the more serious he became.

Sean rarely smiled. He always seemed concerned about one thing or another. Diane used to tell him not to take things so seriously, but it was to no avail. The more Diane tried to get him to just be a six year old, the more he seemed to want to grow up. She told Pat their son took after his Uncle Joe.

Joe McKinney was an intense individual. He fit in very well in the US Marine Corps. Diane admired her brother-in-law, but she preferred her son not follow in his footsteps. Pat said to not worry about him, that he'd grow out of it, but so far, that wasn't happening. Even Pat was starting to worry that his serious attitude might cause emotional problems later in life.

Pat blamed himself for Sean's serious emotional state of mind. When Sean was born, Pat was still in the Navy on the USS *Nevada*, a ballistic missile submarine. At a very young age, Sean would miss his father terribly while he was deployed. The last time Pat came home from sea, Sean was already dreading Pat's eventual departure on the sub again. It took some convincing before he believed his parents that Pat was not going to sea anymore.

As Sean grew, his serious personality became even more intense. When Pat left home for a few nights after an argument with Diane,

Sean blamed himself. He thought Pat wasn't coming back. Now, Pat made it a point to tell Sean where he was heading most times when he left the house. Even so, Sean's face would contort into a twist of concern. He just didn't appear to trust his dad at his word.

"Throw one in here, pal. I want you to make my hand sting." From a catcher's crouch Joe encouraged Sean to throw him a fastball. He hoped the exercise would tire him out so he'd sleep well tonight.

Sean stared at his uncle, then went into an exaggerated wind up and threw the ball as hard as he could. Joe had to reach up quickly to grab the ball before it could sail over his head. He grabbed it and tossed it back to Sean. They'd been at it for about thirty minutes and Sean was ready to call it quits.

He walked towards his uncle, his face scrunched up in a serious look. "Uncle Joe, can I ask you a question?"

"Sure. Ask away."

Sean paused for a moment, "Why does Dad have a gun in his desk?"

Joe's brow wrinkled for a moment as he pondered the question. "Well, your mom and dad want to protect you and Anna from bad people."

"Are bad people trying to hurt us?"

Joe crouched down so his face was level with his nephew's. He didn't smile. He wanted Sean to know they were two serious guys having a serious talk.

"Sean, there are bad people in the world. They aren't everywhere, but your mom and dad want to make sure that if they ever do come around here they can protect you and your sister. That's why your dad has a gun."

Sean thought for a second. "I want to help protect Anna and Mom. I think Dad can protect himself, but what if Dad's gone somewhere and bad people show up. I should have a gun."

Joe's face didn't change, but his heart sank then started to rise into his throat. How could he tell this child he shouldn't worry about the "bad people" out there? He tried to think what might be going through the mind of a six-year old boy that would cause him to worry about his family. Hell, he knew *men* who were far less concerned about their family's wellbeing. He thought his eyes would tear up and show weakness, but he steeled himself as he decided what he needed to say.

"Listen, Sean, when the time comes, when you're old enough, I'll teach you how to use a gun. But you have to be older and stronger . . . and we have to have your mom and dad's permission." He gave his nephew a long look. "Is that a deal?"

He held out his hand and took Sean's.

Sean cracked the slightest smile. "Deal." With a firm handshake, the agreement was sealed.

Joe had no idea how he was going to tell his sister-in-law about the promise he'd made. He figured he'd better tell her first before Sean spilled the beans. Joe wasn't worried about having to teach Sean how to handle a gun. He figured Diane would kill him long before Sean's first lesson.

Chapter 2

"They're failing faster than we can replace them. We have sixteen tanks where we don't know the oil levels because the detectors are faulty or have failed outright. We don't have the manpower to go around to each tank and manually check their level. Corporate is already bitchin' about the overtime."

Ricardo Vasquez, an engineer at the Texas Star Oil Refinery, was pleading with the station manager for funding to replace the antiquated level sensors with a new digital model.

Texas Star was a small producer compared with the mega-refineries built in recent years. It had been the jewel of Texas Oil when initially built, with state of the art technology. But over the years, with the growth of the nation's environmental awareness, equipment at Texas Star was long overdue for replacement. The corporate office deemed it a bad investment to upgrade its systems. The site was in close proximity to a bevy of new commercial and residential development. There was no land to expand oil production at the site, so it could never compete with the newer refineries in the Texas Oil fleet. The company's capital dollars, which were limited by the board of directors, went to its larger refineries. Even with its great location on the Gulf of Mexico, the site was doomed to be among the first targets for cutbacks. Texas Star was on the downside of its useful life.

Much of the housing nearby was lower class rental properties, with strip malls, gas stations, and bars. But south of the refinery a sprawling resort had been built that catered to wealthy clientele. The property was separated from the refinery by tall palms, a privacy wall, and a fake mountain with a waterfall. Once inside, the resort's guests barely knew the refinery existed.

Vasquez continued his plea, holding up one of the new DLD2000 electronic sensors. "These new models are already in use at refineries in Europe and the Middle East. They're extremely accurate and durable."

The station manager listened as Vasquez made his case. He knew the failure rate on the old detectors was high. They were the original equipment that had been installed on the massive oil storage tanks nearly forty years ago. Each tank had three of the aging devices for redundancy. They determined the level of petroleum in each tank by being immersed directly in the oil. Over the years, corrosive elements in the oil began to break down the casing on the detectors, causing them to short circuit. The manufacturing company was no longer in business and no suitable direct replacement existed.

The manufacturer's specifications on the DLD2000 were impressive. They were easily attached to the exterior of fuel tanks and used ultrasonic pulses to determine the fluid level in each tank. And they were guaranteed for thirty years. Their biggest advantage was that they used a transmitter to send the level information to a panel in the control room. That eliminated the need to run new electrical cables to the tanks. That savings alone would pay for the sensors and their installation.

"Rich, this sounds great, but I don't know if the big wigs will go along with it."

The expression on Vasquez' face said it all. "You know if we don't replace these things, we won't even know the oil level in each tank. How can we keep an accurate inventory?"

His boss turned his palms upright and shrugged his shoulders. "I'll present it to the board today and see if we can push it through. From what you've shown me, it looks like we can cost-justify it." He paused and gave Ricardo a look that didn't exude much confidence. "The biggest sticking point that I can see is they don't like purchasing big ticket items without putting a project out for bid. But we already know nobody else makes detectors like these."

Vasquez was nearly pleading with his boss. "If you need me to go to the meeting with you, let me know. I'm glad to help."

"Thanks, Rich. I may take you up on that."

Later that afternoon, Vasquez was surprised to hear the good news that the board approved the project. The funding would be available within the week. They directed that Vasquez cut the purchase order for the new detectors immediately. Installation was to begin as soon as they arrived on site.

Vasquez thanked his boss for his support. He said he'd contact the vendor immediately with the news.

* * *

Victoria Garcia, with a fresh Margarita in hand, glanced around the resort from her private balcony. The sandstone-colored walls matched the dry, hot day. She'd just returned from the pool at the base of a fake mountain, where a waterfall provided a beautiful backdrop to a southwestern desert theme. It also separated the expensive resort from the grimy appearance of the old Texas Star Refinery.

The prevailing winds from the Gulf helped push the foul odors produced by the refinery north towards the eastern suburbs of Houston and away from the luxury resort. The developers counted on this in order to draw wealthy families to the vacation destination. They had to compete with resorts with far better locations. Their promotions paid off. The resort was well known among wealthy circles as a great vacation destination. Many of the residents lived at the resort year-round.

As she took a sip of the golden drink, she brushed back her straight, auburn hair. Her dark, olive skin still glistened with a thin layer of tanning oil. The pearl-colored nail polish contrasted with her skin color and dark brown eyes, but matched her smile perfectly. She savored the lime flavor mixed with salt from the edge of her glass. Setting her drink on the table, she read the letter again. Before she finished the first paragraph, her cell phone rang. She placed the letter under the paperweight to prevent it from being blown off the balcony by a Gulf breeze, and looked at the name of the caller on her cell. Smiling, she flipped the phone open. Before she spoke, her demeanor turned from relaxed and happy to serious and businesslike.

"Ola, Ricardo."

"Ola, Victoria. I have news."

He sounded upbeat, but she didn't want to have this particular conversation over the phone. "When can we meet?"

"I finish at four. I can meet you by five-thirty if you are close."

"I'll pick you up at La Casona's at five. Be there on time."

Victoria Garcia flipped the phone shut. Her face twisted into a wicked smile. Things were coming together.

* * *

At precisely 5:00 P.M., Victoria, sporting bright red sunglasses, a bright red tank top, and white capris, pulled her 1998 red Corvette convertible into the parking lot at La Casona's. The thin man with short black hair and black sunglasses, stood near the entrance to the local eatery. She motioned for him to come to the car.

"Get in. We're going somewhere else."

Vasquez opened the passenger door and slid in. Before the door clicked shut, the Corvette was moving. Victoria didn't say another word as he searched for a seat belt. He was getting concerned as the car gained speed. She turned a corner and headed for West Highway Six. The wind racing past their heads made talking in a normal tone impossible.

He shouted, "Where are we headed?"

She said nothing, but looked at him through her dark sunglasses. He thought her lips curled up in the slightest smile, but he wasn't sure. For the next fifteen minutes, they cruised north until they were in the Houston metropolitan area. She finally brought the car to a stop in the parking lot of a strip mall.

She turned to Ricardo. "Well?"

"Did we have to drive half-an-hour for you to ask me this?" A smile slowly spread across his face.

She returned the smile. "I thought we'd go somewhere and celebrate. La Casona's won't do it. We need someplace special."

As Victoria pulled back into traffic, Ricardo smiled at his luck. His day was getting better and better. He leaned back in the passenger seat, enjoying the remainder of the ride.

They pulled into the parking lot of an upscale restaurant. The parking lot was filled with Cadillacs, BMWs, Lexus', and Jaguars. Vasquez looked around the lot, a bit surprised by Victoria's choice. He wasn't even sure he could get in the door without a sports coat, or maybe even a tie.

"Relax. I have a coat that will fit you just fine." She reached behind the passenger seat and pulled out a plain, light sports coat. "This should match your shirt just fine. Try it on."

Ricardo was amazed. The coat matched his shirt and pants perfectly.

The evening turned out fine indeed. Victoria paid for a very fine dinner. She mentioned that her employer was really paying, that she had a generous expense account and could use it as she saw fit, as long as she got results. After sipping her Merlot at the end of dinner, she said, "I want to thank you properly. So I hope you don't have any early plans for tomorrow."

Ricardo nearly choked on his Crown Royal on the rocks.

Later that evening, Vasquez drifted off to sleep after a very good day indeed. Victoria Garcia made a call. "Everything is going as planned."

A man with a Middle Eastern accent replied, "Excellent."

Without another word, she disconnected the call.

Chapter 3

"Are you declaring anything today, Mr. Ramirez?" The Canadian Customs agent at the Pearson International Airport in Toronto, Ontario eyed the olive skinned man with interest. He'd just looked over the gentleman's passport and carry-on bag and found nothing that would indicate he needed to look further; but it was his job to scrutinize every non-Canadian passing his post. In his nine years of service not a single article of contraband had made it past his watchful eyes, even in the random checks that seemed to be more frequent each year. The states seemed almost nonchalant about security from what he'd heard. They were more interested in protecting the individual's rights. But he didn't have to be concerned about rights for U.S. citizens. He was concerned about the safety of Canada and her citizens. Individual's rights were a distant second, in his opinion.

"No." That was all. No smile, no frown, no raised eyebrow. Just a stone-cold, unblinking stare.

The agent had a gut feeling he should look further, but Mr. Ramirez gave him no reason to continue asking questions. With reluctance, he stamped the passport, closed it, and handed it back. With as much chill as he could muster, he said, "Enjoy your stay in Canada."

Without a word, the olive skinned man with a clean-shaven face and dark eyes took his passport, his bags, then left the customs table. When his back was turned fully away from the customs officer, he murmured, "Infidel pig." He smiled at the ease at which he'd entered the country that would be his doorway to the land of Satan.

* * *

An hour later the man checked into his room at the Sheraton Gateway Hotel. He thought the name of the hotel appropriate since this was his gateway to the United States. It wouldn't be long and he would leave Canada and join his family.

The rooms at the Sheraton had been recently remodeled. The scent of new paint, new carpet, construction glue, and a lot of room deodorizer hung in the air. The beige and cream striped vinyl wallpaper made the room appear bright, even though the lighting in the room was limited to a floor lamp, a desk lamp, and two lamps on each end of the king sized bed.

Ramirez, whose real name was Sheik Al Salil, spread his prayer mat on the dark brown, commercial grade carpet. Kneeling on the mat, he faced east towards the Holy Kaaba in Mecca. He wasn't able to pray while on the flight to Toronto or during his brief stop at Heathrow Airport in London. But he reasoned that Allah would forgive him, given the circumstances. Besides, once he carried out his mission, which, as all good followers know, was Allah's will, he would be justly rewarded.

In a voice that was almost a whisper, so he wouldn't be heard in the hallway or neighboring rooms, he proclaimed, "Allahu Akbar," meaning God is Most Great.

He continued to recite the first chapter of the Koran. Then he read a second passage, concentrating so hard he was sweating, even in the relative cold of the air conditioned room. He continued his prayer ritual through the second Rak'a, his voice growing louder. His concern with anyone hearing him disappeared, his confidence in the power of Allah to protect him growing with every verse.

Finally, he finished his official prayer with, "Allahu Akbar."

He sat back on his heels, kept his eyes closed and began to quietly recite, from memory, the Fatwa of Osama Bin Laden. After five minutes, he stopped.

Turning to his right, he said to no one in particular, "Assalamu alaikum wa rahmatullah." *Peace be upon you and God's blessings*. He turned to his left and repeated the blessing.

He opened his eyes and stared straight ahead for several minutes. Mentally ticking off the steps in the plan, he smiled. Everything was ready except a few minor details. He had yet to receive the final payment for a few supplies, but his financial sources had never before failed him. *Yes, God is Most Great.*

Sheik Al Salil rolled up his prayer mat, and sat down on the edge of the hotel bed. He dialed his wife's telephone number. She answered before the second ring finished.

"Hello?"

"Ah, that sweet sound that I've longed to hear."

The woman at the other end of the line smiled. She'd been expecting the call from her husband. His timing was perfect as she was home alone and didn't need to worry about anyone listening in.

"The pleasure is all mine, my love."

He smiled at her rather forward response. She must have picked up some western traits after living in the United States for so many years. He didn't care. He just wanted to be with her. It had been too long.

"It pains me to be away from you, but it won't be long now. The first leg of the journey is over. Tomorrow will be the last flight."

"That's wonderful. Are you still scheduled for the same flight or has the schedule changed?"

He smiled. She was still a stickler for details. "Everything is as planned. The flight, the room, the car are all the same."

Salil's wife smiled, but she was nervous. She worried the long separation might cause her and her husband to grow apart. Would they still be as committed to each other as before? Would he still find her beautiful? Would their love stand the test of time? The brief silence between them caused her anxiety level to rise.

"I love you."

He was surprised to hear the words. She would not have said this to him over the phone before. Before this, she'd only said *I love you* in person and in private.

He almost said it back to her, but it wasn't supposed to be expressed in public. Even though the phone line was a private line, one had to use caution.

Instead, he said, "I miss you, too. I've thought about you every hour of every day."

When he didn't return her declaration of love, her heart sank just a bit, but he wasn't an American. She hoped he would not think less of her.

He paused. "How is Ahmed?"

"He is fine. Things are going well here. He finished his project with only minor difficulties. I'm sure he'll want to tell you all about it when he sees you."

Sheik Al Salil listened to his wife's voice, wishing he could be with her even now. But that wasn't possible. He had a mission to complete. The timing was critical so he needed rest now, after he finished his other calls. "That is very good news indeed. Is he home now?"

"No. He had to work late this evening. But you can call again tomorrow at this time. I'm sure he'll want to tell you all about it. They are giving him much more responsibility now, which is good. He fits in very well with his co-workers. His supervisors are saying that he'll make a very fine engineer."

Sheik smiled. His wife had just confirmed the plan was moving along well and there was no reason to worry. Another piece of the puzzle was in place, or very nearly so.

After a few more minutes of mostly idle talk, they said their goodbyes. As they hung up, each felt a pit in their stomach and a tug on their heart. The time had been too long, but they would soon be together again.

After he finished talking with his wife, he dialed a second number. Another female voice answered. "Ola?"

Sheik disliked talking with the woman. She was arrogant and disrespectful of men. He'd hoped he could put a man in her place, but there was no time and she had the right connections to make the plan work. So his options were limited.

"How is your project coming?"

"As I told you yesterday, my part is right on schedule. You need not worry. Is everything in place on your end?"

Her question had a condescending tone. No matter the topic of discussion, this woman spoke with an air of defiance. It drove him crazy, but no matter. She had her reasons for her personality flaws. He could tolerate them for another five days. Then the mission would be over and he could celebrate. He, his wife, and his son would be together again. And he would be rid of this rude woman. Her usefulness was nearing its end.

"Everything is proceeding as planned. You will get your supplies by the end of the day tomorrow."

The woman's voice again became irritating to Sheik. "You're not leaving me much time. We should have had the shipment by now. There's a lot of work to be done and it's being held up by not having supplies. How do you expect—"

"Stop!" He caught a glimpse of himself in the mirror above the cheap dresser as he barked into the phone. He saw the anger in his own eyes and realized he had to maintain better control of his emotions.

Salil lowered his voice. “I will make some calls to better the delivery time.” He paused, waiting for her to reply. She remained silent. *Finally, she knows her place.* “You must move quickly over the next four days. The timing of your project is critical to our success.”

At the other end of the phone, the young woman rolled her eyes. She’d heard that Middle Eastern men were chauvinistic, but dealing directly with them was far worse than she’d expected. It would be difficult to keep her cool for the next few days. The stress level would be high. She’d been under pressure before but this was unusual, even for her. But she would do anything to make sure she was successful.

She tempered her response. She wanted to ask Sheik if he thought she was an imbecile, but decided instead to speak in an even tone. All she said was, “I agree.”

She allowed Sheik to hang up first so he wouldn’t assume she was being disrespectful.

Salil disconnected and dialed the number for the Imam Khidir Khadduri. The aged cleric answered on the fifth ring.

After a respectful greeting, Salil provided a cryptic update on their progress. If the Imam was pleased, no one listening in would know. But Salil knew he approved of the status report.

Sheik hung up the phone, thinking about the mission. He’d told the Imam that everything was going according to plan. The time was quickly approaching. It would be glorious to strike at the devil in his own land as the enemy had done to Islam over the years. After going over the plan in his mind once more, he turned on the flat panel TV to watch CNN News. The story was about the rise in crime in America, particularly murders. The news anchor spoke about the most deadly cities; Detroit, Cleveland, Washington DC. *American fools. They cannot even stop the killing in their own capital. They do Allah’s work for us. No matter. We will continue with our plan. It is our duty.*

Sheik turned off the TV and leaned back in his bed. He began to quietly whisper the Fatwa of their leader, Osama Bin Laden. The message was clear. The great Satan must be destroyed.

Chapter 4

"Play it again from the beginning. Pay attention to the details. Before we call in other agencies, I want this thing thoroughly analyzed."

Following the directive of her boss, Colonel Sheila Warner, Nancy Brown concentrated on the screen where the video was about to play for the fourth time. Colonel Warner stood in the back of the conference room while technicians cued up a digital version of the recording they'd received that morning. It was unlike any they'd reviewed before.

First, when a video of a beheading was delivered, terror groups fell all over each other to claim responsibility. On this particular video, no one claimed to be the jihadists. On the contrary, very few people even knew the video existed.

Second, the media, *Al Jazeer* in particular, was the primary conduit for the delivery of such horrifying clips. Islamic terrorists believed this gave them credibility with their counterparts. If you got the Islamic media to make the delivery, then you had hit the big time in your journey to shower death on the evil supporters of Satan. Not using this method of delivery didn't make the act any less terrifying for the victim and their families, but it did cast some doubt on the authenticity of the group performing the act.

This particular tape was delivered directly to the Anti-Terror Unit at Quantico, Virginia, completely bypassing the major media outlets of every nation. That alone placed the authenticity of the tape in question. Every terror group in the world wanted publicity, especially if it was a heinous act perpetrated against the great Satan, the United States of America. Members of the Anti-Terror Unit believed there were reasons why this group may not have wanted this tape made public.

A clear voice came out of the overhead speaker, "Ready, Colonel."

"Please turn up the volume a bit and be ready to freeze it on my cue."

"Yes, Ma'am."

The video started again. It was being displayed on a brand new, seventy-two inch, high definition digital screen at one end of the twenty by twelve conference room deep in the confines of the offices of the newly formed agency. The image was very clear. It hadn't been altered yet by specialists who would clean up any interference in the tiny pixels of the video.

On the screen, Nancy noted that a breeze shook tall pine trees, filling the air with pollen, the yellow film coating the pine needles on the forest floor. Thin rays of sunlight filtered through the trees at an angle that cast eerie shadows on the sparse shrubs in the forest. A constant, low-level roar from the breeze filled the audio. The only other sounds were the birds chirping and chattering back and forth in their mid-morning songs. It was like the introduction to an environmental film.

Then the camera shifted. White sheets, one on the ground, the other hung by ropes from two trees, formed a small, make-shift stage where a man was held up with his ankles wrapped together with duct tape, wrists bound behind the back, and a dark canvas bag over his head. A group of men threw him to the ground and ripped the bag from his head. His mouth was covered with duct tape. He briefly stared into the camera, fear etched on his powdery white face.

The men, dressed in black with black hoods, stood around him, just within view of the camera. From his prone position, he was looking up at his assailants. No one on camera spoke.

Nancy and the other members of the Anti-Terror Unit in the conference room took notes as they watched the scene. The heat of the room and sweat caused by anxiety gave the room a musky odor. Everyone was uncomfortable even though they'd already reviewed the film multiple times.

This was the fifteenth graphically violent murder of a westerner by various alleged Islamic extremists that had been videotaped and sent to the U.S. Government. Agent Nancy Brown had seen them all. This was the first video that involved a very close up, vivid, good quality image. Although she knew that the man in the video was already dead, her instincts made her want to help him get free. As it played, she shifted in her seat. She looked around the room. Several of her peers were having a similar reaction. She'd taken a moment before this fourth viewing to reconcile her thoughts. If she wanted to do her job well, she had to dehumanize the situation and analyze the data absent the emotion. It was tough, but she would manage.

Back on the screen, the victim's expression went from fear to terror. His eyes darted from one of his captors to another. He knew he was about to die, but did he know why these men wanted to kill him in such a brutal way? Maybe he knew why he'd been kidnapped. Did he know too much? Did he know his captors? These were the questions at the forefront of Nancy Brown's mind.

Concentrate on the terrorists. The man on the ground is dead. His expressions are inconsequential to the case. We need to concentrate on his captors.

One of the men spoke to the others. Nancy was taking lessons in Farsi, but she didn't recognize this language. The men hurriedly formed a line along the sheet that had been used as a backdrop.

"Stop." Colonel Warner walked to the front of the room next to the screen. "The backdrop has no insignia, no flag, and no identifying marks of any kind. This is out of character for Islamic groups looking to make their mark. From this point on, be looking for other signs that depart from past practices." She paused, looking around the room at her team. As she walked to the back of the room, she said, "Continue."

On screen again, the young man looked over his shoulder. He seemed to pause for a moment, as if he recognized something. Then he continued his struggle against the duct tape that bound his arms and legs. Two of the men held guns across their chests. Only one had an ammunition belt. The condemned man turned his head back towards the camera.

One of the captors who had established himself as the leader adjusted the camera. He centered it on the sheet being used as a backdrop and zoomed in. That must have been the signal it was time for action. Two of the men in the line reached down and grabbed the bound and gagged man under the arms and stood him up so that his face was centered on the screen. The leader walked slowly in front of his prisoner and faced the camera. He started to speak again.

Behind the leader, the young man's terrified eyes wandered, looking at the forest, apparently trying to think of a way to escape. He looked back at the man who was speaking to the camera.

Nancy studied the video intently, searching for any details that were missed during the first three viewings. The tension still rose as she watched.

On the screen, the leader held a large, serrated knife in his right hand. He was apparently making a speech that he'd practiced many times. He was becoming more animated with each word. He pointed at the camera in an aggressive motion, shouting what appeared to be threats. Then he repeated his words in a staccato manner. Finally he raised the arm that held the knife and made a motion across his own throat. He slowly turned to face the prisoner and nodded. The men again roughly threw him to the ground.

The camera was adjusted again to focus on the terrified prisoner. His eyes nearly bulged out of their sockets. His face turned a ghostly shade of white. His nostrils pulsed, fighting for more air. He tried shouting through the tape covering his mouth, his screams muffled. Tears poured from his eyes Then his face turned bright red as he struggled in vain to free his arms and legs.

The camera had been adjusted so the man's head was at the center of the screen. They positioned him on his side so that the top of his head was facing the back-dropped sheet. He bucked and squirmed, trying to break free. One of his captors grabbed a handful of his hair, holding his head down. Another of the men straddled his legs to keep him as still as possible. The others moved to the side, their legs still remaining in view. The man with the knife knelt behind their prisoner and started to repeat the words he'd last spoken. The others chanted in unison.

The leader slowly lowered the knife until it was touching the condemned man's neck. He applied pressure so that the knife made a slice in the skin and blood started to ooze from the wound. The terrified man tried to buck his captors from his body, but his flailing only made the knife cut deeper. More blood flowed from the widening gash. The leader applied more pressure to the knife, starting a sawing motion, cutting deeper with each move. The blade pierced his windpipe, allowing blood to get sucked into his lungs. The muffled screams turned to a gurgling sound that filled the surrounding forest. The blade then cut into the jugular vein. Blood pumped from his neck in bursts, hitting the white sheet in a grotesque, pulsating spray.

With his own blood running into his eyes, the young man began losing consciousness. His blood stopped pulsating from his neck and was now a continuous flow. The man with the knife finished the gruesome task of hacking off the head.

One of the captors began to heave uncontrollably. He ripped off his mask just as he stepped out of view. He could be heard retching off camera. A second man, seeing the first, began to convulse. The leader stood, faced the camera and said in broken English, "Death to America."

The video stopped.

Colonel Warner nodded to a soldier at the back of the conference room. He turned on the lights. She looked around thc room at the Anti-Terror Unit under her command. She'd made some notes, but she wanted to hear from her team first.

"Observations?"

Nancy Brown shifted in her seat. She hoped another would speak up first, but Colonel Warner noticed the look on her face. "Ms. Brown?"

Nancy sat up and looked at her notes, but wasn't really reading them. She had two lines on her paper underlined. "What kind of terrorists wear highly polished wingtips and new Nike running shoes to a beheading?"

Chapter 5

"Honey, come in here. You've got to see this."

Lisa Goddard listened over the sound of the dishwasher and the running water in the sink. The moist, hot air surrounded her, making her sweat. She was having a hard time moving around the kitchen with her belly sticking out. Their child, still tucked safely in her womb, decided tonight would be a great night to use her bladder as a soccer ball. She wasn't paying close attention to much else except the acute aroma of dill in the air. For some reason, she could smell dill pickles anytime she was near the kitchen.

She yelled back to Joe, "What did you say?" As she yelled, she waddled towards the living room. Joe was sitting on the couch, a laptop opened on the coffee table. Pat and Diane's children, Sean and Anna, were playing in the family room.

As she turned the corner to the living room, Joe shouted, "There are a couple of stories at Yahoo.com about Superior Shores Nuclear Plant. One of them is about an engineer at the plant. He's been missing for nearly a week."

"You don't have to yell, I'm right here."

Joe turned to his fiancé and smiled. "Sorry. I thought you were still in the kitchen."

She moved closer to Joe and turned to sit on the couch next to him. She held out her hand so he could help ease her onto the cushion. It took a few seconds for her to get seated, then a few more to get as comfortable as she could. "So, what's so important you had to drag me in here?"

Joe felt guilty watching her twist and turn, trying to find a comfortable position. He took her hand gently and kissed it. Her gaze let him know a kiss on the hand wouldn't cut it, so he leaned over and kissed her cheek. The big, tough ex-Marine smiled sheepishly. Then he turned to the computer and said, "Superior Shores is where Evan, that friend of Pat's, works. An engineer's been missing for a few days."

Lisa frowned. "It figures your brother is heading there." *He's got a knack for finding trouble.*

"Pat said his friend's family has lived up there their whole lives. Evan wanted to get out of there so he spent twenty years in the Navy. Now his folks have deeded him the house and they moved to Florida. He got a job at the nuke plant. He's been there about five years now."

"Maybe you should call him, see if he knows anything about it." Lisa rubbed her belly as she spoke. "Do they have any idea what happened to him?"

"Not really. It just says he disappeared. Check it out."

Lisa read the story on the computer screen.

> *Alex Corbin, a twenty-eight year old engineer from Ashland, Wisconsin has been missing since last Tuesday at 6:45 A.M. He was last seen wearing dark slacks, a white button shirt, black wingtips, and a navy blue wind-breaker. He is a white male, approximately five-foot-eleven, one hundred seventy-five pounds. He is employed by Northstates Power-Wisconsin at the Superior Shores Nuclear Power Plant in Bayfield County, Wisconsin. A spokesperson for the Sheriff's office in Bayfield County is asking that anyone with information on the whereabouts of Mr. Corbin contact the Sheriff's office at . . .*

Joe turned to Lisa. She'd stopped reading. She was now watching her belly move from side to side as the nearly full term baby squirmed, maneuvering for a more comfortable position. She rubbed her taut skin through the light weight silk blouse. Joe watched in fascination while Lisa's expression turned from a smile, to a look of pain, then back to a smile again. He was amazed at the transformation of his soon-to-be wife. When they first started dating, she was a rough and tumble young woman who loved to jog, lift weights, and swim daily. Now, as a mother-to-be, she watched her every step, always protecting her baby from even the slightest possibility of being bumped. Joe smiled in spite of himself. She seemed oblivious to his stare. Slowly, he reached an arm around her shoulder, leaned over and kissed her on the side of her head. She looked up and smiled, then leaned into his side, and yawned.

Joe gave Lisa a look of concern. "You look tired. Are you sure you're up to taking the kids to the park?"

They planned to take Sean and Anna to Disney's Magic Kingdom for a day. Pat and Diane thought it was a great idea. They knew the kids would love it but were concerned that it might be too hard on Lisa. But they left the decision up to Joe and Lisa. They were keeping the trip secret from the children in case Lisa didn't feel up to the task. Joe was becoming more concerned each day. Lisa looked like she was ready to go into labor at any moment.

"I'll be fine. Besides, there are plenty of places to rest. And they have air conditioning in many of the restaurants and shops. If I get tired, I can stop and rest while you and the kids tear up the park."

"Are you sure?"

"Yes, I'm sure."

Joe's face was still stern, his jaw jutting out slightly. He wasn't fully convinced she could stand the all-day adventure, particularly in the Central Florida heat this time of year. The temperatures could easily reach ninety degrees with high humidity. That would be rough on her. But he'd never known her to back away from a challenge either, so he resigned himself that the trip was on, no matter what he said. In a sing-song voice, he said, "Okay. If you're bound and determined to go, then we will. I just want to make sure we have plenty of cold water. And we need to see where all the hospitals are in the area. I'd hate to get in the middle of the park and all of a sudden you go into labor."

Lisa let out a long yawn, then rubbed her belly. "I already checked it out. There's a hospital at Celebration right outside the park entrance. They can get us there in no time. They even have a maternity ward. All we have to do is notify a park staff member. They're all trained to get the right medical help to you when needed. How's that for service?"

Lisa smiled at Joe who was still not convinced this was the best idea, but who was he to argue? She already had her mind made up they were going and nothing short of the baby being born beforehand would change it. He pulled her close again and planted another kiss on her head. She tried to reach over and rub his chest but it was too uncomfortable, so she rubbed her own belly instead. Just then, the baby kicked. A bulge in her skin the size of a hard-boiled egg appeared then just as quickly disappeared.

"Did you see that?" Her voice had a tone of excitement even as exhaustion consumed her mind and body. She closed her eyes, a smile on her face.

Joe smiled, too, amazed that her belly was so big. *How could a child fit in there without being crushed?* He thought about the wonders of a mother's body being the life support system for another human being. What a miracle, the creation of life. He'd helped give life to their child. But Lisa was the sole source of life support for their baby. Emotions overwhelmed him and his eyes started to water. He smiled and wiped his eyes. *Good thing your Marine brothers aren't here to see this.* He hugged Lisa even tighter until he heard her breathing become heavy. He looked down at her peaceful, relaxed body. She'd fallen fast asleep. He dared not move, letting her sleep as long as she needed.

Now he had plenty of time to think. His first thought was *I'm the luckiest guy on the planet.* He relaxed his arms but didn't let go. He cuddled his whole world in his arms.

As Lisa slept, Joe thought about Pat and Diane in Wisconsin. *Pat sure manages to step right in the middle of it. I'll call later. Maybe there's a simple explanation. Maybe that engineer just wasn't happy at home and took off. It happens . . . right?* He heard Sean and Anna playing in the back room. He thought about what an awesome responsibility it would be to have to raise his brother and sister-in-law's kids if something bad happened to them. *Where the hell did that come from? Man, I've got to get more sleep.* He looked back at Lisa and her bulging stomach nearly covering her lap. He lightly put his hand over hers as it rested on her belly. She made a soft, low moan and her lips curled up in a slight smile. Then, apparently still asleep, she winced as their baby decided to move again. Joe's and Lisa's hands rose as the baby maneuvered around inside her. Joe's emotions rose again, like a coaster heading to the top of the first big hill. *Fatherhood, here we come.*

Chapter 6

"Diane, tell me again how you ended up with this guy?"

Frank Clarion, a friend and former shipmate of Pat's on the USS *Nevada,* was having lunch with the couple at the *New Bremen Coffee House and Book Store*. The little shop on the main drag in New Bremen, Ohio was popular throughout much of the west-central part of the state. Their specialty coffees and gourmet sandwiches drew lunch and dinner crowds rivaling many of the big chain restaurants in the region. Shelly and her staff hustled between tables taking orders, serving sandwiches, and refilling drinks. Coffee, in one flavor or another, was the drink of choice. Pat lifted his mug, sipping a hot Columbian brew. He liked his cup of java the old fashioned way, black, no sugar.

Diane placed her own mug of mocha flavored coffee on the table, smiled at her husband, then turned to Frank. "He used to be charming." She turned, leaned towards Pat and smiled, enjoying the chance to tease her husband. "Really, I remember our first date. He was nervous as a cat. He went to kiss me and . . ."

Pat cut her off. "Enough with the mushy stuff. Just face it, she fell for me and chased me down. I couldn't get away."

"Ha! Right. Good one." Diane was clearly having fun. She was relaxed, joking with Frank at Pat's expense. She could tell that they were good friends who shared the bond of being in the submarine service together. "So, Frank, do you know Hatch?"

Frank's smile broadened. "Yeah. I know Hatch real well. He's quite the character. I spent a week at his place by the swamp." He spoke about Hatch's beat up log cabin in the Okefenokee Swamp outside of Moniac, Georgia. "Man, that was fun! We fished, shot guns, fished again, and shot more guns. We even shot fish."

He paused and his expression turned less jovial. "That was when his sister and parents were still living there. They were the nicest folks. Weird, like Hatch, but they treated me like I was their son. It was the best week I ever spent away from home and away from the boat." His expression tightened. "It's a damn shame. They were the best."

Frank was referring to the murder of Hatch's parents and the murder-rape of his younger sister that had happened while Hatch was out to sea. Pat wasn't sure if Frank knew the story of what happened to the two men who committed the crimes. But Hatch found out who the bastards were and took care of them, shooting them both in the groin, watching as they bled to death. Hatch was never questioned about the murders. Apparently, the local county sheriff felt that justice was served. Everyone in Southeast Georgia knew those boys killed Hatch's family. And everyone figured Hatch had returned the favor. So, according to the Old Testament, the score was even. Only once did he confide his real feelings to anyone, and that person was Pat McKinney. They shared a bond that could only be shared if you had vengeful blood on your hands.

"You know, Hatch still lives there," Pat said, trying to lighten the mood.

Frank's expression brightened. "He does? I'm surprised. I thought he'd move after that, but what a great place. Man, the bugs are quite the science experiment, though. When did you talk with him last?"

"He was at our house a few months back. We had a barbeque and he stopped by. He does some odd jobs for different folks. Sometimes, he helps out with investigations. He's good at snooping around." Pat smiled as he said this.

"No kidding?"

Pat told Frank the story about the investigation of the couple who were taking advantage of young soldiers and sailors just getting out of boot camp. He described how the woman charmed the young military men who'd been isolated from everything except other men for nearly three months. Pat told his friend how beautiful the young woman was and how easy it must have been for her to literally charm their pants off. Frank couldn't believe anyone would be so brazen. As Pat continued about how Hatch, Pat, and his brother, Joe helped investigate the crimes, Frank's mood darkened.

"This country's going to hell in a hand-basket. I just don't get what makes some people tick." There was silence at the table as they all took sips of their brew.

Just then, Shelly walked up and asked, "Anything else I can get you folks? Maybe a slice of apple or pumpkin pie?"

Pat's eyes lit up at the sound of pumpkin pie. He turned to Diane who rolled her eyes and said, "Sure. Why not? You're on vacation."

Shelly smiled then asked, "How about you, Ma'am? We have a great selection of ice cream and cookies."

Diane opted for a double chocolate chip cookie. When it arrived at the table with Pat's pie and Frank's ice cream, the hot chocolate chips were melting on the warm plate. The cookie was at least five inches in diameter and half an inch high. "Oh my," she said with a surprised expression.

As they ate their dessert, Frank asked where they were headed next. When Pat said Port Clinton, then Wisconsin, he asked, "What's in Wisconsin?"

"Were you on the boat with Evan Jones? He was there when I first got to the ship. He works at Superior Shores Nuke Plant up there."

"Yeah, I know. As a matter of fact, he and I still keep in touch. We hunt up there every deer season."

"Really? I remember some of his hunting stories. Don't his folks own a bunch of property up there?"

Frank said, "Yeah, but that's all Evan's now. His folks moved to Florida and left it all to him. Said they couldn't take the winters anymore."

Pat smiled at Diane as he said, "I understand that. It's got to be bitter cold in the winter."

"Yeah. I'll be up there in November. The season is right around that time."

Pat wolfed down a mouthful of pie, then said, "Well, he said he might give us a tour of the plant while we're there. I think it'd be cool."

Diane rolled her eyes as if to say she wasn't that interested. She took another bite of the gooey cookie.

Frank's face took on a serious look. "He said an engineer friend of his is missing. Was supposed to be home right after work the other night, but never showed up. It's like he vanished. Evan said it's real weird."

Pat frowned, gulped down the last of his coffee. Then he ran his finger over the pie plate to get the last bit of pumpkin. He stuck his finger in his mouth and made a popping sound as he withdrew the finger. Diane looked at him with a stunned expression, her mouth partially opened, eyebrows scrunched together. Frank just laughed.

"You haven't grown up a bit since you left the boat."

Pat smiled. "And I don't plan to, either." Diane smacked him on the arm.

He paused for a minute then asked, "So, do they know anything at all about this missing engineer?"

"Nope. It's like he fell off the face of the earth. He's been missing for about five days, but according to the guy's wife, he's always home after work like clockwork. Not a word, not a sighting, not a sound. I mean, he lives about fifteen miles from the plant, but it's not like there's a half dozen interstate highways leaving the plant."

Pat rubbed the scar on his chin as he listened. Diane grabbed his arm to stop him.

Frank continued, "There aren't five thousand people living within a twenty-five mile radius of the plant. I mean, it's wilderness up there. Everybody seems to know everybody else. Folks are generally pretty friendly."

"That's what he said when I talked with him last month. That's when we made the plans to drive around the lake and stop in to see him."

"Well, these folks know when a stranger comes into town. They fought tooth and nail to keep that plant from being built. They don't want any industry up there. It's disrupted their peaceful existence."

Pat asked, "Do you think one of the locals went psycho and killed him, maybe hid the body?"

"Nah. The guy was the son of one of the locals; said nobody would want to hurt him."

Frank finished his coffee and set his cup down. Both men leaned back in their chairs and rubbed their stomachs. "Wow. That was good." He turned towards Shelly and said in a loud voice, "Shelly, that was excellent, as usual."

"Thanks. Would you all like anything else?"

Pat and Diane both raised their hands and shook their heads. Frank said, "I guess we're done, sweetheart."

"I'll get your check, sugar."

After the bill was paid they stood out in front of the shop and looked up and down the handsome, clean main drag through downtown, admiring the buildings. They were again impressed by the cleanliness and the general feeling that people in New Bremen were proud of their city.

Frank asked, "When will you get to Evan's place?"

"We're staying overnight in Grayling, Michigan after a visit to Port Clinton. Then we're heading to Evan's. So we'll be there tomorrow, probably late in the afternoon. We plan to stay there just a couple nights then head west around the lake. Then however long it takes to get around the lake and back over the Mackinac Bridge, and back down to Florida, that's how long we'll be on the road."

"Sounds like a great trip. Should be fun. When you get back, send me some pictures. I know it's going to be beautiful. When you see Evan and his wife, tell them I said hi and I'll see them in November."

"Hold on a minute. He's married? He never said a word when I talked to him."

"Yeah, well, he doesn't say too much about it. She has a kid from a previous marriage. Up there, stuff like that has people talking. Besides, the kid's a grown man now, in his twenties. Evan's no spring chicken. But his wife must have been pretty young when she had the kid. She's only about forty and her son's got to be twenty-five or so." He shrugged.

"I never thought he'd marry. Wonders never cease."

With that, Frank leaned over and kissed Diane on the cheek and shook hands with Pat. The couple turned and headed for their Explorer.

* * *

After forty-five minutes back out on Interstate 75, Diane was already fast asleep. Pat thought about the early dinner with his old friend, Frank. But his mind kept going back to the missing engineer. He'd seen the maps of the area at the most northern point in Wisconsin and it was definitely isolated. While there was plenty of area to hide out, if anyone saw you, word would get around. Why would an engineer want to leave work and not head straight home? From what Frank said, the guy was a homebody. It didn't make any sense. As he thought, he rubbed his scar harder. He suddenly shook his hand and moved it under his leg, trying to hold it down. *I've got to break this habit.*

Chapter 7

"So, my buddy Sammy is supposed to work this job, but this engineer, Ricardo Vasquez is trying to get me on the job." Danny Wilkerson took a long pull on his beer then wiped his mouth with the back of his hand. He brushed his hand up across his forehead, sweeping his brown hair back away from his eyes. Since leaving the Navy several years back, he'd let his hair grow longer, but only so that it covered his ears. His face was long, pale, and narrow. His eyes were blue and always moving, taking in the surroundings, analyzing everything he observed.

"I don't know why. I mean, I don't have a dog in the fight, but I wouldn't mind working the job. It just isn't my call."

"Why do you suppose your buddy . . . what's his name?" Hatch said.

"Sammy. He's the lead tech in the shop."

"Why is he so intent on doing this job?"

William "Hatch" Hatcher and his friend, Danny, sat at a table in Loco Pedros' bar near Danny's apartment in Lake Jackson, Texas. They'd just finished a dinner of burritos and were nursing a couple of Coronas. The air was filled with a smoky haze, most of it from cigarettes, though the acrid aroma of Mexican weed could also be detected in the mix. The bar had pool tables, darts, a handful of video games, and half a dozen TV monitors mounted on the walls. Four of them showed the Astros playing at home against the Dodgers. Hatch didn't care for baseball, but Danny would stop and holler at the game midway through a sentence. Hatch just smiled and rolled his eyes.

The bar was nearly three quarters full and most of the patrons were cheering right along with Danny so he figured it wouldn't be too smart to make any wise comments about what a stupid game baseball was. He waited for Danny to have his fun, then steered him back to the conversation, giving him a look as if saying, *and then?*

"Where were we? Oh, yeah. Sammy's the senior tech in the shop. He usually gets the cream-puff jobs. He's been buddies with the shop foremen for a long time. Both of them, the foreman, I mean, came from the shop so they let the guys get away with a lot of stuff. It's not like when we were on the sub. Anyway, they like him so he usually gets to pick his jobs. I think one of the reasons Vasquez doesn't want Sammy on this particular job is because he tends to milk 'em. I've never seen a guy who could take a twenty minute job and turn it into overtime." Danny paused, a wry smile on his face. "I've seen a lot of guys put off shit they don't like to do, but this guy is in a league of his own. It's weird, too, because I think he likes the work. He just wants to stretch his retirement income. He's got his time in and I think he's got a pretty good nest egg."

Hatch knew guys like that in the Navy, but they didn't stay that way very long. Shipmates didn't protect guys who didn't pull their weight. You had so much time to do a job. If it didn't get done, you didn't sleep until you finished. Milking jobs and turning them over to the next crew wasn't tolerated. Besides, the pay was the same if the job took you twenty minutes or twenty hours. Though there were different reasons for making sure everyone did their job. It wasn't just a paycheck. One wrong move by a shipmate could cost an entire crew their lives.

Hatch looked at his beer, thinking about his time back on the Trident submarine, USS *Nevada,* where he and Danny were shipmates. Danny was better suited for life on the sub. He was fairly short, five-foot-eight and he weighed about a buck fifty.

He was a damn good technician. Hatch recalled a number of troubleshooting incidents where the young, baby-faced tech had found problems in minutes after more experienced technicians had scratched their heads for hours. The senior men probably would have been pissed off if they hadn't been so tired.

In one incident they'd been up running drills for hours. Then the senior man stood watch for six more hours before a problem was discovered in the control rod circuitry. He'd been working on the cabinet for five hours and was starting to fall asleep when Danny, looking over his shoulder, pointed to a diode on the schematic. He told the senior man the diode had failed and that's what was causing the erroneous reading. Sure enough, when the diode was replaced, the system readings went back to normal. Problem solved.

Hatch said, "So this engineer, Vasquez, wants you on the job so it'll get done faster?"

"That's the way it looks. Vasquez is trying to be subtle about it, but it's obvious he doesn't want Sammy on the job. I thought our boss, Bud Yantzy, was going to toss Vasquez out of the shop, but he thought about it and finally agreed it was a good idea. I guess there's pressure from management to get the job done before somebody from corporate pulls the funding."

Hatch frowned. "But they already bought the parts, right?"

"That's never stopped 'em before. I've seen 'em toss hundreds of thousands of dollars of inventory into the dumpster. Supposedly the parts were all obsolete, but I saw some of 'em. They were brand new, in sealed boxes. Nothing surprises me anymore."

Hatch raised an eyebrow. That seemed like a huge waste. *No wonder the price of gas is so high.* But he figured what the heck? He didn't drive that much anyway.

"So what's so special about these detectors that they need to be installed so quickly?"

"It's just that the old ones are failing fast. We ran out of replacements for 'em nearly a year ago."

Danny told Hatch about how the company was cutting back on maintenance funding, but the cost was so low on the replacement project they felt it was worth the expenditure.

"All new technology. No wires. Everything's transmitted over the air to the control panel so the cost of replacement is small, at least, compared with running new wires to every detector. Besides, we can't get direct replacements anymore. Supplier went out of business."

Hatch smiled. He liked playing around with electronic gadgets. When he was only eight years old, he built a shortwave radio from an old kit his father had bought him. His dad was amazed when he completed building the radio in less than half the recommended time in the instructions. Over the following months, he played around with the circuitry and increased the range of the signal. From that time on, Hatch was hooked. It led him to an eight year hitch in the US Navy on trident submarines. But that was history.

"I'd like to see one of these wireless gadgets. It's got to be a detector, transmitter, and receiver in a single unit." Hatch scratched his chin as he thought about what one of these units would look like. He turned back to his buddy. "How do they work?

"That's one of the cool things about it. They use a sonar pulse to detect the liquid level in the tank. You attach 'em using a metallic epoxy. We clean a spot on the tank's exterior with metal oxide sand paper and basically just glue 'em on. We tested one in the shop. Once it cures, they don't come off. I was impressed." He frowned for a second. "But these things are bigger than I expected and they've got some kind of insulating stuff encasing the electronics. I've never seen anything like it."

Hatch frowned. He'd read up on sonar pulse technology and some of the different uses. Most of the time they were used in enclosed spaces. Maybe the insulation was some type of weatherization technique since the units weren't protected from the elements. But his interest was piqued. "Could I get a look at one?"

Danny smiled. "Sure. I don't see why not. I'll talk to my boss in the morning. If he's okay with it, I'll call you. I can meet you at the gate tomorrow."

They raised their bottles and finished off the last of their beers. Danny reached for his wallet, but Hatch already had forty bucks on the table. Danny started to protest but Hatch smiled and waved him off. They headed out the door at 10:15 P.M thinking this used to be the time they were getting ready to go bar hopping. In the dim lights of the parking lot they watched several girls walking towards the bar, giggling as they went. To the ex-sailors, they looked like they were in junior high school.

Hatch looked at Danny. "Man, do I feel old."

Danny just shook his head and turned towards his Ford Explorer, waving at Hatch over his shoulder.

* * *

The next morning at 7:45, Danny escorted Hatch into the Instrument and Controls maintenance shop. The fluorescent lights made the entire shop area brighter than it needed to be. A greasy film covered the walls, doors, desks, and filing cabinets. The room smelled of oil, burned solder, and a number of other odors that couldn't be identified. Hatch wasn't sure he wanted to know their source. With all the fumes, he wondered how anyone could smoke or do anything else that caused a spark without sending the entire site up in a fireball.

He was introduced to the five I&C techs who were looking over their work packages and gathering tools. He also met the two shop foremen. Danny explained there were twelve men in the shop, but two were on vacation and two more were on the backshift. The others were already out at job sites. They sat on bar stools in front of Danny's workbench, looking at his collection of pictures under a plexiglass cover. He had a good mixture of family and friends, including one of several crew members of the USS *Nevada* with the ship in the background. Hatch, Pat McKinney, Danny, and several others were on the gangplank on their way to board the ship. Hatch remembered that day. They were readying the ship to deploy, which meant they had several long months ahead of them.

Hatch smiled. "I sure don't miss those days."

"Me either." Danny's smile brightened. "I do remember we had a great time the night before this picture was taken. Those nurses from Jacksonville sure were looking for some fun."

Hatch's smile grew even more. As they talked, a man who looked to be in his fifties entered the shop and strolled up. He stuck a hand in Hatch's direction and said, "Hatch, Sammy Helzer."

Hatch took the hand and gave him a firm shake. "Sammy. Nice to meet you. I understand you're the senior tech in this shop."

Sammy smiled. "That just means I'm the oldest. But these kids are pretty sharp, like Danny here. He learned his stuff pretty good when he was in the Navy." He turned and smiled at his fellow tech. "But he tells me you're the best."

"He stretches the truth from time to time." Hatch grinned at Danny.

"He also tells me you live in a log cabin in the Okefenokee Swamp?"

"That part is true. My folks lived there their whole lives so when they passed away I decided to stay there. It's not too bad if you don't mind the bugs, snakes, and gators."

The men laughed.

Danny said, "Hey, let's look at these detectors."

On Danny's bench, a one foot square by half inch steel plate was welded to a couple triangular pieces of steel so that the plate stood vertically on the bench. Attached to the steel was a plastic rectangular gray box.

Danny motioned with his hand like he was a game show host demonstrating a prize. "Here it is. Looks kind of like an old Kodak

110 camera, don't you think?" Then he paused, watching Hatch's reaction.

Hatch rubbed his chin as he looked at the wireless gadget. He leaned in closer, looking over the device from left to right. It didn't look like much. "The whole thing is sealed, except a tiny hole."

"Yep. You can adjust the signal strength using a screw driver; a very small screw driver. Like I said last night, the coolest thing is they work on pulses, just like active sonar. It sends out two pulses, one at a high frequency and one at a very low frequency. If the low frequency pulse returns from the tank wall at the far side, then the oil level is . . ." Danny looked up at Hatch and stopped talking, seeing the perplexed look on his face.

Hatch said, "Somethin' ain't right." He rubbed his hand across his face, trying to remember his electronics training. "Why's it so big?"

Both technicians frowned. Danny said, "I told you they were bigger than they needed to be. I thought they'd be more compact."

Sammy chimed in, rubbing the back of his neck as he spoke. "I agree. For this type of equipment, they're pretty bulky."

Hatch nodded. "They don't need to be this big. Seems like a lot of wasted space." Maybe there was a legitimate reason for its size, but he couldn't think of one. "Maybe we should take one apart and see what's inside."

Danny shrugged. "Why not?"

Hatch looked at the men. "Hey, it's your call. I'd just like to see what makes these things tick."

Danny reached in his workbench and pulled out a handful of small tools. He set up a mini vise and put the detector in place. He was about to attempt to pry off the cover when Ricardo Vasquez walked into the shop. When he saw what Danny was about to do his eyes widened and his face paled.

He shouted, "What are you doing?"

All three men stopped and turned towards Vasquez. For a moment, no one said anything. Then Sammy asked, "What does it look like we're doing? We're taking one of your gadgets apart, you know, to see how it's made."

"Stop." He paused. It appeared to Hatch he was searching for a reason that they shouldn't disassemble the detector. "We don't have any spares. We need every one of them."

Not wanting an argument, Danny stopped and put his tools away. He turned to Vasquez. "Okay, dude. Settle down already." Then he took the detector from the vise and placed it back in its box.

The engineer looked each man in the eyes, then turned and went into the foreman's office where he complained about what Danny was about to do. After a few minutes the foreman nodded. That appeared to satisfy Vasquez, who turned and left the shop area, closing the door a bit louder than necessary.

"That was odd." Danny looked at Hatch who'd watched the entire episode without saying a word.

Hatch asked Danny, "Why?"

"I've never seen him lose his cool like that. Even when he has a big project, he's pretty calm. I wonder what the big deal is. We have a few spares."

Hatch and Sammy didn't reply but Hatch was deep in thought. He'd seen men in many different situations. He knew anger, rage, horror, even terror. He knew what each looked like in a man's eyes.

Ricardo Vasquez was terrified.

Chapter 8

The handsomely papered walls of the meeting room were covered in photographs of the Superior Shores Nuclear Power Plant in various stages of construction. The first pictures were of a large tract of flat ground. Trees had been cleared to make way for heavy equipment and trucks of all types to haul in stone, concrete, wood, steel, and all manner of building materials. As the group of students from Globe University moved past the pictures, the power plant grew before their eyes. Buildings appeared, roadways were paved, electrical towers stood tall, and the concrete and steel reactor building rose. Moving from picture to picture, the structure started as no more than a hole in the ground. With each successive photo it grew as if rings of concrete were dropped into place. After twelve photos, the large, gray cylinder dominated the site, dwarfing smaller buildings around it.

One of the students commented, "The cooling tower is smaller than I thought it would be. Why is it so small compared to others I've seen?"

Jimmy Smith smiled. "We don't really need one at all at Superior Shores because of the cooler waters of Lake Superior. But it does give us a little extra cooling margin. So it was added to the design." He looked around the room at the juniors and seniors from the engineering school. Most appeared surprised. Jimmy continued, "In reality, most all power plants, regardless of the type of fuel used, nuclear, coal, natural gas or oil, don't need the large cooling towers. As long as they have an adequate supply and flow of cooling water that can dissipate the heat from the heat source, there's no need for a tower. But we'll talk more about that later in the day. If you'll take your seats, we'll get started with the presentation."

The students looked around the tables set up so that they were angled towards the front of the forty-by-forty-foot room. A projector screen lowered from the ceiling when Jimmy clicked a button on the remote control. Another click, the lights slowly dimmed, and the projector came on. A film clip started with the CEO of Northstates

Power-Wisconsin welcoming the students to Superior Shores. It lasted just a few minutes, encouraging them to continue their studies, wishing them well, and asking them to consider a position with NPW. "We're always looking for bright, new talent. If you've got what it takes to be part of a great team of engineering professionals, you can map out a great future here at Superior Shores. This plant has consistently been in the top quartile–that's the top twenty-five percent of the United States nuclear industry in safety and power production. We need talent like you to continue that record into the future."

The projector went off, the lights came on, and Jimmy Smith turned toward the dozen young faces. He wasn't much older than the students before him. He'd been hired at Superior Shores only four years ago as a student intern. Jimmy was also a graduate of Globe University, as were a number of the other engineers at the plant. Lon Phillips, another engineer at Superior Shores, was scheduled to give the first tour. But he was nowhere to be found. It seemed he was always missing. So the engineering manager had decided Jimmy would be the best person to give the tour of the plant and facilities. They were looking for new, young talent and what better way to lure young engineers than to have one of their own provide the details of working for a financially solid, stable company. The starting pay and benefits were more than competitive.

But it was the location that scared most of the talented prospects away. Situated at one of the northern-most points in Wisconsin on Lake Superior, access to the leisure activities most young folks enjoyed was lacking, and there was little the company could do about it.

"Are there any questions before we begin the tour of the plant?"

One young woman asked, "Are you afraid of the radiation from the reactor? I mean, we're only about one hundred yards from the core."

Jimmy glanced at her nametag. "Jenny, that's an excellent question. Let me tell you we're actually receiving less radiation right now, where we sit, than if we were out in the sun. So, no, I'm not afraid of the radiation." He paused then continued, "But that doesn't mean we don't take safety very seriously. If we were to have an accident like Three Mile Island or Chernobyl, and our lines of defense that are in place to protect the public and our employees fail, then that would be cause for alarm. As you take the tour we'll talk about those barriers. It's generally called *Defense in Depth.*" He looked around the room again and asked, "Anything else?" When no one offered a question, he said, "Okay, then let's get going."

The group toured the control room, the turbine building, and the maintenance shops before sitting down to a complimentary lunch in the cafeteria. They stopped at the entrance to the radiological restricted area that housed many of the systems that contained radioactive fluid. Jimmy explained they couldn't tour that part of the plant, including the reactor building since, by law, students weren't allowed to receive any occupational radioactive exposure, regardless of how low the dose might be.

Finally, they toured the administration building. They skipped the Human Resources area and the Quality Assurance Department. They continued on to the Information Technology center, then to the Engineering Department.

As with the other support areas in the admin building, engineering work spaces were divided up into cubicles. The office space for each worker had plenty of open space and the dividing panels looked brand new. Jimmy explained each cubicle had everything it needed to perform engineering tasks for the power plant, including access to a vast number of technical manuals and drawings on-line. Northstates Power had invested well over one million dollars to upgrade engineering for two reasons. The first was to provide the staff with the latest in technology so they had the tools necessary to keep the plant in top operating condition. The second was to impress young prospective engineers so they would want to join a company that provided really cool tools to do their job.

As they toured the area, a number of Jimmy's peers walked by, some smiling, others all but ignoring the tour group. A man with a large manual walked up to Jimmy and said cheerfully, "New meat?"

Jimmy returned the smile. "Funny, Evan." He turned to the group, pointing his thumb over his shoulder, "When you hire on, remember this name, Evan Jones. He says he's an engineer, but he's more of a practical joker. Plus, he's crazy from riding around in submarines all his life."

Jimmy smiled, turning back to Evan. In a quiet voice he asked, "Any news on Alex?"

Evan's expression quickly changed to serious concern. "Nope. Nothing new."

They both paused. Jimmy realized the subject of the missing engineer would not be a good topic for the tour group. Evan forced a smile and said to the group, "This really is a great place to work. Look me up when you hire on. I'll give you a real tour." He punched Jimmy lightly on the arm as he turned and walked away. Jimmy rubbed his shoulder in mock pain then waved the group on.

As they passed one cubicle entrance, a short, olive-skinned man with a tight fitting turban and a black beard rushed out and nearly knocked over one of the students. He dropped a handful of papers, which scattered among the group.

The man looked at the student and nearly spat in broken English, "Watch what you are doing." Two of the students leaned over to pick up the papers. With an angry expression he exclaimed, "Leave them. I will get them after you have left my area. Watch where you walk. Do not step on them."

Jimmy rolled his eyes and waved the tour group onward. As they continued, several students exclaimed, 'What a jerk' and 'That dude looks like a terrorist. Why would they have a creep like that working here?'

Jimmy heard the murmurs. Once they were out of earshot of the Muslim engineer he addressed the group. "That was Yusef. His personality leaves a lot to be desired, but he's a good engineer. Trust me, he's not a terrorist. Everyone's background is thoroughly checked before they start work here."

"If I was hired would I have to work with him?" The question came from a young woman with dark hair and plastic black framed glasses.

Jimmy smiled. "Yusef likes to work alone. He rarely works closely with anyone. So while there's always a chance you could be required to work on a project with him, that chance is pretty slim. I sure wouldn't let that little incident sway your decision. Working for Northstates is a fantastic career opportunity."

Jimmy turned and continued the tour. The rest of the day went off without another incident. There was one other engineer who wore a turban and the students took note of it. This man, Bashir El-Amin, smiled at the students and spoke nearly perfect English. He bowed slightly to the group, commented that they would make a wise choice joining the engineering team at Superior Shores, then moved on to continue his work.

One of the group asked Jimmy how many Muslims worked at the plant and if that concerned him. He reassured them about background checks and that he knew of four Muslims total working at the plant. There was a small population of Muslims in northern Wisconsin. He also mentioned that the vast majority of employees at Superior Shores were Christian. He looked at the group for any reaction to his comment. Seeing none, he continued the tour.

As they headed back to the conference room where they started the tour, they again passed Yusef. He looked up, bushy eyebrows furrowed. A sheen of perspiration glistened on his forehead. He looked as angry as when they'd seen him earlier. He walked on quickly, as if in a hurry to avert a crisis.

One of the students asked if he always looked so nasty. Again, Jimmy said it was just his personality and they shouldn't read anything into it.

At the end of the day, Jimmy walked the students to the administration building exit and took their visitor badges as they left. The students seemed to appreciate the hospitality and thanked Jimmy for the tour. At least two members of the group expressed interest in career opportunities with NPW.

After the group left, Jimmy smiled as he thought about the encounters with Yusef. His outwardly nasty disposition was almost comical to the young engineer. He realized it made all Muslims guilty by association, even though the other Muslim engineers were most pleasant to the students. It made the job of recruiting young talent that much harder.

Now he had to tend to his real job. The tour left little time for real work.

Chapter 9

Colonel Sheila Warner was known to be a tough woman who ran her department efficiently. She set high standards and even higher goals for her people. She accepted no excuses for failure. Her favorite saying was '*There is no such thing as failure unless you stop pursuing success. That's not failure, that's being lazy.*' Being lazy in her department was not tolerated. If she detected weakness in one of her people, they were advised they had a limited time to exhibit strength of character and purpose or they were transferred. And there were plenty of examples as evidence that she was serious. She gave a speech to every member of her department upon their arrival to her command. *The business of fighting terrorists is extremely important and serious. Our country is relying on us. We will not fail on my watch.*

Nancy Brown had just recently resigned her commission to become one of the lead investigators in the relatively new Anti-Terrorist Team. She'd proven her value immediately upon joining. Colonel Warner liked her work ethic and her tenacity. Nancy didn't let any of her male counterparts bully her. The Colonel appreciated Nancy's position in a male dominated field and liked how she handled herself in meetings. She also knew Nancy was thorough. She'd read her NCIS file in which she was given high marks for her work in tracking down several perpetrators who had robbed and killed young servicemen. It was good work on a tough assignment.

Nancy was standing in the Colonel's office waiting to be addressed.

With a stern expression, Colonel Warner said, "Miss Brown, please take a seat. How is the assessment coming?"

Nancy launched into a ten minute dissertation on the most likely locations for an attack by 'Islamic extremists' on U.S. soil. There were about seventy-two civilian targets on the list. There were many hundreds of less likely targets that could move onto that list depending on a number of factors. But the identified targets in the top seventy-two were further broken down into very high likelihood, high likelihood, medium likelihood, and low likelihood. Nancy stressed that even the targets with low marks in the list were still higher than any of the others beyond the seventy-two.

"I just gave you this assignment. How did you come up with this list so quickly?"

"We used a combination of computer models and personal evaluation. We had much of the work completed before you requested it, but the evaluation process wasn't complete, not until we were given the directive. Since we had a lot of data, we just had to make sure it was correct and organized so it would work with the computer models."

"You said you had personnel review the results and add a human perspective?"

"Yes, Ma'am. Computers are only as good as the data provided. We felt we needed to validate the results with human input from a number of key specialists."

"How confident are you we have an accurate top ten list?" The colonel stared directly at Nancy as she replied. She wanted to see if she was as confident as she appeared.

Without missing a beat, Nancy said, "I put a 70% confidence level in the list. Of course, we can't be sure because we're not inside these lunatics' heads, but we have profiled them extensively. So we know some of what makes them tick."

Colonel Warner didn't smile, but the corner of her mouth curled up slightly. Nancy kept her game face on. She wanted the colonel to know she was very serious about her job. Colonel Warner had no doubt.

"Nancy, this is good work. Next, I want you to review the names and records of the top terrorists and the likelihood of them directing and financing attacks on these targets. I want to know who is capable of pulling this off and how soon they might make an attempt. We need better forecasting of these events and we're not likely to get any help from any of the other federal agencies. When can you have this back to me?"

Nancy had to think about this one. Colonel Warner was demanding and very aggressive. But Nancy liked knowing where she stood and so she appreciated the Colonel's straight forward approach. "We can have this information to you by tomorrow evening."

"Excellent. Bring your report to me directly. No leaks. Understood?"

"Yes, Ma'am."

Nancy went immediately to her own office. She had a lot of work to do in a short period of time. The colonel's no-nonsense approach gave Nancy all the encouragement she needed to get the job done fast. But it also had to be as accurate as supposition would allow.

Back in her office she called a meeting of her staff and laid out the challenge. She looked at each person as she spoke. Every member of the team accepted their assignment without question.

"One last thing. This assignment is *Eyes Only*. Nobody is to know anything about it. Is that clear?" She looked around the room, making sure she received a positive response from each team member. "Let's go."

The team scattered to their cubicles and started their research. As she watched them go to work she was amazed at how they partnered with each other, depending on their specialty.

The most demanding job was on two computer technology specialists. They had to produce reports and data for the team to analyze. The noise level in the office was high while the team rushed to create Nancy's report. The databases they used for their research held thousands of organizations, tens of thousands of names, and terabytes of data gathered as part of the government's anti-terror effort. The slightest actions of anyone with known ties to suspected terrorist groups were entered into the database. As more information was gathered on them, it was added to their profile.

That was the start of a long process of data accumulation. It caused the amount of information to grow rapidly. If not for the technicians who knew how to mine the data, it would remain just a bunch of individual bytes of information. But their ability to enter criteria that searched key information for the reports was legendary. These techs were the best the government could find.

One had a prior conviction for hacking. After he was shown the error of his ways, he was hired by the federal government. He was watched closely, but had shown no signs of turning back to a life of malicious mischief. Nancy chalked up his former hack-oholic tendencies to being too smart and too bored. He now appeared to be on the straight and narrow. He was told the option would be a prison term and it wouldn't be one of those country club joints.

Within a few hours, the team had a preliminary list of sixty-six people with the means and desire to finance an attack on United States soil. The list was further divided by personal wealth, suspicious activities over the past five years, ties to known terrorists, travel, and commentary from various spy organizations throughout the world.

The technicians ran the list through a program with weighting factors for the data. The program ranked the people on the list in priority order, from one to sixty-six. Once the program completed its analysis, the team reviewed the list. They were ready for the second meeting with Nancy.

"Okay, we're going to review each of the top ten names on the list and the supporting data. We need to validate that this list is the best we think it can be. I'll need solid reasons why a name should be moved up or down the list. Is that clear?"

Heads all around the conference room nodded.

Nancy continued, "Everyone has looked at the list, right?"

Again, heads nodded.

Nancy turned to her team leader, Eric Lederman. "Eric, lead the team through the list. Read the name, country of origin, net worth, organizational ties, and reasons why they want to attack the United States."

Eric was a former Marine Staff Sergeant who worked in Naval Criminal Investigative Services for a brief time before taking a job with a defense contractor. He'd been well paid, but hated the work. When the opportunity to be on the anti-terror team was offered, he jumped on it. He was an expert in Islamic culture and Middle East history.

The muscular man with dark, close-cropped hair stood and moved to the front of the room. His loud, staccato voice commanded everyone's attention. "Thank you, Miss Brown. We'll start with Osama Bin Laden. He is a very wealthy, very influential man. When in public, he lives like a pauper. His family is from Saudi Arabia and his fortune comes from Saudi oil. He uses passages in the Quran to justify his desire for a holy war against the west. He's opposed to Saudi Arabian policy allowing U.S. military bases on Saudi soil." The report on Bin Laden went on for several more minutes before moving on to number two.

The second man on the list, Imam Khidir Khadduri, an elderly Muslim Cleric, was believed to be Syrian. He'd traveled quite a bit over the last fifteen years to stay out of sight. His wealth was from oil and weapons sales. He used his wealth to fund terrorist training camps in several countries, including Syria and Libya. No intelligence agency had successfully tracked his whereabouts for years. He remained hidden, like a ghost, but his influence was evident in several terror plots around the world.

The next six members of the list were also wealthy extremists from various Middle East countries, all of whom had an ax to grind with the United States government.

The ninth man on the list stood out from the first eight. This man had a fraction of the wealth of the others. He made the list because of his ties to five of the top eight men. He was more of a middle man than a financier. A number of team members felt he should be moved further down the list, possibly as low as number twenty. But Nancy and several of the members with military background were against that move.

Nancy said, "What good is all the money of the first eight if they don't have a funnel to the troops. I think we're underestimating the importance of this man if we move him off the top ten. I suggest we move him up to number five." She paused and looked around the room. "Anyone have an opinion?"

"I think number two would be more appropriate." It was Eric Lederman. He also looked around the room for reaction.

After a number of sighs and deep breaths, several side bar discussions started to take place. Nancy let the discussions go for about thirty seconds, then held up her hands. "Okay." Everyone gave her their undivided attention. "So, let's have your comments for the record. Where should we place Sheik Al-Salil?"

He wound up at number six, but Nancy put a mental star next to his name.

Chapter 10

Vasquez had just walked in the door to his apartment at 6:30 P.M. when his cell phone vibrated in his pocket. He looked at the number and smiled. Tossing his keys in the tray on the table by the door, he flipped the phone open.

"Ola, Victoria."

"Ola, Ricardo. Working late I see. Does that mean you've got our detectors installed?"

His smile faded. But he put on his professional demeanor and said, "Yes. Well, almost. We're making good progress. I expect we'll have them installed on ninety percent of the tanks by Friday. They're very easy to install."

Victoria had just finished making a margarita in the kitchen of her condominium on the Gulf of Mexico before making the call to Ricardo. Her smile lit up the oval shaped mirror that hung on the wall in her living room. A small piece of salt from the rim of her glass hung on her lip. She licked her finger and picked off the white crystal. Tucking the salt crystal in her mouth with the tip of her finger, she savored the taste. Her smile returned at the news that her end of the plan was coming together nicely, even though Salil had been late with the shipment. If all went well, her piece of the plan would be in place well ahead of schedule. "And they should last for the remaining life of the refinery." *Which shouldn't be long if all goes well.* That thought made her smile broaden even more.

She continued, "Is there anything you need from me? Support in the field for installing the rest? Consider it a professional courtesy."

Vasquez thought about the offer for a moment. He was hoping she'd offer some help of a personal nature. His mind drifted to her beautiful, dark eyes and olive skin, and his view of her legs when they rode in her Corvette. *What a classy, sexy woman.*

"Ricardo?"

"No, we have everything under control. We'll start testing the units we installed today first thing in the morning. Like I said, it's so easy it hardly takes any time at all." He paused. "We may need an extra detector. One may be damaged. The tech we have doing the work was trying to take one apart."

Victoria tensed. She gripped her cell phone tighter as her mind raced with the possibility that one of these yokels might find and recognize the extra component under the cover. She was about to yell at Vasquez and ask him what the hell he was thinking. What if they went to the authorities? The FBI could be battering her door down at any second. Her mind raced.

"So, what's this guy's name?"

"Danny Wilkerson. But don't worry about him. He didn't even get the cover off and I made it clear t we didn't have any spares."

Victoria asked if he knew how to get in touch with Danny. He told her the tech's favorite hangout was a bar not far from his apartment. Victoria grinned. *It may not be such a bad day after all.*

Vasquez tried to shift the conversation to more personal topics. He suggested they go out for dinner, go to a movie, or just go out for a drink. Victoria deflected each suggestion by claiming she was tired and would probably stay in for the evening, alone. After a few more minutes of awkward conversation, punctuated by more awkward silence, he said good night and flipped his cell phone shut.

He wondered why this beautiful woman turned so cold so fast. She was always close to him, even when they grew up together back in Mexico. Since they were close to completing the job, she'd cooled off. *She's just uptight. She'll get over it once we've completed our work here.*

On the other end, Victoria flipped her phone shut as well. A blank stare looked back at her from the mirror as she formed a plan. She couldn't take the chance that he learned the real purpose of the devices. They were too close to fail now. As she held the antenna of the phone to her lips, more pieces of the puzzle fit into place. Slowly, the blank stare turned to a serious frown, then to a wicked smile. She knew what she had to do.

* * *

At 10:00 P.M. that evening, five miles north of Victoria's condominium, Danny Wilkerson had just walked into his favorite bar, Loco Pedro's. Lynyrd Skynyrd blared from the juke box. The cigarette smoke was heavy in the air. He was about to head up to the bar when he noticed a young woman looking at him. She sat at a booth, apparently alone. She lifted her drink and slowly took a sip. From the shape of the glass, the salt on the rim, and the golden liquid it contained, he knew she was drinking a margarita. She was stunningly beautiful and stood out among the regulars in the crowd. He looked away, heading towards the bar when he stopped to chat with a couple friends. He couldn't help but glance back at the woman. To his surprise, she was still looking his way. This time she cocked her head slightly, her smile just a bit more pronounced. Danny smiled back. He went to the bar and ordered a Corona and headed for the booth. She kept looking at him as he approached.

Even though her glass was over half full, he asked, "Can I buy you another one?"

"Sure."

He motioned for the bartender, who nodded.

Danny turned back to face the beautiful lady dressed in a red pull over blouse, cream colored capris, and red pumps with three inch heels. She wore bright red lipstick and nail polish. Her olive skin was perfect, not a blemish in sight. He looked up into her dark brown eyes set in a slim face.

"My name's Danny. What brings you to this dive?"

She glanced around the bar, still wearing the smile that had reeled him in. She wasn't uncomfortable in this bar, but it was easy to see it wasn't her style. She seemed the type who preferred something a little more upscale.

"I kind of like it. Has a real friendly atmosphere."

Just as she finished, two guys playing pool in the back room got into an argument. One of them accused the other of cheating. The bartender, a large, overweight man, looked their way. After a few seconds, the dispute cooled and everyone went back to their own private conversations.

Danny couldn't let the moment pass. "Yep, a real friendly atmosphere." He smiled.

She continued to smile at him.

Danny asked, "So what's your name?"

"Victoria. Victoria Sanchez."

"Where are you from, Victoria Sanchez?"

"I live in a condo on the Gulf. My great-grandparents are from

Mexico, just north of Mexico City. But my grandparents moved to Texas a long time ago." She continued that electric smile. "What about you, Danny . . .?"

"Wilkerson. I live around the corner from here. I work at Texas Star."

With as much phony sincerity as she could muster she said, "That's cool. What do you do there?" She knew, but she didn't want to push too hard. They had all night to talk. For the next half-hour, Victoria and Danny chatted. He drank another Corona. She sipped at her second Margarita, not making too much headway.

Victoria asked, "How would you like to take a ride?"

"That's okay. I can walk home from here."

"Who said anything about going home? I thought I'd take you for a spin in my new Corvette."

He smiled and immediately agreed. He was thinking fast car, fast woman. He was feeling pretty lucky. Was he going to score tonight? His chances looked pretty good right now, but he'd just met this woman. Maybe he was making a mistake. *What the hell, it's worth a shot. She's a beautiful, sexy woman and she has a Corvette. And she is with me.* He bet it was a red one and that's why she used red lipstick, red nail polish, and wore red. *Red hot.*

"Well, hell, yeah. Let's get going."

They headed for the parking lot and Victoria's bright red Corvette.

I knew it!

* * *

Twenty minutes later, Victoria Garcia and Danny Wilkerson were heading southwest on Highway 59. They'd just passed through the town of Edna. Victoria sped up. There were no cars visible in either direction. Danny saw a sign that said *Victoria-27 miles*. He smiled to himself at the irony. *I wonder if I'll have to wait that long?* Victoria hadn't said much since leaving the bar, but she still wore that infectious smile. He decided to be adventurous, touching her leg just above the knee. She turned his way and smiled even more as she put her hand on top of his. He began caressing her leg. She put her hands back on the wheel and didn't protest.

After another two miles, she slowed the car, preparing to turn off the highway. He didn't see any intersecting roads, but he was more concerned with trying to make sure this lady was in the mood before they stopped. As she turned the car off of the main highway, the headlights shone on a gravel road. She accelerated down the drive that went between a stand of trees. He looked ahead but didn't see anything. The trees formed a dark, leaf-lined tunnel. Finally, a creek came into view off to the left of the road. The gravel got rough as it followed the creek deeper into the woods. She had to slow down as the bottom of the car bumped the weeds and gravel that was slightly mounded between the tire grooves of the road.

The road was little more than a wide path now. Victoria slowed the car and turned to the right. A small house, little more than a cottage, came into view as the headlights swung around. She turned the engine off, opened the driver's side door, and got out. She headed towards the building.

Danny was a bit confused. He wondered what they were doing out in the middle of nowhere when she had a condo back in town. "Where are we?"

In the dark of the night, she noticed the confused look. Standing in front of the car, her smile was still visible in the headlights. The air was warm and still. Danny was a bit nervous now. What seemed like a great night was getting a bit weird.

"Come on inside. I think you'll be more relaxed once we get out of this heat."

Danny hesitated, not sure about Victoria's intentions. What if there was a group of men in the house waiting to mug him? He shook off the thought. This woman had a Corvette. She didn't need to mug guys in bars to pay her bills.

"Are you planning to get out or are you just going to sit there?" He sat motionless for a moment longer then opened the passenger door. As he stepped out, his foot caught a small, fallen branch and he stumbled.

Victoria laughed with a tone that was more mocking than playful. She headed towards the house, encouraging him to follow.

The moon was bright. There were eerie shadows of trees across the creek. The water made little noise as it moved on towards the Gulf. The only sound came from a chorus of insects playing their nighttime screeching tune.

He was still about ten feet behind when Victoria unlocked the door to the house. She went inside and turned on a light in the living room.

He followed her in, still feeling insecure, his nerves firing pulses throughout his body.

He entered the house and looked around. She closed and locked the door behind him.

Chapter 11

"Mom, Ann, how was the drive?"

Joe greeted his mother, Emma McKinney, and Lisa's mother, Ann Goddard at the front door of his and Lisa's home. Ann had flown to Ft. Myers from northern Ohio earlier in the week to visit Emma. They decided that a trip to Winter Garden, Florida to see Emma's grandchildren was in order. Ann also wanted to make sure her daughter was taking care of herself now that her pregnancy was nearing full term.

Ann smiled. "It was great. We stopped in Sarasota for lunch at a wonderful little diner. Then we decided to take a detour through Wimauma and Plant City."

Emma took over, a bright smile on her face, "And we have gifts." She pulled a plastic bag from behind her and handed it to Joe. "I think you'll like them."

Joe reached inside the bag and pulled out two tee shirts. The dark blue tee was an extra-large, the olive green shirt was a small. Joe held up the larger shirt across his chest and read the slogan under a picture of a run-down building. It said, *Ft. Lonesome Grocery – The Coldest Beer in Town.* Joe smiled. "They mean the only beer in town."

Lisa held hers up and read, *We Get All Our Supplies at Ft. Lonesome Grocery.* Lisa smiled. "Where is Ft. Lonesome?"

"Ask Joe," Emma replied. "He used to be a regular."

"It's a long story. Not to mention boring." Joe gave his mother a look that said *Now's not a good time.*

Just then, Anna ran into the entry yelling, "Gwamma, Auntie Ann!"

"Saved by the bell," Joe whispered, smiling at Lisa.

Sean followed, the perpetually serious look planted on his face.

Lisa maneuvered her belly next to Joe so she didn't have to lean over too far and quietly said, "You're not getting off that easy. I'll torture it out of you."

"Is that a promise?"

Lisa started to tickle Joe. Emma looked cross at the two lovers. "Cut it out, you two. There are children in the room." She smiled at her grandchildren. "We have gifts for you, too."

"Yea!" Little Anna screamed, delighted, not even knowing what her gift was. Emma handed over a box with the latest Barbie Doll on the market. It was one of the Independence Day special release dolls. Barbie was dressed from head to foot in red, white, and blue, with silver sequins running down the side of her slacks. An assortment of accessories came with the doll, including an American flag, high heeled shoes, and a patriotic, red, white, and blue top hat. Anna again screamed, "Yea!" Emma helped her get Barbie out of the box and Anna sat down to play.

Sean remained calm, his expression locked on serious. When Emma handed him what looked like a dark green book with a pen attached, Sean gave her a puzzled look. She leaned over to him said, "It's a journal. Whenever you feel happy or angry, or for any reason at all, you write it in your journal."

Sean considered what his grandmother said. "Do I have to write something down every day, 'cause that sounds like a diary. Girls have diaries."

She smiled at her grandson who seemed in a big hurry to grow up. "No, Sean. A journal is more like a story. You can write in it as often as you want and you can write whatever you want. You don't even have to keep track of the dates. Just write when you feel like it. If you want, I can help you get started."

"That's okay, Gramma. I can do it." Then with the slightest smile he said, "I'm going to start right now."

Sean headed back to his bedroom, then turned around, still smiling. "Thanks Grandma, I really like it."

Tears gathered in the corners of Emma's eyes as Sean headed down the hall to his room. She wasn't sure how he'd handle being given a journal. After all, he wasn't even seven. But his manner was more like that of a twelve-year old. Her hope was that writing would help him get his feelings out in a positive way. She'd mentioned her idea to Pat and Diane. They had no objection but were afraid he would find it stupid. It surprised Emma how readily he'd accepted the gift and it appeared he was planning to use it. But he was young. Only time would tell.

Ann walked over to her daughter and leaned over to get a hug. As she did, she noticed Lisa's belly shift, a bulge moving from one side of her daughter's stomach to the other. "Oh, my! That child sure is active, and big. I'll bet that baby weighs over eight pounds by the time he's born. Or is it a she?"

Lisa smiled. "She. We found out for sure this past week. We wanted to surprise you." The baby kicked. Lisa winced at the pain.

"It looks like you've got a soccer player there." Ann and Emma both smiled.

Joe motioned to the moms, "Can I get you anything to drink? We have pretty much anything, iced-tea, lemonade, sodas, water, even an adult beverage or two."

Emma said, "Normally, I'd say no, but I think I'll have an iced-tea."

Ann chimed in, "Make that two."

"Coming up."

"I'll help." Emma followed Joe into the kitchen.

Ann again looked over at her daughter as Lisa slowly eased into one of the recliners in the spacious living room. Her own pregnancies had been relatively difficult and Ann was concerned it might be a family trait. But she quickly pushed that thought from her mind. Lisa looked tan and fit. She moved slowly, but with confidence, careful to avoid obstacles. "So sweetie, how are you feeling?"

"Like I swallowed a basketball and our daughter is dribbling it down the court. She is so active. I'm hardly getting any sleep."

"You look good, considering you're about to pop." Ann's smile had a touch of empathy. Her daughter was in the home stretch, but that was the most difficult time of most pregnancies.

"I just wish I didn't have to pee every twenty minutes."

As Emma and Joe returned with a pitcher of ice tea, the phone rang. "Here, Mom. Can you handle this? I'll get the phone."

They all heard Joe answer and say, "Pat, how's the trip going?"

After the usual greetings, Joe passed the phone to Anna, then hollered to Sean so they could talk with Diane. After Joe and Pat let the women and children talk, they were back on the line.

Pat asked, "So is Lisa up to the trip to the park?"

"Yeah, I think. She's a trooper. She doesn't want to disappoint the kids. Anna's really excited about seeing the mice. Sean, well, he's your son. He's trying to act all macho."

Pat shook his head and looked over at Diane in the passenger seat. She was looking at him, but he turned his attention back to the call. "He'll loosen up once you get him to the park."

Pat turned serious. "Diane and I were talking with a guy I know from the USS *Nevada* in a coffee shop today. His name's Frank Clarion. He knows Evan Jones, my buddy who works at Superior Shores. Evan told Frank that an engineer who works at the plant is missing."

"Yeah. I saw it on the internet. I was looking up information on the nuke plant and it was one of the stories. How long's he been missing?"

"Five days, according to Frank. He said the whole thing is real suspicious. Nobody's seen or heard from him, like he fell off the planet. Left work one afternoon and never made it home." Pat paused for a moment then continued, "Evan told Frank this guy's wife claims they were planning a shopping trip to Chicago the next day. They had tickets to a show and a list of things they planned to do. Then he came up missing."

"If that's true, doesn't sound like she had anything to do with him going missing. But you never know."

"According to Evan they were a very happy couple. Nobody suspects the wife. Everyone agreed there weren't any issues at home."

There was silence on the line for a few seconds. "There's a lot of wide open space up there. Somebody could get lost easy in those woods."

"Yeah, but this guy knew the woods. Like everyone else up there, he's an outdoors kind of guy. He hunts, fishes, and camps. He knows how to survive. He had a cell phone. According to Frank there's patchy coverage in spots, but he would have known where the phone worked and where it didn't."

The more Pat talked, the tighter Joe's square jaw got. Maybe the couple wasn't as lovey-dovey as everyone thought. Funny things happen behind closed doors. But he and Pat weren't there, and they didn't have any hard facts. He reminded himself not to jump to any conclusions over a brief telephone call.

Pat spoke, "Hey, you still there?"

"Yeah. You sure know how to find trouble. Hell, you drove half way across the country into this mess. Remember Pat, you're on vacation, trying to relax. Don't get yourself tied up in this."

"It's not like I go looking for trouble."

Joe smiled. "Well, it sure seems to find you." He paused again. "Anyway, it could be just a domestic dispute. If it is more, leave it to the Mounties or the Wisconsin State Police or whoever the law is up there."

Pat had to agree. He was on doctor's orders to relax. More important, he was on his wife's orders to relax. If he started to get too involved, she'd do him bodily harm for sure.

"So you and Lisa are having fun with the kids?"

"Yeah, absolutely. I can see where raising kids can be tough at times, but your kids are easy. Sean hardly says a word." He paused. "He's one serious young man, especially for his age."

Pat tensed slightly at Joe's remark. "Yes, he is. He's serious for a twenty-year old. We don't understand it, but we hope he grows out of it."

"I wouldn't count on it. He gets it honestly. His grandpa was a serious guy. Remember Dad when we talked about going into the orange-growing business? He nearly had a fit."

"Yeah. And look at his Uncle Joe. He's a real serious Marine Corps dick-head." Pat laughed into the phone.

"Real funny, brother. We should probably drop this. Anyway, have a great trip around the lake. Bring back some souvenirs and try to stay out of trouble."

"I will. You think Diane is going to let me get involved? She's watching everything I do."

Joe could hear Diane in the background saying, "You're damn right I'm watching you. You're going to relax if it kills both of us."

"See what I mean? She woke up just to tell me that. She's relentless." Pat turned and smiled at Diane who punched his shoulder.

"Ouch. That hurt."

Joe said, "Wimp."

Pat rubbed his shoulder in mock pain and said to Joe, "Hey, we've got to run. We want to head up to the northern part of Michigan, around Grayling, before dark. We've still got a couple of hours to go. Kiss the kids, the grandmas, and the mom-to-be for us."

"Will do. Later."

When Joe hung up, his mind went to the missing engineer. He thought about Northern Wisconsin and wondered what could have happened, especially to someone who supposedly knew the outdoors. People like that took precautions. He thought about going on the internet to see if any news had come up on one of the major network websites. It was worth a shot. It wasn't like he was real busy, just a few home projects. Maybe he could find out something before Pat and Diane got there that would keep his brother from looking deeper. Pat didn't need the stress and Joe didn't want his sister-in-law charged with murdering his brother.

Chapter 12

Nancy Brown stood in front of the briefing room. Most new hires would be nervous addressing a team of specialists with more experience. But Nancy was comfortable with her knowledge and skills in her chosen profession. She looked directly at the audience, challenging them to question the content of the report she'd just delivered in her usual, no-nonsense, manner.

"We have a lot of data from a number of sources who've reviewed the video. It's a mixture of good news and bad. The 'experts' had relatively little in the way of new information."

Colonel Sheila Warner looked around the room as her newest member addressed the team at 0730 hours in the briefing room at Quantico. Much of the information in the rapidly growing file came from the dozen people in the room. The new data came from intelligence agencies with expertise on radical Islamic groups. They were able to deliver their preliminary reports within twenty-four hours. Specialists from the Central Intelligence Agency, the National Security Agency, the Marine Corps, and the Army determined that the beheading was not performed by any of the jihadists on their lists. They also backed the belief of the Anti-Terrorist Unit that the scene of the crime was not in Iraq, Iran, Afghanistan, Pakistan, or anywhere else in the Middle East. It wasn't in any Arab or predominantly Muslim country.

Nancy continued. "Based on analysis of the video, the victim was beheaded in the United States or Canada. The highest probability is the Midwestern United States, specifically northern regions of Minnesota, Wisconsin, or Michigan. The other possibility is western Ontario or southern Manitoba."

The team members believed it to be true based on the type of plants and trees that were observed as well as the background noises made by wildlife and insects.

Nancy continued her briefing. "These 'terrorists' also appear to be amateurs, maybe even imposters. The leader of the group appears authentic, based on his accent, his delivery of parts of Bin Laden's Fatwa, and the apparent elation in his expression during the entire episode. The supporting cast did a poor job of playing along. All of our counterparts at the other agencies said they'd never seen personnel at a beheading puke at the first sight of blood like this bunch."

The rest of Nancy's brief took less than fifteen minutes. It was at a summary level since the team had sat through hours of review the previous day. Except for confirming what the team had already suspected, only a few points were new. None of the usual groups were claiming responsibility. No reports appeared on Al Jazeera or any other news agency. The video hadn't appeared on any internet sites. The report all but endorsed their professional opinions.

They'd made quick progress on their initial hypothesis. Whoever killed this guy did a lousy job of appearing to be seasoned jihadists. They looked more like school kids pulling a prank on video. But the beheading was real. Even Hollywood couldn't fake what they'd seen.

Nancy continued. "Since we believe this is not the work of a hardcore terrorist organization, and all the feedback that we have confirms our suspicions, we've contacted the FBI. They've gathered information on missing persons meeting the description of the victim. They already have a number of leads. We expect to hear back from them this morning."

One of the veteran members of the team, Alfred Harple asked, "Miss Brown, shouldn't we just turn this over to the FBI and call it a day? We've already determined that this isn't a real, or developing terrorist situation. Isn't it out of our jurisdiction now?"

Colonel Warner bristled at the comment. She was about to rip into Al Harple when Nancy replied, "No, it's still our case. Per our procedures, we have jurisdiction until there is an official turnover of responsibility and exchange of data. We haven't done either in an official capacity. We're not pulling off this case. Not yet anyway."

Nancy looked around the room for any reaction, but everyone was stone-faced. She continued, "Just because these subjects look like amateurs, they did violently and brutally commit murder. They did cite passages from the Koran, and they did recite Bin Laden's Fatwa. Just because they don't meet our expectations of what a terrorist should be, doesn't make them any less of a threat."

No one else pushed the issue. Colonel Warner's face remained stern. Nancy had calmly said exactly what she intended to say though she would have said it with more force. If nothing else, she wanted to find out who these well-dressed terrorists were. Maybe they were real and were just good at mixing in with western culture, hence the dress shoes and pants. Regardless, these people were apparently on U.S. or Canadian soil. If they were in the United States, that constituted an invasion by an enemy force. That was an act of war, assuming the victim was a U.S. citizen.

"Thank you, Miss Brown for the update and your analysis." She nodded in Nancy's direction. "We will be keeping this case, and we will pursue these subjects until they are apprehended and prosecuted. It is my hope they stand before a military court and we keep the civilian legal system out of it. But we can't do anything until we find them and apprehend them. So our first move is to wait until we get more information on the identity of the victim or we have a definite crime scene. As soon as we hear from the FBI, we'll put our plan in motion."

Al looked at Colonel Warner and asked, "What plan is that, Colonel?"

"The plan that you and Miss Brown are going to put together today, starting right now." She looked from Al to Nancy and back. "Any questions?"

In unison they said, "No, Ma'am."

* * *

Angela Corbin blew her nose again. It was red and sore from the constant assault from her draining sinuses caused by hours of continuous crying. She wiped her bloodshot eyes with the back of her left hand, then dialed the number for the FBI field office in Milwaukee. She threw the tissue into the trash beside the kitchen table. It was already overflowing with used Kleenex. The phone rang once, then again. It seemed like the ring was in slow motion, as if the next ring were delayed a second or two longer than the first. The third ring seemed to drag on forever when the ring was finally interrupted by someone answering the phone.

"Federal Bureau of Investigation. Milwaukee field office."

In a raspy voice, Angela Corbin asked to speak with the agent in charge of her husband's case. She was placed on hold, then the call was disconnected. She dialed again and the same person answered with the same greeting. Angela repeated her request.

This time, a man answered, “Special Agent Kowalski.”

“Agent Kowalski, this is Angela Corbin.”

She paused, expecting that Agent Kowalski would recognize her name and know it was about her husband. When he didn’t respond, she continued, “I reported my husband missing several days ago. I haven’t heard anything from you. Have you found my husband yet?”

Again, Agent Kowalski didn’t respond for several seconds. At first, she thought the connection might have been broken, but she heard him sigh. Finally, he said, “Mrs. Corbin, I’m sorry, but we haven’t located Mr. Corbin yet. I can assure you we’re doing everything we can to find him.”

Angela thought he was being evasive. She shifted the phone from one ear to the other and picked up a pen, preparing to take notes.

“Agent Kowalski, exactly what is the FBI doing to find my husband?”

Again silence followed by another sigh. “Ma’am, we are going through the standard procedures for a missing person. We have not turned up anything at this time. When we get information we will contact you.”

She didn’t know what else to say so she meekly said, “Thank you,” and hung up the phone. She immediately began to sob again, feeling helpless and alone.

In Milwaukee, Agent Kowalski thought back to the original call from Angela Corbin, reporting her husband as missing. He tried to tell her the FBI didn’t handle missing person cases unless there was evidence of a kidnapping or other crime that crossed state boundaries. As he looked at the printed “Request for Information,” he felt a twinge of guilt for putting her off. The agent read the form for the third time. A man had apparently been brutally murdered, and they believed that it might have happened in his jurisdiction. The federal agency that sent the request, the Anti-Terror Unit, was trying to determine the decedent’s identity. The physical description – size and hair color—and the clothing worn by the dead man matched Alex Corbin in every detail, right down to the wedding band on the ring finger of his left hand.

Kowalski picked up the phone and dialed the number for the Anti-Terrorist Unit at Quantico, Virginia. It was going to be a long, busy day.

Chapter 13

Evan Jones sat on his screened-in back porch staring out into the thick pines that ringed the back of his house. The sky was overcast with odd-shaped silver and gray clouds so low they seemed to touch the tips of the swaying pines. The breeze was chilly for late May, even by northern Wisconsin standards. The pine pollen was thick in the air.

Evan shivered, then stiffened as his thoughts went back into the woods where he'd been walking several hours before. His jaw tightened. It was sore from gritting his teeth. The scene was burned into his brain so vividly he was certain he would never forget.

He'd been out on his property scouting the area for signs of deer. He knew where he'd had luck with placing his tree blind in the past, but he wanted to try a different location this year. It was good to change things up so the deer didn't get used to you setting up in the same location, year after year. Deer seemed to have a keen sense of where danger lurked. They learned that hunters, like wild animals, had certain habits. The clever creatures changed their habits in order to avoid that favorite blind. It was uncanny how a hunter could sit and observe deer traffic for weeks before hunting season officially opened, and the deer would nearly walk up to you. Then on opening day, they all disappeared. Word was out on the wilderness network that hunting season had arrived.

Evan had been walking on his property in the heavily wooded Chequamegon National Forest in Wisconsin, about five miles southwest of Muskellunge Lake. It was early morning and the temperature was in the mid-40s. This particular walk in the forest was easy since he had no gear to haul. He was the owner of the land. His parents, now retired in Florida, had deeded the property to him last year. He could hunt to his heart's content, when in season of course. Since deer season was about six months down the road, he didn't even carry a rifle. The plaid cotton shirt and Carhartt hunting jacket he wore, coupled with the energetic pace he kept, provided plenty of protection from the chill. He planned on returning home long before sunset.

As he scouted the area, he spotted numerous deer, a flock of wild turkeys, and countless other animals. None of them appeared frightened. *They know. It's not time yet. Damn.* He shook his head, wiped his nose with a handkerchief and continued along the nearly invisible path.

A twelve point buck crossed Evan's path not fifty feet in front of him. He froze in his tracks, the buck stopped and looked directly at him, pausing for several seconds before calmly continuing on his way.

Evan shook his head and started walking again, looking after the handsome animal. He walked in silence for a few more minutes, observing the trees, trying to decide which one would make the best vantage point for the path that big buck had just used.

He noted this area was a good possibility for the coming season. After walking a bit further he noticed that someone had baited the area with salt licks. He left them in place, but he planned to remove them before hunting season began. If he found out who set the salt licks, he'd ban them from hunting on his property for good. Deer should have a sporting chance. Shooting an animal at a salt lick was like shooting fish in a barrel. *What's the point?* You could buy them already cleaned and filleted at the grocer.

As Evan walked on, the breeze rustled through the trees. The sounds of the forest came alive. A number of birds called out as they flew overhead. He spotted a pair of bald eagles high in the sky through an opening in the tree cover and stopped to catch a better glimpse of the great birds circling. He smiled. *Beats sitting in front of the boob tube.*

When the eagles disappeared beyond the treetops, he continued down the path. It was getting more difficult to actually see a path as the brush grew thicker.

A dark object about twenty feet ahead caught his eye. It looked unnatural in this setting. Evan moved in for a closer look. It was a black knit cap, the type that covered the entire head with openings for a person's eyes and mouth.

What the hell is this doing here? It looks almost new. This can't have been here for more than a week.

He decided he would pick it up on the way back, if he remembered. If not, the earth would reclaim it soon enough.

The breeze picked up again. Tall pines swayed as the sound of the wind grew louder. The canopy of several maple trees leaned with the rush of air, their newly sprouting leaves rustling. It had been a thoroughly enjoyable walk to that point.

Then Evan frowned. He stopped in mid-stride. He raised his head and sniffed the air. No mistaking it. Something was dead. Judging from the strength of the odor it had to be a large animal, like a deer or bear. Whatever it was, it wasn't too far from where he stood.

The path led to an area heavily wooded with white pine. The forest floor was carpeted by brown needles, muffling the sound of his steps. As Evan walked, the scent of decomposition grew stronger, his nasal passage assaulted by the foul odor. He was about to stop and turn back when he spotted a number of turkey vultures about fifty feet ahead. He moved closer. One by one, the vultures turned towards him. As if on cue, they all took flight at the same time and took their places in a large pine tree about one hundred feet away.

Evan turned his attention back to the path and the spot where the vultures had been feeding. The smell was nearly overpowering. Finally, the gruesome scene came into view. He stopped as nausea welled up in his stomach and he heaved.

He dropped to his hands and knees, heaving again. He came up for air and looked again at the scene. Several minutes passed before Evan got himself together enough to approach the badly decomposed human body.

From the clothes, he guessed t it was a man, about six feet tall. He noticed duct tape around the man's legs and arms. The head was separated from the body. At first he thought the vultures may have caused the separation, but then he saw the marks on the vertebrae. Someone had cut this poor guy's head off. Duct tape had been placed over the man's mouth, too, though the tape had been partially torn away. Somebody wanted to make a point with this murder, but they didn't want anyone to hear the man's screams. This scene reminded Evan of the beheadings he'd heard about that had appeared on the internet recently. But why would anyone do this in northern Wisconsin?

Evan thought for a moment , then cursed, remembering he hadn't brought his cell phone. Out here, they were useless anyway, as the closest tower was over twenty-five miles away. He knew his property well, so he was sure he could find his way back to the body after he contacted the sheriff's office.

Fear welled up in his chest. *What if the killers are watching?* But they wouldn't watch for this long. He had to get back to his house and call the sheriff's office. They'd know what to do. Evan wiped his mouth, then lifted his Brewer's ball cap, pushed his hair back, and put his ball cap back on. He'd been sweating even on this cool morning. Now he had a chill. *Best get walking. It's gonna take time to get the sheriff back out here.*

It took him nearly twenty-five minutes to get back to his house. As he walked along, it hit him. *The shoes, the clothes. It's probably Alex. Oh, God. Somebody killed him on my property.*

When Evan got to his house, he took a deep breath then dialed 911.

"911, what is your emergency?"

"I found a body."

The operator calmly asked, "Is the person breathing or do they have a pulse?"

"Uh, no."

"Have you tried CPR?"

Evan held the phone away from his ear and looked at it as if it was diseased. He had a vision of the decomposed body causing a wave of nausea. Into the phone he said, "No, ma'am. The body smells. It's been dead for at least a few days. It's out in the woods about five miles southwest of Muskellunge Lake."

"Sir, please stay away from the body and give me your location. I will contact the sheriff. May I have your name, please?"

Fifteen minutes after his call, a Bayfield County Deputy Sheriff pulled into Evan's long, gravel driveway. After questioning Evan for a few minutes, the deputy called Sheriff Madeline Wymer. He repeated Evan's gruesome description of the condition of the deceased. Twenty minutes later, his place was crawling with law enforcement personnel. The entire group followed him to the location. They set to work with crime scene tape, as if there was anyone around to disturb the sight.

After nearly an hour of questioning, Evan was allowed to head back to his house.

Sitting on his back porch, he wondered at the evil that must have possessed the killer—or killers—to commit such a crime. And would they be back for him now that he had discovered their evil deed? He couldn't erase the sight of the dead man branded into his brain. He wondered if he'd get any sleep that evening. His new companion by the bed would be his loaded twelve gauge shotgun with a round chambered.

Evan was glad his wife was gone for a few days. One less thing he had to worry about at the moment. He would eventually have to tell her and her son, Jimmy Smith. Hopefully the perp would be caught by then and Evan wouldn't be afraid to leave her home alone. Then he'd have to call his parents in Florida and tell them the terrible news. It wouldn't affect them directly, but they'd be shocked, to say the least. Crimes like this didn't happen in northern Wisconsin.

One other thing was certain. If this was Alex Corbin, the missing engineer, he didn't just wander off and get lost. Some sick bastard had made sure he was dead.

Chapter 14

"Anybody know where the hell Danny is or why he's late?" Shop Foreman, Bud Yantzy, yelled out into the shop where his technicians sat at their workbenches, awaiting their assignments for the day. He'd been peering out in the shop area, waiting for Danny Wilkerson to clock in, but he was late.

Sammy Helzer, his feet propped up on his workbench, looked up from the morning paper towards Danny's seat. He moved his feet, his work boots hitting a cup of coffee, spilling a bit on the Plexiglas that covered the surface of his bench.

Damn it. At least it didn't get on my pictures. He grabbed a rag and started to clean up the mess. He looked toward his foreman as he soaked up the coffee. "Hey, Bud, what's up?"

"Where's Danny? He should be in by now. Did he tell you he was calling off?"

Helzer hesitated. Danny hadn't said a word to him about being late or missing a day. Not that he would have. Everyone in the shop knew you called your foreman, not your buddy in the shop, if you were calling off sick. "No. He didn't call me. Last time I talked with him was at the end of shift yesterday. He didn't say anything about being late or calling off today."

Bud rubbed a burly hand across his face. He had more work than he had workers and one of his jobs required skills for which only a handful of guys were qualified. Now he had to have someone work overtime, and that assumed nothing else went wrong the rest of the day. But he had to get his techs out in the field working or the situation would get worse. *Damn management. We're already short staffed. How do they expect us to get this maintenance done without trained workers?*

He handed one of the newer technicians a manila folder. "Okay. You're not really officially qualified"—he put quotes in the air with his fingers—"to calibrate the gas relief valves, but there's no one else. You need to read the procedure first, then come see me and I'll give you some instructions on how to do it right. I'll be overseeing your work, so we can meet the requirements without your being qualified. Can you handle it?"

"Sure, Bud. I've helped Sammy do it before. It's not rocket science."

"Listen, son, if you screw this up, you could blow up half the plant, so don't get too cocky. Understand?"

"Yeah, I understand."

He must have turned white as a ghost because Bud looked at him and asked, "Are you gonna get sick? You look like crap."

"No. I'm good. I just ate some real hot wings last night and they're catching up with me. I'll be fine." He laid the folder on his desk and started to read the instructions.

Bud looked at him a little longer, then went back to reading the next folder in the stack. He yelled out another name, and another technician walked into the office.

Sammy headed back to his workbench, wondering where Danny could be. He pulled out his cell phone and dialed his friend's home number. The answering machine picked up after five rings and a mechanical sounding voice said that no one was home, but to leave a message at the tone. Before the beep sounded, he hit the end button.

Technicians being late in the maintenance shop wasn't unheard of, but Danny being late without calling in was unprecedented. He was the most punctual and reliable person in the shop. You could always count on him, without fail.

Something isn't right. He'd have called in. The only thing unusual about yesterday was that Danny's buddy, Hatch, had visited the shop. Then that deal with Vasquez, but that was nothing. *Maybe he's just running late and his cell phone battery is dead. I'll give him a little longer and see what happens.*

But another hour passed and Danny was still a no-show. Worse, Bud Yantzy paced in the foreman's office, scratching his head, mumbling to himself. Sammy's anxiety rose. The folder on his workbench with his work assignment was all but forgotten. He wondered if Hatch might know Danny's whereabouts. *How can I reach him?* He walked over to Danny's workbench and scanned the pictures, notes, and manuals. There were no phone numbers.

The shop phone rang. Sammy took four quick strides and answered, "I&C shop."

"Yo, Sammy."

Helzer recognized Hatch's voice immediately. "Hatch, have you seen Danny this morning? He didn't show up for work."

In his southern twang, Hatch said, "No, I haven't. Knowing Danny, this isn't good news."

"Yeah. He never misses work. If he's going to be late, he always calls ahead."

"I'll go to his place and see if he just overslept or something." Before Sammy could say anything he asked, "Did he say where he was going last night?"

"Sometimes he goes to a bar near his apartment. He can walk there and stumble home if need be."

"You mean Loco Pedro's?"

"Yeah, that's the place."

"We were there the other night. Okay. Here's what I'm gonna do. I'll try his place first, then I'll head over to Loco's and see if anyone's at the bar this morning. Maybe one of the employees saw him. He's a regular, so they probably know him."

"Call me when you find him."

"Oh, yeah. You can count on it."

* * *

Fifteen minutes later, Hatch pulled up to Danny's apartment building, a tan, three-story, stucco building. The stucco finish had some wear and tear, but the building looked solid aside from being due for some maintenance. The windows were due for an upgrade. The landlord was obviously saving his capital.

There were two apartments on each floor. The main entrance was in the center of the building.

Hatch parked his rented Ford Taurus on the street. Even this early in the morning the oppressive dry heat hit him as he stepped out of the car. He hit the clicker to lock the car doors as he approached the building. He walked through the apartment building entrance, noting the mailboxes in the hall on the right. The hallway ran the length of the building to an identical doorway at the rear. He looked over the names on the six boxes. Five of the small brass doors had names. One looked like the name label had been recently scratched off. Danny lived in 3B.

He looked around for an elevator, but saw none and headed for the staircase. It looked solid enough, but creaked with each step that he took. He looked up and noticed the building had ten-foot ceilings. *Well, I guess I'll be gettin' my morning exercise.*

Mariachi music came from behind two of the apartments as he made his way to the third floor. When he got to 3B, he stopped, looked around, and listened. There wasn't a sound coming from Danny's apartment. He looked across the hall at the apartment that had no name. It, too, was quiet.

No better time like the present. Hatch took one last look around. There were no security cameras and he didn't see anyone. He shrugged, placed a hand on the door knob, readied himself to force the door when the doorknob turned and the door eased open. A young Mexican girl gazed up at Hatch. A small dog with golden fur ran out and sniffed at Hatch's pant leg. The girl said nothing but continued to stare at him.

Hatch finally regained his composure. "Hello there, pretty lady. Is Mr. Wilkerson home?"

In perfect English, the young girl said, "No. He was supposed to come home by midnight. I watch his place when he goes out."

Hatch raised an eyebrow. This little girl couldn't have been more than twelve years old.

"He's not a perv. He just pays me to watch the place, feed his dog, and take him out to poop." She paused while Hatch considered this new information. She continued, "He was supposed to pay me last night when he got home, so I'm pissed."

"Hey, you should watch your mouth. Little girls shouldn't talk like that."

She shrugged. "I talk like that all the time. I'm gonna say a few things to Danny when I see him, too, the bastard."

Hatch shook his head, smiling. The kid had spunk, that's for sure. "What's your name?"

"Alisa Maria Lopez."

"Okay, Miss Lopez, can you tell me where Danny went?"

"Same place he always goes. To Loco Pedro's. Sometimes he brings girls back here, you know, to . . ."

Hatch covered his ears in mock horror. Then he said, "Is there anyone at Loco's that he knows especially well?"

"Well, let me think. Maybe the owner, you know, Pedro!"

Smart ass kid. “Okay. Thanks. I’ll head over there and see if he knows what happened to our buddy.”

“First, he isn’t our buddy. He’s a prick for stiffing me out of my pay. Second, Pedro won’t tell you anything. He doesn’t trust strangers and you are a stranger.”

Hatch considered this little girl for a moment. “How much did that prick, pardon my language, stiff you for, Alisa?”

“Twenty bucks.”

Hatch reached into his wallet, pulled out a Jackson and handed it to the girl. “Okay, he’s all caught up. Now, where do you live? Aren’t you supposed to be in school?”

“I’m home-schooled.”

“Well shouldn’t you be at home . . . being home-schooled?”

“Look, mister, just because you gave me twenty bucks doesn’t mean you can run my life.” He frowned at her. “Anyway, I start at four in the afternoon, when my mom gets home from work. I’m already doing high school Algebra and English.”

“Sounds to me like you’re doing real well in the English, too. At least you got the cursing down.”

She stuck her tongue out at him. “I have to get home. I have some chores to do. And I have to get lunch ready for my brothers.”

At this revelation, he raised both eyebrows. He decided it was time to go before he learned any more about little Alisa Maria Lopez. He made his way down the steps and out to his car. Three young, tough–looking Chicano boys were standing there, two of them leaning on his rental car. He took a deep breath, rolled his eyes and walked right up to them.

“Ya’ll havin’ a nice mornin’?”

The tallest of the boys said, “Yeah, Homes. We’re having a fine day. Better than you, anyway.”

“What makes you say that?”

“Cause we like this car, and I think we’re going to borrow it for a while.” He smiled and said, “You got a problem with that?”

When he finished, all three stood up straight and started to form a circle around Hatch. He just smiled and stood still, but he looked each kid over, judging who was leading and who was following. “Yeah, I got a problem with that. Tell ya’ll what, I’m goin’ to give you a chance to walk away, but it won’t last long.”

When the first kid started to speak Hatch swung around and grabbed one of the others around the throat. He pulled a switchblade from the kids pocket, then cut his belt in two. His baggy pants fell on the ground at his ankles. Lucky for him, he had on a pair of boxer shorts, decorated with marijuana leaves. The other two stared first at their friend's pants, then back at Hatch who was still smiling.

"Times up."

The two kids, their jaws hanging open, stared at Hatch, then slowly backed away a few steps. After putting about ten feet between themselves, their friend, and Hatch, they turned and ran, disappearing between two nearby apartment buildings.

Hatch let go of the boy, his pants still around his ankles. He moved in front of him and said, "You can pull your trousers up now. You shouldn't really advertise that you're a dope head. And I think you should follow your friends."

The kid cleared his throat and said in a scared, shaky voice, "Si." He reached down with one hand.

"But before you go, do you know the man that lives in 3B?"

The kid was still scared. When he opened his mouth nothing came out. Hatch smiled.

"Look, I'm not going to hurt you. I just need to know where my friend is."

"Danny's a friend of yours?"

"Yeah. The girl who takes care of his dog said he didn't come home last night. Know anything about that?"

The boy got his voice back, though it sounded a bit dry. "You must be talking 'bout Alisa. She talks too much, but she's cute. She's my sister."

Hatch raised an eyebrow. "Seems like everybody's brother and sister around here. When we're through, you should go home. She said something about fixing your lunch."

"I'm telling you the truth. She takes care of our little brother while Mama works. And she's tellin' the truth. My man, Danny didn't come home last night. That's not like him. He's a pretty solid dude. He's good to us, buys us beer to watch his place."

"Okay . . . I didn't catch your name."

"I didn't toss it." With that he pulled his pants up and walked away.

Hatch shook his head, turned and headed off down the street towards Loco Pedro's.

Chapter 15

"This is it. The walleye mailbox is a dead giveaway." As he brought the Explorer to a stop Pat nodded towards the oversized fish on a four by four post at the edge of the road.

"Right, since that's only the fifth one we've seen since turning off the highway."

"You're such a skeptic. Look at the driveway. He said you can't see the house from the road."

Diane looked straight ahead. All she could see on either side of the road were tall pine trees. The trees were so thick that only a scant bit of the blue sky was visible. Since the time they'd turned onto this gravel road, there had been no houses visible on either side. Diane shook her head. "Did he happen to give you the address?"

Pat looked at his wife like she'd just grown a third eye. "Dear, real men don't need addresses. But I happen to have it right here." Sitting behind the steering wheel of the Ford Explorer, he tried to straighten his leg and reached into his pocket, pulling out a ragged and worn piece of folded notebook paper. "Let's see . . . 63695 Musky Lake Road, Iron River, Wisconsin."

"That's what the fish says." Diane pointed to the scaly, plastic mailbox.

"Pardon me?" Then Pat looked where his wife was pointing. Sure enough, on the side of the fish was the matching number with the name Evan Jones. "I told you it'd be easy to find."

Diane rolled her eyes. They'd been in the area for about an hour and had just found Musky Lake Road in the last ten minutes. Pat turned and headed down the drive. After thirty seconds, they were still driving along, beginning to wonder if it was the right drive.

Pat said, "Maybe his drive was across the road back there. It sure doesn't look like there's a house back this way."

Just as Pat finished his sentence, a large log home came into view. "I knew it was back here."

Diane rolled her eyes for the second time in less than three minutes. But they were quickly drawn back to the massive log home. It was a sight fit for the cover of *Log Home Digest*, if there was such a publication. The pines had been cleared for at least one hundred feet on all sides of the home. A well-manicured, green lawn surrounded the structure. A fence made from rough cut beams edged the beautiful lawn. The shade from the pines made Diane wonder how the grass received enough sunlight to grow.

Pat pulled the Explorer in behind a four wheel drive Ford F150 and parked. The air was cool with a strong pine scent. Several stacks of firewood in varying stages of curing ran along the edge of the pine trees to the right of the house.

As they got out of the Explorer, a middle-aged man with salt-and-pepper hair, and wearing a light-weight coat came around the house from the back. He approached Pat, smiling.

"I thought you got lost or something!"

"Nah. Just took our time, that's all."

They shook hands, then the man turned to Diane. "You must be Pat and Diane's daughter." He turned to Pat and asked, "Where's your wife?"

Diane smiled and blushed all in the same moment. He held out his hand and introduced himself. "I'm Evan Jones, one of Pat's former Navy buddies." He lightly shook her hand. "I can see Pat is a very blessed man. It is nice to meet you, Diane."

"Nice to meet you, too. You have a lovely place."

"It was my parents. They turned it over to me when they moved to Florida. They swore they'd be back in the summers but so far, they've missed the first two. Dad likes his golf and Mom likes the beach, so there you have it."

Pat commented, "That's a pretty good deal if you ask me."

"It works great for me. The only thing is it's a pretty long drive to the plant each day. But with no mortgage payment, I guess I can afford it. I love the drive through the woods. It's beautiful no matter what time of year. Winters get a little dicey at times. The snow's pretty deep up here and sometimes the plows take their time getting out this way. But the neighbors work together to clear the local roads."

"Nice." Pat and Diane smiled and nodded their approval.

"Let me help you with your luggage. You are planning to stay here tonight, right?"

Pat replied nodding towards the large home, "Well, if you have room."

"I think I can squeeze you in."

Pat and Evan grabbed the suitcases and they all headed inside. When they walked into the entry, Diane was awestruck. The two story entry was spectacular, with windows from the top of the doorway to the second floor ceiling, ending in an A-frame at the peak of the roofline. The light entering the windows was subdued by the shade of the pines. The natural light coming through the windows danced on the walls in the entry with the swaying of the trees.

Pat noticed Evan appeared a bit tense, that his smile wasn't as relaxed as he remembered from the submarine. He wondered if there might be some problems on the home front. He hadn't mentioned his wife or her son at all. Pat did notice some feminine touches around the house, but most of the décor had a hunter's lodge feel rather than a family home.

Evan and Pat dropped the bags at the foot of the stairs. Evan then gave them the grand tour. Every inch of the log home was beautiful. Diane noticed the mounted deer heads and trophy-sized fish on the wall. It was obvious their host was a big outdoorsman.

When they settled in the family room off the kitchen, Pat and Evan talked about their days in the Navy on the USS *Nevada*. Diane had heard most of the stories before, but from Pat and Hatch. Evan's versions were similar, but he added a few new details. She made a mental note to ask Pat about them later.

Then Pat asked about the missing engineer.

Evan's mood changed in an instant. His smile flipped to a frown.

"He's not missing anymore. He was found this morning."

Pat spoke up. "Is he alright?"

"No. He's dead." Evan looked down for a moment and took a deep breath. "Actually, I found him."

"Oh, my God!" Diane's hand shot up to cover her mouth. Pat frowned.

"Where did you find him . . . and how did he die?"

"I'm not sure you want to hear this, at least I don't think Diane will." He looked from one to the other. "He was murdered." He took a deep breath and continued the tale of how he came across the body of Alex Corbin on his property. He left out the part about the buzzards, the smell, and the beheading. He figured he would tell Pat when they were alone, and Pat could decide if his wife could handle the details. He talked about how the sheriff came out and surveyed the scene before calling in the FBI. “The county sheriff’s office and the Feds just left about an hour ago.”

“How far are we from where the body was found?” Pat was getting that familiar itch to help investigate.

He was focused on Evan when Diane interrupted. “Pat, don’t you think we should leave that to the FBI and the sheriff?”

“Sure, honey. I’m just curious.”

Diane forced a smile. Pat and Evan could tell she wasn’t happy where this was going. “Remember the last time you got ‘curious’ about a crime? I think you’re still getting reminders about that.”

She was referring to his nightmares. He’d been recovering recently. The last thing she wanted was for him to get involved in a murder investigation. She was pretty sure that the Feds or even the local sheriff’s office would shun any attempt by him to offer his ‘expertise,’ but you never know. In a rural area like this, they might welcome someone with previous investigative skills.

After talking about the crime and the discovery for about ten minutes, Evan suggested they talk about a different topic. He wanted to know about their plans for the trip around Lake Superior. He asked when they planned to head out, which direction they wanted to go, and how long they figured the trip would take. He suggested several stops along the way, including the shipping port at Duluth, the locks at Sault Ste. Marie, and the Pictured Rocks Lakeshore. There were countless other beautiful places along the lake, particularly in Canada where the land looked the same as it must have before the country was settled.

Evan told them they were in for a real treat that evening because he planned to cook dinner. When Diane asked about the menu, he said, “It’ll be a surprise.” Diane looked at the mounted deer heads on the wall and had a good idea what was in store. About that time, she was thinking a burger would be nice.

* * *

To Diane’s surprise, she enjoyed the venison stew. Their host told them cooking wild game was an art. If you tried to cook it like beef you were making a mistake. He recommended they look for wild game cookbooks in the small shops around the lake. Maybe even try some of the local favorites at the small diners.

After dinner, Evan fixed drinks. They talked about his work at the plant. He mentioned they needed to take a tour of the plant before heading off around the lake. Diane said Pat would, but she would take a rain check. After some mock disappointment, Evan turned to Pat and asked, "Are you still in?"

"Heck, yeah. I wouldn't miss the chance to see a nuke plant in operation."

"Then it's a date . . . kind of."

Diane didn't care too much about the plant, but she was concerned Pat would use the opportunity to dig into Alex Corbin's murder. She would talk with him about it before they went to sleep that evening. Her biggest concern was whether Pat's nightmares would return. *Maybe this trip wasn't the greatest idea after all.*

Chapter 16

Haji Madu had been with StarPower-Ohio for just over two years. Considered bright and reliable by his peers, many thought he had a great future with the company. He'd been willing to spend extra hours working on issues many new engineers were afraid to tackle without oversight from more senior staff. But Haji was energetic, intelligent, and resourceful. He was one of the many new college graduates hired to replace experienced, retiring engineers. He seemed eager to learn. Many believed that Haji was destined to be part of the future management team at Erie Shores Nuclear Power Station on Lake Erie in northern Ohio.

About two-thirds of the engineers hired over the past two years had quit and went on to other companies. During their exit interviews, many stated they were leaving due to the stressful working conditions at the power plant. Erie Shores had just completed the requirements of a Consent Order, which included increased regulatory oversight by the Nuclear Regulatory Commission. The heightened attention had been warranted, the result of some poor decisions and alleged deliberate acts of hiding major plant equipment problems. The entire senior management staff at the plant had been fired or moved to lower level positions with less authority. The new management team established a series of strict policies aimed at turning the plant around. It took nearly three years to accomplish, but the plant was restored to top condition and finally taken off the NRCs watch list.

But the long hours required to accomplish this task took its toll on most everyone at the facility. Patience was in short supply and trust was still not totally restored in management, even with the complete change of personnel in key positions.

Then, just as the attention shifted to other troubled plants, StarPower, the parent company of Erie Shores, announced their intent to license two new nuclear plants at the site. Morale at the plant was low, people sensing that an increase in workload was coming at a time when employees were already stretched to their limits. They couldn't afford publicity that would cause a reversal of the progress they had made to date.

So when Haji Madu calmly walked into the NRC resident inspector's office at Erie Shores Nuclear Power Plant and made his claim, management was stunned. The claim hadn't been made public, but it was only a matter of time. He'd just completed signing the complaint about a flaw at the plant he claimed would cause a primary coolant leak that could not be isolated. In other words, all the coolant covering the reactor core would be lost. In his complaint he alleged that management at the plant knew about the problem and ignored his pleas to investigate. He named names and accused at least one individual of deliberately covering up the problem. It was exactly what the plant didn't need, especially after they'd just completed their recovery from a very public and highly scrutinized nuclear safety problem.

Edgar Williston sat at his desk in the small NRC office near the turbine deck at the Erie Shores plant. He was watching the young engineer's every move. These were extremely serious allegations. Rarely did employees bring complaints directly to the NRC. Williston couldn't remember anyone so young and new to their position making such a claim. The seasoned NRC inspector knew this was going to make national headlines, given the situation with the company's past actions and the state of their recovery. No one would come out of this new round of issues without scars; not plant management, not senior executives at the company, and certainly not the resident NRC inspectors who were supposed to provide oversight for safety issues at the plant. As he watched the young man sign the complaint, he wondered where he would be assigned since this new problem happened on his watch.

When Madu finished signing the complaint, the NRC inspector said, "Mr. Madu, we will make every effort to keep your identity confidential. If necessary because of certain conditions, we may have to disclose your name to the company, the news media, or other agencies. Do you object to us releasing your name in the event one of these conditions occurs?"

"No, sir, I have no objection."

"Do you understand the serious implications of the allegations you're making and the potentially serious nature of the flaw that you have identified?"

He calmly looked the inspector in the eyes. "Yes, sir, I understand."

The resident inspector was surprised by the demeanor of the man making the complaint. Either he didn't understand or he didn't care. *Or he's got big balls.* Williston had been an inspector for the NRC for over twenty years and he was nervous as hell. *How could this kid remain so calm?*

Haji Madu left the inspector's office. His smile was so slight no one would have noticed. He was almost done with his work here. All hell was about to break loose at Erie Shores.

* * *

Back in his office, Edgar Williston reopened his policy book and re-read the section on receiving complaints from plant personnel. He was to immediately contact the regional office where an Allegation Coordinator would be assigned. This person would assign a number to the allegation and log it in a tracking database. Then they contact the person who submitted the complaint. The NRC would assemble an Allegation Review Board. This board would determine if action was required and contact the operator of the plant, known as the licensee. If the issue was serious enough, the NRC could request immediate action by the licensee to protect the health and welfare of the general public. In other words, they could order the plant shut down.

Williston determined this issue was of major safety significance, so he dialed the number for the NRC's Region III office in Lisle, Illinois to inform his boss of the nature of the complaint. It was a call he sincerely wished he didn't have to make. His hands shook as he signed the witness line at the bottom of the page.

* * *

Within thirty-five minutes of the call to the NRC Region III office in Lisle, Illinois, Elliot Simpson, the Senior Resident Inspector at Superior Shores Nuclear Power Plant in northern Wisconsin, had orders to board a plane and get to the Erie Shores Nuclear Power Station. He was to assist Edgar Williston with the investigation of the claim made by a junior engineer. He shook his head at the order. He knew the situation at Erie Shores, and feared this might be the death knell for the troubled plant. Even if the claim turned out to be false, scrutiny of the plant's new management would be an ongoing, nearly insurmountable burden to bear.

He made a call to his partner, Jim Riske, at the Superior Shores Nuclear Power Plant to let him know he would be on his own for a stretch. Riske was a very junior inspector, but very bright. Simpson didn't know how long he would be gone. It would almost certainly be for a minimum of three weeks, but most likely longer. Riske said he understood. Simpson planned to make his own call to Lisle, Illinois and request an additional inspector be assigned to Superior Shores in his absence. He was hopeful they would comply, but he knew even the NRC was working short-staffed due to tight budgets. He wished Riske the best of luck.

Before they disconnected, Riske said, "Hey, Elliot, I hope this turns out to be a false alarm. We don't need any more bad press."

Simpson replied, "Jim, even if it does turn out to be a false alarm, we're still going to get a black eye. You know how the problems at Erie raised all kinds of hell." He sighed, then continued, "The anti-nuke community latches on to anything that will further their cause."

"True, but if it's false, can't we go on the offensive?"

"It's not in the cards, my man. You'll learn. We're the watchdog. We can't even afford the appearance of being in bed with the industry."

Riske had to believe the senior inspector knew what he was talking about. They said their goodbyes amid the rising level of anxiety and hung up.

Jim Riske, junior resident inspector for the United States Nuclear Regulatory Commission, felt like he'd just been abandoned. He had a routine to follow each day and Elliot promised to call and talk him through any issues that arose. But there was nothing that kept your confidence up like a senior man acknowledging you were making the right decisions. That assurance was flying to Ohio on the first available flight. By default, Jim Riske was now the Acting Senior NRC Resident Inspector at Superior Shores Nuclear Power Station. *Holy crap.*

* * *

When Haji Madu left the inspector's office he headed straight for his supervisors office. The door was open, but he knocked on the door jamb anyway. Gail Martin, the Engineering Manager looked up, smiled, and said, "Come in Haji. Have a seat and let me finish here. It'll take just a moment."

Haji smiled, nodded, and sat in one of the chairs at the table that extended from Gail's desk. He passed the few moments looking around the office, noticing the Engineering Certificate on the wall, University of Toledo, School of Engineering. That was where he'd received his education in engineering as well. He continued looking around, and saw the pictures of what must be Gail's family. Of course, with the way Americans divorced at will, it could be pictures of step-children or even someone else's children. Regardless, it didn't matter. He had a job to do and it didn't have anything to do with engineering.

She finished adding her signature on one of the hundreds of forms used at Erie Shores. She looked up and smiled. "So, what's on your mind?"

Haji smiled. Without saying a word, he handed a copy of the NRC complaint to his boss.

With her smile still on her face, she asked, "What's this?" Then as she read the document, her smile disappeared. Without saying another word to Haji, she picked up her phone and dialed the number for the Director of Engineering. When his secretary answered, Gail said, "Janice, is Mr. Grace in?" A pause as Janice replied. "When he gets off the phone, tell him I will be down to his office immediately." Another pause. "No, this can't wait."

As she said it, Janice heard Randall Grace slam his phone down and yell, "Son of a bitch!"

She hung up her phone and said to Haji, "Let's go." Gail wasn't sure if the buzzing in her ears was a nest of hornets or if she was having a stroke. But one thing she knew for certain; the shit was rolling down hill, picking up speed, and she was at the bottom looking up. The arrangements she'd made to have dinner out with her husband and kids just went out the window.

Chapter 17

Nancy Brown received the call about the discovery of the body of Alex Corbin, and immediately called Colonel Sheila Warner.. The body was found within the area they'd deduced where the murder had taken place. Now it was her job to find out why. She feared there was more to come. Nothing about this case followed the typical pattern of an attack on a westerner by Islamic extremists. Nancy wondered, *Why Alex Corbin and why northern Wisconsin*? Her team was getting ready to assemble for the final time before some of the members would be deployed to Wisconsin to look at the scene and review evidence. It would be a time-consuming task.

Nancy asked for details about the scene, but the sheriff of Bayfield County, Wisconsin had few. Her orders were co-lead a combined team of Anti-Terror Unit and FBI members and investigate the murder. Madeline Wymer, the Bayfield County Sheriff was already expecting the assistance, and it appeared she was happy to have it.

Within the hour, a private jet took off from a runway at the newly renamed Reagan National Airport. The six Anti-Terror Unit members were already reading briefing papers they'd received just before leaving their office. When they leveled off at thirty-two thousand feet, the team assembled at the table in the center of the fuselage.

Nancy opened her folder. A photo of the decomposed body of Alex Corbin greeted her. She closed her eyes and took a deep breath to clear her head. She had to concentrate on the task at hand. To do that, she had to block out all emotion, all anger, all feelings of hate for whoever destroyed this young man's life and the lives of his family. She took another breath. As she did, she smelled fresh coffee. When she opened her eyes she noticed one of her team had brought her a fresh cup. Nancy sipped at the steaming brew. She acknowledged her agent with a nod and a hint of a smile as she set her cup down next to the file.

Now detached from her emotions, she had the analytical part of her brain engaged. The picture was no less gruesome, but she could look at the details and not get bogged down with emotional interference. Like the film of the actual beheading, the pictures of the decomposed body showed the brutality of the murder. It was hard to imagine the video and the pictures were of the same man. Alex Corbin had suffered a horrific death. Then his remains were left in the woods like so much trash. Even this act was different than previous beheadings.

Nothing in the package provided new information. There was a preliminary coroner's report that merely confirmed the approximate date and time of death and the cause as exsanguination, meaning the loss of blood.

Nancy discussed logistics for when they reached the sheriff's office in Washburn, Wisconsin where interviews would take place. It was eight miles from Superior Shores Nuclear Power Plant where Alex Corbin worked and over thirty miles from where his body was found. That seemed like a long distance to transport him in broad daylight without someone noticing something out of the ordinary. But this wasn't Washington, D.C. or New York City. The entire population of Bayfield County was short of fifteen thousand. That was a very small population density for one of the largest counties, measured by land area, in Wisconsin. Still, in broad daylight, someone should have seen or heard something.

The jet landed at John F. Kennedy Airport southwest of Ashland. The FBI was already waiting there with four black Suburbans for ground transportation. From the airport they headed north on County Road 112, west on US 2, then north again on County Road 13, to Washburn. Talk during the trip was subdued. There was a noticeable air of tension between the FBI and Anti Terror Unit. Nancy wasn't sure if it was a built in distrust between the agencies or if it was due to directives from their respective managers. There was also disparity between the seniority levels of personnel within each team. The ATU was new on the scene as far as federal agencies go. The FBI was obviously well established, and their team members exuded an air of superiority. While that didn't sit well with Nancy, she expected nothing different. Her team would have to prove themselves in the field and in everything they did.

Nancy was the designated team lead for the ATU. The FBI's team was led by a much more senior agent. Add the Bayfield County

Sheriff's office to the mix and this assignment promised to be as awkward as a first date. Nancy expected getting the FBI to share information was going to be a challenge. Sheriff Wymer had personally made the request for assistance from the federal government when it looked like Corbin's disappearance might be a kidnapping. Nancy wondered how Wymer would feel when not one, but two federal agencies took over her investigation. Now, with the possibility that this was a terrorist attack, Bayfield County, Wisconsin would get much more attention from the federal government. There hadn't been this many feds in the county since the start of construction on Superior Shores Nuclear Plant. Nobody had wanted them here then, and their feelings probably hadn't changed.

When they arrived at the Bayfield County Government Complex the building was smaller than Nancy expected. But in a county with a very small population, facilities were bound to be smaller and designed for multiple purposes.

Sheriff Madeline Wymer welcomed them. Nancy was surprised to see a young, slender, woman. She couldn't have been over thirty-five. She looked as if she were gritting her teeth. Nancy wondered whether it was nerves because of her new guests or if this was her normal demeanor. Being only twenty-nine, Nancy had to remind herself Sheriff Wymer's perception of her was probably the same.

As the teams piled out of the Suburbans, they stood back and naturally formed two groups, the FBI on one side and the ATU on the other. Nancy walked up to Sheriff Wymer and introduced herself. The senior FBI agent, Randall Scott, also introduced himself. He walked up and nearly stepped in front of Nancy, as if to cut her off from direct contact with the sheriff. He added he was the AIC, the agent in charge, and would be coordinating the efforts for the federal government. Nancy's jaw tightened, but she let the comment pass without a challenge in front of the two teams and the sheriff. She wondered who'd given Special Agent Scott that authority.

After the brief introductions, Sheriff Wymer motioned that the groups should follow her into the brownstone building housing the County's Administration. The building looked relatively new, but it blended well with the turn of the century brownstones further down the street. The trees all around the city were just showing new leaves as they emerged from a long, northern Wisconsin winter.

When the team reached the basement, Nancy was happy to see temporary cubicles set up as office space for the team. She also noted the two private conference rooms, phones, internet connections, and three projection screens. Everything she'd requested was available and then some.

As they started to settle in, Randall Scott gave orders for his team to take the office cubes on the right side of the room. He turned to Nancy and said her team could have the cubicles on the left. He planned to use one of the conference rooms for an office.

"Nancy, you can have one of the cubicles near your team. Will that work for you?"

Nancy didn't crack a smile. "No. I'll be in that office with you. Also, our orders are to work as a single team ."

"That's not going to—"

But Nancy raised her hand ."As I was saying, our orders are to work as a single team. Therefore, each agent from ATU will be teamed with an agent from the FBI. Either you can make the assignments or I will. If you have any questions, we can get on a conference call with my boss and yours and clear this up."

Agent Scott's face turned beet-red. "Ms. Brown. Step into my office, now!"

Nancy turned her back to Scott and told her team to introduce themselves to their FBI counterparts and get to know them. They would, after all, be working closely together.

During this entire exchange, Sheriff Wymer stood back, maintaining her serious look and taking mental notes. She liked Agent Brown and that she was apparently playing by the book. She wasn't taking any crap from the FBI's top man, to whom Sheriff Wymer had taken an immediate dislike. He was obviously trying to push his weight around. That was establishing a hostile work environment for everyone involved which was going to make it difficult to get anything accomplished. Maybe this could work out after he and Nancy talked privately.

Nancy turned back to Agent Scott. Without a trace of anger she said, "We have to talk with Sheriff Wymer. I'm heading to her office. You should join us."

Nancy turned to the sheriff who motioned towards the stairs. The women headed up. Randall Scott went back inside the conference room for several minutes, then reluctantly headed up the stairs to join the women. He was still fuming.

* * *

The call came to Sheik Al Salil the morning after the discovery of Alex Corbin's body. It was not good news. Salil didn't show any outward signs. He simply acknowledged the message and hung up.

The news confirmed something he feared would happen. The financial assets of Imam Khidir Khadduri and the Saudi Prince, who was the primary source of funding, were frozen in the United States and Europe. The money supply had been cut off. Salil had funds available for several more days, but the largest purchase of weapons was not yet complete. He needed about $90,000 to complete the deal. He knew it was time to go to his secondary source of funding, though it pained him greatly. He picked up the hotel room phone and dialed.

Victoria Garcia answered. "Ola."

"Victoria, how is your part of the plan coming?"

"My part of the plan is ready except for a few minor details, Salil."

He hated it when she addressed him so. This was going to be more painful than he first thought. He wished there was another way, but time was short and he needed the weapons right away. Victoria's offer was his only short term solution.

"We've run into a little problem. In order to complete our transaction, I need to take you up on your generous offer, the one we spoke of last month."

"I know, Sheik. I read about your situation."

The freezing of a Saudi Prince's assets was all over the national news. Victoria suspected Salil might come running for cash. She had already made a call to her friend Carlos Esposito, a man high up in the Contrada family cartel. He'd assured Victoria that whatever she needed, she could have. 'Whatever you need, just call. Any enemy of the North Americans is a friend of mine,' he'd said.

"How much, when, and where?"

And with that, Sheik Al Salil was back in business. He didn't like doing business with a drug dealer. For the time being, it couldn't be helped.

Chapter 18

A bright flash lit up the Emergency Reactor Cooling Room #2 at Superior Shores Nuclear Power Plant. Evan Jones squinted, wrinkled his nose and held a manila folder between his face and where a worker was finishing the last few centimeters of the weld. Smoke from the reaction between the metal pipe and the weld rod filled the room with an acrid odor.

Evan adjusted his hard hat and safety glasses, then twisted the ear plugs that protected his eardrums from the loud roar of the pumps and motors all around him. The welding was a plant modification that would allow temporary cooling water to be supplied to the reactor vessel during an extended shutdown where radioactive fuel remained in the reactor vessel. The Nuclear Regulatory Commission had determined there might not be adequate cooling water in the primary storage tanks during certain maintenance activities involving the Shutdown Reactor Cooling System. Alex Corbin had been the backup engineer on the modification. Evan was watching the work because the new backup engineer, Yusef Hassan said he had a personal matter to tend to. The primary engineer was Evan's stepson, Jimmy Smith. He'd been at the job site on and off since the job began, but wasn't here to see the final weld.

Evan had stopped in so he could stay abreast of the status of the work. He wasn't a supervisor and he was only needed if Jimmy had to be away from work for an extended period. He knew Jimmy was a very competent engineer, and since the job was nearly complete, he wouldn't be taking over the final engineering reviews. With the news of the allegations at the Erie Shores nuclear plant, there would undoubtedly be increased scrutiny of everyone's work. But that increased oversight wouldn't start until the Senior NRC inspector returned or was replaced. The very junior Resident Inspector, Jim Riske had stopped by briefly to look in on the job, but it was just a cursory look. He wasn't even sure he had the authority to do anything, if there was something wrong with the job, except to report it to the regional NRC office. But everything looked in order so he went to the control room where he would review the Senior Reactor Operator's logs.

Evan felt that his project was well in hand and would be delivered in plenty of time for their next refueling outage. He wasn't worried, but you never knew when the Engineering Manager would toss a new challenge your way. So he headed back towards the administration building to attend to his own workload.

The corridors in this part of the plant were lined with pipes, conduit, electrical panels, and steel supports. Employees had to pay attention when walking through this area, known as the radiologically restricted area, or the RRA. As he made his way along the corridor, Evan thought about Alex Corbin in the Emergency Reactor Cooling Room making notes about the modification that was now being installed. He shook his head, not wanting to believe Alex was dead. Preoccupied, he ran into a steel pipe support. His hardhat hit the support hard enough that he nearly fell over. He stopped, took off the hat and looked where the support made contact, noting the gouge out of the hard plastic. He raised an eyebrow, shook his head, put the protective hat back on, and headed towards the stairs, paying closer attention to where he was walking. When he was at the door to the stairs, the door burst open.

Yusef plowed through, carrying a folder that was nearly three inches thick. He sported the usual scowl on his face, his dark eyes magnified by the large safety glasses. His hard hat was loose fitting over his turban. Evan noticed particles of food stuck in the dark, disheveled beard. He nearly knocked Evan out of the way as he passed.

"Yusef, watch where you're going, man!"

"You were in my way. You watch where you are going!" His English was laden with a heavy Middle Eastern accent as he spat the words. "I have work that can't wait."

"Yeah, like nobody else does. Did you want a turnover on the weld job?" Yusef kept walking, all but ignoring Evan's question. "Well have a nice day." Evan turned back to the stairwell then mumbled under his breath, "Jerk."

When Evan reached the Engineering Department, he saw movement in Yusef's cubicle. When he stopped and looked in, Jimmy Smith looked up, an anxious expression on his face. When he noticed it was Evan, he relaxed a bit.

"Hey, Jimmy, what are you doing in here?"

Jimmy moved towards Evan, looking up and down the aisle, then said in a near whisper, "I need to show you something."

He turned back towards the surly engineer's desk. Evan followed. Yusef was busy in the plant, but Evan felt uncomfortable in another man's private space.

Jimmy turned to Evan and said, "I found something that isn't right." Then, with another nervous look around said, "Look at this drawing."

Jimmy pulled a drawer open that was part of a five-foot wide table. A large sheet of paper with a very detailed drawing lay on top of a hodgepodge of paper clips, pens and pencils, post-it notes, and fluorescent labels. Jimmy pointed to the paper and said, "Check this out. It looks like the Stator Cooling System for the main generator, but it's been modified."

The drawing may have been hand-made, but the detail was extraordinary. The notes were nearly perfect block letters near arrows pointing to different components.

Jimmy was right. It was a portion of the Stator Cooling system which used hydrogen as the cooling medium because of its ability to efficiently transfer heat. And the drawing showed a new component. He looked at the label. It read "Ignition Source."

Evan drew in a deep breath and frowned. He took another look at the drawing, then closed the drawer. He grabbed Jimmy by the elbow and guided him out of Yusef's cubicle and down the hallway to a small, empty conference room just large enough for a group of six. After they entered, Evan closed the door.

A thousand questions ran through his mind. Was it true? Was Yusef planning to blow up the turbine using the hydrogen in the Stator Cooling system as the fuel? Was he truly a terrorist? Was he working alone? This was definitely a security matter, so a call to the Security Shift Supervisor was the first call to be made. How could they do it and not alert Yusef they had discovered his plan?

Evan turned to Jimmy. "How did you find out about that drawing?"

"He had the drawer open. I had a question about the modification in the Emergency Reactor Cooling Room. I walked in while he was on the phone. He didn't notice me, at first. But when he saw me near the table he ended his call and nearly pushed me out. I got a quick look at the schematic. I remember that system because, during training, I thought it odd that hydrogen would be used in a generator for cooling. Seems like one little spark would blow the whole thing up." He paused then said, "I guess Yusef thinks it's a good idea."

Evan tensed at the thought of the 850 megawatt generator exploding into a huge ball of flame. A chill ran up his spine.

"We have to call security. I just passed him down by the job site. He was heading in as I was coming out."

Evan thought about the drawing again. He tried to visualize the physical location of the piping in the system and where this ignition source might be placed. Then he realized the system had an enclosed room where the hydrogen coolers were located. In the drawing in Yusef's cubicle, the ignition source was close to the cooler. Some of the piping in the room was behind the cooler, so the igniter could be placed out of the line of sight of anyone entering.

He turned to Jimmy and said, "I have an idea where he's planning to put it. Contact security by phone. Tell them exactly what you've seen. Tell them they need a bomb crew to meet me in the Hydrogen Cooling room in the turbine building. And do it now."

"Are you sure about this? What if we're wrong?"

"If we're wrong, then Yusef will have a lot of explaining to do. At this point, I don't think there's any doubt."

Evan left the conference room and headed towards his cubicle to grab his hard hat and safety glasses. He made a beeline for the turbine building.

Back in the conference room Jimmy closed the door and picked up the phone. He dialed 5911 for security.

He heard a woman's voice, "Security."

It was Ingrid Shaw, Jimmy's fiancé. He didn't like that she worked in security. But she was adamant that this was the best place for her. It was a continuous source of friction between them.

"Ingrid, this is Jimmy."

She smiled. "Hi sweetie. What can I do for you?"

"We've got a big problem. I think there might be a bomb in the plant."

Ingrid hesitated before answering. "Jimmy, you shouldn't joke about stuff like that. It isn't—"

"Ingrid, this isn't a joke."

He had her attention. He described how he had found the drawing in Yusef's office and that Evan was on his way to see if the bomb had actually been put in place.

As Jimmy talked, Ingrid relayed the details to her supervisor. They were already trying to locate Yusef Hassan. Based on where he'd used his badge in the plant, they determined he'd not only left the Radiologically Restricted Area, he'd left the security controlled area. There was no way to locate him because he didn't need to use his badge once he was out of the areas with controlled access.

Instructions were sent out advising security personnel to locate and detain Yusef Hassan. The Security Shift Supervisor instructed two of his officers to cut off access to Hassan's cubicle. Two other security officers were instructed to perform a search of the administration building and find the surly engineer.

Hassan figured that all the security officers from the plant were searching for him. He also knew their efforts would be fruitless as he drove away from the plant. He was under immense stress and doubted he would ever return to the plant again.

Chapter 19

At 10:50 AM, Hatch stood on the sidewalk in front of Danny's favorite bar, Loco Pedro's. The bar occupied the first floor of a building with whitewash wood siding weathered to a light gray in the Texas sun. The yellow sign above the door was only two feet square with red lettering in a script that at one time may have been considered classy. The red coloring on the letters was starting to wear off. He tried the front door. It was open so he walked in.

The acrid scent of recently burned marijuana filled his nose. Hatch smiled and closed the door behind him. The barroom was dark now, the only light came from the small windows in the swinging doors to the kitchen and one small porthole sized window in a north-facing wall. The narrow stream of light illuminated the layer of bluish smoke that hung in the stagnant air. He looked around, allowing his eyes to adjust. He thought back to the other night when he and Danny had a few beers and talked about the "old Navy days" back on the sub. The floor looked like it hadn't been swept since last night's crowd left.

The bar was straight ahead, a horseshoe shape ranging out from the back wall. A mirror ran the length of the wall, fronted by liquor of nearly every popular brand. The pool tables were in a separate room to his far right.

Hatch heard at least two men talking in Spanish in the kitchen. He had no idea what was being said. He took several steps towards the kitchen, peanut shells crunching under his boots. After a few steps, the chatter in the kitchen stopped. The kitchen doors swung open and two men with serious faces strode through. One of the men kept his right arm behind his back. Hatch figured it was a gun or a baseball bat. It didn't matter to him. He wasn't looking for a fight.

With both hands held about head high he said, "Hey guys, I come in peace. I'm just lookin' for a friend who was in here last night."

The men kept coming towards Hatch, but slowed their pace. They eyed him, suspicion etched on their faces.

Both men appeared to be of Spanish descent. The man in front was slender with tattoos on the side of his neck and down his left arm. Hatch couldn't make out the design. He also had diamond earrings in both ears and a nose stud. His hair was straight and long, nearly to his shoulders, and jet black. He wore a black tee shirt and blue jeans.

The man following, the one hiding something behind his back was overweight, probably three hundred pounds. His hair was also long but wavy. He had no jewelry or tattoos and wore a gold sleeveless tee shirt with the number thirty-three on the front. A sheen of sweat glistened on his upper lip and forehead. They maintained their sneer as they rounded the corner of the bar. Hatch kept his cool, his hands still in plain view. There were tables with chairs turned upside-down on top of them on his left, the bar and bar stools on his right. He was very close to a post that supported the ceiling. The men stopped about eight feet in front of him.

The skinny guy asked, "Why you lookin' for this dude?"

"He's a friend. His name's Danny. Word is he was here last night. He didn't show up for work this morning."

"You his boss or somethin'?"

"No. Just a friend." Hatch wasn't in the mood to explain, but he also didn't want these guys to get too agitated. He wasn't looking for trouble. But he was burning time; time that could be better spent finding Danny. "He lives down the street and I heard he spends a lot of time here."

Hatch didn't recognize either of these men from when he and Danny were here two nights ago, but maybe one of them had seen the two of them here. "We were here the other night and had dinner. We sat in that booth over there." He pointed to a booth across the barroom.

Hatch saw the fat man's face change to recognition. He nodded. "Yeah, I remember you. You was with Danny." He turned to his partner, tapped him on the arm, and said something in Spanish. It sounded like he said Danny's name in the middle of the sentence.

His friend didn't smile or change his expression, but he nodded and turned to the big man. He said something back in Spanish, then headed to the kitchen. The big man relaxed and his right arm came out from behind him. The Louisville slugger looked like a thirty-six inch Alex Rodriquez autographed model. It also looked like it had hit a few homeruns, probably right here in the bar and not with baseballs. Hatch's eyebrows rose slightly.

Hatch walked towards the big man and extended his hand. "Name's Hatch."

"Pedro. I own the joint." Pedro grasped Hatch's hand with a firm grip and shook it once.

"So Pedro, I don't mean to sound in a rush, but was Danny here last night?'

"Si. He wasn't here very long, though. He hooked up with a very beautiful lady and left."

Hatch's eyebrow hiked up another notch, Danny with a beautiful woman. That was interesting. When he and Danny spoke the other night, he didn't mention anything about dating anyone. But that didn't make him celibate. "Is this woman a regular?"

"No, man. I never seen her before. She drew a lot of stares though. I mean she was real fine. She isn't the kind of babe we see here, you know. We have some regulars who are lookers, you know. But this babe . . . I mean, she was trying to dress down to fit in, but it wasn't workin'. Some of the regular chicks were smackin' their boyfriends' arms because they kept starin' at her. I mean she was freakin' smokin'." Pedro licked his fingers and touched his butt, then made a sizzling sound to emphasize the point.

"And Miss Hotty was interested in our boy, Danny?"

"Si. I mean, Danny's not ugly or nothing' but there were other guys that could show her a good time. But she had her sights on Danny, almost as soon as he walked in. I know 'cause I was tendin' bar with one of my boys when he did. We both noticed it. She was here about an hour before Danny. Had one Margarita. Had another one while Danny drank a beer, then they left before she finished her second one. If he's still with her, he's one happy hombre."

"Did anyone see them when they left?"

"Yeah. One of our regulars came in and said they left in a bright red Corvette. See what I mean? Ain't nobody in this joint drive a car like that. This crowd's into used cars, you know, Ford Taurus, Chevy Impala. Ain't nobody drivin' a Vette or a Beamer."

Puzzled, Hatch looked around the bar then asked, "Where were they sittin'?"

Pedro pointed to a booth next to where he and Danny sat the night before last. "Right there, bro. She sat there facin' the door and chased off any dudes tryin' to talk with her. Then when Danny came in, she turned on the charm. Thinkin' back, it was kinda strange, but it was busy last night, so I didn't think nothin' of it."

"Did your buddy see which way they headed when they left?"

"Si, towards the 288, but who knows where they went from there? He didn't say if they went north or south."

"Damn," Hatch cursed under his breath. Danny wasn't home or at work and he was last seen leaving the bar with a beautiful woman. Maybe he shouldn't worry. After all, Danny was a grown man. He could take care of himself. *Or could he?* There were a couple of pieces that didn't make sense. One, Danny never missed work. His boss confirmed that. He'd never been late for watch on the USS *Nevada*, either. It wasn't his nature to be the least bit irresponsible. As a matter of fact, he was one of the most reliable people Hatch knew.

But that wasn't the most troubling thing. The beautiful woman at the bar . . . . It was like she'd been waiting to meet up with him specifically.

Danny wasn't exactly a worldly guy. He had some experience with women. He once told Hatch he'd only had one serious girlfriend and that he'd nearly ejaculated in his pants when she slid her hand down the inside of his thigh. She broke up with him because all he talked about was geek stuff, like computers and electronic gadgets.

If this woman was as beautiful and worldly as Pedro described, his friend was in trouble. He'd be putty in her hands. But he had no idea why she singled out his friend. That was what concerned Hatch the most.

He turned back to Pedro who'd been watching Hatch "Pedro, if you see Danny, tell him to call me. If you see this woman, whether Danny is with her or not, call me."

Hatch scribbled his cell phone number on a cocktail napkin and handed it to the bar owner. They shook hands and Hatch headed for the door.

Before he pushed the door open, Pedro asked, "You think our boy's in trouble?"

"I don't know, Pedro, but something smells funny and I ain't talking about the air in here."

Pedro gave a half smile. He was concerned about Danny and if he ended up missing, the police would be around asking questions. That would be bad for business, the kind they did under the table. It wouldn't be good for the bar business, either.

As Hatch reached for the door, a young man pulled it open and yelled, "Hey, Pedro." When he saw Hatch standing there he said, "Oh, sorry, homes. Didn't mean to yell in your ear."

"That's okay." He started for the door again when the young man yelled, "Hey, I got some pictures of that honey that was in here last night."

Hatch turned around and smiled. He decided he might stay a few minutes longer.

Chapter 20

Nancy could tell that Angela Corbin's sniffles bothered Special Agent Randall Scott as they questioned the young, pregnant widow. Her eyes and face were puffy and red from crying.. Angela was being questioned about the time leading up to his disappearance.

Angela's mother sat next to her on the floral couch in the small living room with her arm around her daughter's shoulder. She tried her best to comfort her daughter, but her eyes were puffy and red from hours of crying, sharing grief and pain with her only daughter. All a mother could do in these circumstances was offer her unconditional love and support.

Angela barely remembered what day it was, much less specifics about events nearly a week old. But as the questions came, she started to recall details. As she recounted certain events, the tears flowed anew.

"He was so distant for days before he disappeared. How could I not have noticed? All I could think about was why he didn't pay more attention to me. I kept thinking, he should be helping out more. He must have known something was wrong, that somebody was after him." She looked up at the two agents, tears trickling down her cheeks. "Who did this to him?"

Angela took a tissue from the box that Nancy offered to her, blew her nose and wiped her cheeks. When she laid her hands across her rounded belly, Nancy saw that her nose looked painfully raw, as if she'd been rubbing it with sandpaper. Losing a husband to a violent murderer had been devastating for this young mother-to-be.

Special Agent Scott's attitude made the situation worse. He acted bored at best. His body language all but said, *I don't believe a word you're saying*. Nancy wanted to pull him aside and throttle him. She did her best to take control of the interview and keep Angela concentrating on her husband's movements until he disappeared. She leaned forward and placed a hand lightly on Angela's knee, noticing her jeans were cold to the touch. Angela asked for another tissue and

Nancy obliged. After a moment, her crying was again under control.

"That's why we're here, Mrs. Corbin. We need to find the people who did this and make sure they're brought to justice." She paused then asked, "Did your husband talk about any specific people just before he disappeared, maybe someone you'd hadn't heard of before?"

Angela Corbin stared straight ahead as if in a trance, deep in thought. After a moment she frowned and said quietly, "He didn't mention any names, but said things at work weren't going well. I just figured he was going to have to work more overtime." Her face tightened and she started crying again. Between sobs she said, "All I could think of was he wouldn't be home to help if he had to work all these hours. I was afraid I'd go into labor while he was at work and he wouldn't get home in time."

She blew her nose again then wiped her eyes with the back of her hands. She tossed the soggy tissue in the general direction of an already overflowing trashcan.

Special Agent Scott turned his head and made a face when she blew her nose yet again. He was tiring of the kid-glove-treatment. His counterpart wasn't being direct enough. He turned back to Mrs. Corbin and asked in a voice that bordered on interrogation, "Who did your husband piss off? He must have been threatened in some way to be brutally killed like he was."

Surprised by his tone, Angela turned to him with a shocked expression. She hesitated for just a moment, trying to make sense of his harsh manner. Then she said with surprising force, "No! My husband had no enemies! He was easy going, quiet, polite to a fault. He never said a bad word about anyone and no one said anything bad about him." She stared at him.

Nancy thought that Agent Scott was going to jump right in with another question, so she again asked, "I know I've asked this already, but it's very important. Did you hear him talk about anyone in particular, like a co-worker he wasn't getting along with? Maybe his boss?"

As Nancy asked, Angela shook her head slowly. "He just seemed distracted. That's all. We didn't talk at dinner, either. And he was coming home a little later than he had been. Like fifteen to twenty minutes later. Not like hours or anything. I just figured work was starting to get to him. It isn't unusual for him to work overtime, but before all this, he would talk about projects he'd been working on."

"Was he working on anything recently? Maybe it wasn't going well."

"That's just it. He hadn't talked about any new projects for months." Her eyes opened wider "I remember the first time he came home and he seemed troubled. I could tell his mind was back at the plant. I asked him what was wrong and he said, *Nothing. Just a little problem at work. Nothing to worry about.* Then he kissed me and went out back to the garage."

"Did he continue to act 'troubled' after that day?"

"Not right away. But after a week or so, I noticed he was deep in thought more often. I'd watch him. He'd frown for no apparent reason. He wouldn't even notice me watching. That was odd because, before that, he would always look my way and smile. From that moment on, he was wound so tight he didn't even notice me; like I wasn't even there. That's when I started to worry something was wrong." Her face twisted like she was going to cry again. "I thought he might be having an affair. That he didn't find me attractive anymore." She folded her hands across her belly and her eyes watered, but no tears escaped.

Nancy thought she was going to start crying again, but Angela maintained her composure. Her eyes opened wide again. When Nancy asked her what it was, she shook her head and said, "Nothing. It's nothing really."

Agent Scott said, "Tell us. We'll determine if it's anything or not."

"Well, when Alex was watching the news after dinner, I heard him say *stinking bastards*. I walked into the room and a commercial was on. I asked him what he said. He said *Nothing babe.* Then he changed the subject."

Scott said, "That's it?"

"Yes. It's totally not like Alex. He never swore, ever."

Nancy asked, "Did you ever find out what he swore about?"

"No. But the week before he disappeared, he was reading the paper and he balled it up and threw it across the room. He didn't know I was watching and I didn't ask what was making him so angry. He was actually scaring me at this point."

"Did you find out what he was reading about when he tossed the paper?"

"I'm not sure, but there were only three stories in the paper on the page he was reading."

"What were they about, do you remember?"

"I'll show you."

With her mother's assistance, Angela Corbin got up slowly. She went out to the utility room and came back with a newspaper that had been crumbled up then flattened back out. She handed it to Nancy, but Agent Scott grabbed it. He scanned the front page while Nancy rolled her eyes. A story about the local anti-nuke movement was prominent about midway down on the left side of the paper. Nancy and Angela watched as Scott read through the article.

He shifted to another story about a local volunteer group, but quickly moved to a third story about contamination sites on Lake Superior. Another local activist group planned to picket several companies with manufacturing plants along the lake in Wisconsin. One of the sites was Northstates Power Company's Superior Shores Nuclear Power Plant.

Smiling, Agent Randall Scott said, "I think we have a solid lead. May we keep this paper ma'am?"

Angela just nodded.

They questioned her for another fifteen minutes, but the answers were getting vague and Angela Corbin looked exhausted. Her mother's body language was getting more defensive. Nancy felt it was a good time to let her rest. Maybe she'd remember something once the pressure of a direct interview was relieved.

Nancy asked if they could look around the detached garage. Angela gave Nancy the keys.

The agents left Angela and her mother inside to rest. Nancy carefully opened the service door and flipped on the lights. It was a relatively new garage with a workbench taking up half the twenty-four foot length of the garage. Alex Corbin had a decent assortment of tools. A layer of sawdust covered tools, the floor, and several shelves of spare parts. They stood in the center, looking around for anything out of place.

"Agent Scott, look at the filing cabinet," Nancy said.

He turned and looked where Nancy was pointing. He nodded. The black filing cabinet was a short, two-drawer style was made for legal size paper. The top was clear of any sawdust. The area in front of the cabinet was also clear. Maybe Alex Corbin had been doing more than wood-working recently.

They opened the top drawer. Agent Scott said, “Let me take a first look. If I find anything, I’ll pass it on to you.”

“How about you take half the files and I’ll take the other half.”

He couldn’t think of a sensible argument, so he reached and passed Nancy a handful of the hanging folders. She found a stool and dusted the seat off with her hand. She spread the folders out on the workbench and began looking through them, one page at a time. Her half was about nine inches thick.

Most of the folders were of woodworking projects. Alex apparently had planned to build several pieces of fine furniture. Angela had mentioned he was quite skilled at several trades.

Nancy moved to the next folder. The drawings in this folder showed the layout for a house, including the foundation and the rough lumber, like the floor joists and the stud walls. Another drawing showed the truss arrangement for the roof. The next folder showed the plumbing for the vent and drain lines. The next two folders were also related to the house.

Then she came to a folder that showed plumbing, but this one was different. A lot of pipes ran through a large square, presumably a room. There were too many pipes for the drawing to be for a house. Maybe it was a geothermal ground piping arrangement, but the symbols looked commercial, not residential. This drawing appeared to have been produced on a copy machine, where the previous ones were hand-made with precision. The drawing appeared to have been copied multiple times causing them to lose their definition and clarity.

She turned to Agent Scott and said, “Look at these. Everything else in here was for house plans . . . except this.” She handed the drawing to Scott.

He frowned. He’d just been through a number of folders that also contained house prints. This was obviously out of place. He noticed one handwritten note on the drawing. It said, *Different than approved.* Scott thought, *What the hell does this mean?* There were no official markings, but it looked like it might be a small section copied from a larger diagram. That would explain the lack of detail and the grainy appearance.

“Let’s keep looking. This may be nothing, but we’ll have our teams look at it. Maybe one of them has an idea.”

Nancy just nodded and went back to her search. She was perturbed that her counterpart still thought of this task force as separate teams. She intended to address the problem soon. But this was not the right time or place.

They didn't find any other information in the file cabinet. That was because they failed to pull out the bottom drawer and look beneath it. It would have made all the difference in the world.

Chapter 21

The condominium was cool at seventy-four degrees. The humidifier was set to maintain fifty-five percent, but the arid climate made this nearly impossible. The small rock fountain on the kitchen counter helped add needed moisture to the air, but the air conditioner dried the air out again. There was a floral aroma from a number of air fresheners plugged into outlets in three rooms. It was a nice living space, but it was only temporary. It was nearly time for Victoria Garcia to move on. *Just a couple more days.*

She flipped her cell phone closed. She'd had second thoughts about making the call. But then her resolve had kicked in, as she'd remembered the reason for it. If she succeeded, this first move would be followed by many more steps to make the North Americans pay. They would wake up each day feeling the despair and fear that she had felt as a young girl in Mexico, as she watched her brother beaten to death. Her partnership would expand, this time with her people. It would also strengthen her position with her other partner. Together, they could accomplish much. They could bring the United States down a few notches.

It was ingenious, using money made from drug users in the United States to punish them. *They're so spoiled and weak minded. All they want to do is get high and scramble their brains.* She'd learned the concept from Salil. He told her of the many businesses devout Muslims owned in North America. Much of the money made at these businesses was sent to his partners in his country to train fighters and to buy weapons and supplies. So, she'd made the call.

It was easier than she'd imagined. One call to Carlos Esposito and she not only had more money than she needed, she also had manpower and weapons. She could now tell Salil she didn't need his help, but he needed hers. She had the money, so she had the power. She looked around her condominium. *Time for a little celebration.* She grabbed the bottle of Patron tequila and mixed a margarita. She raised her glass and was about to take a drink when her cell phone rang. *It can wait.*

She took her celebratory drink. When she finished licking her lips, savoring the tangy taste mixed with salt, she looked at the number on the phone. She smiled and flipped the phone open.

"Ricardo. I've been expecting your call. How is our project going?"

"Ola, Victoria. The installation is nearly complete and we've tested most of them. They work just fine. I expect they'll do exactly what we need them to do."

"I told you they would. You'll probably get a promotion and a raise, if only for a few hours. We should talk about other refineries. They could use an upgrade."

Vasquez thought about that for a moment. He would probably be able to get a job at another refinery and make the same modifications. What a surprise it would be when they found out the extent of their changes. He smiled.

"We do have a small problem. The technician who was doing the installation didn't come to work today."

"Why is that a problem? Just have someone else finish the job."

When Victoria had left Danny he was in no condition to go to work. The drug she'd given him had strong side effects, especially after a night of drinking.

Ricardo frowned. Victoria didn't understand that it wasn't that simple. It would be at least a day before another person could be trained on how to glue the detectors in place on the remaining storage tanks. It wasn't hard, but the training took time. The paperwork to record the training took longer. Government regulations. Not to mention that other jobs had to be delayed in order to reallocate the manpower to complete the modification. They had enough detectors in place so Ricardo wasn't concerned. He decided to lie. She didn't need to know the details anyway.

"We should be done by the end of the day tomorrow."

Victoria wondered how many tanks were left to complete the job, but she didn't want to appear too pushy. After several seconds she asked, "So how close are we to completing the job?"

"We only have three tanks left. If Danny makes it in tomorrow, it'll be done by noon. If not, maybe by 8:00 P.M."

Victoria smiled. Even if the three tanks didn't get finished, that meant that over thirty tanks were completed. That would be more than enough. She took another sip of her drink. "That's excellent, Ricardo. You've done well. We should meet for dinner day after tomorrow. My special treat." The last line was delivered with a seductive tone.

He smiled and anticipated a special evening indeed. They talked for a few more minutes, but it was mostly small talk. When the call ended, Ricardo thought about her 'special treat.' Then he thought about how she'd again changed her demeanor. Last night she was cold and distant. Tonight was a different story. It was almost like she was coming on to him. He shook his head. *Women.*

* * *

Victoria's confidence soared. Now for the call she looked forward to the most. She hit the speed-dial button. The phone rang four times. She was ready to disconnect when a male voice answered with a crisp, "Yes?"

She was annoyed he took so long to answer. After all, she was now in the driver's seat. She thought briefly about hanging up, but then decided to talk with her partner. It would give her an opportunity to gloat.

"Salil, I have good news."

On the other end of the line, Sheik Al Salil cringed. He wanted to yell at her, but he needed to hear what she had to say. His sources of funds had been cut. He needed cash. He had arms dealers waiting for him to complete the deal. If he didn't come through, they would take their business elsewhere. Worse, it would get around that Sheik Al Salil couldn't be trusted. That would put a serious dent in his plans.

"Tell me, what have you found out?"

"We've been able to obtain financing for our project, and we have a contractor who will supply manpower as well."

Drug dealers who sell poison. But, at least, it's to the children of Satan. Common goals make for strange partnerships. "This is very good news. When can I expect delivery of the funding?"

Victoria wanted to make him sweat, but there would be other opportunities for that. "I will wire the funds within the hour."

Salil smiled. Despite his hatred of the Garcia woman, she had connections and she shared his hatred of the North Americans. Their partnership might not be ideal, but it would work since the American government wouldn't suspect that Muslims and Mexican drug lords could work together.

"I'll be waiting."

They both hung up. Victoria held the closed phone to the side of her mouth, thinking about the possibilities. There was a lot of work to be done after this first project. Their enemies wouldn't see it coming. Then her thoughts went back to a minor detail, the technician, Danny, not showing up for work. She'd had fun toying with him, getting information so easily. All it took was a little touch here, a little kiss there, and a little dose of the date rape drug, HGB. He was such a puppy dog. *I wonder why he didn't show up for work. He wasn't that hung over and didn't seem sick when I dropped him off.* She stood thinking a bit longer, then took another long drink of her Margarita. She smiled. "I'm in control. With more money and manpower, this is just the first step."

Then she thought about Ricardo Vasquez. He was another puppy dog, maybe more so than Danny. *He wants me bad. That makes him an easy mark.* She smiled, realizing just how much power she wielded over the two men.

Her mind shifted again. She visualized explosions that engulfed cities. Her smile widened.

* * *

At the Best Western Hotel in Superior, Wisconsin, Sheik Al Salil smiled. He was already thinking about the virgins that would greet him in Paradise. He was doing Allah's work and certainly he would be rewarded. That he had to partner with heathens would be forgiven. That he had to work with this Garcia woman was most painful. She was vain, so full of herself. But she had come through with funds and more. Maybe this would work, at least for a while, until he got his own source of funds restored. He wondered how the Imam would manage that, being under such close scrutiny. He had to trust in Allah, the Great Provider of all things good.

Yes, there had been a few snags, but the plan moved along quickly. In less than forty-eight hours the plan would be in motion. *Praise be to Allah.*

Chapter 22

Salil pulled back the curtains to the hotel room for the fifth time in the past ten minutes. Anticipation made every nerve ending in his body spark. It had been several years since he'd last seen his wife. He looked at her picture often, remembering their life together. In the beginning, times were difficult in southwestern Syria, still in the shadow of the Israeli war machine. The fear of a military attack was always in the back of his mind. But he and his wife had it better than most of their neighbors. Salil's affiliation with Imam Khadduri allowed him privileges not enjoyed by the masses. Early in his life he'd been selected as a man who could lead the fight against the enemies of Islam. He was trained in battlefield tactics, but more importantly, he was trained to deceive the enemy, to make them feel as if he were a friend.

Closing the curtains, he looked around the hotel room again, searching for any device that might be there to record his presence or his words. He was constantly on guard, looking for cars that looked too official, or too casual, and faces that looked his way one too many times. It had served him well. He was still alive and bore few battle scars, unlike the enemies who'd crossed his path, like the fools in Virginia who'd broken into his home and stolen the funds to be used in the war on his enemies. The first fools suffered, but they were the pawns of the real perpetrator. The real thief suffered a far more painful death at sea. Salil allowed himself a brief moment of satisfaction thinking back on the bloody scene.

He looked towards the curtain again, but looking out too often might attract attention. He thought of his beautiful wife, Salma, again. Allah had smiled on him because he was a key soldier in the battle with Satan.

Salma Nidal was the most beautiful creature Salil had ever seen. Her dark brown eyes and olive skin were perfect. She was the image of purity and modesty when in public. When they were alone together, she was passionate. She was more a partner than a subservient mate.

Salil was assertive at home and played the part of head of the Muslim household, but when Salma spoke to him on important matters, he listened. She was educated and clever and knew how to get her point across in a manner that allowed him to maintain the appearance of being totally in charge. They both knew how to play the family game among their peers.

When she became pregnant early in their marriage, they both believed it was the will of Allah that their children were destined to be soldiers in the fight against their enemies. She had a relatively easy time carrying the child to full term. But when their son was born, Salma had difficulty in delivering. The umbilical cord wrapped around his neck placed him in danger throughout the delivery. When she finally gave birth, all attention was paid to ensuring his health. Salma was attended by only a single nurse with little previous training and the placenta was not expelled for an extended time, resulting in a severe uterine infection. Two days after giving birth, she was near death. After several days, while her recovery was still tenuous, she began to improve. It took nearly a month before she made a full recovery. She and her husband believed Allah had intervened.

The boy lived and was a healthy baby, but she never conceived another child. The doctors weren't sure if her inability to get pregnant again was related to the difficulties during birth or the infection after, but it didn't matter. Ahmed Salil was their only son. He would be a great warrior in the fight against their mortal enemies, the imperialist Americans and their bastard stepchildren, the Jews.

He looked out the window again and saw the car pull into a parking spot below. It was a green Ford Taurus. After nearly a full minute a woman got out and looked up at the room where Salil stood. After another brief moment of hesitation, she headed for the hotel steps. He smiled and allowed the curtain to close. He shook with nervous excitement. His Salma was here.

* * *

Salma Nidal Salil sat in the car for several moments in the grip of nervous anxiety, thinking about her husband. She'd been counting the days since the New Year began, but she was nervous. She'd been living amongst the Americans for so long she was afraid her true husband would disown her. She and Sheik had talked about the separation with Imam Khadduri. He assured her it was necessary to gain their trust and therefore, truly blend in with the community. She asked the Imam several times if her actions would be sinful and cast her into the fires of Jahannam. The Imam insisted she was doing the work of Allah. He said she was blessed to be able to strike at the heart of the devil and that these actions were preordained.

Now, sitting in her car, bought by her American "husband", she had doubts. She enjoyed her physical relationship with her American "husband," and that fact tormented her. Shouldn't she hate making love with him? At least, she tried to minimize the times she had to do it by claiming all manner of excuses. Regardless, it was still exhilarating. She reasoned part of the excitement was that she was literally screwing the enemy, though he didn't seem like much of a threat to Islam.

She took a deep breath, looked up at the second floor of the hotel room and identified the door where her true husband waited. She closed her eyes and said a brief prayer, asking for forgiveness for her sins. The sun had warmed the car. Perspiration formed on her forehead as tension combined with heat sent her nerves into high gear. After one more deep breath, she exhaled, opened the car door, and stepped out into the sunlight.

Her head was covered with a tan hijab, hiding all of her head except her face. She wanted her husband to see that she remained faithful and modest. And she needed to ensure that no one would recognize her.

The air felt cooler than the stagnant heat from the car. She closed the car door and took another deep breath, still tense with anticipation. *How can he forgive me for giving myself to another man?* She stood there a moment longer, then gathered the will to climb the steps of the hotel and face her husband.

Salil had asked for a room near the stairs so he could get away quickly in an emergency. So far, that precaution had not been needed. Salma approached the door ready to knock, when it opened before her. Sheik Al Salil smiled and held out his hand to her, guiding her inside, closing the door behind her.

They spoke very little as they held each other. It had been a long time. Slowly, they explored each other's bodies. He wanted to ask if she'd had to submit to her "husband" frequently, but he didn't. He didn't want to know the answer, and it was part of her job to get her

American "husband" to trust her fully. To gain and keep his trust, there were things she must do. He didn't want to know, but it was there in the back of his mind. She was here with him now. And so they made love in this cheap hotel room with pressboard furniture, and dark, commercial carpet.

Salma gave her entire self to her true husband. She hungered for him. She hated her current living arrangements and looked forward to the change that was soon to come. The sex was good physically, but the guilt was starting to eat away at her resolve. Living in the United States allowed her to have many material things she would never have in Syria. It was easy to see why American women were spoiled. They acted as if having thirty pairs of shoes, a wardrobe with an outfit for nearly every day of the year, and more makeup than a queen was their birthright. They acted like whores, throwing themselves at men. And they were training their daughters to continue this pattern of decadence when they grew up. It was a cycle that would never be broken unless they were taught a lesson.

Salma was treated like a queen in the United States, even by the man she despised. One day she looked into the bathroom mirror and asked herself why she shouldn't enjoy this lifestyle. Back then she'd only been with her American "husband" for a short time. Later that day, her son was hurt at school. A bully had knocked him down and broke his arm. The incident passed without much drama. The bully was suspended. Over time, the boy and her son became friends. But she took it as a sign. She was being punished for her impure thoughts. From that day on, when she was tempted, she locked herself in her room and prayed for forgiveness.

She and Sheik lay side by side, relaxing, smiling, feeling as one again. She rolled onto her side, facing her true husband, stroking his chest. "It is good we are together again. I have missed you."

He tilted his head and looked deep into her dark brown eyes. There was a glow about her, as if an aura outlined her entire being. "It is as if we were never apart. You are as beautiful as the day we met."

Her smile brightened and she laid her head on his shoulder. She thought back to that fateful day when they walked along the dusty road to Damascus. They were among the survivors of the vicious Israeli attack on their homeland.

"I'm afraid I wasn't so beautiful that day. I was covered in dirt and grime along with the blood of my little brother. My clothes, my hair, everything was . . ."

Sheik lightly put a finger to her lips. "Shhh. Even then, to me, you were the most beautiful creature on earth. I saw into your eyes and your soul touched mine. I knew then that you would be my wife."

They were silent for a time. Her mind drifted, thinking of what was ahead of them. Knowing the time they had together was short, she wished to make the best of it. She moved on top of him and they made love again. This time, with more intensity and passion; as if they needed to make it right. They worked each others' bodies as if this might be the last time ever. They both believed it to be true. Slowly, they moved their hands over each other, arousing every tingling sensation. Exploring every centimeter of flesh, they ignited pulses of energy that ran the length of both their bodies. The temperature seemed to rise in the room as they worked harder and faster. This time had to be the best time. As they neared the pinnacle of their love, they locked eyes, searching for each other's soul, just as they had on the road to Damascus. They gripped each other tight, completing the bond that made them one. They collapsed, their energy drained from an exhaustive climax. They held each other in a euphoric embrace, finding it hard to imagine that Nirvana would be nearly as pleasurable. Within seconds they fell into a deep, dreamless sleep.

* * *

Sheik awoke to the sound of the shower. He looked where Salma had been, remembered the moments preceding his restful sleep and smiled. When he heard the shower stop, he rose and went to the bathroom door and knocked lightly before entering. He stepped into the shower with his wife where they showered together, holding each other under the hot stream of water.

Finally, they dressed and sat at the cheap, small table. The talk was now serious. They spoke about the plan. And the brevity of their mortal future was now before them.

"So, are we on schedule?"

Salma regarded her husband's question and smiled. "Yes. What time is it?"

Sheik looked at his watch. It was nearly four in the afternoon. He showed Salma and she smiled. "Less than forty-two hours. We will strike the first blow with our mighty army."

Sheik smiled. "I have good news. We have another source of funds. Our new partner is not of the best character, but we have a common enemy. They will carry out their attack at the same time we execute ours. I believe that, after we succeed, we'll have even more people wanting to join our fight."

"That is wonderful. Tell me more of this partner."

Sheik's smile disappeared. "She is a vile woman, arrogant. Back home, she would be sentenced to death for her promiscuity." His smile returned. "But she has connections with the Mexican drug lords. They have lots of money supplied by the foolish drug addicts of this condemned country. They supply the very resources that will destroy them."

Salma smiled at her husband. She liked that he was so confident and committed to their cause. "So we are ready then?"

"Yes. After I wire the money we will have weapons at our disposal. It's coming together just as we planned."

Salma had one change to their plans that she wished to discuss.

Salil noticed the tension in her look. "What is it, love?"

"I want to kill my American husband. I cannot stand another night with him."

Salil smiled at his wife and nodded, sealing the fate of the man who had no clue of the danger that lived in his home.

Chapter 23

Sheriff Madeline Wymer walked through the back door of the Bayfield County services complex heading for her office. She'd just returned from a lunch meeting with the first deputy to respond to the Alex Corbin murder scene on Evan Jones' property. She hadn't arrived on the scene until nearly thirty-five minutes later. The vision was still vivid in her mind. She wanted to know if there were any details that he remembered, now that he'd had time away from the murder scene. There were none. The only comment he made was that Special Agent Scott had questioned him at length about what he saw while on the Jones' property. She asked if Agent Brown was there with Agent Scott and he'd said no. *The Feds are supposed to be working as a team. Looks like one team has an "I" in it.* She headed for her office until she noticed Agent Nancy Brown standing by the coffee pot, staring in the direction of the pot, preoccupied. The sheriff headed in her direction.

She tried to ease into Nancy's field of vision to gain her attention without startling her. Nancy caught sight of Madeline and looked up. Distracted from her thoughts, her jaw and neck relaxed.

Madeline smiled and spoke first. "Hey, Nancy. I thought you were having a seizure from drinking that swill. It'll kill you if you're not used to it."

Nancy returned the smile, but it was brief and a bit forced. She raised her cup a bit. "I work at Quantico. Compared to what we have there, this is like Columbia's finest." Her blank stare returned.

After a few moments of awkward silence, Madeline asked, "Want to talk about it? My office is soundproof. I guarantee no one will hear us." She poured herself a cup of the dark brew. A brief sniff made her frown, but she took a swig anyway. With cup in hand, Madeline tilted her head towards her office. They both headed in that direction.

The sheriff's office was small, but not cramped. The walls were painted institutional beige with dark brown wood trim. Official pictures of the President of the United States and the Governor of

Wisconsin hung on the walls, but nothing else. The American Flag and the bright blue flag of the state of Wisconsin were posted behind her desk against the wall. Nancy looked around before taking a seat in front of the metal, government-issue desk. She noted the lack of family pictures of any kind. Madeline closed the door behind her and noted Nancy scoping out her office. Instead of sitting behind her own desk, she sat next to Nancy in one of the cheap, but comfortable guest chairs.

"Divorced for seven years, no kids. I had two miscarriages and that was more than I could handle. Apparently, it was more than my ex could handle, too. He left almost as soon as I was out of recovery with the second."

Nancy's face flushed a light shade of pink. This woman could read a person exceptionally well. "Sorry. I should've just come out and asked. Must have been a real prick."

The sheriff smiled. "Not really, just weak. And he really wanted kids. He figured the odds were slim with me." A brief silent moment followed. Then Madeline asked, "How about you? Married to the job?"

"Can you read everyone like this?"

Her smile broadened, but she didn't reply to Nancy's question. She shifted gears. "I can see by the look on your face something's bothering you. Want to tell me about it?"

"That obvious?"

"Yeah. So, you want to tell me or are we local yocals gonna be kept out of the loop?"

Nancy's face hardened at the notion she was keeping anything from a fellow law enforcement agency, especially one that needed to know the details. Besides, she didn't think she could get away with lying to this woman. It was exactly why she was tense in the first place. Her counterpart, Special Agent Randall Scott, was keeping certain details from her and her team. She was just thinking what an ass he was.

Earlier in the day, one of her team recommended interviewing certain members of the local Muslim community, including the few who were employees at Superior Shores. It seemed only logical, given that the film of Alex Corbin's murder appeared to be carried out by Muslim extremists. When Nancy proposed the idea to Agent Scott, he said she should discuss it at the next meeting of the task force. She was a bit put off by his recommendation due to the urgency in gathering information.

Then she learned the real reason for his dodge. After they talked, he instructed one of his men to schedule the interviews, but without any participation by Nancy's team. Having just learned this, she hadn't had time to confront Agent Scott, but she had every intention of doing just that. It had crossed her mind to report the incident to Colonel Warner, but she decided it could be handled locally. If necessary, she'd put it in her report and let the colonel know how she had handled the situation.

Nancy looked directly at Madeline, whose face was set in stone. She returned her look with equal steel. "It appears the FBI is treating you like a second class citizen. I know because my team's been relegated to the same position." She paused and took a sip of coffee. "The FBI doesn't want to play nice. Special Agent Scott," she rolled her eyes as she said it, "believes that he's the lead on the case and that my team and your department are too naïve to be equal players." She paused, looked away briefly then said, "He's a dick."

Madeline's lips curled ever so slightly at Nancy's description. "I read up on you. I also called your last C.O. at NCIS. Seems he's pretty confident of your abilities, but he also said you're sometimes too hard on yourself."

Nancy's jaw slackened slightly. She was surprised that a rural sheriff could make that kind of connection. It also made Nancy's level of respect for the sheriff jump up a few notches. "You talked to Major Griggs?"

Madeline nodded. "Yes, but its Lieutenant Colonel Griggs now. When I spoke with Colonel Warner about you, she recommended I talk with Griggs, said I'd get a better overall assessment from him." She paused to get a reaction. The only thing Nancy did was close her mouth tight and wait. "I can tell you, Griggs is more confident in you than Agent Scott's boss is in him."

That brought a smirk to Nancy's face. *This woman is good. I want her on my side.* She leaned forward and set her coffee cup on the sheriff's desk. It was time for some serious data sharing with the Bayfield County Sheriff's office.

"What else did Colonel Griggs say?"

"He mentioned you worked a case for NCIS where you tracked

down a couple of real sleaze balls. They were stealing from young recruits and embezzling life insurance money?"

"Yeah. It was tough. I had a great team."

"He mentioned one particular guy. Joe . . ."

"McKinney," she finished for the sheriff. "He's a former Marine sniper, but he's also one smart guy. I'm not sure we'd have been successful without him."

Nancy was wondering where this was going when Madeline asked, "Any chance we can recruit him for this case?"

She picked up her cup again and took a sip. She hadn't spoken to Joe in a few months. Not since she was at a barbecue at Pat and Diane's house in Dunnellon, Florida. She recalled that Joe's fiancé was pregnant. She'd probably be due about now. *Maybe he could just be in on conference calls. It's doubtful he'd be willing to leave his wife alone if she's still pregnant or has just delivered their child.*

"I'll give you the lowdown on Joe McKinney. He's a very serious guy. When he's focused on a problem, he is intense. And he knows his work. But his wife's . . ."

". . . pregnant." This time, Madeline finished for Nancy. "She's due within a month, from what we know. But I understand he's got a brother, Pat?"

"Yep. He's different than Joe. Not nearly as intense, but he's also very good at solving problems. He was also involved in that case for NCIS, in an unofficial capacity. But he was very helpful, too."

Madeline took a sip of coffee while looking at Nancy. The silence became a bit awkward, as if she were waiting for Nancy to respond to an unasked question.

Finally Nancy asked, "Are you suggesting I ask for the McKinney's to get involved in this investigation?"

"I'm not suggesting anything." She paused for a few seconds then said, "Well, maybe I am. Do you think they could help?"

Nancy shook her head slowly, but a very quiet "yes" escaped from her lips.

After a few more minutes of small talk, Nancy told the sheriff she would call Joe and ask if he and Pat could provide some long distance support. She wasn't promising anything, especially with Joe's situation. She had no idea where Pat was at the moment. She hoped they'd jump at the chance to be involved. Nancy left the sheriff with a promise she would call Joe right away. She also suggested that she and the sheriff have a serious talk with Agent Scott. Working together was essential. Right now they had a murder. But this situation had the potential to be much more serious.

* * *

Twenty minutes later with the afternoon sun bearing down, Nancy flipped open her cell phone and dialed the number for Joe McKinney. A little girl answered, “Hewwo.”

Smiling, Nancy said, “Hello, young lady. Is Mr. McKinney there?”

“Hewwo,” the voice said again, then a bit of noise crackled in her ear.

“Hello?” A man’s voice came on.

“Hi, Joe, Nancy Brown here.”

”Good to hear from you. How are you?”

“Pretty good. How’s Lisa holding up?”

“She’s a real trooper. She’s ready to have this baby, though. You know how energetic she is. Well, this has been a lot tougher than she thought it would be.”

“Any idea on how soon she’ll deliver?”

“Could be within a couple of weeks. But the doctors keep telling us it isn’t like a clock. It’ll happen when it happens. We’re pretty excited.”

Nancy could hear it in his voice. That was unusual for Joe. He was always very serious and methodical. But this was a different role for him. She cleared her head and decided to get right to the point.

“We have a situation we need help with. I know you’re not available to travel or get directly involved in the field, but would you be interested in being a long distance consultant for our team?”

Joe was silent. She could almost hear the wheels turning. Then he said, “What kind of a case is it?”

“First, this is classified confidential. You can’t talk with anyone.”

“Okay, I get it. Get to the point, please.”

Now that’s the Joe McKinney I know. “There was a murder we’ve been called in to investigate.”

“A murder? I thought you were on an anti-terrorist team.”

“I am. I’m getting to that.” She described the murder of Alex Corbin, the video tape of the murder, and some of the suspicions she and her team had about the perpetrators. She also told Joe they were working with local law enforcement and the FBI, though it wasn't going as smooth as she'd hoped. "The sheriff here in Bayfield County is sharp. She's the one who recommended that I ask you to join the team."

On the other end of the phone, Joe's brow wrinkled. "How does she know me?"

"She doesn't. But she knows about you. She did some homework and talked with Lieutenant Colonel Griggs. Apparently, he recommended I call you and your brother. He said you two would make a good addition to the team."

"Well, Pat's out. He and Diane are on vacation. They'll be gone for several weeks."

"Oh, that's right. I remember them saying they were taking the time off. Pat really needed a break. Where are they headed?"

"They're taking a circle tour around Lake Superior. Right now they're visiting an old Navy buddy of Pat's way the hell up in northern Wisconsin. The trip's off to a rough start, though. A co-worker of his friend went missing last week. They found his body—"

Joe tensed as he suddenly realized Pat and Diane were right in the middle of Nancy's investigation.

Nancy smiled. "I'll give Pat a call on his cell. And Joe, I'll conference you into our next meeting."

Chapter 24

Hatch left Loco Pedro's and sat in his rented Ford Taurus. The heat was unbearable, so he started the engine and turned the air conditioning on maximum cool. For nearly a full minute it blew scorching hot air. Finally, it cooled to the point where he could sit and think of something besides burning up.

Back at the bar, Pedro's young friend with the pictures of "Miss Hotty" hadn't been able to stop talking about her. Hatch actually had to pay him for the best three pictures of the young woman and a fourth of her Corvette.

Pedro was right. She was a classy, beautiful woman who definitely looked out of place at Loco Pedro's. But he needed to know where she and Danny went and he needed to know now. His friend was in deep trouble. But that's all it was . . . a gut feeling. At least he had a starting point, the three pictures of the woman and a picture of her Corvette. The license plate was visible, but the numbers were a blur. Joe McKinney had experience with photography and image enhancement from his time in the Marine Corps. He would have a good chance to narrow down the possible license plate number combinations. Hatch's only concern was that Joe might not have the time since his fiancé was about to have a baby. *I guess I'll find out one way or another if he can do it.*

He dialed Joe's number. Joe answered on the first ring.

"Hello?"

"Mr. Joseph McKinney, I presume?"

"Hatch! How in the heck are you?"

"Doing just okay, my friend. I wish I could say great, but circumstances as they are, I just have to stick with okay."

"That doesn't sound good. What can I do for you?"

"My friend, Danny, didn't show up for work today at the Texas Star Refinery. That's a big problem, because it's totally outta character. And the last person to see him was a woman. She might have been stalking him." He paused. "Any other guy, I'd just think he was having a good time, you know, relieving a little tension, enjoying . . ."

"Yeah, Hatch, I get it. But that doesn't fit with what you know about your friend?"

"Right." Another pause. "I'm worried. Real worried. It isn't like him to disappear. But, some guys at a local bar down here got a couple pictures of the woman and her car. They got the license plate on one picture, but it's blurry. I was hopin' I could send it to ya' and you could do a little photo magic on it. Maybe tell me if you could narrow down the list of possible plate numbers."

Joe thought for a second, then said, "Sounds like a challenge. Send it on and I'll see what I can do."

Hatch was pretty confident Joe could help. But he had work to do while waiting for the results. He'd gotten directions from Pedro to the local library. He was surprised that Pedro knew where the library was. Pedro had noticed the look and told Hatch he read at least one book a week. "I may look like some poor Hombre to you, but I make good money with the bar. You have to stay up on your game or you'll be out of business in a hurry. I can't be estupido."

Hatch had extended his hand to Pedro and said, "You ain't estupido, I'll give you that."

"Hatch, you find our hombre, Danny. Good luck."

* * *

At the library, Hatch asked a young lady with raven hair and bright red lipstick what the highest scanner resolution was that he could use to send a picture over the internet. While chewing her gum, and in a heavy Texas accent, she explained in detail why it was best to use a lower resolution. *The more pixels in the picture, the bigger the file. The bigger the file, the longer it takes to send. If it's too big, it won't make it to the recipient. You see the internet only has so much bandwidth and when your e-mail exceeds that bandwidth* . . . She went on for a minute more when Hatch held up his hand. Realizing she'd been a bit too technical for her customer, she smiled, exposing a mouth full of bright white teeth. With her red lipstick and white teeth all she needed was a bit of blue and her mouth would have looked like an American flag. She kept smiling and batting her long eyelashes at him. He was getting uncomfortable.

"So, miss, what's your name?" She couldn't have been more then seventeen.

"Cassandra. What's yours?"

"My real name's William but everybody calls me Hatch. You seem to know your way around computers and stuff. Do you like working here?" He was in a hurry, but a few kind words went a long way in gaining peoples trust and cooperation.

He handed her the e-mail address and a brief set of instructions for Joe. While he talked, she scanned the picture of the red Corvette, attached the picture file to the e-mail, and typed up the message. At the same time, she smiled up at Hatch and continued to chomp away on her gum. He was amazed that she could do all this and still hold a conversation.

She said, "Multi-tasking."

"Pardon?"

"I'm multi-tasking. You're wondering how I can do all this and still hold a normal conversation. I'm good at multi-tasking." Her smile broadened, even as she continued to chew her gum.

"That's amazing," he said, trying to keep the amusement off his face. "You can do all that and read my mind. I can hardly walk and chew gum at the same time." That was not altogether truthful. Hatch was very good at multi-tasking, but he called it *doin' lots of stuff at the same time.*

To keep from having to endure the woman's stare, he looked around the library, taking in the layout, trying to gauge the age of the building. It appeared to be many decades old based on the high ceilings and older light fixtures. A recent renovation was obvious. New book shelves with dark-stained wood and new carpet were just a few features used to try to modernize the interior. Looking the building over also helped keep his mind from worrying too much about Danny. It would do him no good to flood his brain with negative thoughts.

He was just about to turn around when Cassandra said, "Alright, the e-mail's on its way." With her bright smile she asked, a bit too seductively, "Is there anything else I can do for you, Mr. Hatch?"

Hatch just smiled back, "No, Miss Cassandra. I think that'll do it. Thank you, Ma'am."

Her smile turned a little less fluorescent, but her accent remained pure Texas. "Well, thank you, Mr. Hatch. If you change your mind, you know where to find me."

"Yes, Ma'am, I do." He smiled, nodded, and headed for the main entrance.

Once outside, Hatch called Joe to let him know the file was on its way. Joe said he'd call back when the e-mail arrived. With a file as large as Cassandra described, it might take a while.

He decided to go back to Danny's apartment, maybe he'd missed something, maybe a sign that Danny and "Miss Hotty" had been there and left. But if the little girl, Alisa, had seen them, she would have said something. Of course, Danny could have paid her more than twenty bucks not to say anything to anyone. "Miss Hotty" could have convinced her to keep quiet, too, but little Alisa didn't seem like the kind of kid to hold secrets too close. It was worth a shot.

Then it occurred to Hatch he didn't even know what kind of car Danny drove. He pulled out his cell phone and dialed the I&C shop at Texas Star. Bud Yantzy, Danny's foreman picked up after only one ring.

"Yantzy."

"Hey, Bud, this is Hatch."

"You found Danny yet?"

Hatch thought *How you doin', Bud. Nice day today.* But instead he answered, "Not yet. That's why I'm callin'. Do you know what kind of car Danny drives?"

A brief pause, followed by, "No, but let me ask. Sammy just walked in." He heard the sound of scratching material on the phone as Bud held the phone to his shirt. After about twenty seconds he came back on the line. "He drives a gold Ford Explorer, fairly new. Maybe two years old. Nothing fancy."

"Okay. That may help. Call me at this number if you think of anything else." Hatch recited his cell phone number then disconnected.

A gold Ford Explorer. There are probably only about a thousand in the greater southeast Houston area. Hatch headed towards Danny's apartment and parked on the street near where he'd parked before. He looked up and down the street. No gold Ford Explorer. The three teens he'd encountered earlier were nowhere to be seen. He locked his car and made his way to the apartment building. Climbing the steps more slowly this time, he looked around for any sign that Danny might have been there since the night before. Nothing caught his eye.

He again tried Danny's apartment door and it was still not locked.

This time, Alisa was not in the apartment, but a small gold-colored collie ran up to him, wagging his curly tail. He let out a few barks, but they were friendly barks, the kind that said *Come right in, sit down and pet me a while. Maybe while you're here you can feed me, too.*

Hatch liked animals and crouched down to pet the little guy. "So, little fella, where's our boy Danny?"

The little gold ball of fluff laid down and rolled over on his back, begging for a tummy rub. Hatch smiled and obliged the puppy for about ten seconds. As he stroked the pooch, he looked around the apartment for signs of change or anything he might have missed on his previous visit. Nothing caught his eye right away. The apartment was clean and organized, something that surprised him. Danny was a bachelor and a tinkerer. He liked to experiment with things. Hatch expected he'd have all kinds of tools, puzzles, models, or some other hobby junk around the place. There was nothing like it anywhere in the living room or kitchen. *Maybe in the bedroom?* He stopped petting the collie, much to the pup's disappointment. The dog hopped up on all fours and stood at Hatch's side while he made another more deliberate scan of the two rooms. Still nothing hit him as being out of place.

He carefully searched both bedrooms, trying not to leave any fingerprints. Technically, he'd entered the apartment uninvited, which meant the police could make a case for breaking and entering against him. But he worried more about finding his friend. So he continued the search, still not knowing what he expected to find. He turned away from a dresser and nearly tripped over the golden ball of fur at his feet, still wildly wagging his tail.

Back in the kitchen, he scanned the countertop. The usual small appliances: a coffee maker with old grounds still in the holder, a toaster, can opener, blender, and a scented candle on the glass top stove. Hatch had never seen one of these new stoves and just shook his head. *What will they think of next?*

On the kitchen walls were a few paintings of country roosters and a clock. After Hatch noticed the clock, he heard the methodic tick, tick, tick. Why hadn't he heard it before? Now, it was starting to annoy him. Below the clock was a wooden wall hanger designed to hold mail, reminder notes, and honey-do lists. There were a few hooks on the bottom for keys and other small items. There were two sets of keys, a dog tag, and a pair of nail clippers. Hatch looked at the keys more closely. One looked like a spare apartment key. It was on a key ring with a smaller key, possibly for a storage room. The other set looked like they might be Danny's main set. Hatch looked closer. The large key with electronic door lock controls was for a Ford. *If the keys to his apartment are here, where is my man, Danny?*

The sound of someone slowly turning the apartment doorknob captured Hatch's full attention. He silently and quickly made his way to a spot behind the door. Not that it mattered, because Danny's dog was at his feet, gazing at him and wagging his tail. Trying to shoo him away by waving both hands did no good. Hatch took a deep breath, held it for several seconds then slowly and quietly exhaled. The door inched open while he waited, his hands at his side, relaxed but ready to pounce.

The fluff ball moved towards the door as it slowly opened. *Good, a distraction.* As the door opened further, Hatch flexed his knees and prepared to leap at the intruder. The dog started barking with excitement, wagging his tail even faster. The intruder's hand was visible now, reaching for the little puppy. It was a child's hand. Hatch looked around the door. His little friend, Alisa was back.

"Hi there, Miss Alisa."

She jumped up and made a startled yelp. When she saw that it was Hatch, she took a swing at him and shouted, "You scared the crap out of me! Damn it!"

"Well. I see you've been studyin' your English."

"It's not funny you . . ."

Hatch cut her off, hoping to avoid the inevitable stream of profanity. "Okay. I'm sorry I scared you. I thought you might be a bad guy and I had to be ready." He paused while Alisa settled down a bit. "Have you seen Danny in the last hour or so?"

"No." She looked around his apartment, then back down at the collie. "Are you getting hungry, Patrick?"

The pup continued to wag its tail, but it turned and headed towards the kitchen and looked up at the refrigerator. On top of the fridge, an open bag of dog food had Patrick's full attention.

"Patrick's a smart little dog. Did you teach him about looking for food when he's hungry?"

"No, he just knows." She looked sad now "You haven't found Danny yet?"

“Not yet. But we will. When was the last time you saw his car?”

“About a minute ago.” Hatch gave her an odd look. She continued, “It’s in the parking lot out back.”

Hatch grabbed the keys off the letter holder. “Can you show me?”

They left Danny’s apartment, walked quickly down the three flights of stairs and headed out the back door of the apartment building, opposite from where Hatch parked on the street. In a small area to the left of the doors was a parking area for the tenants.. On the far side of the small parking lot was a gold-colored Ford Explorer.

Hatch turned to Alisa. “Are you sure that’s Danny’s car?”

“Yes.” She looked worried now. Hatch thought something bad had happened, or was about to happen.

“Alisa, can you stay here, please?”

She took a deep breath. “Yes.”

Hatch walked over to the gold SUV and walked around it, trying to look in the windows. They were tinted a dark black. He couldn’t see anything inside. He thought he caught the scent of a familiar odor. The car was close to the dumpster. That made identifying the source of the smell more difficult. He pressed the button to unlock the doors and heard the click as all four door locks popped up. He took a deep breath and pulled open the driver’s side door.

The scent of death was strong. He shut the door, then went down on one knee, placing his head in his hands. Danny was slumped over the center console with a large hole in his head and a gun in his left hand.

Chapter 25

Special Agent Randall Scott listened to one of his agents give him the lowdown on Yusef Hassan. The agent read the charges from a single incident in his police record.

"He has one arrest for *persistent disorderly conduct, assault, and disturbing the peace,* all from the same incident. He threw a drink at a patron in a restaurant in Washburn. Continued to yell at the responding officers that all Americans were pigs and that they thought they owned the world. Shouted something the officers couldn't make out, but it says here that it sounded like he was asking Allah to destroy America. Yelled that he wished he was back home in Dubai."

"That's it?"

The agent leafed through the few pages in the file and shook his head. "That's it. This happened back in 1994. Nothing before or after."

Randall Scott leaned back in his chair and looked up at the ceiling. His sources in Washington hadn't responded to his inquiry yet. He expected it to be faxed within the hour. If Hassan was a terrorist, he wasn't being very cautious. Most Muslim extremists tried to keep out of the limelight and away from law enforcement. That didn't mean Hassan was innocent. Agent Scott said quietly, "Maybe he thinks he's bullet proof or something."

"What?"

"Nothing. Just thinking out loud." He hadn't realize he'd spoken loud enough for anyone to hear. "How about that other Muslim engineer? What's his name?"

The agent picked up another file and started to open it when there was a knock at the office door, then it opened. He stood just as Nancy Brown walked in. She looked at the men and read the guilty looks on their faces. "Am I interrupting something?"

Agent Scott gave her a look of contempt. "Not at all. Back from lunch so soon? You and the sheriff exchange any good recipes?"

The junior agent smirked. Nancy looked at him and said in a firm voice, "Out, now."

When he didn't move, she slowly reached out as if to shake his hand. He naturally extended his. She took his hand and began to apply pressure, then grabbed his wrist with her free hand. With a quick motion, she had the agent on his knees, his arm twisted behind his back, and his face against the wall. Agent Scott stood.

She yelled, "Stop!"

He did.

"I'm just going to explain the rules to your agent here. Apparently, he didn't get the memo." She bent close to his ear and spoke. "I am in charge here, along with Agent Scott. I have as much authority and command responsibility as he does. So if you think you can ignore a direct order from me, think again. In the field it could get you or one of your peers killed. Do you understand?"

He didn't say anything, but grunted in pain.

Nancy put more pressure on his hand. "When I ask you if you understand, the correct answer is 'Yes, Ma'am.' Do you understand?"

"Yes, Ma'am."

"Now, I'm going to let you up. If you try anything stupid, you'll be back on your knees. Don't try my patience."

With that, she released the pressure on his wrist. He pulled his arm around to his front and slowly stood, rubbing his arm and wrist. His look pretty much said, *We're not done, bitch.*

"If you're smart, you'll forget about what just happened and figure out how we can work together. Next time I won't be so nice. If you think I'm kidding, have Agent Scott read you some of what's in my file. I'm sure he's already done that, so he knows what I'm talking about," Nancy said.

The agent slammed the door as he left the room. Nancy took a deep breath, then turned to Scott. "So when do our joint interviews start with our Muslim engineers?" Her stare burned holes in Randall Scott's head.

He stared back, not speaking at first. Then he tried to change the subject.

"I could have you charged with assault for what you just did to my agent. How dare you attack one of my men! And you want my cooperation? Think again."

"Pick up that phone and dial this number." She rattled off a telephone number with a Washington, D.C. area code. When the receiver was in his hand he realized it was his boss's direct number. He put the receiver down.

"I don't need to talk with the Director. We already spoke this morning. He's pleased with the way things are being handled up here."

Nancy's lips curled slightly and she leaned across the desk. "Funny, because when I spoke with him moments ago, he didn't remember your conversation. And he suggested that if we have any further problems working together, that I should just let him know." Her face grew hard as she continued to stare at him. "We aren't going to have any more problems, Agent Scott. You and I are going to solve this case. You'll get a little feather in your cap and maybe get that last promotion before you retire, and I'll get some bad guys off the streets. You see, if we work together, we both win." She walked to the door and opened it.

Sheriff Madeline Wymer walked in. "Hello, Agent Scott."

Maintaining her stone cold demeanor, Nancy said, "If I find out you've kept even one piece of information from me or the sheriff, no matter how insignificant you think it might be, I'll make sure your career ends up in the crapper."

Randall Scott remained behind the desk. Outwardly, he was confident and cocky. Inside he was worried. He'd seen just how quickly Nancy had handled his junior agent, both physically and psychologically. He didn't want to be on her wrong side. And somehow she knew he'd read her file, or reasoned that he had. It was impressive. She was smart, serious, and quick on her feet. She'd received high marks on her officer fitness reports from every senior officer under which she'd served in the Marine Corps. He'd wondered if she'd slept her way up the ladder, but when he'd inquired he found out different. She was the real deal. She wasn't anyone to be trifled with.

Now, in the makeshift office, he stared back at Nancy. He hardly paid the sheriff any mind. Heck, she was in law enforcement in a county that had less people in it than the few city blocks where he lived in D.C. He decided to hold his cards close. No need to worry about anything this early in the investigation. So he eased back in the worn office chair and relaxed a bit.

"Agent Brown, Sheriff, you have my full cooperation from this moment on. We have interviews set up with a number of employees from Superior Shores this afternoon. I also have reports coming from Washington on Yusef Hassan and Bashir . . ." He looked around his desk for a file. "Here it is, Bashir El-Amin. We have El-Amin coming in tomorrow morning. As I'm sure you already know, Hassan is missing. He left the power plant about an hour ago. We have an agent checking that out. But we're suspending all interviews with anyone outside the local Muslim community."

Nancy was annoyed at his narrow view of the possibilities. "Why are you only interviewing local Muslims?"

"Because it's becoming real obvious Hassan is our man. We believe he has ties to a terror organization in Dubai. Why do we even have to play this 'no profiling' game?"

"Agent Scott, the reason we have to 'play this game' is because we're not sure that radical Muslims are the perpetrators any more than a group of skinheads, or some nuns from the local Catholic Church. And until we find the real killers, we shouldn't limit ourselves to one group over another."

Scott's face twisted into a half-smile combined with a look of disbelief. "So, according to your plan, we're going to let the Muslim extremists walk while we hunt down Nuns and school kids? Some plan, Agent Brown. Now let's talk seriously. These guys have a much higher likelihood of being our perps than some little old ladies, or even some of the local hoods. So why should we waste our time on regular Americans?"

Nancy took a deep breath. Before she could answer, Sheriff Wymer chimed in. "First let's get rid of all this proper title protocol. My name's Madeline. Call me Maddie. I'll call you . . . ?"

"Randall."

"Nancy."

They all seemed to lighten up a bit with this suggestion. "Randall, Nancy's reasoning is this: on the video, our 'Muslim Extremists' wore wingtips and tennis shoes. If they were real Muslim Terrorists, don't you think they'd have played the part better, more realistically? I know these terror cells become "Americanized," but the video clearly shows at least two members couldn't handle the bloodshed. They gagged at the first sight of blood. That's pretty weak for a seasoned terrorist, wouldn't you say?"

He rubbed his chin a moment, as if thinking it through. He

hesitated just long enough to anger the two women. Finally, he decided it was time to tell them about the drawings found in Hassan's office area.

"It appears some suspicious drawings were found in Yusef Hassan's cubicle."

Sheriff Wymer asked, "So, exactly when were you planning to tell us about this?"

"I'm telling you now."

The Sheriff continued, "What was in the drawings that has you concerned?"

"The sketch had a reference to an ignition source. According to Evan Jones, one of the plant's engineers, there's no such device in that system. And the system contains hydrogen gas, so it would make one hell of an explosion if it were ignited."

This time Nancy took aim at Agent Scott. "Where is your team looking for Hassan?"

"So far, we checked his home and the local mosque. No sign of him."

Nancy shook her head. She hadn't been impressed with Agent Randall Scott from the beginning. His reputation as a loose cannon preceded him, and he was living up to it. His specialty was kidnapping cases. Why his boss had put him in charge of this team baffled her. But they had to work together to find the killers of Alex Corbin. She was determined now, more than ever, to make sure they succeeded. They owed his wife that much.

Based on this new information it looked like Hassan might have been planning to sabotage the Superior Shores Nuclear Plant.

Scott said, "We should have more information on Hassan when we receive his file from Washington. It should be here within the hour."

He looked at Nancy first, then at Madeline. They still looked skeptical but nodded.

The two women headed for the sheriff's office and closed the door to discuss what had just happened. They both agreed Randall Scott was still a scheming bastard and needed to be watched. They planned to make sure at least one of them was with him as much as reasonably possible. But when the cat's away, the mice will play. As far as they were concerned, this guy was a rat.

Madeline's phone rang as Nancy was about to leave. She motioned for Nancy to take a seat. Nancy listened to one half of the conversation as the sheriff nodded, then thanked the caller before hanging up.

"One of my men reviewed the drawing from Hassan's office. It definitely looks like he planned to plant an explosive." She paused. "It looks like Agent Scott may be correct in his assertion about Hassan."

It might look that way, but Nancy still wasn't convinced. She'd already read the file about Hassan's only encounter with the law. Not much of a track record for a terrorist.

Chapter 26

After Nancy left Madeline's office, she headed for the office she shared with Randall Scott. When she arrived, the door was open and the office was empty. She stepped in and closed the door. Her side of the office was cramped. Her inbox was full of files to review in preparation for more interviews. She ignored them. She picked up the phone and dialed Pat McKinney's cell phone. He answered on the second ring.

"Hello."

"Pat, this is Nancy Brown. How's your trip going so far?"

"Hi, Nancy. Going pretty well. We're supposed to start our trek around the lake in a day or two. Who spilled the beans about our trip, Hatch or Joe?"

She smiled. "I can't reveal my source, but your brother is a pushover."

Pat turned to Diane and mouthed to her that Nancy Brown was on the line. They'd just parked in the Memorial Park picnic area overlooking Chequamegon Bay,

At first Diane smiled. Then she frowned. Why was Nancy calling? She knew they were on vacation. Her mood dipped even more.

Pat continued. "You should see Northern Wisconsin. There's not much in the way of people. Most of the towns up here are what you'd call "quaint." It's beautiful, if you like wilderness. We're sitting here looking out at Chica-something bay."

"That's *Chequamegon Bay* and it is beautiful. And I love small towns. As a matter of fact, I'm looking at one right now." Through the lone window in the makeshift office she glanced at the house across Sixth Street from the Bayfield County Services Building. The shrubs were overgrown, the house needed paint, and the lawn was more weeds than actual grass.

"Come again?"

"Well, I just walked out of the Bayfield County Sheriff's Office in Washburn, Wisconsin. It's one of those quaint, small towns, though some of the homes in this one could use a little TLC."

There was a long pause as Pat processed her comment. He hoped Diane couldn't hear her talking, but from the look on her face, he was beginning to worry. It finally dawned on him why Nancy was in Washburn. *The murder*. The hairs on the back of his neck stood up.

"Nancy, are you there about the dead engineer?"

"Yeah, and I'd like to talk with you about that." She took a deep breath and plowed right in. "I know you're on vacation . . ."

"I hear a 'but' coming."

"I'd like you to help us . . . in an unofficial capacity, of course. Would you be willing to review the information we have so far and give us your opinion? That's all, nothing in the field, just paper reviews."

Pat turned away from Diane, trying to shield the conversation from his wife. If he took an assignment while he was under doctor's orders to relax and stay away from any stressful situations, he wouldn't have to worry about his mental health. Diane would kill him. Even so, he was torn. He already had ideas on what could have happened to Mr. Corbin, but he needed more information to see if he was on the right track. He turned to see if Diane was listening. She was, and she was straining to hear as much of the conversation as possible.

Diane liked Nancy, but she knew what the agent did for a living. She didn't want Pat to get involved. What good did it do to drive from Florida to Wisconsin if trouble followed him? But he had a knack for getting involved in touchy situations most normal people would avoid.

Pat turned to look at her for just a moment. The look on her face confirmed his fears. If he accepted Nancy's offer, he was a dead man.

Pat spoke loud enough so Diane wouldn't miss a word. "Nancy, I'm sorry, but I can't. My doctor and Diane both agreed this was a relaxing vacation away from all stress. I just have to say no."

Nancy changed gears . She knew he'd met with Evan Jones, and that he and Diane were staying at Evan's place. She took the opportunity to pry a bit.

"How do you like Evan Jones' place? Nice spread and the house is like a hunting lodge."

Pat said, "Yeah, it's nice. A little spooky with the body having been found on his property, though. I mean, why would someone drive a man all the way there to commit a murder?"

"You mean a beheading, trying to make a political statement?"

Pat wasn't sure he should continue with Diane looking over his shoulder but he said, "No, I mean a murder. Joe told me about the video and the amateurish way these supposed terrorists acted. Except for the leader. Since when does a terrorist yank off his—what the heck are the masks called—anyway, he pretty much exposed his identity and then barfed? What's up with that? A real terror group would have kept that one for a training film and beheaded the barf guy for being such a wuss."

"Did Evan take you back to the murder scene?"

"No. He hasn't even been back there since the day the body was found. He's thinking about selling off that section of the property. I wouldn't blame him. I'd have worse nightmares than I'm already having."

He looked over his shoulder again. Diane's jaw was tight, her brow furrowed. He had to end the call soon.

"Hey, Nancy, I have to go. Good luck with the investigation. We sure hope you get these guys; even if they aren't real terrorists. It still takes balls to cut off someone's head."

Nancy's mind raced as she tried to think of anything to keep Pat on the phone. She really wanted him to review the evidence, even if just a cursory look and comment. It was very hard to justify having her anti-terror unit in Wisconsin when everything, with a few exceptions, pointed to a murder investigation instead of a terrorist plot. Something had to turn up or they'd be ordered back to Washington to wait for another 'real' opportunity. The only real evidence they had were drawings from Yusef Hassan's cubicle and others from Alex Corbin's garage. But the drawings weren't even of the same systems. Unless they came up with something else quick, they might as well pack up their gadgets and head for home. She doubted the FBI could handle the situation, if it turned out to be a real terror threat. She had no faith Randall Scott could handle a murder investigation. But that opinion was tainted by his lack of a personality.

"Pat, could I interest you and Diane in dinner this evening at one of Washburn's finest restaurants? My treat."

Pat smiled, knowing Nancy was trying to pull him in. And he was game. There was just the small problem of his potentially homicidal wife if he were to get involved. But they had to eat, right? And Nancy had offered to pay. What could it hurt?

Pat turned to Diane and said into the phone, "We'd love to meet you for dinner. Name the time and place. We'll be there."

As soon as the words were out of his mouth, he knew he was in trouble. Diane stomped her foot, rolled her eyes, and looked away. She opened the passenger door of the Explorer, jumped out, and headed towards the water. Pat watched his wife stride away.

Nancy was talking, but Pat didn't hear what she said. He was busy trying to figure out how he was going to calm his wife. That might be tricky, and he had to do it before dinner that night, or it was going to be a long night.

"Pat, are you listening?"

"Oh, yeah, Nancy. What did you say?"

"I said there's a steakhouse off the main road in town. It's called the Steak Pit. Rumored to have the best steaks this side of Oklahoma. That's probably a stretch, but it beats that sub place, and it's the only steakhouse in town."

"Sounds great. What time?"

"Let's say around six. That'll give me time to wrap up our day here. We've got a lot of notes to cover. And I'll bring the sheriff, too. She'll be great company."

"She?" *Man, I'm in trouble. Dinner with three women?* "Okay, we'll meet you there."

When Pat closed his cell phone, he looked out at his wife. She sat on a picnic table top, looking out at the bay. From here she looked relaxed. Probably because she was plotting how to get rid of his body after she killed him. But the damage was done. He wondered just how quickly she'd explode when he told her the sheriff was also coming to dinner. *Well, might as well get it over with. At least if she kills me, I'll die in a beautiful place.*

Diane was calm about the entire arrangement. She said they had only tonight and tomorrow left here in Washburn and that they'd hit the road on their tour of the lake the following morning. Then they could both relax. Pat sat on the table next to her and put his arm around her shoulder. She leaned her head against his and they watched the bay, trying to snuggle to keep warm against the chilled air.

As he held Diane even tighter Pat said, "We ain't in Florida anymore."

Diane smiled. "You got that right."

* * *

Eight hours later they were at the Steak Pit, a plain looking building from the outside. Once in the door, the restaurant looked large enough to seat two hundred people. The décor was 1960s. It apparently hadn't been remodeled since then, but it was clean and welcoming.

Nancy introduced Pat and Diane to Sheriff Madeline Wymer. Nancy made a point of highlighting Pat's skills when it came to investigations. As she spoke, Madeline noticed the thinly veiled strained look on Diane's face. Diane was not the least bit pleased by the course Nancy was setting.

They were seated towards the back at the request of Sheriff Wymer. A blonde waitress with a round face and too much pink lipstick passed out menus and took their drink orders. Once drinks were delivered, the three women and Pat settled into polite conversation. After several minutes of small talk Nancy asked Pat a question about the case. He tensed. He wanted a nice quiet dinner with no talk of murder. Diane was going to be ticked off, but she kept her anger to herself as Nancy pressed on.

"Are you enjoying Evan's hospitality?"

Pat tried to steer the conversation away from the case. "Yeah. Under the circumstances, he's been pretty accommodating."

Surprising everyone at the table, Diane spoke up. "It's weird, though. I mean, his cabin looks so nice and neat, but we haven't met his wife yet. She hasn't been home. Neither has his step-son."

Sheriff Wymer answered, "She's a bit different. She smiles a lot but keeps quiet most of the time. Her son is pretty outgoing though. He talks all the time. I'm surprised you haven't met them. Did Evan say when they'd be back?"

Pat and Diane looked at each other, then shook their heads. Diane said, "No. But the place has a woman's touch. I mean, there are throw rugs and candles everywhere. The beds were all made when we arrived, the dishes were put away, and everything had a fresh smell. Men can't do that."

Pat shot her a skeptical look. Just then a waitress came over to take their food orders. Once she turned away and headed to the kitchen, Pat said, "That's pretty sexist, don't you think?"

"I'd say it's pretty observant," Sheriff Wymer said. "Evan got married soon after he got back home from the Navy. His parents weren't real thrilled because his wife already had a son who was in his twenties."

Diane said, "Really? He hasn't said much about them since we got here. But we've been out driving around the area and he's at work all day. So we haven't seen him much."

Nancy watched Pat's reaction as Diane talked about Evan and his home. When Diane and Madeline finished, she said, "What's on your mind, Pat? I can see the wheels turning."

He was silent for a second, the question catching him by surprise. He sipped his water while he gathered his thoughts. "Evan mentioned something to me. It happened at work." He paused and looked around the restaurant, then leaned across the table a bit. "He said one of the young engineers found some drawings in the desk drawer of the engineer, Yusef Hassan, who works next to him. The drawings appeared to show some kind of electronic device attached to a pipe. When the kid checked the real drawings, there's not supposed to be anything there but a stretch of pipe."

Madeline said, "Yusef Hassan's name has come up before. He's got a temper and a short fuse, figuratively, that is. But he's been in trouble only once before for making threats, saying Americans are dogs or some such thing. He hasn't had any trouble with the law since then and that was a few years ago. The FBI has a file on the guy. We were supposed to get a copy of it this morning but we haven't seen it yet."

She paused. "But my sources say he's just a hot head, not a terrorist. He doesn't have any known contacts that would make us believe he's involved with the Corbin murder. But discovering the drawings might change things. We just heard about them earlier today."

Pat wasn't finished. "Thing is, Evan said the drawings were in a desk drawer that wasn't locked. Actually, it couldn't be locked. Evan thought if someone were trying to hide them, they were doing a terrible job of it." He paused then asked, "Who found the drawings?"

Nancy answered. "Jimmy Smith."

Madeline looked straight at Pat. "Jimmy Smith is Evan's stepson."

Pat tried to process this new piece of information. Just then their waitress approached with their salads and a loaf of fresh baked bread. All conversation stopped while they were served. When they were satisfied that no one could hear again, Pat asked. "Are you planning to interview this Hassan guy?"

Nancy replied, "We were." She looked at Madeline, who nodded. She continued, "Hassan disappeared from work this morning and hasn't been seen since."

Pat asked, "Any idea where he's gone?"

Nancy caught a glimpse of Diane's face out of the corner of her eye. She saw her mood darken. "Pat, maybe you should let us worry about that. You should probably keep away from details of the investigation."

Pat was a bit surprised at the sudden change in the direction of the conversation, until he looked at Diane. Then he realized that he'd been completely absorbed in the discussion. He reached over and touched his wife's hand.

She pulled it away while trying to appear calm. Inside, her heart was pounding and her head was spinning. Pat was being sucked in again.

The conversation turned to light topics. The women started talking about how Madeline got into law enforcement. She told her tales of woe in marriage and that it was a natural to pick up a gun and hunt down men after all her marital problems. Pat didn't hear a word. He was deep in thought about drawings of nuclear plant piping and Evan's concern that it was too easy for the kid to find them. Nancy said she'd ask more questions of Evan, but Pat planned to beat her to it.

Pat's cell phone rang. He looked at the display. It was Joe. Pat motioned he was taking the call and headed for the front door. When he opened the door and stepped outside, he answered, "Hey, Joe, what's up?"

"Hey, Pat. I just got a call from Hatch. You know that friend of his he was visiting? Danny Wilkerson?"

"Yeah. He was on the Nevada with Hatch and me. Weird kid."

"Well, now he's a dead kid."

"What? No! How?"

Joe told Pat how Hatch had found Danny's body and the circumstances with the woman at the bar. A thought crossed Pat's mind, but he quickly dismissed it as coincidence. *A murder in Texas, a murder in northern Wisconsin. Both under very strange circumstances and close together. Could they be connected? No way.*

But the nagging thought persisted even as he returned to the table to finish dinner.

Chapter 27

The heat from the mid-afternoon sun, coupled with the dry air, made for a miserable afternoon. The sky was clear and bright blue, so there was not even a temporary respite from a passing cloud. The only shade was from Danny's apartment building. The crowd that had gathered jockeyed for a spot in the real estate beyond the crime scene boundary.

The police worked quickly to gather evidence and get Danny's body out of his Explorer. The car was to be towed to the impound lot where it would be secured for further processing should the need arise.

The good news was that Joe McKinney was able to get a partial set of numbers on the red Corvette's license plate. A friend of Joe's who made a hobby of hacking into government databases was able to narrow down the remaining three numbers to just a handful of combinations. Only one of them owned a red Corvette. The bad news was that the person on the registration was a man named Victor Garcia and he lived in Del Rio, Texas, nearly three hundred fifty miles away from the Gulf Coast of Texas. Hatch sat back in the rented Taurus and scratched his head.

He was beside himself. His good friend was dead, and he had no idea why. It had to be linked to the woman in the red Corvette, but what was she doing driving a car owned by some guy from across the state? Was she some high priced hooker and Garcia was her pimp? Hatch knew Danny could afford a woman like that, but it wasn't his style. Besides, Pedro and his guys said Danny didn't seem to know her, but she'd sure had her eyes on him. It also didn't appear to be a coincidence. She was waiting for him. Then he wound up dead.

Poor little Alisa, who was so quick with the sarcastic and witty comments earlier, had screamed when she saw Danny's body slumped over in his car. She'd never seen a dead body before. Seeing her friend in such a state scared the life out of her. When the police arrived and searched Danny's apartment, Alisa asked what would happen to his dog. When they said that the dog warden would take him to the animal shelter, she begged the officer to let her keep him. The officer looked at Hatch who nodded his approval. The cop shrugged and handed the puppy over to the sad little girl. He even helped bag the dog's food and bowls for her. Hatch's heart nearly broke as he watched her hug the puppy tight and cry into his fur.

The police questioned Hatch at length. He fielded their questions with relative ease. After nearly an hour, they apparently scratched him off the suspect list. As soon as they finished with him, they returned his cell phone and keys, and said he was free to go. He gave the officer in charge his number in case they needed him for further questioning. He doubted he'd hear from them again.

As he reached the bottom steps of Danny's apartment building, he again ran into Alisa, standing at the foot of the stairs. She was still clutching the golden ball of fur, rocking back and forth. For the third time that day, his heart was ripped from his chest. As he watched the tears stream down Alisa's face, he thought about his own little sister. Many years ago, when his sister was about the same age as this pretty little girl, her pet rabbit died, probably of a heart attack from being obese. She used to feed the creature constantly. When she found her precious bunny still and lifeless, she cried for hours, hugging the white ball of fur in much the same way Alisa hugged her new best friend. She would cherish her new puppy. It was the only reminder she would have of her boss and friend. Eventually, she would recover and this event would harden her. Her world was tough, but Danny's murder would eventually make her stronger. It would take time.

"Ya'll might want to loosen your grip on Goldilocks. He has to breath, ya' know."

She stopped rocking and looked up at him with bloodshot eyes. He smiled back at her to let her know he was just playing with her, trying to cheer her up. It was tough because he wasn't all that cheerful himself. But he had years of practice after the murder of his little sister and parents in a home invasion gone horribly wrong.

She opened her mouth to say something, but she closed it and looked back down. She started rocking again, another round of tears escaping her eyes.

"How 'bout you and me sit down and talk for a bit? I'd like to tell you a few stories about our friend Danny. And I need to ask you a few questions."

She nodded slightly and made her way to the bottom step, still clutching the dog. He must have sensed that something was drastically wrong. His head stayed still against Alisa's arm and his tail wound up under his bottom. Hatch wondered if the poor dog thought he'd done something wrong.

Hatch told Alisa about Danny and some of the things they did while on the USS *Nevada*. If she was listening, Hatch couldn't tell. She kept her head down, occasionally wiping her nose with her wrist. Much of the goo ended up on the poor puppy's fur.

Finally, Hatch asked, "Sweetheart, is your momma still at work?"

A nod.

"Is your brother home?"

A shake.

"Well, I'll stay here with you until you say you're okay. Would that be alright?"

A nod. Then she leaned over and put her head against Hatch's arm. He reached over and lightly patted her head.

Hatch looked at the dog who stared back, still looking afraid and confused. Hatch lightly stroked the pooch's head and spoke in a quiet voice. "You didn't do anything wrong, boy. None of this is your fault. Alisa's gonna take good care of you. The good news is she'll always be home since she's home-schooled. So you two will be fast friends. You can cheer each other up when you get sad."

As he continued to stroke the puppy's head, his tail began to slowly wag back and forth.

"Alisa, can I ask you a couple questions about Danny? I mean, are you feelin' up to that?"

In a voice as quiet as a mouse she said, "I guess."

"Now, this might be tough thinking about what I'm gonna ask you, but it's real important. When was the last time you saw Danny? Was it last night?"

Without taking her head off his arm, she said, "Yeah. It was right before he left to go to Loco's."

"That's right. You told me that. Are you sure you didn't see him after that, like early this morning?"

"I'm sure. Momma made me go to bed, and I fell asleep right away. Then this morning I saw you at his apartment."

Hatch nodded. He smiled to himself remembering her smart

mouth. "So, besides me, was anyone hanging around the apartment?"

She paused. "My brother and his friends. They're always hanging out. And the mailman. He was there after you left."

Hatch's gaze wandered around the hall, looking for any clues, any ideas that might jump out at him. He was thinking of what to ask Alisa next when a police officer made his way down the steps. There was enough room for him to pass. When he reached the main floor and headed towards the front door, the officer stopped and turned to face them. He gave them a sad look then moved on.

The sadness in the apartment building was like a lead weight on everyone. Hatch looked up at the ceiling, took a deep breath then looked down at Alisa again.

Just then, the front door to the apartment building opened and Alisa's brother and his friends walked in. One of them said, "Maybe we'll see that hot chick in the 'Vette' again."

Hatch's back straightened as adrenaline shot through him. The boys noticed him and stopped in their tracks. They looked ready to bolt, then they saw Alisa sitting next to him. Alisa's brother frowned.

"Hey, homes, what are you doing with my sister?" He looked at Alisa and said something in Spanish. She said something back that had a little pepper in it. Hatch didn't know what was said, but at least she was out of her malaise. That was a good thing. Alisa's brother started to say something else, but Hatch cut him off.

"Hey, what did you say when you walked in?"

"I said, 'What are you doing with my sister?' "

"No, before that. When you were just walking through the door you said something about a hot chick in a 'Vette.' "

"Oh, yeah. There was this smokin' hot senorita in a bright red Corvette driving around the neighborhood last night. Some guy was with her."

"You mean Danny?"

"No, some other dude I never seen before. They wasn't from around here. But she did drop the dude off down the street. Dude was either brave or stupid."

Hatch asked, "Why's that?"

The boys looked at each other then one of the friends said, "Because he parked his Beamer on the street. It was a nice car." The boys laughed at the inside joke.

"What do you mean *was*?"

Alisa's brother said, "Because a couple of the local home boys tagged it."

Hatch looked at them and raised his eyebrows like he didn't get the joke.

"You know, gave it a custom paint job. You can't miss it. Got a big Gila monster on the hood." The boys laughed again.

"Can you tell me what this dude looked like?"

"Sorry man, we was looking at the babe. We didn't hardly notice the dude."

Then one of the boys said, "I did." His friends stared at him. "He was Chicano, like us. But he had money, you could tell. He had long hair, almost to his shoulders. I seen him once before. He was sittin' across the road in his Beamer, kinda like he was casin' the apartment building. I watched him for a while 'cause it was weird. I thought maybe he was some undercover dude, or some government inspector, but why would he be sittin' there in broad daylight? And what G-man drives a Beamer?"

Hatch and Alisa stood. Alisa's brother noticed that his sister was holding Danny's dog. He asked, "Where's Danny?"

Immediately, tears trickled down Alisa's cheeks. She leaned against Hatch, still holding Danny's dog. Hatch answered, "He's dead. He was shot out back, probably early this morning."

In unison, the three said, "Oh, man. No way."

Hatch left Alisa with her brother. The news of Danny's murder seemed to take the swagger out of his step, and he immediately became more protective of his sister.

* * *

On his way to Loco Pedro's, he dialed the number for the I&C shop at the Texas Star Refinery. Danny's foreman, Bud was shaken badly by the news. He didn't know how to tell the guys in the shop, but it had to be done. Within seconds of hanging up from the shop foreman, Danny's friend, Sam called Hatch.

"Hatch, what the hell . . . is it true?"

"I'm afraid so, Sammy."

"Was it a robbery or something?"

Hatch took a deep breath. "I'm afraid not. He had a wallet with nearly a hundred bucks on him."

The line remained silent for some time, then Sammy said, “I need to talk with you, but not over the phone.”

He had Hatch’s full attention.

Chapter 28

The heat in the office of Nuclear Regulatory Commission Resident Inspector Edgar Williston was stifling. The office, located just off of the turbine deck of the Erie Shores Nuclear Power Plant in Northern Ohio, was designed to contain three small desks and a set of filing cabinets. Being close to the steam-powered turbine naturally caused the heat load in the office to rise. Even when only two of the resident inspectors were at their desks, the heat buildup made the room uncomfortable.

Now, with fifteen people squeezed into the twelve by twenty foot space to review the findings of their reactor compartment inspection, the heat was more than Elliot Simpson could stand. He had just downed a bottle of cold water but sweat still soaked his work clothes. He and several other NRC inspectors and members of plant management had spent the last hour in the reactor building where the temperature was close to one hundred thirty degrees. Now, jammed into this office with all these people, he was close to passing out. He looked around for an open chair. There were only six in the office and they were occupied by four women, and two men older than him. He sucked in deep gulps of air trying to stave off the coming nausea.

"Hey, Elliot. You gonna be okay?" Edgar Williston saw his counterpart from Superior Shores struggling with the heat. "You need another bottle of water?"

Barely able to speak, he shook his head slightly and grunted, "Nah. I'll be alright."

"Okay. Hey, Ginny, let Elliot take a seat for a bit."

The short, hefty young woman stood and nearly knocked two other men over in the process. Another NRC inspector helped Elliot to the seat. As he did, Elliot signaled he needed another bottle of water. The water was passed across the room from a small, office sized refrigerator. The man who had helped him to his seat opened the bottle then handed it to him. Elliot drank nearly half the bottle in five quick gulps. He leaned back in the chair and took a deep breath.

After taking a final, concerned look at his colleague, Edgar Williston said, “Let’s get this meeting started. I know the folks who entered the reactor building to perform the inspection want to get out of here to a cooler place.”

Heads nodded as many of them continued to sip cold water from plastic bottles.

“Randy, lead us through the inspection review. Hold on a second. Lisa, are you taking notes?”

The young clerk answered, “Yes, sir.”

Randy Carlson waited for his boss to nod, then proceeded to lead the group through the long, tedious inspection process. He started with their entry into the reactor building. It was a large, concrete building lined with a steel shell. The reactor was shut down shortly after Haji Madu’s signed allegations were received by the Plant Manager. A few years ago, the Plant Manager would not have taken the plant off line over an allegation from an inexperienced engineer. Now, there was no other option.

Less than two months earlier, the plant had just completed all the requirements of a consignment order from the Nuclear Regulatory Commission. That milestone signaled the end of the recovery from a major safety issue that drew national attention. If he refused to shut the plant down now, the company would be back in the national limelight and his career would have gone down the toilet. He made the right decision and said the right things. *Our primary concern is for the safety of the general public and our employees.* And he meant every word of it. He and all the employees at the plant lived with the burden of safely operating the reactor each and every day. They understood that the safety of the public was always their first mission.

So they vowed they would perform the needed inspections and repairs. They would do whatever was needed to ensure that the plant was safe before it was restarted.

Randy was meticulous in his descriptions of what the team did as they approached the area where Haji Madu gave a detailed description of a serious flaw in the primary system piping. The inspection required that thin steel shields be removed from the twenty-four inch piping, followed by several inches of insulation. Mechanics from the maintenance shop performed the removal under the close watch of plant management and NRC inspectors. They understood that they were under intense scrutiny, so they did their best to use caution when removing the shields. The process took nearly twice as long as usual.

Even though the reactor had been shut down for nearly a day, the reactor coolant system piping emitted tremendous heat. The team had to retreat from the reactor building after only an hour. They changed out of their protective clothing, cooled off, rehydrated with cold water, then went back in while the mechanics removed the layer of insulation. Once the insulation was removed, the heat from the pipes intensified. Stay time, the length of time workers were allowed to remain in the intense heat, was cut in half.

Randy continued his report. After nearly nine hours and four trips into the building, the inspection team was able to get a good look at the piping that Haji Madu said had a defect and was near failure. The inspectors looked at the pipe then back at the drawing. They looked at the pipe again. What they saw was . . . nothing. The three inspectors moved away from the intense heat of the pipe and looked at the drawing again.

Elliot Simpson thought back to the moment that Randy Carlson was describing. Elliot was the lead inspector on the team that was brought in to investigate the serious allegations of a flawed section of piping. The drawing they referenced was made by the young engineer, Madu. It was hand drawn in very clear and precise detail, pointing out the exact location of the "fatal flaw" in the steel alloy pipe. It even gave a detailed description of the corrosion eating away at the primary system piping.

Simpson and other members of the team had looked around at the reactor vessel and the system piping that looped out towards the reactor coolant pumps and the steam generators. They had to be absolutely certain they were on the right pipe in the right location. Simpson, after a moment of getting his bearings down, had nodded. They'd been in the right place all right.

He looked back at the piping that had been cleared of all insulation, dust, and anything that could possibly obstruct their view. But there was nothing to see. The "massive corrosion on the primary pipe," as Haji Madu had described it, didn't exist.

With sweat rolling down into his eyes, he had turned to his team and said, "Take pictures of every square inch of this pipe where the insulation is removed and make sure we get pictures of the surrounding area. Use the highest possible resolution. I want to be able to see every detail and every speck of dust on that pipe. When you're done, put the pictures on the best computer you have."

He turned to the rest of the team and said, "Let's get out of here. We don't want anyone passing out."

Now, in the confines of the crowded NRC residents' office, Elliot Simpson thought back on the events leading up to this non-discovery. *Why in God's name would anyone make a false report?*

Randy Carlson was just finishing up his rundown of the day's events. Elliot finally felt like he had enough fluid back in his system. He stood and said to Edgar Williston, "Contact the FBI. Tell them to pick up Haji Madu and have him detained for making a false report."

Williston looked at him through the throng of people. "Can we do that?"

"We have an obligation to do that, now get on that phone. And let's get out of this office. It's hotter than hell in here."

* * *

Forty minutes later, a team of FBI agents knocked on an apartment door in the Emerald Gardens Condominium Complex near the Erie Shores Nuclear Power Station. There was no answer. Their orders were to bring Madu in, so they broke down the door and searched the apartment. The condo was empty, except for the furniture that came with the unit. It looked as if Haji Madu had never lived there at all.

* * *

At that moment, Haji Madu neared the crest of the Mackinac Bridge to the upper peninsula of Michigan. He was about half way to his destination in northern Wisconsin. He was at peace as he viewed the sunlight against the bridge's towers and on the pipes that supported the roadway that crossed the Straits of Mackinac. At 5:50 P.M. there was still plenty of daylight. The sunshine that came with the longer days of the northern hemisphere held on until late into the evening this time of year.

Once on the other side of the bridge, Madu stopped for gas, a bottle of water, and a snack. As he left the convenience store, a Michigan State Trooper was coming in.

He said to the officer, "Good day, Sir. It is going to be another a beautiful night, isn't it?"

Surprised by the manners of the young man, the Trooper said, "It sure is." He nodded to Madu and entered the store.

Haji Madu smiled as he walked to his Mercury Marquis. He got into his car and headed west. He still had a long journey ahead, but he would enjoy the trip. His first mission was a complete success. *The fools at Erie Shores fell for the ruse. They had no choice since they put themselves in such a bind with their foolish actions.* He conceded that it wasn't the current management's fault. They had nothing to do with past failures, but they had to live with the sins of their predecessors.

Madu's next assignment would be easy compared to the acting he'd had to do at the power plant. He also wouldn't have to be the supporting cast in a beheading. Tonight, he would drive to Bayfield, Wisconsin and carry out the first part of his new mission. Then he would get a room for the night and say his prayers to the Most Holy One. Sleep would come easy. In the early morning, he would finish his mission. Haji Madu was the main event for this part of the plan.

His most recent orders were not part of the original plan, but had been added at the last minute. He didn't like last minute changes without more planning, but he had to trust the leader of his cell. He'd learned a lot from Sheik Al Salil, who had the training and the contacts. Someday, he would take over the cell when Salil was promoted to handle greater responsibilities.

He would recruit other men to carry out his bidding. The more foolish ones would be used to deliver a single blow to the infidels. The more intelligent ones would be assigned greater duties. The Army of Allah would grow. All this would be done in enemy territory. With this government's foolish laws about profiling and privacy, Madu was certain there was no way to stop the growing Islamic movement in the United States.

He smiled. *We are winning!*

Chapter 29

Within minutes of arriving at the Texas Star Refinery, Hatch felt as if his skin was covered with a thin film of oil. The air was heavy and had the scent of rotten eggs. The heat had not retreated, making the assault on his senses even more unpleasant. All these factors together were still not as depressing as the task at hand. Talking with Danny's friends and coworkers was going to be tough. Hatch had to find out if they knew anything about this mystery woman or where Danny planned to go last evening.

Hatch was escorted to the I&C shop where he met with Danny's foreman, Bud, his friend Sammy, and a handful of technicians who had a close association with Hatch's friend. He watched them as they assembled around a table in the foreman's office. They looked as shocked as he was that Danny had been murdered. Every one of them swore Danny didn't have any enemies.

"Did Danny have a steady girlfriend?" Hatch said, trying to see if any of his coworkers were aware of the woman who picked him up at Loco Pedro's. He got the response he expected. Danny's hobbies, the trips to Pedro's, and playing with his dog filled his free time. He didn't seem real interested in finding a woman. He dated, but not often. Most times it was when Sammy or one of the shop guys set him up. He seldom went on a second date with any of those women, even though many of them would have made a fine catch for most young men.

After nearly half an hour of asking questions and getting nowhere he was getting frustrated. It was like no one really knew Danny at all. Everyone said he was a great kid, that he knew his stuff when it came to electronics, and that he didn't seem overly interested in women. He would go out with the guys and have a few beers, but that was about it. They'd never seen him get really angry with anyone. They'd never seen him drunk. He was always happy and easy going.

Bud spoke up, "I've only seen him really upset once. He got a call from his mom that she had to have an operation on her back. He was shaken up about that. He actually came in and asked me what I thought he should do. I told him to take the time off and be with her if he wanted. He had enough vacation built up. He never took any personal time off, so he had it to burn, if he wanted. Hell, that little talk cheered him up and that was it."

Hatch asked, "Did he go?"

"Yeah, but he arranged it so he only missed a few days. He was happy so who am I to complain." Bud leaned on the table on his thick, hairy arms. He raised his hand to his face and wiped across his eyes. "I can't believe anybody could do this to him. Are you sure this wasn't just a robbery gone bad?"

Hatch nodded. "Yeah, I'm sure and so are the police. His wallet was still on him and there was plenty of cash in it. Credit cards, too." He paused. "Whoever did it made a real poor attempt to make it look like a suicide. The cops are all over that one. He was shot from about four feet away."

Hatch stood and stretched. The guys around the table leaned back in their chairs or stood, mostly to break the tension or to stretch tight muscles. They'd been at work all day. A couple of the guys said they had to head home. They promised to call Hatch if they remembered anything out of the ordinary. But they were pretty sure that they'd covered everything, which was very little. There just didn't seem to be a motive behind this senseless crime, at least not one that they could see.

Hatch asked if there was a vending machine close by. Bud told him they had soft drinks and bottled water in a refrigerator in the back of the office. He headed in that direction. Sammy Helzer followed him.

"Hatch, I just don't get it. Danny was a great kid. He was special. He had more talent in his little finger than most guys have in their entire bodies. And everybody liked him. How does this happen to a guy like him?" Sammy shook his head.

Hatch opened the refrigerator door and grabbed a bottle of water. "What'll it be? I'm buyin'."

Sammy replied, "Water's good for me." Hatch passed him one and they both turned back towards the table.

As they passed Bud's desk, Hatch noticed one of the level detectors sitting on top of a manila folder. "Hey, Sammy, isn't this one of the level detectors Danny was looking at?"

Sammy nodded. “We’re just about done installing them. There’s only a handful left in the shop storage room. Danny was intent on taking one apart.”

“You know, that engineer seemed pretty upset when he was taking that one apart in the shop. What was that all about?”

Sammy took a gulp of the cold water, then he said, “That’s what I wanted to talk to you about. That was Ricardo Vasquez. He’s a dick sometimes. That day, he was even more of a dick than usual.”

“Yeah? What do ya’ mean?”

“This level sensor project is his baby. He was in charge from the get-go. He actually found these replacement detectors and convinced management to install them. It’s pretty amazing since this place is slated to be mothballed before too many more years. Hell, it’s a real dog as far as the company’s concerned.”

“Hmm. Why’d they need replacin’ in the first place?”

“The old detectors were failin’ one right after another. We ran out of direct replacements a year or two back and we haven’t been able to find a suitable substitute since then. Then Vasquez, the wonder engineer comes to the rescue. He finds these gadgets that are cheap, durable, and don’t need any wiring. If we had to replace all the cable like the old detectors had, it would’ve cost a fortune. Management wouldn’t bother.”

Hatch nodded. He’d found it odd that the engineer, Vasquez, would get so upset about Danny taking the one device apart. Hell, they did that kind of thing all the time in the Navy. Danny probably would have recommended some changes to improve the design of the thing. But the look on Vasquez face stuck in Hatch’s mind. At first, it seemed like panic, even fear. But he wasn’t sure. It only lasted for a split second then his expression turned to anger before he stormed out of the shop.

“Do you know if Danny ever finished taking that one apart?”

Sammy stopped and looked around. Bud wasn’t paying attention and was still out of earshot. Sammy turned back to Hatch and said in a near whisper, “Danny took one home with him. He said he was going to see how they worked and bring it back today.” He shook his head with the realization that Danny would never be back.

“It wasn’t in his apartment or his Explorer.”

Sammy frowned. He knew Danny hadn’t returned it to the storage area in the shop. He also knew that he hadn't given it to his foreman.

Hatch said, "That ain't the one there on Bud's desk, is it?"

"Nope. That one is for tomorrow morning's work. It's one of the last few that need to be installed."

Hatch was starting to wonder if Danny's disappearance had something to do with his taking the detector. He looked at Sammy and guessed he was thinking down the same line. Now Hatch wanted to see what made these things tick.

"Do you think I could borrow one of the spares from the storage room? I promise to return it." He thought for a moment then added, "It might not be in perfect working order but you'll get the pieces back anyway."

"I can live with that. I'll get it for you."

Sammy turned towards the shop and was nearly out of the foreman's office when Hatch asked, "By the way, has anyone seen Mr. Vasquez today?"

Bud answered. "He was supposed to watch the rest of these detectors get installed but his supervisor said he called off. Something about needing to take his car in for some work."

Fireworks went off in Hatch's head. "What kind of car does Mr. Vasquez drive?"

"A Beamer."

Damn, that's one hell of a coincidence.

* * *

Hatch left the refinery with one of the detectors jammed into his pocket. He planned to head to a home improvement store and purchase a variety of small tools, including a utility knife, needle-nose pliers, an electric drill and bits, a portable vice, and a magnifying glass. He would then head back to his hotel room and set to work.

Turning onto the road that ran alongside the Texas Star property, he looked around at the neighborhood. At one time the homes would have been considered well built. They were close to the refinery, so the workers were within easy walking distance of their job. Their wives stayed home to care for and raise the children. Most likely, it was predominantly white families. Hatch shook his head, wondering where the folks from the old neighborhood were now. *In the suburbs most likely.*

He was about to pick up speed when he saw it. The bright red

Corvette sat just two blocks up the street from the refinery. In this neighborhood it stood out. Hatch went to the next block, took a left turn and drove for two blocks. He doubled back one block and parked about one hundred yards from the beautiful car that was so out of place.

He had a clear view of the car. He waited a few minutes to see if anyone would approach the Corvette. When no one did, he got out of his car and headed straight for it. He tried to calm his racing pulse, but the thought of Danny with a hole in his head made that difficult.

He was only ten feet from the car now. 'Miss Hotty' was nowhere in sight. He examined the houses closest to the car. Nobody came out to challenge him. He moved in closer, then went to the back of the car to look at the license plate. It was definitely the car from Loco Pedro's. But where was she hiding?

When he looked up, she was about one hundred feet away, walking right towards him.

Chapter 30

Ingrid Shaw gazed out across Chequamegon Bay at Madeline Island. The view from the Pier Plaza Restaurant in the city of Bayfield, Wisconsin was beautiful on this crystal clear day. It was 7:20 P.M. and the dinner crowd had thinned out. She sipped her nearly full, ice-cold Corona, savoring the taste of lime. The surface of the bay was calm. Sailboats cruised between the mainland and the island. A few others swayed in their berths at the pier which extended out from the end of Rittenhouse Avenue.

She smiled as her fiancé, Jimmy Smith, returned with a Dos Equis lager and a tray of calamari. Setting the appetizer down on their table, he looked out over the bay, seeing what made Ingrid smile. He smiled as well, but she noticed a hint of sadness in his expression. Was he thinking about Alex Corbin and all the scrutiny that personnel at the plant were receiving? Engineering, where Alex had worked and where Jimmy still did, was the primary focus of FBI interviews. It must be difficult to work under those circumstances. Bad enough that a friend and colleague had been killed in such a brutal manner, but to be questioned at length about your relationship with the man had to be stressful. Then to have to justify your whereabouts nearly every minute of every day for the week prior to the murder . . . Jimmy said it was nothing, but she'd noticed a change in his manner after the interviews.

She turned her attention back to the view from the deck. The bay was a deep blue, an outline of trees making a green backdrop in the distance. The breeze blew towards the bay. The temperature had dropped to a comfortable seventy-five degrees. Grateful the long, cold winter was finally over and the last days of spring promised to usher in a warm summer, she wished it hadn't started with such tragedy, especially for Jimmy. He had known Alex far better than she.

She reached across the table and laid her hand on Jimmy's forearm. He tensed briefly, then relaxed. He turned to Ingrid. "Are you going to take the promotion?"

She was surprised to hear him ask about her recent offer of a promotion to Security Shift Supervisor. She thought it was the murder that preoccupied him. She took a deep breath and prepared to answer. Ingrid knew that Jimmy didn't want her to take the job. Hell, he said he wanted her to quit. Life as a security guard at a nuclear power plant wasn't exactly dangerous work. But you never knew when some group of whacked-out protesters would take out their frustrations with the nuclear industry on the workers. And those workers who walked the perimeter of the plant's fenced-in area carrying military grade small arms were the easiest targets of all. Jimmy had expressed his preference a number of times and was still pushing the issue, but not with as much passion as before. There was a time when he would argue his case for hours. He explained he was worried that if she ever got pregnant she might hurt the baby while doing the strenuous training. *And what about the sounds of gunfire? Might that cause the child to grow up nervous and tense?*

Ingrid had countered that they had never even talked seriously about a wedding date. They were engaged, but that was as far as the discussion had gone. She wasn't ready to be a mother, but with the right amount of encouragement, she might change her mind. But that moment hadn't come . . . yet.

"I'm pretty sure, yes. It's a great opportunity. It's more money, and I'd have less time in the field. It would be more of a desk job than patrolling like I do now."

She knew he wouldn't like her answer. She hoped he would keep it civil.

He turned towards the island again. She followed his gaze, strands of her fine, platinum hair trailing across her face.

The breeze and the ambiance seemed to calm him. He didn't have much of a temper, but he did have a stubborn streak. She hoped to convince him her promotion was a good thing for them both.

"It's beautiful here. This would make a great place to settle down and raise a family, don't you think?" She wanted to find out if he was truly serious about their relationship or if he was just stringing her along. He always treated her with respect in public and with affection, even passion in private. The only tension appeared to be her job. They both worked at the power plant which meant they both made a good living. She still lived with her parents and had planned to get her own apartment this past spring, but she'd decided to hold off when their relationship appeared to be getting serious. She hoped she had made the right decision.

He turned to her and smiled, again with a hint of sadness. She saw it, but couldn't figure out the source. He didn't hold her gaze long, turning back towards Madeline Island.

He spoke as if directing his words to the mass of land in the bay, "It is beautiful, but not as beautiful as you."

She wondered, for a moment, if he meant her or the island. He looked up at the bright blue sky. Taking a deep breath, he smelled the scent of the grilled beef from the restaurant's kitchen. He again smiled.

Turning back to face her, he said, "Yes. This would be a great place to settle down and raise a family." He looked around again at the bay and the surrounding town. "It's so peaceful. It can be tough in the winter, but that builds character, toughens you up, makes you strong."

She stroked his hand lightly. They had planned to go back to his step-father's log cabin later that evening. It was a little over an hour, so they had plenty of time, but she had the morning shift at the power plant, starting at 5:30 A.M. and he had to be in an hour and a half later. She hoped he wouldn't say anything more about her quitting or about her pending job offer. She had another week to decide. It had surprised her when her manager told she could take her time in making her decision. The only right answer in her mind was 'yes,' until Jimmy acted like he disapproved. She hoped, in the long run, he'd see it was the right decision.

But what she wanted most right now was to hear him say how much he loved her and that he wanted to make love to her. They could get a room right here at the inn. She stroked his hand a bit more passionately, urging him to return the gesture.

He reached over and patted her hand.

She thought, *Please, don't stop now.*

Jimmy turned again to look out over the bay. He removed his hand and her heart sank. He took a drink from his beer. With a fork, he picked up some calamari, dipped it in Cajun sauce and dropped it in his mouth. A bit of the sauce ended up on his chin. She wanted to reach across the table and wipe it away, but she was disheartened by his manner. He seemed distant, today more than most days. *Is he growing tired of our relationship?* She decided to be bold.

"Jimmy, let's get a room here for tonight."

His head turned quickly towards her. At first, she thought he was angry. But his expression was blank more than anything else, as if he hadn't heard her suggestion. Then slowly a smile crossed his face.

"Alright. Yeah, that sounds like a great idea."

"We'll have to get up early for work, but that's not a problem. I'm up early anyways."

Jimmy thought for a moment. He smiled and said, "Then we'd better finish this calamari."

* * *

"That guy with the knife doesn't look anything like Hassan or any of the other Muslims at the plant. Look at his eyebrows. They're trimmed close. None of the engineers from the plant keep their eyebrows trimmed. They're all bushy."

Nancy nodded as Sheriff Wymer made her observations. This was the second time through the film for the sheriff. Nancy had lost count of the number of times she'd seen it. She'd watched it at regular speed, slow motion, stop action, frame by frame. You name it, she'd seen it. But Madeline noticed details the other "experts" had missed.

"There. That woman's not used to handling a weapon. Look how she's holding the stock. Look how her hands are gripping the barrel. See?" Madeline pointed to the computer screen where the film was stopped. "Her hand isn't anywhere near the trigger. That gun's too heavy for her. She can't weigh more than a buck twenty. No way she can hold a real AK the way a trained soldier would hold it."

"Maybe she works out." Nancy knew the comment was weak. Madeline was right on most every point. This was a rag-tag group at best. But this rag-tag group had killed a man in a brutal way.

Madeline gave her an incredulous glance. Nancy shrugged. *You're right, but I had to say something.*

After watching the video through one more time, they reviewed clips of the interviews with personnel from the nuclear plant.

It felt like a waste of time. It was a tedious and time-consuming process that was frustrating for both women. The Muslim engineers at the plant had nothing in their backgrounds that would indicate contacts with known terrorist groups. It was getting late in the evening and the ladies were exchanging yawns. They both stood and stretched when Nancy's cell phone rang.

She flipped her phone open in the middle of the second ring, "Agent Brown."

The voice on the other end of the phone was nearly a whisper. "Nancy, this is Pat McKinney. Is Sheriff Wymer with you?"

She smiled at the sheriff as she answered, "Yes, she is, Pat. What's up?"

Maddie gave Nancy a quizzical look. She mouthed back, "Pat McKinney."

"Well, I've been thinking about the Corbin murder and I remember a couple things Evan said that didn't register earlier. He was saying how the drawings the young kid showed him were real easy to find. I mean, they weren't out on his desk or anything, but he wasn't making any effort to hide them." He paused. "It just seems real odd. If he is a terrorist, he's not real good at it. I mean, who would work on a terror plot at their work desk?"

"So, if he didn't keep those drawings there, how did they get there? You think he was being framed?"

Pat's mind raced. He stood in the hallway outside the bedroom in Evan Jones' cabin, trying to talk quietly so he didn't wake his sleeping wife. He opened the door a crack and gazed in. Diane was still sound asleep as far as he could tell. He closed the door as quietly as possible. In the dark, he walked a few feet and kicked something hard. Pain shot through his big toe and it immediately began to throb. He groaned. It was all he could do to keep from yelling out.

"Pat, are you alright?"

After a moment of silence, Pat said, "Yeah. I just kicked something hard and it hurt like hell. Sorry. I'm trying not to wake Diane."

Nancy covered her mouth to stifle a laugh. "Okay, Pat. Just wait until you get over your pain. Also, I'm putting you on speaker phone so we can both hear you."

After a moment and several deep breaths, Pat started again. "Where was I? Oh, yeah. Yeah. I think he was framed. He's an easy target. He acts like everyone's idea of a crazy terrorist. All you have to do is picture him with a dynamite vest strapped to his chest and you could put him on the cover of the Jihad Monthly. I just don't buy it."

Pat heard a noise coming from the kitchen, like a door opening. He knew that Evan was in bed and he'd just seen Diane in deep sleep.

"I think someone's at the kitchen door to Evan's house. Hold tight."

Pat and Diane's room was on the second floor loft which looked down on the living room. The living room was open to the kitchen. His eyes adjusted to the darkness, now, he headed for the edge of the loft and looked down just as the kitchen light came on. A woman walked in and laid a set of keys on the counter. She was in her late thirties to early forties, and very beautiful. He eased away from the rail, just out of sight. Then he heard the door to the main bedroom downstairs open.

He heard Evan say, "Hi, sweetheart. How was your trip?"

"It was fine. I'll be right in and tell you about it. I'm just getting a glass of water. I see your friend and his wife are here."

Pat heard Evan reply as he quietly backed towards the bedroom door. He was in a real pickle now. He didn't want to let his hosts know he was on the phone and he didn't want to wake Diane. He slowly made his way to the bedroom and eased inside the dark room. With his eyes being exposed to the light from the kitchen, he had to wait for them to adjust. He tiptoed to the bathroom door, opened it and went in, closing the door quietly behind him.

Whispering into the phone, he said, "Nancy, Maddie, you still there?"

"Yes. What's going on?"

"I think Evan's wife just got home. Evan called her sweetheart. "

Nancy said, "It must be Sally."

Pat's mind was racing now. He heard Diane stir. "Listen, I've gotta go. If Diane hears me in here, I'm dead."

Nancy said, "Okay. We'll talk more tomorrow. Is your plant tour still on for tomorrow morning?"

"Yes. I really have to go now."

Pat hung up the phone and made his way to the bed. He eased the covers back and slid in beside his wife. He moved ever so slowly, trying to get comfortable when Diane said in a quiet, sleepy voice, "You're right, you're dead. Were you talking with Nancy about this murder?"

Busted. How the hell does she do it? In a whisper, Pat said, "Uh, yeah. I just thought of something and I wanted to tell them before I forgot."

"Them?"

"Yeah, uh, Nancy and Maddie."
"Maddie? You're on first name basis with the sheriff now?"
"Uh, well . . . no . . . uh . . . not really."
"Jeez, Pat. Just go to sleep. We have a long day tomorrow."
"Good night, dear. I love you."
But Diane was already asleep again.
How does she do it?

Chapter 31

Back at the office, Nancy and the sheriff discussed what Pat had just told them. It made perfect sense and coincided with what they were thinking. They, too, felt Hassan was framed. From the inspection of the piping in the plant, no explosive device was found where the drawings said it would be. But why go through all the trouble to frame someone for nothing? Unless . . .

Nancy asked, "Why would Hassan run if he wasn't guilty of anything?"

"Maybe he thinks he can't get a fair shake from our legal system, being a Muslim with a prior and a bad attitude."

Nancy considered that for a moment. *He looks like a terrorist and talks like a terrorist, at least most people's idea of what a terrorist looks like. But what if he was framed? Who would want to frame him? Someone from the plant? What purpose would that serve?* From what she had observed of Yusef Hassan, he wasn't afraid of his co-workers. Most likely, he'd take the drawing right to them and start screaming, asking them what they were doing in his work space.

Maddie asked, "So who does that leave and how does this tie into Alex Corbin's murder? If someone wanted to frame him for something, why not try to pin the murder on him, too?"

"Maybe they thought he'd be accused of the murder once that drawing was found?" Nancy murmured.

"What did you say?"

Nancy shook her head. "Nothing. I must be getting tired."

"Hassan's co-workers don't think he killed Corbin. But who would want him dead? We're missing a big piece of this puzzle. Unless we get a break, we're stuck."

Nancy said, "Maybe we're going at this all wrong. Everyone we're looking at doesn't have a motive. Or they have a good alibi. So who would profit from killing an engineer at a power plant? And why a beheading? Why wouldn't you just kill him and get rid of the body? Why the film and all the theatrics?"

Maddie thought for a moment. “Maybe they’re trying to gain credibility as a real terrorist group. Maybe they were players and somehow got disgraced. Now they’re trying to get their honor back. Could be that’s why they didn’t go public with the film, because they botched it.” Maddie paused. “What do we know about Hassan’s family?”

“His son works at the plant as an intern, an engineer like his dad, except he’s in Maintenance Engineering. He works directly with the skilled craft guys, like mechanics and electricians. Why do you ask?”

“Did we interview his son?”

“No, but he’s on the list for tomorrow. What are you thinking?”

“I don’t know. It’s just that, if Hassan is innocent, then something else made him bolt like that. We should question his family, especially the son, in their home. Maybe they know why. It’s worth a shot.” Maddie paused. “Should we tell Agent Scott?”

Nancy thought for a moment before saying, “Nah. He’s probably got the interview scheduled already. If we find anything, we’ll tell him then.”

The call from Pat gave the women a burst of energy. They combed through dozens of file folders containing background information on a number of plant personnel. After another half hour fatigue caught up with them again. Maddie’s head started to bob. She was exhausted. The words in the files ran together.

Shaking her head, she looked up at the clock and swore, “Damn. 11:15. We’ve been going at this since early this morning. It feels like we’re moving backwards.”

Nancy stood, stretched, and looked around the office. The room appeared smaller and darker now than it had earlier. Her eyes felt pasty. She glanced in a small mirror on Maddie’s desk. “I could carry your luggage and mine in the bags under my eyes. This is crazy.”

Maddie agreed it was late and they weren’t accomplishing a thing. They were about to call it a night when Nancy’s cell phone rang. For the second time that evening, it was a McKinney.

“Hi, Joe. What’s up at this late hour?”

“Just me around here. Lisa’s in bed trying to get some sleep. This baby better come soon or she’s never going to get any rest.”

Nancy smiled. “Don’t worry. She’ll start to catch up on her sleep in about eighteen years.”

Joe didn't laugh. He was tired, too, but he knew better than to complain. He saw what a toll the pregnancy took on Lisa. The time would come when this would be a distant memory. That time was so far into the future Joe didn't even want to think about it.

"Anyway, I've been going over some of these files and I have some things that I think you should check out."

"Fire away."

"I'll tell you about the lesser of the two mysteries first. Ali Malik Hassan is an intern at the plant. He's been there for just over a year, working in Maintenance Engineering."

Nancy said, "We discovered that just a bit ago."

Joe continued, "He likes to tinker with electronics. He has a degree in Electrical Engineering with a minor in Finance. He went to school at that local university up there . . . Globe University."

"Nothing unusual there. Half the Engineering Staff came from Globe, according to these files."

"True, but half the Engineering staff didn't spend their summers in Syria at a terrorist training camp."

That bit of information got Nancy's attention. When Maddie saw her face change, she motioned the call should be on speakerphone.

"Joe, I'm putting you on speaker. I think Maddie needs to hear this."

"No problem, Nancy."

A moment later, through the tinny sound of the speaker phone on Nancy's cell, Joe explained the connection between Ali Malik Hassan, a terrorist wanna-be and another man, Bashir El-Amin.

"It seems El-Amin is the young Hassan's spiritual leader. He accompanied Ali to Syria, but he didn't stay there. He actually went on to Israel. Apparently, he has family in the Gaza strip."

"Did he make contact with anyone on our terror suspect list while there?" Nancy asked.

"Not that we know of. That doesn't mean he didn't, but we don't have a trail."

"So where do we go from here?"

Joe said, "I'm not finished. Let me tell you about a real mystery."

Maddie and Nancy looked at each other. They turned to the phone and in unison said, "Well . . .?"

* * *

Ali Malik Hassan received the call at 11:30 P.M. He had never heard of an intern being called into work at the power plant in the middle of the night, but he was game. The caller said he'd get overtime for his efforts. He could use the money. Maybe he wouldn't need to ask his father for money next week if he got a little extra in his check.

He told his mother he had to go into work and he didn't know when he'd be home. She, too, was surprised. But it was a sign he was trusted and that was important in America. The Hassan family was making a good name for themselves, despite the discrimination and prejudice that persisted against Muslims. She told him to drive carefully as he walked out the door to his beat-up Ford Escort.

The drive north on Highway thirteen out of Washburn wasn't a bad drive except when fog blanketed the area. This evening, the sky was clear and the air was cool, having dropped into the high sixties. The cool air helped to invigorate Ali. His only concerns were deer and drunk drivers. The young engineer made good time as he thought of what challenge awaited him at the plant. Regardless of the work the supervisor would assign, he would have time to ask if it were true his father was suspected of being a terrorist. And if it was true, then someone had found the drawing he had placed in his father's cubicle. Someone had to be the 'red herring.' What better man than someone who embraced the homeland of the enemy. If a family member turned their back on Allah, they were the enemy.

Hassan thought about how his father had turned away from his religion and now pursued material wealth. Yusef preached to his son about the great fortune they would amass in America. He spoke of making sure the family was well cared for.

Ali would argue with the old man, but his religious overtones fell on deaf ears. His father was on his way to Jahannam, where great flames would engulf but not consume his being. He would suffer for eternity for his greed.

As he made the curve past McCulloch Road, a car approached him from behind. He saw the headlights of an oncoming car in the lane heading south. As soon as the oncoming car sped past, the car following him went into the passing lane. It sped up and pulled alongside his Escort, then slowed and matched his speed. Hassan started to get nervous, and wished the driver would just pass. No other cars were in sight in either direction. He glanced at the car next to him, but couldn't see the driver's face.

Unnerved, he slowed down, and hoped the other driver would continue and pass, but he also slowed, matching Hassan's speed. There were still no other cars around.

He rolled down his window, turned towards the other car and yelled, "What are you doing, you fool? Are you trying to get us killed?"

The driver didn't even turn in his direction. He maintained his speed. Up ahead, Hassan saw headlights in the on-coming lane. *Finally, another car. Maybe this fool will get moving and leave me alone.*

The car to his side sped up and pulled into his lane ahead of him, just as Hassan had hoped. He began to relax. When the car that was headed in the opposite direction passed, he watched its taillights in his rearview mirror. He looked ahead just in time to see that the car in front of him had slowed dramatically. He hit his brakes hard, but still bumped into the car in front of him. The collision was not hard enough to deploy the airbag, but he nearly hit his head on the steering wheel. When he looked up, the other car, a Mercury Marquis, had pulled over to the side of the road. Hassan pulled off the road about thirty yards behind it.

Ali stayed behind the wheel for what seemed like an eternity. He thought for a moment how angry his father would be he was in an accident. He briefly wondered if being late the first time he was called in during off-hours might put his job in jeopardy.

Then he thought about the car in front of him. The driver of that car caused the crash. It was like he'd done it on purpose. Maybe he was drunk. No one had gotten out of the other car yet, so maybe they were hurt. He should check on them. Then, if they were alright he could give them a piece of his mind.

He stepped out into the night air. It felt much cooler with a breeze blowing off the Chequamegon Bay. A shiver ran through him as he slowly approached the Mercury.

Chapter 32

Victoria looked through her binoculars at the tanks in the yard at Texas Star Refinery. They looked old and run down, just like the neighborhood where she stood, adjacent to its western fence. White paint with the Texas Star logo on the side was faded, chipped, and oil-covered. Pathways between the tanks were slick with oil buildup from leaks in the system and residue from the burn-off stacks. Rust decorated the upper rim of several of the tanks; something that should worry the neighbors of the ancient plant.

She noticed most the homes in the surrounding area were in worse shape than the tanks inside the compound. Many of the front porches held old refrigerators or stoves that should have been hauled off to the landfill. But the tenants were either too poor or didn't care what landed on their porch. Some of the wooden decks sagged under the weight of the discarded appliances. Others sagged from age and wood rot. Many houses were too dangerous to be occupied, but people were evident in several of those. Some of them stared out their windows or doors at her. At first she wondered why. Then it hit her. In this neighborhood, she stood out like a bright red rose against discarded dead brush on a compost pile. She turned and walked in the shade of overgrown trees towards the refinery two blocks away.

Her Corvette was three streets over and she wondered about the wisdom of parking the car in the street in this neighborhood. Would it still be there when she returned? Or would it be stripped down, sitting up on blocks? She was nearly finished with her business here. She'd return tomorrow for her final trip to Texas Star.

Victoria stopped on the corner of a street less than a block from the refinery's perimeter fence. Several of the storage tanks loomed large in front of her. She held the binoculars to her eyes and searched the exterior of the tank closest to her. Starting at the top and slowly moving down to the base, she tried to find the prize. The tank was so large it was like looking for a tick on an elephant. She was amazed at the amount of black, liquid gold that must be stored in each one.

The North Americans are busy raping the rest of the world of its resources. If I were philosophical, that alone would be enough to make me mad . . . there it is.

She adjusted the field glasses to get a closer look at the level sensor. This particular sensor was mounted at the base of the tank, not one hundred fifty yards in front of her. She looked at the next tank and quickly located its detector. Her smile grew. Seeing the fruits of her labor, she was satisfied. Now it was time to go.

Turning crisply, she noticed two little girls in dirty clothes playing hopscotch on the sidewalk near the road next to the perimeter fence. They were less than thirty yards from the first tank. They laughed and sang as they used pieces of the broken sidewalk to redraw the squares on their makeshift hopscotch board. One of the girls noticed Victoria staring at them. She grabbed the sleeve of the other girl's blouse and guided her to where Victoria stood.

When they were about thirty feet from her, they slowed down, staring at her as they approached. Victoria stood still, wondering what had them so curious. When the girls were within ten feet, they stopped.

The girl who guided her friend looked Victoria over from head to toe, her mouth hanging open as if in awe. The other girl tended to look away, never quite making eye contact.

"Who are you?"

The little girl's question caught Victoria off guard. Her face twisted in such a way that the girl laughed. In a voice that must have seemed harsh to the girls she asked, "Why are you laughing at me?"

"Your face, it was all wrinkled up. You shouldn't do that. My mom says it'll stay that way."

Victoria hiked her eyebrow at the girl. Something about the girl's manner was familiar. She couldn't put her finger on it. But she asked, "So where do you two live?"

The shy girl whispered to her friend, then looked up at Victoria with a defiant expression, almost like she was trying to appear angry.

"Gina says we're not supposed to talk to strangers." Gina elbowed her friend for giving her secret away. "Ouch. Cut it out."

"So you're Gina," Victoria said to the shy girl. She turned to the talkative girl and asked, "So what's your name?"

"Madonna."

Gina looked at her friend and said with disdain, "It is not. It's

Marianna."

Marianna laughed at her friend. "But I'm going to change my name to Madonna when I grow up, so I might as well start calling myself that now."

Victoria nearly laughed out loud. Now she knew where she'd seen such spirit in a young girl. Every time she looked in the mirror she saw it. She remembered when she and her friends played games on the streets back in La Purisima every morning. But the streets weren't paved. They were dry clay, baked to a hard pack by the intense sunlight and dry heat. They'd take a break from their games during the middle of the day. Then, after dinner, when the dishes were finished and put away, they'd be back on the street playing games.

In the evening, they had to avoid the older kids. They were tough, or they thought they were. Victoria always thought she was tough. But she knew her brother was tough. Javier worked hard all day at the ranch in Texas, then came home and gave his money to their mother. He never complained. He even smiled about it. He was proud to support the family. Yes, Javier was tough even when his friends made fun of him for giving away his money. He worked for it, he should enjoy it.

But he did enjoy it. He was happy to help his mother and little sister make ends meet. He even helped them get ahead . . . until that day.

"Why are you angry?"

Marianna was very perceptive. Victoria snapped out of her momentary haze and smiled at the little girl. The smile was drenched in sadness. This little girl had no future unless she broke out of this neighborhood. Odds were that she wouldn't leave here without some scars, if she got out at all. With all her spunk, she at least had a chance. Her friend Gina had little unless she found a way to come out of her shell. Neither child had a chance at all if they played hopscotch the next morning on that same sidewalk near the refinery.

"You never told me where you live."

The girls looked at Victoria again, this time a little less apprehensive. Gina said, "You're still a stranger. You never told us your name."

"My name's Victoria Garcia."

Marianna smiled. "That's a pretty name. Are you a model?"

Victoria blushed, “No. I sell equipment to places like the oil company over there.” She nodded her head towards the tanks.

The Madonna wanna-be continued in a matter-of-fact manner, “Victoria, you should be a model. You are very pretty.” She paused for a second then continued, “Do you think I could be a model?” She put her hand on the back of her head striking a pose and smiling.

Victoria leaned over and said, “I think you’d be a lovely model.”

Gina piped up, “What about me?”

“You, too. You’re both very pretty.” She straightened up. “So, are you going to tell me where you live or not?”

Gina pointed at the corner house closest to the refinery perimeter fence. “I live there with my mom.”

Victoria’s heart sank. She turned to Marianna and raised her brows as if asking the question without words.

“I live about three blocks that way.” She pointed away from the refinery. “My mom and her boyfriend live together. Me and my brother live there with them.”

Yes. Maybe there’s hope.

“Wow. Will your mom mind if Gina stays with you tonight and tomorrow?”

“Gina stays with me sometimes and I stay with her sometimes. I can ask Mom if that would be okay.” Marianna became suspicious. “But why should Gina spend the night with me? Why can’t I stay here with her?”

This might be tough. “I heard the fire department is going to practice on the street right there tomorrow. They’re going to be real noisy. But, once they’re here and it’s safe, you can come down here and look at them. What do you think?”

“I don’t like fire trucks.” Gina was pouting now with the revelation there might be fire trucks outside her window.

“Don’t worry. Mom will let you stay with us. Let’s go ask now.” They turned to Victoria again and said together, “Bye, Victoria.”

“Bye, girls. Remember, stay at Marianna’s house until the fire trucks get here.“

“Okay.”

With that, the girls ran off to get Marianna’s Mom’s permission to spend the night. Victoria drew in a deep breath. She hoped when tomorrow’s events unfolded that Gina and Marianna would be far enough away to remain safe.

Walking quickly through the run-down neighborhood to where she'd parked her car, her thoughts were divided between her childhood when she'd witnessed her brother's murder, her mother, who died a painful death with cancer, and the two little girls she'd just met. She thirsted for revenge, so much so that she didn't even think about the poor people of this neighborhood.. But then she had to meet Gina, the pretty little girl who was so shy she would hardly look up at her. And then there was Marianna, so much like herself, so full of life and curiosity she would walk up to a total stranger and start a conversation. How could she be sure that the children would stay at Marianna's house? Victoria stopped in mid-stride as her car came into view.

A man stood next to it. He wasn't just looking at the car, he was looking at the license plates, and he was on his cell phone. That was real trouble. But the trouble worsened. He looked up and saw her when she was within one hundred feet.

Her first thought was to flee. Then she thought better of it. She walked straight towards him, formulating a plan as she closed the distance. She looked around at the houses near her car and noticed several men sitting on the porch a few houses down from where her car was parked. When she was within ten feet of the stranger, she stopped and gave him a wicked smile. It quickly turned to an angry look.

* * *

Hatch stood by the driver's side door of the bright red sports car. He kept a straight face as the woman approached, the one who'd met Danny at the bar. She was as strikingly beautiful as her pictures. But he wasn't swayed by her looks. He wanted answers.

Before he could say a word, the woman shouted something at him in Spanish. It was so loud and harsh the three men on the porch turned and looked. All three came off the porch at once, heading in Hatch's direction. They arrived in seconds. Hatch tensed. It was one thing to handle a couple of punk kids with an attitude. It was a different matter encountering three grown men defending a woman, even though they probably didn't know her from Eve.

One of the men said something to her in Spanish, nodding towards Hatch as he did. She answered. As the man listened, his expression and that of his friends grew more serious. Hatch checked each man over for any obvious bulges in their pockets where a gun or knife could be hiding. Two of the men carried knives or had cell phones or both. It didn't appear any of them had guns, unless they were tucked in the waist band of their jeans. But two of the men's jeans sagged so much he doubted they could be carrying.

Not sure if they'd understand him, he held up his hands, and said "Hold on, fellas. I'm just lookin' for a friend of mine. I think this lady might know where he is."

Victoria gave Hatch a look that could kill, then turned to the men and spat out something that, even in Spanish, had to be nasty. She was accusing him of something, and it was working, because the three men started to move around the car towards him. He slowly backed away from the car and into the street to get some maneuvering room. In seconds he'd have to decide whether to fight or run. He knew he could outrun them, but he wasn't sure he could win a three on one fight.

As he watched the men approach, he said to Victoria, "So, why are you sickin' these goons on me? All I'm trying to do is find out who killed my friend Danny and why."

Her expression immediately changed to one of dismay. She tried to put the angry face back on, but it didn't work. "I don't know what you're talking about."

Hatch backed further into the street. "Oh yeah, you do. My friend Danny met you at Loco Pedro's. Now he's dead. Why?"

Victoria's face changed again, as if she was surprised by the news. "He was alive and happy when I left him off at his apartment. But you're not going to be if you don't get the hell out of here."

He was still watching the men who were nearly all the way around Victoria's car now. "Why Danny? Why did you need to meet him?"

"Because I liked him. And I needed some information from him." She looked at the three men. "You should probably leave while you still have a head start."

"What's your name?"

With the plan less than twenty-four hours away, she had no reason to lie. "Victoria. Now run before they kill you. Go!"

Hatch turned and ran. He didn't like running from a fight, but the odds were too poor. These guys had no dog in this fight except they'd been egged on by a beautiful woman. She was convincing, he had to give her that.

As he ran, he turned to see the men starting to fall behind. He also saw Victoria pull away in her bright red Corvette. She smiled and waved.

He didn't wave back and he had nothing to smile about.

Chapter 33

"We're headed to the plant. Diane's going to hang out in the admin building while Evan gives me the nickel tour. She doesn't want to see a working nuclear power plant. Can you believe that?"

Pat was on his cell phone with his brother Joe, who was about as interested in taking a tour of a power plant as Diane. He understood Pat's interest, being on a nuclear powered submarine for a time, but he also understood why Diane couldn't care less.

"So Pat, I'm looking at this map of northern Wisconsin. Tell me again, where in the hell is this plant? And why do they have one in the middle of nowhere?"

In an excited voice, Pat said, "It's just north of Washburn right on Lake Superior. It's actually the Chequamegon Bay, but most people would just say it's Lake Superior."

Joe looked the map over, running his fingers past the western tip of the Upper Peninsula of Michigan heading west. He came to the point where the land wrapped north for a short distance into Lake Superior. Washburn had a circle instead of a solid dot indicating it was the county seat of Bayfield County. There were a few other towns scattered about. The town of Bayfield was north of Washburn. Offshore were the Apostle Islands. Joe remembered hearing about those islands somewhere, but he couldn't put his finger on it, maybe junior high geography.

Pat talked the entire time Joe examined the map. He still didn't understand why any company would build a nuclear power plant that far north, but it wasn't his money so he really didn't care.

"Joe, you still there?"

"Yeah, Pat." He stopped his review of the map and looked at the computer screen showing the official seal of NCIS, the Naval Criminal Investigative Service. He wasn't officially in the military anymore, having been discharged after his and Pat's last adventure, but he still had the clearance and Nancy provided the connections he needed to allow access to lots of classified information. That included files on anyone suspected of being linked to terrorists, no matter how slim the link.

"So your friend, Evan Jones, is married? When did you find that out?"

Pat thought Joe's question a bit odd. "In New Bremen. My buddy Frank mentioned it. Said he was married to Sally Smith. She has a son who's an engineer at the plant. Jimmy."

"Yeah, well, interesting thing about Jimmy. He's black."

"No, he's not."

"Well, according to his parents, he was black when he was born and he remained black until he died. He was ten when that happened. Then he turned white and he's alive again."

Pat frowned. They were pulling into the parking lot of the Administration Building for Superior Shores Nuclear Power Station.

Diane looked his way and asked, "Something wrong?"

"No. We're just talking." Then into the phone he said, "Let me get parked. I'll go in and give Nancy and Maddie a call. Then I'll call you back." Pat flipped the phone shut.

Joe yelled, "Pat, wait. I'm not done. Pat?" *Damn*.

Diane gave her husband a stern look. He was now deep into the investigation and he wasn't even trying to hide it now. It was as if he couldn't help himself. She followed him into the lobby of the building. Diane was on the verge of grabbing her husband by his coat lapels and throttling him. Pat was about to pick up a phone to call Evan and ask him to escort them into the locked building when he spotted his friend through the glass door. Evan opened the security door. Diane put on her best, fake smile and played along. *Damn*.

Evan greeted them, and walked them around the vestibule which doubled as an information center. He pointed to the history displays of the electric industry, particularly the growth of nuclear power. After several minutes, Pat excused himself saying he had to make a phone call. Evan showed him to a room off the vestibule where Pat could have some privacy.

He dialed the Bayfield County Sheriff's office and was transferred to Maddie. "So what's this about Jimmy Smith?" Pat asked.

"I see you've been talking with Joe." She put Pat on speaker phone so Nancy could join the call. The sheriff continued, "Well, he's white, but we're pretty sure he was born black."

"That's not possible, physically, I mean."

Nancy and Maddie both rolled their eyes. Nancy picked up a file from Maddie's desk and started to read parts from it. While he listened, Maddie grabbed two more cups of coffee and set one down in front of Nancy.

Pat frowned as he listened. Nancy described the copy of James Smith's New York State birth certificate with date of birth and social security number.

Pat asked, "So how do you know he was black? Nothing on his birth certificate says so."

"That's true, but we did some searching. His school records at Globe University list his mother, Sally Smith, as a single parent from Eau Claire, Wisconsin. But there's no record of a Sally Smith ever living in Eau Claire. There's also no record of a James Smith ever attending secondary school in or around Eau Claire. So we searched on his social security number and dug a bit deeper. It turns out this particular Smith family is from Amsterdam, New York. They haven't moved in nearly thirty years. They had a child involved in a schoolyard accident about eighteen years ago. The kid was ten years old. Fell off the monkey bars and broke his neck."

Pat grimaced. "So you're telling me that our Jimmy Smith is using a stolen identity?"

"Yep, that's what we're telling you. We called the parents and they said they'd been getting credit card applications for their dead son as recently as two years ago, but then they stopped coming. They were going to contact some of the companies, but when the applications stopped they decided to drop the matter."

"Wouldn't the utility do a thorough background check and find out about this before they hired him?"

"Even the nuclear industry only goes back so far. Jimmy Smith's identity was consistent all the way back to junior high."

"Do we have reason to believe that Jimmy Smith is . . ."

A loud commotion erupted outside Maddie's office. Maddie grabbed her door knob and jerked the door open. A short man in a turban shouted at the deputy at the front desk. He was yelling so fast and loud she could barely understand him. All Pat heard over the phone was "My son" and "kidnapped" and "brainwashed" in the midst of the long rant.

Maddie walked over to the desk and put her hand on her deputy's shoulder. The man in the turban continued his tirade. Maddie put up both hands in an effort to try to calm him. It took nearly a full minute of her coaxing, but he finally calmed down enough to speak in a nearly normal tone. His speech, even when calm, was laced with anger and venom.

In broken English he spat, "Ali did not come home last evening. He has been kidnapped. That goat herder, Bashir, is responsible. My son follows him like a puppy dog. He believes every foul word coming from his mouth."

Maddie didn't want to say anything that might cause him to go off the deep end once again. "Mr. Hassan, are you talking about your son?"

His voice immediately acquired a confrontational tone. "How do you know my name? You spy on me. That's how. My son is missing. Not me. And yes, his name is Ali Malik Hassan. He is twenty years old. He has been playing the fool to that pompous bastard, Bashir."

"Why do you think Mr. Bashir had anything to do with your son's disappearance?"

He got red in the face. Just as he was about to speak, Agent Randall Scott and two of his agents appeared. They walked towards the front desk. He had a broad smile on his face.

Nancy knew there was going to be trouble and said into the phone, "Pat, I have to go. Call later."

Pat was about to say good-bye when the dial-tone sounded in his ear. He raised an eyebrow, then flipped his cell phone shut and left the private room.

* * *

Back at the sheriff's office Hassan continued his rant. "Because he is evil. He is trying to get my son to join the enemies of America. He must be stopped."

Agent Scott smiled. He walked right past Nancy and Maddie and looked Yusef Hassan right in the eyes and said, "Mr. Hassan. Yusef, right? Can I call you Yusef?"

Hassan turned quickly and growled, "No. You may not call me Yusef. You call me nothing. You must find my son before he is completely lost or worse."

Agent Scott continued to smile. "We'll find your son, Yusef. But first, tell us why you had drawings in your cubicle that appear to indicate you were planning to plant a bomb and blow up the turbine?"

Hassan's face turned bright red as he stared at the FBI agent. He spoke in a low tone filled with barely controlled rage. "I did no such thing and you will not call me Yusef. I am Hassan."

Randall Scott's grin grew wider. Nancy knew where this was going. She looked at the sheriff to see if she was going to intervene before Hassan went off the deep end again. She could see by the look on her face she wasn't quite sure what to do. So Nancy jumped in with both feet.

"Agent Scott."

The interruption threw the agent off his game plan momentarily and his smile disappeared. "Not now, Miss Brown, I have to talk with Yusef here. We need to find his missing son, and we need to know why he's attempted to commit an act of terrorism." His broad, sarcastic-looking smile returned.

Hassan turned towards Agent Scott, apparently ready to lunge when Nancy stepped between the men. Maddie joined her. They formed a human wall between Hassan and Scott.

Maddie spoke as calmly as possible. Hassan was sweating profusely, his eyes like lasers pointed directly at the FBI agent. If looks could kill, Agent Scott would have been cremated.

Hassan started yelling at Scott, "I come to the police for help and all I get is accusations! I am not a terrorist! Did you hear me? I am not a terrorist! Did you help kidnap my son?"

The FBI agents standing behind Scott looked nervous. It seemed they weren't in on their boss' antics. Their eyes darted from Hassan to Scott, then back to Hassan.

Agent Scott, still with a smirk, said, "Yusef, why would I do anything like that? He's just the son of a suspected terrorist. This is America. We don't do stuff like that."

Hassan lunged at the agent, trying to get past the blockade. He was shorter than the women so he didn't make much headway, but he screamed at the top of his lungs. "You accuse me of being a terrorist? How dare you? I'll show you terrorist, you pig, you coward! You hide behind these women! I should kill you for such accusations!"

Hassan continued shouting and trying to get at Agent Scott's throat. He flailed his arms and caught Nancy on the jaw with his elbow. It cut her lip slightly and blood began to flow. She'd had enough. She took Hassan by the arm and with one swift move placed him on the floor on his back. "Stop!"

Hassan was so shocked that he immediately stopped fighting and yelling. Nancy turned to Maddie and said, "Keep him here!"

Then she turned to Agent Randall Scott. She wiped blood from the corner of her mouth with her hand then wiped it on her pants. Two steps and she was right in his face. As she spoke, spit mixed with blood sprayed in the agent's face. He backed away, but she moved in closer.

"You planned this whole episode." She pointed a finger at his chest, as her voice took on a piercing tone, "Your director is going to hear about this! Plan to be on the first flight out of here!" She turned as if to leave, then turned back. "If I were you, I'd retire because your career is finished."

"You don't have that kind of pull, little lady."

Almost as soon as the words left his mouth, Nancy grabbed Agent Scott's right arm and spun him around. She put a knee to the back of his leg, causing him to buckle. Before his knees hit the floor she pinned his face against the front counter where Hassan had been making his complaint. She pulled his arm high up on his back. He was too shocked to say anything, but he did groan at the pain in his shoulder and arm. His agents didn't make a move to defend him.

Nancy spoke quietly into his ear, "I told you we were going to cooperate and work together as equals. Don't ever call me "little lady" again. Or I'll show you what this "little lady" can do. Understand?"

"You're going to be awfully sorry t you did this."

"If you want your arm to remain attached, you'll shut your mouth. When I let you up, you're going to apologize to Mr. Hassan. We've already checked him out. He's not a threat to anyone but himself. But that's because of his temper. He's no more a terrorist than you or I."

"Would you bet your life on that?" Scott was trying to talk but his words were more grunts than anything else as Nancy kept the pressure on his arm.

"Yes, I would. Now, we need to find out what's going on with his son, and a few other people we have on our list. We don't have time to keep playing these little games of yours." She put more pressure on his arm. "Are you getting my message?"

"Ahhh!" The pain got worse on his arm and face. "Yeah! I got it!"

"Last chance, Agent Scott. I'm not playing with you. One more screw-up and you're done."

"Okay. Okay, just let me up."

Nancy relieved the pressure on his arm and backed away. She didn't turn her back on him, but asked Maddie, "Is Mr. Hassan calmed down yet?"

Maddie glanced at him. He was now standing, staring at Nancy in awe.

Maddie said, "Yeah, I'd say he's calm."

"Good. Now let's see what we can do to help him."

Maddie's office phone rang. The sheriff trotted into the office to answer.

Randall Scott stared at Nancy, seething in anger, but realized he couldn't retaliate, at least not for now. *How can she trust this Muslim freak? He's an obvious choice for a suspect. But she'll be the one to screw this up.*

Nancy asked Hassan a few basic questions about his son's disappearance when the sheriff returned. She looked grim.

"Mr. Hassan, please be seated."

His forehead furrowed and his bushy eyebrows nearly covered his eyes. The fire that had ignited within him was now dying, as if ice cold water had doused his spirit. He eased into the nearest wooden chair. He looked up at Maddie. Before she said a word, he knew. Right before he blacked out, Maddie confirmed that Ali Malik Hassan was dead.

Chapter 34

Members of the anti-terror team, the FBI, and the Bayfield County Sheriff's Office sat around the table in one of the small conference rooms discussing what they now knew about Yusef Hassan, Ali Malik Hassan, and Bashir El-Amin. They had a lot of information, but still no clear motive for the murder of Alex Corbin, and now, the murder of Ali Hassan.

What was clear was that Yusef Hassan had no known ties to any terror organizations. He spent long hours at the power plant and, since moving to the United States, had never traveled back to the Middle East. He was a hard working engineer who'd moved his family to the United States to find a better life. His family had lived in the shadows of war for a lifetime. At an early age, Yusef grew tired of the constant drumbeat of war against the Jews. So he concentrated on his studies and his desire to become an engineer. When the opportunity came knocking to move his family to America, he seized the moment. It was a dramatic change moving from the hot and arid desert of Dubai to the frigid winters of Northern Wisconsin. But when the plant was under construction, the company needed engineers. Hassan filled one of the company's positions. Management liked his work. He was a good engineer so they tolerated his poor disposition. Though many of his coworkers joked about him looking like a terrorist, none of them ever believed it. Their comments were for the entertainment of watching Hassan's blood pressure rise off the charts.

Sheriff Wymer sent a deputy to Hassan's home to deliver the bad news to Mrs. Hassan about her son's death and her husband's collapse. Yusef was taken to the hospital by ambulance. He had regained consciousness when he left the sheriff's office, but his skin was so pale, it was hard to believe that his skin was normally a deep tan. Mrs. Hassan was distraught and overcome with grief when the deputy told her about her husband's condition. She became hysterical, sobbing in deep gasps, when told about the death of her son. Her daughter tried to comfort her. She told the deputy that she would take her mother to the hospital so that her mother could be by Yusef's bedside.

At the office, the team members talked about Bashir El-Amin, the Muslim engineer who appeared to have ties to someone in the Gaza Strip. Until now he'd been way down on their suspect list. With the latest accusations from Yusef Hassan, and the information they had received from Joe McKinney, he moved up a few steps. But with no known ties to any terrorist organizations, it was hard to make a case for moving him to the top.

Even though her lip was sore and slightly swollen, Nancy led the group in a serious discussion, sorting through all the information and evidence they now had.

"According to everyone we interviewed, El-Amin's a great guy, very cordial and likable. He comes across like your grandpa or a kind neighbor. We had no grounds to suspect that he had ties to any radical groups. But, according to Joe's research, he did travel to the Gaza Strip several times over the past three years." Maddie and two of her deputies, Agent Scott and two FBI agents, and two members of Nancy's team all listened intently.

She continued, "Even though he's made these trips, he was monitored. He apparently didn't make contact with any people or groups on our watch list. So he wasn't flagged as a risk. But on the last two trips, he took Ali Hassan with him. He was supposedly acting as his spiritual advisor. But they would split up at the Damascus Airport. The young Hassan would travel to parts unknown while El-Amin made his way to the Gaza Strip to do his 'charity work.' "

"Do we have any reason to believe the young Hassan was involved with any terrorist training groups?" The question came from the now very cooperative Agent Scott.

Nancy replied, "No, except that his whereabouts in the Middle East couldn't be tracked. He landed in Damascus and dropped into a black hole until he came out to fly back to the states again."

The tension in the room was evident. The team thought they were starting to get close but they were missing a few pieces of the puzzle. One big one was motive. First, what was the motive for the Alex Corbin killing. And why did the killers make it such a production? Then, where was the connection between the Corbin and the Hassan killings?

While they talked, a deputy came to the door for Maddie. Joe

McKinney was on the phone and needed to talk with her as soon as possible. She punched the button on the speaker phone in the conference room and told Joe he had an audience. He asked who was there.

When he was satisfied there were no bad guys, he asked, "Sheriff, have you talked with Pat this morning?"

"Yes. We were on the phone with him about thirty minutes ago. We had to cut the call short. We had a bit of an interruption. What's up?"

"Well, you need to be looking for two people immediately. The first is Ali Malik—"

"Hassan. We found him . . . at least we found his body."

"What do you mean?"

"He was killed early this morning, or maybe late last night. His throat was slit."

"Well, I guess you won't need that picture I just e-mailed to you. But you are looking into Jimmy Smith, right?"

"Yes."

Agent Scott shifted in his seat. "When did Jimmy Smith become a person of interest?" He looked directly at Nancy, his eyes burning through her.

Nancy didn't flinch. "We just found out about him this morning, right before Mr. Hassan came in."

Joe chimed in. "I did some investigating and determined he's is using an alias. I don't know who he really is yet, but he isn't Jimmy Smith. That also means we don't know who Sally Smith is. She may be his real mother or she may just be playing the part."

Scott asked, "So is Evan Jones who he says he is?"

Joe said, "Yes. He's definitely legit. My brother Pat served with him in the Navy for a few years. My guess is he doesn't know his wife and stepson are frauds. The only question is *Why*?"

That question hung in the air.

Joe spoke up again, his voice sounding mechanical over the speaker phone, "Pat and Diane are at the power plant now. Diane's staying in the Admin building while Pat gets his tour. I'm worried. Has anyone found Jimmy Smith or seen his mother either last night or this morning?"

Heads shook. Nancy said, "No." There was silence on the phone and in the conference room as the anxiety level jumped up a notch.

There was a loud knock at the door. The Crime Scene Investigator who'd been to the murder scene of Ali Hassan came into the conference room. He set a manila folder down next to the sheriff and said quietly, "Photo's of Hassan." He opened the folder and showed her a few details as the others looked on. Joe waited while the CSI gave a brief report to the sheriff and the rest of the team at the table.

Hassan's murder was not as gruesome or dramatic as Alex Corbin's. His throat had been slit and he'd bled to death. But it didn't happen where the body was found. There wasn't enough blood at the scene. He was left in a public place; the same park where Nancy had sat on the picnic table only yesterday morning. A chill ran up her spine.

Nancy stood and looked at the photos over the sheriff's shoulder. Her and Maddie's expressions changed at nearly the same instant. They both recognized the young Hassan. She held up the high resolution photo so the rest of the team could see. Except for the nasty gash across his neck, there was no mistaking it. Ali Hassan was the terrorist at the beheading of Alex Corbin who couldn't stomach the brutal murder. He'd ripped off his mask and heaved. Whoever witnessed his weakness had made sure that if he was recognized, he wouldn't be able to tell a soul. The investigator nodded to the sheriff and left the room.

Almost right after he left and the conference room door closed, there was another knock. Maddie shook her head and mumbled, "Now what?"

A female deputy leaned in and said, "Angela Corbin to see you, Sheriff."

Angela's mother guided her as they made their way into the crowded conference room. She looked tired and frail, as if she hadn't slept in weeks. This much stress couldn't be good for her baby. But what could she do? She couldn't just ignore the fact her husband had been brutally murdered.

A deputy stood, offering his seat to the young widow. Angela eased onto the wooden chair. An FBI agent in the seat next to Angela offered his seat to her mother. She thanked him, sat, and moved the chair closer to her daughter. Everyone forgot about Joe on the conference line until he cleared his throat.

Nancy said, "Joe, we have to call you back. Mrs. Corbin is here."

"Before I go, you need to locate Jimmy Smith and his mother ASAP. If I find anything else I'll call."

"Thanks, Joe. We'll keep you posted." Nancy hit the button disconnecting the conference phone.

Angela had already handed the sheriff the still sealed envelope. "It's from Alex. It says to give it directly to you, not to open it."

Maddie handled the envelope by the edges, as if it might contain something fragile. Using a letter opener, she slit the top, then pulled out and unfolded a standard letter sized sheet of paper. As she read the note, her face grew serious.

She looked up at Angela. "Mrs. Corbin, thank you for bringing this in. We're going to need access to your garage again. Will you give us permission?"

"Yes, whatever you need."

"Thank you, ma'am. We appreciate this very much."

* * *

When the team left the office, Maddie and Nancy rode with two members of the Anti-Terror Team in the back seat. Their car was followed by the two deputies, Randall Scott, and the two FBI agents. When the parade of law enforcement vehicles arrived at the Corbin residence, they headed right to the garage behind the house. Per the letter's instructions, they removed the bottom drawer of the file cabinet. Taped to the underside of the bottom drawer was a large manila envelope. When they emptied the contents, several drawings spilled out onto the workbench. They appeared to be piping schematics and electrical drawings. The lower right corner of one diagram said "Emergency Reactor Cooling System." Another drawing, this one looked to be of an electrical system, said RPS (Reactor Protection System).

Nancy said, "I wish Pat were here. He's worked with this stuff before."

She picked up the large envelope and spotted a letter-sized piece of paper inside. Nancy took it out and read it aloud.

> *The modification on the Emergency Reactor Cooling System is designed to allow a direct path from the Reactor Coolant System to the Chequamegon Bay. The lead engineer on the project, Jimmy Smith, knows*

> *this. I think he's trying to purposely cause an accident. If he's successful at finishing what he's started, if he's really trying to do what I suspect, he could conceivably cause a meltdown. I've been asking a few questions about his project, but I think he suspects I'm snooping around too much. If he isn't stopped soon, I'm afraid he may actually succeed. He's planning to override the manual and automatic scram functions, which means that it will be difficult, at best, to shut down the reactor. A loss of cooling water with the reactor still at one hundred percent power would be devastating. I'm going to plant management and the police tomorrow. If you find this note, it means that I'm dead and it may be too late.*

Agent Scott spoke, "We need to get these drawings to the plant now. And we need to call plant security so they can locate this nut-job."

Chapter 35

Hatch leaned back in the desk chair and stared at the ceiling in his hotel room. He was angry with himself for allowing Danny's stalker to get away. He wondered if Victoria was her real name. It was impossible for a woman who drove a bright red Corvette to blend into such a poor neighborhood. But she'd used her beauty and charm to get the locals to side with her. He wondered if he would ever see her again. Something told him he hadn't seen the last of Victoria Garcia.

But he had to focus his efforts on another matter. The detector Sammy Helzer had given him was clamped tight in the small vise on the desk. Hatch had started the slow process of reverse engineering the small, black box. Could it hold the key to why his friend was dead? One thing was certain, the trouble started when these gadgets showed up at the Texas Star Refinery.

Through the magnifying glass over his right eye he saw tiny scratches and dust particles on the cover. He worked the fresh blade of a utility knife down the side of the thin, metal cover. He moved slowly, not applying too much pressure, maintaining a straight line as the blade sliced the soft metal. After several minutes of repeating the same motion in the original cut, he had to stop and relax. Sweat beaded on his forehead from the pressure of concentrating on the straight, shallow cut. He also had no idea what he expected to find, but he needed to be sure that whatever it was didn't get destroyed by cutting it to pieces.

Finally, back at the task, he completed the first slice along one edge. He adjusted the position of the detector in the vice and started the second cut, a long, tedious process. After the second cut was completed Hatch leaned back in his chair, removed the magnifying glass from his eye, and relaxed again.

Moving his head from side to side to stretch tight neck muscles, he thought about Danny. A mental image of his friend's body slumped over in his Explorer flooded into his mental view. Could this Victoria Garcia have done that? When he'd called out to her, telling her Danny was dead, she'd looked genuinely shocked. Maybe she didn't have anything to do with his death. If she didn't, then why had she stalked Danny? Why had she chased other guys away and insisted on hooking up with him? And how in the hell would this little contraption provide the answers?

Hatch got his second wind, turned the detector once again in the vice, and started to cut. He was concentrating hard on the task at hand when the room phone rang, startling him. He dropped the utility knife. It rolled off the desk and into his lap, the razor piercing his jeans. A trickle of blood seeped from the tiny slice in his pants just three inches below his crotch. *Damn!* He removed the magnifying glass and answered the phone.

"Yo."

"Hatch, how's it going?"

"Well, Joe, I just cut my leg with a utility knife and I'm bleeding. Other than that, it sucks. Hang on for a second while I go get a tissue."

Joe was about to say something when he heard the phone hit the desk so hard the sound of it hurt his ear. He jerked the phone away from his head.

Hatch came back on the line. "I guess I'll live. What can I do for you?"

"What, were you making a sandwich in your room? I know you're cheap, but that's going a bit far, even for you."

"You're a barrel of laughs. But I've nearly got this here gadget I'm working on apart, and I need to get back to it. What can this poor boy do for ya'?"

"The company that sold the detectors to Texas Star doesn't exist. I searched Thomas Registry and all the other business resources I know of and there's no listing. I made dozens of calls and came up empty."

"Hmm." Hatch processed this new information.

"Plus, there are about three hundred women named Victoria Garcia in the greater Houston area. If I were trying to hide my real identity, that would be a great name. Of course, so would Lopez, Perez, Martinez, Hernandez, and a dozen more."

"Victoria wouldn't fit you. Your bright, white, male self would stand out a bit with that name. But it does fit our Miss Garcia. And she is one smart cookie. She enlisted the help of some local goons to protect her, almost on the spot. If they'd have had their pants pulled up and not saggin' around their crotches, I might have had to get a little dental work earlier today."

"Yeah? What happened?"

"I'll tell you what. Can you wait on that story? I'm in the middle of something here I hope will give us some answers."

"So what's so important that you can't talk for five minutes?"

"I'm doin' a little investigatin' on a level detector. Seems like all this trouble started when the refinery started to install 'em. Let me call you back in ten minutes."

"Okay, Hatch, but one more thing. They found another body up in Wisconsin. A young Muslim engineer named Ali Malik Hassan. He was an intern."

Hatch raised an eyebrow. "Joe, there's something awful fishy in the water up there. Are Pat and Diane safe?"

"Yeah. They're at the power plant. Pat's about to take the tour with Evan and Diane's waiting for him in the admin building. When Pat finishes, they're on their way around the lake. I think you're right, though. The sooner they get out of there, the better."

Hatch had hoped Pat and Diane had already left the area, but there was nothing he could do about it. "Joe, if anything else happens, you call me right away. Thank the dear Lord you and Miss Lisa are safe at home."

"Yeah. Thank God for that."

"And Joe?"

"Yeah?"

"Can you do a little more checking on our 'Vette owner? I'm wondering how our little lady was able to get her hands on that car. Just seems real odd. Ya' know what I mean?"

"Sure. I'll get right on it."

Hatch used the tissue to dab some blood from his pants, then went back to work. He had to stop twice, once for a bio break and once to relieve his aching muscles. Finally, he was on the last quarter inch of the detector's cover. He made the cut and the cover came loose. He took a deep breath and set his tools down, then eased off the cover, exposing the internal components.

Like he'd seen through the tiny adjustment hole, the internals were covered with a gray, putty-like substance. At first, he thought it was some kind of plastic explosive, but it didn't look like any explosive compound that he knew of. He wasn't one hundred percent sure, but he was up on explosives and his confidence was in the high ninety percent range. But the million dollar question was still unanswered. Besides the basic components of a wireless level detector, the pulse generator and receiver, and the transmitter to send the signals to the control room, there was another electronic board that was completely out of place.

Hatch used the magnifying eyepiece to inspect the circuit cards mounted to the small board. It looked like the inside of a mini-computer with a tiny motherboard. He spotted a small nameplate with a model number, a serial number, and a lot number along with a military specification, or mil-spec number, and the manufacturer's name. He wrote down the information on the notepad by the phone, then started an internet search. While that ran, he called Joe back to enlist his help with the company search.

"Hey, Joe, long time, no hear—"

Joe cut him off. "I've got news and it can't wait."

"Hit me, my man."

"Victor Garcia, owner of a 1997 red Corvette was a rich kid who lived in Del Rio, Texas. He was found dead in his parents' home about five weeks ago. Turns out his folks were killed instantly a few years ago when a road grader pulled out in front of them while working the night shift repaving Interstate 10. He won a wrongful death lawsuit against the paving company."

Hatch took a moment to digest this new information. "So how does Victoria Garcia end up with Victor Garcia's car? Seems like too much of a coincidence that their names are nearly identical."

"Yep, I'd agree with that." Joe continued, "When the police found him, he was on the floor in the living room of his very expensive house. Official cause was heart attack. Any bets that he was helped along?"

"Miss Garcia, or whoever she is, is starting to scare me."

"I agree. You be real careful around her."

Hatch agreed. He then gave Joe the information from the detector's tiny PC board. They hung up, each considering new pieces to the puzzle. Within fifteen minutes, Joe called back. Another piece of the puzzle fell into place. The device was much more than a level detector.

But why would anyone mount a homing beacon on a fuel storage tank? The devices were similar to those used on lifejackets. They generated a signal that could be picked up by search parties looking for persons lost at sea. Danny had suspected something fishy about the detectors, but he'd never mentioned exactly what he suspected. Maybe he wanted to be sure before he went off making accusations. That was probably why he took one back to his apartment to tinker with. That detector was never found.

Then Victoria Garcia all but stalked him. She was seen leaving the bar with Danny in tow. The next thing anyone knew, Danny was dead. This mystery woman was the last person known to have seen him alive. But she denied killing him and now she had disappeared.

Then there was Ricardo Vasquez, the engineer. He apparently knew something about these detectors. He was in charge of the job. If it wasn't for him, the project never would have been funded. And why was he sitting outside Danny's apartment? He had to have left his car for a time. What did Alisa's brother say? Someone did a custom job on it? And Vasquez didn't show up for work the next day saying he had car trouble. Hatch wondered if his trouble was that it needed a new paint job.

That was easy enough to find out. Hatch dialed the number for Bud Yantzy.

A gravelly voice answered, "I&C Shop."

"Hi, Bud."

"Hatch. You found anything yet?"

"Not yet. But let me ask you somethin'. Did that engineer, Vasquez get his car back yet?"

"Nah. It's got to have a second coat. It won't be ready for a couple of days until after the paint's dry. Why do you ask?"

That confirmed what Hatch suspected. The friend of Alisa's brother was right. It was Vasquez who was watching Danny's place. Now Hatch knew why.

"Bud, I need to talk with you right away. Can you get me into the plant?"

* * *

Twenty minutes later, at 8:55 AM, Hatch sat in Bud's office. Just like on his previous visits to the refinery, the air was thick with oil residue making Hatch's skin feel slick. He explained the situation with the detector replacement project. At first, Bud was angry Sammy had given Hatch company property. When he calmed down he was dumbfounded . . . and scared. They both agreed Sammy Helzer should be in on their conversation.

By the time all three men finished talking, they'd agreed on what to do next, and it wasn't going to be easy. Sammy was afraid that someone else would find out and their plan would blow up in their faces.

Hatch looked at the two men. "Time's short gents. Let's get to work. But first, we need to make sure Vasquez is off site. Any ideas?"

Sammy Helzer smiled. "Yeah. I got an idea. I know the guy who owns the shop where his car is."

Hatch and Bud listened. It sounded like a good plan.

Chapter 36

Joe sat in his office waiting for Nancy to call back. The lights were on, but he had closed the curtains on the south facing window. Air conditioning kept the temperature at seventy-five degrees. Even so, Joe was sweating. The stress of combing through the personnel files for Superior Shores and doing the company searches for Hatch was taking its toll. All but one of the files was now stacked neatly on his desk. His shoulders and neck were tight so he stood and stretched. His jaw hurt from clenching his teeth. He rubbed his eyes, then sat back down. He reached for his coffee mug, then realized it was empty and set it back down. *I don't need any more caffeine now anyway.*

He resumed looking through his notes on Jimmy Smith, searching for any clues he might have missed. He nearly memorized his file and the files for Ali Malik Hassan and Bashir El-Amin. Maybe Nancy or her connections would find something on Sally Smith, but for now there was nothing new. Joe had to be content with digging deeper in the files he already had. He should check on Lisa and the kids, but he hated to step away from the phone. *That's pretty silly. We have a phone within ten steps of every point in the house.* So headed down the hall to his and Lisa's bedroom where Lisa was resting.

He quietly peeked in on his fiancé. The clock on the night stand read 9:55. He had to keep reminding himself of the time difference between Winter Garden, Florida and Washburn, Wisconsin. She lay on her side, sleeping with her right arm over her belly. Restless, she didn't stay still for more than a few seconds at a time. Her breathing came in bursts with no rhythm.

Joe wasn't concerned, though. This was the current norm for her. Sleep was difficult so she caught little mid-morning naps when she could. She'd fixed breakfast for him and the kids, a simple meal of cereal for Sean and Anna, and scrambled eggs and sausage for him. She'd had a banana, half a peanut butter sandwich, and a glass of orange juice. That effort had zapped her of all her energy, so Joe let her sleep.

He walked down the hall to the family room where Anna played with her newest Barbie, putting her in a new dress.

Joe quietly asked her, “So, where’s Barbie going all dressed up like that?”

Anna smiled. “She’s going to a wedding.”

Joe smiled back. “And who’s getting married?”

Anna giggled. “Aunt Wisa and Uncle Joe.” She hesitated. “And Mommy and Daddy.”

“But your Mommy and Daddy are already married.”

“Getting mawwied again.”

Sean walked into the room. In his typically serious tone he said, “I tried to tell her that Mom and Dad can’t get married again, but she keeps saying that.”

“That’s okay, Sean. She’s just having fun. So what are you up to?”

He thought for a minute. “When Mom and Dad get home, I want to ask them about going to an all-boys school.”

Keeping a serious expression Joe asked, “Why is that? There’s nothing wrong with it, but I’m just curious.”

“Well, Uncle Joe, they teach you how to do guy stuff, and you don’t have to be around girls.”

Anna giggled at her brother. Sean gave her a dirty look.

In a calm, serious tone Joe said, “You know, Sean, you’re almost seven years old. As you grow up, you change your mind about a lot of things. And I think one of those things is girls. Don’t you like Aunt Lisa, your Mom, your grandma, and your sister?”

“They’re not really girls. Sisters and moms and stuff like that don’t count. And besides, they don’t chase me around and try to get me to play stupid games like the girls at school.”

Joe now knew what the problem was. Sean’s serious side didn’t want anything to do with playing games, especially with girls. He wasn’t sure how to talk to Sean about his little problem. That issue was probably best left to his parents. Joe remembered when he was in second grade and realized Sean was a lot like him in those early days.

What if our child has this kind of struggle? What would I say? Being a parent wasn’t going to be easy.

Someone cleared their throat behind him. He stood and turned in one motion. Lisa stood in the doorway to the family room, leaning against the door jamb and rubbing her belly. She was smiling at Joe’s confused look.

She looked at Sean and Lisa. "Hey, kids. I'm fixing some macaroni and cheese for lunch in a couple hours. Would you like that?"

Anna shouted, "Yeah! That's my favowite!"

Without any emotion Sean said, "Sure."

"Sean, did you want to help me make it? Maybe we could make something to go along with it?"

"I suppose I could do that." Sean thought for a moment. "Do we have any hamburger? I think adding hamburger would make it better."

Lisa smiled. "I think we could try that. What do you think, Anna?"

"I wike it pwain."

Sean put his finger on the side of his face as if in deep thought. "We can make the macaroni and cheese first and put some aside for Anna before we add the hamburger." He looked up at Aunt Lisa for approval. "I think that'll work. What do you think, Uncle Joe?"

Joe nodded. *This parenting stuff will be easy . . . as long as Lisa's here to handle the tough stuff.* He smiled at Lisa, winked, and blew her a kiss.

She grimaced. She rubbed her belly in quick circles as she smiled back. Joe frowned. He stood next to her and whispered, "Baby acting up?"

"You just wouldn't believe. I'm getting kicked every couple of minutes. This child wants out and I'm all for it."

As Joe watched, her blouse bulged out where a tiny foot must have lashed out. "I see what you mean. I wish there was something I could do for you."

"Maybe you can help with lunch while I give instructions. I think I need to be off my feet for a while. My ankles are swollen and the bottom of my feet hurt."

"I'm here to serve. Just tell me what I need to do."

As soon as the words left his mouth, the phone rang.

"As soon as I get off the phone that is."

"It'll be a while before we're ready anyway."

Joe kissed Lisa on the cheek, then headed back to his office and grabbed the phone. "McKinney's."

"Hey, Joe, its Hatch."

"What's up?"

Hatch proceeded to tell Joe about the level detector that he'd taken apart and exactly what he found.

"We still don't know exactly why anyone would put these beacons on the tanks, but it can't be good. So we're removing them as quickly and quietly as we can."

"Good idea, Has anyone at the company called the FBI?"

"Not yet. They're putting together a plan right now. They're trying to do this as quietly as possible. I have a feeling there's some inside help on this job and we don't want to get their attention. Whatever they have planned, we don't want to scare them into action because we announced it to the world." Hatch paused. "They're letting workers go home one at a time, trying to keep a low profile."

"So you think the lady in the little red Corvette is responsible? I mean, she sure seems to be around a lot. Where there's smoke . . ."

"Yeah, I know. But I can't be sure. We have another dude we're watching. He seems to turn up in places he shouldn't be and he was sure scared to death when he saw Danny taking that detector apart. I think he was afraid Danny would figure it out."

"Well, if you need anything else from me, just call. I'll be fixing macawoni and cheese."

Hatch smiled, thinking of little Anna. "Be careful. I've been told you and Pat are both terrible cooks. *Burns water*, if I remember your sister-in-law's comment."

"Diane likes to exaggerate."

"Right."

As soon as Joe hung up, his phone rang again. He picked it up right away. "Hello?"

"Hi, Joe, its Nancy."

"Hi, Nancy. I just got off the phone with Hatch. What's up?"

"We're headed to the power plant. We just found out why Alex Corbin was killed. And we're pretty sure we know who the killer is."

Joe heard Lisa calling him from the bathroom and hollered, "Hang on a second honey. I'm on the phone." Then he said to Nancy, "Shit. Pat and Diane are there. He just had to take that damn tour."

Lisa called out again, "Joe!"

Before he answered Lisa, he said, "Can you get Pat and Diane out of there?"

"We're trying, Joe. We're trying."

Lisa walked in and it looked like she'd wet her pants. Joe looked at her, confused.

"My water broke."

Joe hesitated for a moment as he processed what Lisa had just said. Then he shouted, "We have to get you to the hospital." Without thinking, he hung up on Nancy.

"Joe, please calm down. One of us has to be in control. I'm afraid that has to be you. We have time."

"You're right. Yes. You're right. What should we do?"

"First, you need to call your mom and tell her we could use a babysitter. Then when she gets here, we can head to the hospital."

Joe took deep breaths. He started to calm down. "Okay, I'm in control. We have time."

Lisa smiled and shook her head. This was the first time she'd ever seen her big, strong, ex-Marine, future husband look nervous. She smiled.

"After you call your mom, you should call Nancy back. Tell her everything's okay here."

"Right."

"And apologize for slamming the phone down in her ear."

Chapter 37

At 10:20 A.M. the heat was already uncomfortable. The clear sky meant the sun would again blister the parched earth in southeast Texas. Heat waves rose off of the blacktop of the employee parking lot at the Texas Star Refinery.

Hatch thought hiding in a maintenance storage shed with no windows or air conditioning was a terrible idea. Sweat oozed from his pores, quickly soaking his clothing. Finally, peeking through the slit of the open door, he spotted Ricardo Vasquez heading for the employee parking lot. Maybe he could get out of this hellish shed.

Vasquez was on his cell phone and he didn't sound happy. *Must be Sammy's man from the body shop. Good job.*

The angry engineer stopped near a white Ford van. He was still shouting into his phone, waving his hand in the air in disgust. Finally he flipped his phone shut with one angry motion. He stood on the hot blacktop looking down, shaking his head. After several seconds that seemed like an eternity to Hatch, he slapped his hand on the side of the van. After a few more moments of angry contemplation, he opened the driver's side door, and got in. The windows glided down. The inside of the van must have been scorching hot. As Vasquez started the engine, Hatch slipped out of the shed and made tracks for his rented Taurus. He was behind the wheel with the engine running before Vasquez made it out of the lot. The seats in his Taurus were almost too hot to endure. He let down all the windows, then flipped the air conditioning on maximum hoping to get some relief from the oven-like heat.

The white van took a right turn out of the lot. If Sammy Helzer was right, Vasqeuz would head to the body shop where his BMW was getting a little paint job.

Sammy was right. The body shop was little more than an old gas station where the pumps had been removed. The service bays were open. Each bay was occupied by a car in some stage of body work, from bondo, to primer, to the final coat of paint.

Hatch pulled the car against the curb about a quarter of a block from the body shop. He left the engine running with the air conditioner pumping out cold air. After ten minutes with the air on full blast the car's interior was just starting to get comfortable.

He pulled out a compact set of binoculars and watched as Vasquez approached a man in the bay closest to the office. They walked to the middle bay where a black BMW was parked. By the man's movements and Vasquez' reaction it was clear he was giving the Beamer's owner bad news. Hatch enjoyed the scene. The body shop owner listened for a bit, then shrugged as if to say *What do you want me to do? We'll take care of it, but the deed's done.*

Vasquez continued to complain, but it was apparent the man was through listening. He shrugged again and headed towards the office.

Hatch lowered the binoculars just in time to see a red Corvette pull into the lot. Vasquez turned and watched as Victoria Garcia stepped from her car. At first he smiled, but it quickly disappeared as she strode up to him. She pointed her finger at his chest. It looked as if she was giving him an ear-full.

Hatch wished he had a long range microphone. He was tempted to run up to them, but what would he do when he got there? Too bad Joe or Pat weren't here. Together, they'd have a chance to corner the two of them and get to the bottom of Danny's murder, not to mention all the secrecy about the fake level detectors.

Maybe Sammy could help. He'd have to hurry to get here. But then what? Hatch didn't have a good plan. He needed more time.

As he thought about it, the opportunity evaporated. Victoria headed back to her Corvette and started the engine. She waited for a few seconds, all the while staring at Vasquez. When he turned away, she flipped him off, then laid a stretch of rubber as she sped down the street.

Vasquez had turned to watch the Corvette when he heard the screech of tires. Then he threw his hands in the air and headed for the van. He jumped in, started the engine, and headed off, driving right past Hatch's Taurus, never once looking his way.

Hatch wanted to follow the Garcia woman, but she was long gone. The way she rocketed down the street, no way he was catching up to her. So he followed Vasquez instead. He had no idea where the trip would take him, but at this point, he was running out of options.

Something big was up. He felt it in his bones.

* * *

When Joe and Lisa got to the hospital, they were greeted by a young woman who looked as if she had just graduated from junior high school. She was thin with sandy blonde hair and a long, narrow face with no visible makeup. She asked about the nature of their visit.

Lisa breathed normally and appeared calm. Her color was good. She didn't look to be in any hurry. But when Joe heard the question, he looked at Lisa's belly, then looked back at the young woman with an expression that wore the question *Are you kidding?* Lisa took over from there.

"My water broke this morning. Doctor Epstein said to get here right away if that happened."

In a sing-song, valley-girl voice that irritated Joe, she said, "Like, when did your water break?"

"About forty-five minutes ago."

Miss Valley Girl turned to her left and pointed down a hallway that looked to Joe like it went on for eternity. "Okay, like, you're going to be going down that hallway to the third door on the left. Then they'll, like, get some information from you and, like, get you to a prep room. It used to be called the Labor Room, but somebody thought that name was, like a bit . . . I don't know, harsh, or something."

Joe was getting nervous. Miss Valley Girl took an awful long time to get through the introduction. He wanted to ask her if she could hurry up, but he was afraid she'd get distracted and have to start over.

Then she asked, "Your name please and the last four digits of your social security number?"

Lisa gave her the information which she keyed into her computer. She looked up. "Ms. Goddard, if you'll, like, take a seat there." She pointed to a comfortable looking group of chairs in a waiting area. "Like, we'll get a wheelchair and an attendant will make sure you get to the right place. Okay?"

"Thanks. But is it okay if I stand?"

For just a moment, Lisa's question appeared to confuse the young woman. "No problem. Like, it should only be a minute and the attendant will be here."

She looked down at her computer screen then turned to Joe and asked, "Um, are you, like, Joseph McKinney?"

"Not only am I like him, I am him. But it's just Joe."

Lisa gave him a dirty look. Miss Valley Girl's expression didn't change. "Okay Joe. Like, you'll be able to go with her to the administrator's desk. Then they'll let you know where you need to go from there."

As she finished, a handsome, young black man of about thirty walked up pushing a wheelchair that had more chrome and gadgets than a 1957 Chevy. When he spoke, he sounded Jamaican.

"I'm looking for Ms. Lisa Goddard. That must be you, ma' lady. Am I right?" His smile revealed bright white teeth that contrasted with his dark face. One of his front teeth on the top row was gold plated and flickered in the fluorescent lights of the hospital reception area.

Lisa smiled. "That's me." As she finished, she felt a swift kick from inside. Her face registered pain.

"Oh, mon' we betta get ya movin'. Somebody wants to meet they mom and pop. Are you da fadda?

Joe listened closely, trying to understand the accent. "Yes, I'm Joe."

"My name is William, but peoples here call me 'Wheels.' So Joe, Lisa, get ready for a fast treep. We got to get ya' to Delivery. We ready?"

They nodded and 'Wheels' was off and nearly running. Within minutes they were getting checked in. Joe stayed, but Lisa did most of the talking. This gave Joe time to think about Pat and Diane in Wisconsin and Hatch in Texas.

Two murders in Wisconsin, one in Texas. How in the hell do Pat and Hatch get drawn into these messes? I guess I'm lucky to have to sit these two out. But why kill an engineer and an engineering student? And why was the student involved in the first murder? What's the connection? Did they kill him because he could be identified on the videotape? Or were they afraid he'd talk? Talk about what, though? The murder? If they were afraid of that, why'd they deliver the tape to the Feds?

"Joe. Are you with us?" Lisa elbowed him in the ribs.

"Yeah, I'm listening."

"Okay, then where are you supposed to go from here?"

"Uh . . . well, I guess I missed that part."

In a firm tone, Lisa said, "You pay attention or you're going to be missing some other parts."

She winced, then started to breath in quick bursts. She arched her back a bit, then began to relax again.

"Wow, I think I just had a contraction."

The woman behind the administrations window wore a name tag that said 'Agnes.' She was a heavyset woman in her late fifties with dark red lipstick nearly the color of dried blood and bright red fingernail polish that didn't match her lipstick. With a deep southern drawl, she said, "You need to time the contractions. For right now, Mr. McKinney, I'll go over what you need to do and where you need to go from here."

She nodded to 'Wheels.' "Time to go, mees." He turned to Joe. "See ya' later Joe, mon. You going to make a great fadda."

Joe leaned over and kissed Lisa, grabbed her hand and gave it a squeeze. "See you in a little bit. I love you."

Tears formed in Lisa's eyes. "I love you, too."

"Ah. Das sweet, but we gotta go now. Der's a baby wants to meet you bote."

Joe watched as 'Wheels' headed towards a bank of elevators with his fiancé. The young Jamaican backed her in so they could see each other until the doors slid closed. Joe, the big, tough ex-Marine tried to fight off a wave of emotion, but it didn't work as tears formed in his eyes.

Agnes cleared her throat. For the next five minutes, she went over various instructions. More importantly, she had the papers he needed to sign in order to be in the delivery room during the birth.

As Agnes finished, Joe took a deep breath and thought about how having a child was going to change his life. Agnes smiled at him thinking, *You haven't got a clue.*

Chapter 38

"You're like a kid in a candy store. Quit smiling. People will think you're deranged. You know, they give drug and alcohol tests around here."

Evan ribbed his friend, Pat, as they made their way around the facilities. They'd spent nearly an hour in the control room going over nearly every indicator on the massive control panel. Evan was surprised at how quickly Pat learned the layout of the plant, including temperature and pressure ranges for the primary plant systems. Once they finished the walk around the turbine generator, they toured the maintenance shops, stopping to meet many of the technicians and supervisors. They spent another half hour in the electric shop talking with some of the ex-Navy Electrician's Mates. It was going to be tough getting Pat out of the shop to continue the tour.

"This is great. It feels so natural walking around here with these guys. I could work here."

"Right. And Diane would move to Northern Wisconsin from Central Florida because . . . ?"

Pat shrugged, still smiling. "Hey, it's just a thought. I know the summers are a little short up here, but she's a trooper."

"First off, the summers are usually one weekend long up here. It's going to happen in mid July this year. Then we're right back into fall. Second, the winters are harsh. Why do you think my folks gave me a house and a ton of land and moved to Florida? Cause the weather sucks up here."

"But it's great if you love winter sports, right?" Pat was looking for a bone here, but Evan wasn't about to throw him one.

"Sure, for about the first four weeks. Then you realize you're freezing your ass off, and you think that surfing at South Beach sure would be more fun."

Evan was smiling, but he was serious. He'd really thought he was retiring from the Navy and moving back to Northern Wisconsin to live near his aging parents. Since he was an only child, it was his responsibility to be close and take care of them. When they pulled up stakes, moved to Florida, and gave him the family property, he couldn't very well turn them down. Had his parents not given him the home and land, he would have tried harder to get a job at a plant in a warmer climate. Now he was stuck in Wisconsin, wondering about the sanity of his choice. At least he could hunt on his own property, but with the discovery of Alex Corbin's body, he wasn't sure when he'd feel up to roving the woods alone again.

Evan said, "Hey, we can't go in, but let me show you the entrance to the auxiliary building where many of the support systems are located. It's kind of the transition area between the primary and secondary systems."

"Alright. Let's go."

"I'll show you the latest in electronic dosimetry. You'll get a kick out of them, especially after the archaic tools we used on the sub. The commercial industry can afford a lot of things the Navy couldn't."

As they turned to head for the elevators, an announcement came over the Gaitronics, the site communications system: "Jimmy Smith, line two, Jimmy Smith, line two."

Evan stopped, his eyebrow furrowed. "I didn't see Jimmy last night. I wonder if he's even here." He shrugged and turned to walk again, Pat moving along by his side.

Pat hadn't told Evan yet what they found out about his wife and stepson. He tried to keep his focus on the tour, but it was becoming more difficult to keep this information close to his chest. It wasn't his place to advise Evan he'd been living with two suspected terrorists. But once the tour was over, Pat planned to spill his guts regardless of whether it was his place or not. He'd hoped that Nancy or the FBI agent would take care of it, but so far they hadn't said a word. Pat wasn't about to let Evan go home without telling his friend he was in danger.

A young lady stopped Evan as they neared the elevator and asked if he could review an engineering package she'd prepared. He assured her that he'd get to it later that day. Then she smiled and asked if Pat was a new hire. When he said no, she replied, "Too bad." She smiled again and walked off, her eyes lingering just a bit as she walked away.

As the two men watched her walk away Pat asked, "What was that all about?"

"Her?" He smiled. "That was Angelina. She's an engineer in the mechanical area."

"She seems a bit young for an engineer."

"Yeah. She's been here for about four years now. I think she graduated from high school at seventeen then finished her engineering degree in a little over three years." She was finally out of sight, turning a corner down the hall. "And for some reason, she likes older men. She's quite the flirt."

"Damn. I thought she liked me for my personality." He smiled and turned with Evan towards the elevator.

As the door to the elevator slid open, the Gaitronics sounded again. "Jimmy Smith, line two. Jimmy Smith, line two."

Evan was just about to go over and pick up the handset to the Gaitronics and tell whoever was paging Jimmy that he probably wasn't on site when one of the site guards walked off the elevator. He saw Evan and asked, "Hey, Evan, have you seen Jimmy this morning?"

"No, I haven't. What's going on?"

"I don't know, but if you see him, tell him to contact his supervisor."

Evan frowned. Something was wrong. Turning to Pat, he said, "Let's head down to the auxiliary building, then admin. Maybe Jimmy's out at his desk."

"We can head there now if you like. I've seen enough for one visit."

"No, no, no. We're almost finished. It'll only take a few minutes. I think you'll enjoy this part of the tour." They entered the elevator and the doors glided shut.

Pat's face tightened as he thought this might be a good time to tell his friend the news about Jimmy and Sally, but his friend's mind was on other things now. Maybe he thought his stepson was in danger. The discovery of Ali Malik Hassan's body hadn't become general knowledge around the plant yet, but it was only a matter of time. Also, the news of his father, Yusef Hassan's trip to the hospital was making its way around. Evan was surely concerned as all of the people affected were engineers; people he knew well and worked with closely.

Pat's thoughts were broken by the opening of the elevator doors. They were in a different part of the plant. There were more offices on the left, but there was a large hallway on the right. From where they stood, they couldn't see into the hallway, but there was a woman in a guard uniform standing there with her back to them. She talked with someone out of Evan and Pat's sight. Because of the machinery noise coming from the hallway they couldn't hear what was being said, even though they were only fifteen feet from where she stood.

Evan stopped when he and Pat were only ten feet away. He frowned when he recognized Ingrid Shaw. Her M-16 was around her back, held in place by the gun's strap. Her platinum hair was tied together in a pony tail that was pushed through the opening in the back of her black ball cap. She was pleading with whoever she was talking with. Evan feared that that person was his stepson, Jimmy Smith. He wasn't sure he wanted to take the final four steps and see the person's face. He turned to Pat, leaned close to his ear and whispered, "Let's wait here a second."

Pat sensed Evan's tension, so he just nodded. As they both turned again to wait and see what would happen next, a loud explosion rocked the building. Two loud reports a few feet from where they stood immediately followed, gunshots from a nine millimeter handgun. Ingrid Shaw fell backwards onto the floor directly in front of them. Both men glanced at each other in shock, then took the few steps towards the fallen guard.

A loud, piercing, repeating electronic alarm sounded followed by an announcement.

"The station is under attack. Immediately take cover. Repeat. The station is under attack. Immediately take cover, THIS IS NOT A DRILL." The alarm started again, making it difficult to think.

As they knelt down beside her, they saw blood coming from her forehead and neck. Pat knew it was hopeless. Down the hall, holding the smoking gun was Evan's stepson and Ingrid's fiancé, Jimmy Smith. Evan, bewildered, looked up at him.

Jimmy didn't make eye contact with Evan, but stared at Ingrid's body, apparently trying to understand what he'd just done. Then he noticed Evan and Pat staring at him. He slowly raised his gun.

Pat spun towards Evan and grabbed him by his shirt. He jerked his friend out of the hallway just as another shot rang out, barely missing Pat's head. They scrambled to their feet and pressed their bodies against the wall by the entrance. Over the sound of the alarm, they heard Jimmy's footsteps as he ran down the hall into the auxiliary building. They heard the sound of a door open, then close.

Another explosion rocked the building. Several ceiling tiles fell and dust filled the air.

Pat looked around at the building ."What the hell is going on?"

Evan was still in shock, but his face turned pale with fear. "I think we're being attacked. Jimmy's behind this. I know where he's going." When he looked at Pat, his eyes were filled with terror. "We have to stop him! I know what he's trying to do!"

Chapter 39

Hatch followed the white van at a distance. He didn't want to lose sight of it, but he also didn't want Vasquez to realize he was being followed. It didn't take long to figure out where the engineer was headed as the van made a beeline for the refinery. Hatch didn't know exactly what he was up to or why there was some connection between him and the Garcia woman. But he had to follow his gut and the only lead he had left.

His cell phone rang.

"Yo."

"Hatch, this is Joe. Look, Lisa is heading into the labor room now so I've only got a second and I won't be able to help anymore. I did find one last piece of information you might be able to use. Victoria Garcia's real name is—"

"Joe? Hello?"

Hatch looked at his cell phone. The call was disconnected. He mumbled to himself, "Miss Lisa picked a great time to have this baby."

* * *

Back at the hospital waiting room, a red-headed, middle-aged nurse had grabbed Joe's cell phone, hit the end button, and turned the phone off. She was lecturing him on following hospital rules about cell phone use. Was he trying to get someone killed? Didn't he have any respect for the patients and staff? No wonder kids these days thought they could get away with anything.

All Joe heard was blah, blah, blah, rules, blah, blah, cell phone, blah.

When she finally stopped her lecture, she asked, "Do you have anything to say for yourself?"

"Yes. Can I have my phone back now?"

"If you promise me you'll follow the rules . . ."

With a forced smile and gritted teeth, Joe said, "Yes, ma'am, I will. Now, can I have my phone back?" He held out his hand. She reluctantly handed it over.

With a stern look and two fingers first pointing at her eyes, then at Joe she said, "I'll be watching you like a hawk. Understand?"

Joe held his teeth together as long as he could stand it. He turned and headed towards the elevator, hoping to get outside and quickly make his call before Lisa knew he was gone. The nurses had to get her into her hospital gown, take her vital signs, and talk with her about what to expect over the next hours. They'd told Joe he should come back in about ten minutes and Lisa should be ready. Once Lisa was prepped, he'd be able to stay with her in the labor room.

The head nurse, Belinda, a black woman who appeared to be in her mid-fifties, had told him her team was experienced and he should try to relax. "It won't be long now before you and your wife will take home your beautiful baby girl."

Joe had smiled, but he still felt tense. There was just too much happening all at once for him to relax. His attention was divided between everything happening at the hospital, Pat and Diane's spiraling situation in Wisconsin, and the murder of Hatch's friend in Texas. He needed to make the call to Hatch while he still had time.

After pressing the button for the elevator, he tapped his foot, watching as the lights indicating the elevator's current location seemed to freeze in place one floor below him. He heard a muffled conversation. It sounded like one person was still in the elevator and the other stood outside the doors. The conversation appeared to be about where they would meet after their shift ended. Joe was about to shout at the floor to hurry it up when he heard the doors slide closed.

After a few more seconds the elevator stopped on his floor, the doors slid open and Joe started to get in. He heard a woman's voice yell, "Mr. McKinney?"

He stepped back out of the elevator before the doors closed and looked in the direction of the voice. It was a tall, slender woman in a dark blue business suit. Her brown, unblinking eyes stared right into Joe's. She had the air of a manager.

Joe heard the elevator rising to the next floor. He sighed, resigned to the notion he had to wait longer before he could make the call to Hatch. It would also cause another delay in getting back to Lisa. Joe wondered why this woman was looking for him.

"I'm Joe McKinney."

"Mr. McKinney, we didn't get all of Miss Goddard's information during the check-in process. I just need to get a few additional details from you."

Joe frowned, thinking fast so he could escape and call Hatch. If Hatch tried calling him, his phone would still be off.

"Ma'am, I need to make a quick phone call. Can I meet you back here in five minutes? It's real important."

"I'm afraid this can't wait, Mr. McKinney. Your fiancé is already being prepped for delivery. Since you and Miss Goddard aren't married, we need to make sure the procedure is covered or we need you to sign some forms for financial responsibility. The hospital—"

Joe held up his hand. "Miss, . . . I didn't catch your name."

He looked at her hospital nametag and read her name just as she said it.

"Hollister. Sylvia Hollister. I'm the Admissions Manager."

"Sylvia, we've been coming to this hospital for the last five months. Our doctor practices here. We've got all sorts of paperwork on file here, probably in quintuplicate, if that's even a word. I have to make a phone call. It's urgent."

"Mr. McKinney, so is the birth of your child. What could possibly be more important than that right now?" She looked at the expression on his face, then took a deep breath. "Alright. Please make your call and meet me back at the administration office. I'll have the forms ready for you to sign. It shouldn't take much time."

"I appreciate that, Ms. Hollister."

He turned and hit the button for the elevator again as it had already left the floor. When it arrived back and the doors opened, a man's voice bellowed out his name. "Joe McKinney?"

Joe shook his head. "Now what?" Then to the approaching male nurse he said, "Yes, that's me."

"Sir, please follow me. Your wife's in heavy labor. She's asking for you."

Joe forgot all about Victoria Garcia and Hatch and Sylvia Hollister and everything else that, just moments ago, had seemed so important. He thought of only two things, Lisa and their child.

In an anxious voice Joe said, "Let's go."

* * *

Hatch tried calling Joe's phone again. After the third attempt and having the call go right to voicemail he figured either Joe's phone had run out of battery power or he was inside the hospital and had to turn it off. No matter, he had to focus his attention on the task at hand.

He saw the refinery on the left and the old, beat-up neighborhood on the right. Vasquez drove right past the entrance to the employee parking lot and continued down the road that ran along the western border of the complex. After traveling another three hundred yards, the van turned right into the old, rundown neighborhood.

Hatch whispered. "What are you up to, Mr. Vasquez?"

He drove past the corner where the van had turned. As he passed the street, he saw the van. Vasquez was slowing down, possibly to park. It was the same block where the Garcia woman had parked her Corvette the day before. Hatch looked to see if her three rescuers were on the front porch of the house. He didn't see anyone as he continued past the intersection. Hatch went down one block, then made a right hand turn. He planned to circle the block and try to catch up with the van before he lost it completely.

He was in luck. Vasquez had parked the van only a quarter of the way up the block. Hatch wondered if Garcia and Vasquez had a mutual acquaintance here. He quickly dismissed that notion. They looked too high-class for this neighborhood. Besides, the goons from yesterday hadn't appeared to know who Victoria was, even though they'd seemed more than willing to kick Hatch's ass for her.

Hatch was truly puzzled now. Would Vasquez risk parking a vehicle in this neighborhood for very long, especially with what happened to his BMW by Danny's apartment? Even the neighborhood around Loco Pedro's was a nicer neighborhood than this.

He decided to circle back around the block again and approach the van from behind. He wanted a quiet approach without Vasquez noticing. But instinct told Hatch he needed to hurry.

As he circled the block again, he caught a view of the employee entrance to the plant. Two cars pulled up to the guard shack. The guard stepped out of the air conditioned security hut and approached the lead car. Hatch didn't think anything of it and turned the corner, heading towards the street where the white van was parked just a block away. When he reached the street, he slowed and started into his turn, glancing in the rear view mirror. He frowned when he saw the guard throw up his hands and fall backwards.

He finished his turn just as the rear doors to the white van opened.

It took a moment to understand what he was seeing, then his jaw dropped. Mounted in the back of the van was a missile launcher. In each of the twenty-four launch tubes, Hatch spotted the pointed tip of a short range surface to surface missile The purpose of the "level detectors" became crystal clear.

"Homing signals."

Chapter 40

The shriek of the high pitched alarm added to the confusion throughout the plant. The smell of cordite filled the air from the gunshots Jimmy Smith had fired. A group of three employees walked up as if taking a stroll in the park, until they saw Ingrid Shaw on the floor, a pool of blood forming around her head. One of the women gasped, and covered her mouth with her hands. The two men looked at the body and the blood, not sure if this was a drill with really good props or if the female guard really was hurt. Their faces twisted into confused expressions.

Evan jumped to his feet and yelled at the three employees who stared at Ingrid. "Take cover. Don't you get it? This is real!"

Pat jumped up and grabbed another man who had just stepped off the elevator. He yelled above the piercing sound of the alarm as he pointed in the direction that Jimmy Smith had run, "Except for armed security guards, don't let anyone go down this hallway. Understand?"

The man gave Pat a weak nod, but his face was blank, his skin pale white. Pat wasn't sure the man had understood a word he'd said. The three young employees looked scared. The realization that this wasn't a drill finally hit them.

Evan and Pat knelt next to Ingrid Shaw. Pat searched for a pulse in her neck, but felt none. He shook his head. She was dead.

Evan pulled the M-16 from around her body and laid it by her side. He then took her Glock 9mm and set it down next to the other weapon. He retrieved four loaded 9mm clips from her ammo belt. Then he removed the extra M-16 magazine from her beltpack. He handed the M-16 to Pat along with the spare magazine.

Holding up the Glock, Evan asked, "You know how to handle either of these?"

Pat looked at the assault rifle in his hands and the Glock Evan held. He was well versed in small arms, including military grade weapons, thanks to spending many days at the Swamp with Hatch. "Yeah. I know how to use them both."

"Good, 'cause I have a feeling we're going to need them."

Holding the Glock at his side, Evan headed down the hall to look for his stepson. Pat followed at his heels. They stopped at a Gaitronics unit so Evan could call the control room. "Silence on the line! Guard down at the RRA entrance with at least two bullet wounds, one to the head, one to the neck. Jimmy Smith is headed to the Emergency Reactor Cooling Room. He . . ."

Evan heard another loud explosion. The lights flashed several times. Some of the fluorescent lights went out. More ceiling tiles fell, exposing ventilation ductwork and electrical wiring. A few of the lights that went out blinked and came back on. Dust from the area above the ceiling tiles filled the air, making Pat and Evan cough.

Evan cleared his throat and shouted into the Gaitronics phone to operators in the control room, hoping that they could hear him. "He intends to cause a meltdown! You need to scram the reactor and start emergency cool down!"

The voice on the other end was in a state of panic. "Evan, we're under attack from outside the protected area! All available guards are trying to defend the perimeter!" He paused. "We already tried to scram the reactor!"

"What do you mean 'tried to scram'? Just shut the damn thing down! Do it now!"

A frightened voice said, "We tried! It won't scram!"

"That's impossible!"

"It might be impossible, but it isn't shutting down! We hit the scram button, tried to manually initiate reactor protection. We've tried everything we could think of from here! It won't scram!"

"Oh, shit!" With as much control as he could muster, Evan said, "Bashir is your best Reactor Controls Engineer. You get him on the phone. Do it now! He'll tell you how to shut this son-of-a-bitch down! And hurry!" He paused and took a deep breath before he continued. "If I'm right, you're about to experience a loss of reactor coolant."

He slammed the Gaitronics down. "We have to hurry. Jimmy's trying to melt the plant down. Worse, he's going to drain the primary coolant into the bay. Alex knew it. That must be what got him killed. Let's go. We're almost out of time."

Pat hoped Diane was safe in the administration building. As he and Evan ran down the corridor, he pulled out his cell phone and hit the speed dial for her cell phone, nearly dropping his weapon. She answered before the end of the first ring.

"Pat, where are you? What the hell is going on?"

"I'm not sure, but I just wanted to make sure you're safe."

"Yes, I'm fine. I'm in the engineer's offices."

"Good. Stay there and keep out of sight. Is anyone there with you?"

"Yes. Evan's wife is here."

A cold chill ran down Pat's spine. He stopped in his tracks, his mind racing. Diane was in danger and she didn't even know it. He had no way to protect her.

Evan was nearly twenty feet down the corridor when he turned to see the look of fear on Pat's face. He stopped at the door that led to the Emergency Reactor Cooling Room.

Pat tried to think of something to tell his wife that would let her know she was in danger. But he couldn't think of what to say. Damn, he would just have to tell her and hoped she remained calm.

* * *

Evan motioned to Pat to keep coming. He reached for the door handle. Pat held up a finger. He took a deep breath, hoping his message wouldn't be overheard by 'Sally Jones'.

"You need to get as far away from Evan's wife as you can. She's involved in this somehow." He paused. "Do it quick, but use caution. Don't let her suspect that you know." He paused again, his heart racing.

Diane knew the situation was real. The sounds of explosions and small arms fire were all around her. Pat had never steered her wrong. If he said Evan's wife was involved, then it was true.

Her loss of words left several seconds of silence which seemed like eternity to Pat. "Are you safe?"

In a shaky voice, Diane replied, "For now."

"I have to go. You do whatever it takes to get to a safe place. I'm sorry, babe, but I really have to go."

Diane didn't know what else to say. With tears forming in her eyes, and a voice nearly choked off with fear and anxiety, she said, "I love you."

"I love you, too." He closed his cell phone and sprinted the last twenty feet to where Evan waited.

"Is your husband okay?" asked Sally Jones. She seemed very calm. None of the explosions were near the administration building, but that could change. And this woman acted as if they were having a luncheon.

"Yes. He's with your husband. I think they're safe." Diane paused. "I have to call my children. They'll worry if they see something on TV about a problem at the plant. They knew we would be here on the tour today, and they might get worried."

"Yes, a child afraid of losing their parents is a terrible thing. Evan's office is right here. You can have some privacy." Sally pointed to a cubicle a dozen feet away.

"Thanks."

As Diane stepped into Evan's cubicle, she noticed Sally watched her with that look of utter calm. Evan's cubicle really offered very little in the way of privacy. It was centered among others. A chill ran through her as another explosion sounded in the distance. Moments later, a coffee cup and lamp on Evan's desk rattled. His desk calendar shifted. Diane noticed a folded piece of paper sticking out from under the calendar. She turned to make sure Sally wasn't watching, then she removed the small paper and read it.

> *Sheriff, I suspect my stepson, Jimmy Smith, is guilty of the murder of Alex Corbin. I also believe that my wife, Sally Smith-Jones is complicit in the murder. The shoes on the video of Alex's murder can be found in my house. The murder weapon . . .*

"Are you okay, Diane?"

The calm voice came from directly behind her. She tensed, but did her best to remain calm. She folded the small note paper over and stuffed it down the front of her shirt as she flipped her cell phone open. As she turned she hit the speed dial for Joe McKinney. The phone immediately went to voice mail.

"I'm fine. I just can't get through to Pat's brother, Joe."

Diane looked Sally directly in the eyes. The deep calm looked almost drug induced. Her lips curled up ever so slightly. She was only a few steps away and she had her right hand behind her back.

"Sally, where are the rest rooms? I'm not feeling well."

A voice with a Middle Eastern accent from just outside the cube startled them both. Their heads jerked towards the source. "The restrooms are down the hall on the right. But you won't need the restroom." The man put an emphasis on 'you' as he stared at Evan's wife.

Yusef Hassan walked up to Evan's cubicle. He looked ready to explode. He yelled at Sally, "Why did you have to kill my son? Why? He was a good, young man! He had his future within his grasp!" As he spoke, his face turned a bright red. Even his bushy eyebrows and beard couldn't hide the rage continuing to build inside. "Your son and your husband took all that away from him!"

Diane's fear grew. She didn't know what to do. Sally Smith-Jones and the angry Muslim blocked her escape. Evan's wife was a murderer, and a man who looked like a poster child for a terrorist recruiting campaign was screaming at her. As he yelled at the woman Pat had just identified as a terrorist, another explosion shook the building. The man ignored the blast and continued his tirade. Diane didn't know what to do next.

Just then, she heard sirens in the distance coming towards the plant. They couldn't get here soon enough.

Chapter 41

Hatch couldn't see Ricardo Vasquez anywhere near the van. He didn't have to be close by to launch the missiles. They could be triggered by signals from anywhere in the world, but he had parked the van just moments before. Hatch now wished he'd had Bud Yantzy call the local cops or the FBI. At least they would have an idea of what they were up against.

He quickly dialed 911 on his cell phone.

A female with a strong Texas accent answered. "Nine-one-one, what is your emergency?"

With as much calm as he could muster, he said, "The Texas Star Refinery is being attacked by terrorists. They've entered the site in two cars. I believe they killed the gate guard. And they are about to launch missiles into the refinery to—"

"Sir, making false reports is a serious matter. Your call can and will be traced. Are you sure you want to continue?"

He spoke in terse, but measured words. "Ma'am, this is no joke. It is not a false report. And if you delay in dispatching law enforcement personnel, lots of people are going to die. Do you clearly understand me?"

As the dispatcher weighed the validity of Hatch's call, he noticed a puff of smoke coming from the van. One of the three-foot-long rockets flew from its tube and zoomed right over Hatch's Taurus, heading for the Texas Star tank yard. Within seconds one of the tanks exploded in a fireball. Hatch turned to see black smoke forming over the site. Then he felt heat radiating from within the fenced tank farm.

The 911 dispatcher yelled, "What in the hell was that?"

"It was one of those missiles. Get your people here immediately." He disconnected the call.

He punched in the number for the I&C shop foreman's office.

"Yantzy!"

"Bud, get your guys out of the shop. Find someplace secure and arm yourselves with anything you can find."

“We’re already on it, Hatch. What in God’s name is going on?”

“You’re being attacked. There’s a group of armed men on site and they’re looking to kill whoever they see. Now get your guys . . .”

Another puff of smoke erupted from the van and another rocket whizzed over Hatch’s car. This time he didn’t turn to see the explosion.

“What the . . .”

Hatch yelled, “Bud, just get your people to a safe place and lock it down. I’ve gotta go.”

Hatch couldn’t allow the missile attack to continue. The first missile launches seemed about thirty to forty seconds apart. Each one had to be triggered individually, probably by some wireless signal, maybe a cell phone or pay phone? The second missile had been launched about nearly twenty seconds ago. He had to wait until after the next one before he could make his move.

He looked at his watch. Thirteen seconds passed before the next puff of smoke appeared. The rocket sailed over the Taurus. Hatch pulled his Smith and Wesson .40 caliber pistol from the glove compartment. He opened the driver side door, then ran to the back corner of the van on the driver’s side. He glanced at the van’s side mirror. He was in a bad position if Vasquez was in the driver’s seat and decided to open fire on him. His only escape route would take him across the back of the van, right in the line of fire of the rockets. If he was right, he had about thirty seconds until the next rocket was launched, but he didn’t want to risk his life on that bet.

A strong odor of burnt rocket fuel filled his nostrils, and the smoke irritated his eyes. He examined the launcher, but didn’t see anything obvious that would allow him to stop the rockets.

His next option was to find Vasquez. Odds were very high he was triggering the rockets. Hatch slid alongside the van to the driver’s door. He looked into the side view mirror, but didn’t see anyone in the front seat. He stepped up quickly, pointing his weapon into the cab. It was empty.

* * *

From half a block away, sitting in a rented Toyota Corolla, Ricardo Vasquez smiled, watching Danny’s friend search the van in vain. There was no way for this Hatch character to disable the launcher. The rockets would rain down on the refinery as long as he continued to arm and launch them. He dialed the number to access the launch sequence for the fourth rocket. When he finished, the cell phone signaled the rocket was ready. He hit zero. Vasquez smiled as the tell-tale puff of smoke showed inside the van's front window. A moment later, the rocket, followed by a narrow trail of flames, streaked towards the refinery and disappeared in a ball of fire that, minutes earlier, had been a tank full of oil.

By now, a crowd was gathering on the porches and the sidewalks of the distressed neighborhood. Sirens could be heard in the distance. Vasquez saw Hatch running back to his car. He laughed. *The loser is finally leaving. It's about time to move. I can finish the job from the hotel.*

* * *

In the refinery compound, the armed men stopped their cars in front of the maintenance shop. They ran into the building, brandishing AK-47s and looking for anyone to shoot, but the shops were deserted. The leader yelled an order in Spanish. Several of the men pulled explosives from their belts, armed them, then tossed them into the foreman's offices. The explosions and ensuing fire made short work of the buildings as the men retreated back to their cars. The driver of the first car threw it into reverse and hit the accelerator, until he saw the blockade. Half a dozen police cruisers blocked their escape route. The assailants jumped out of their cars and fired on the police. The officers, already in defensive positions behind their cars, returned fire. They weren't as well armed as the gang attacking the refinery. Their 9mm pistols and twelve gauge shotguns were no match for the Russian military assault rifles used by the attackers, but they held their positions as their cruisers were hammered. The firefight continued as four of the armed gunmen retreated to a warehouse between the entrance and the I&C shop, hoping to find cover and a place to regroup. Two of their compatriots were lying on the ground, apparently dead. They had superior firepower, but they were trapped. The open warehouse door seemed the only way out.

* * *

Another explosion rocked the refinery, the ground shaking from the blast. Bud Yantzy, Sammy Helzer, and the rest of the I&C crew were in the same warehouse as the attackers, but they remained under cover. The warehouse was a large building, with nearly twenty thousand square feet of floor space. Tall shelves, nearly twenty feet high, laden with boxes of replacement parts and specialized tools surrounded an open fifty by fifty foot area just inside the bay door where trucks were loaded and unloaded. A small tool room with a counter that opened into the main section of the warehouse was along the far wall. Bud Yantzy, Sammy Helzer, and the other I&C technicians now hid there. They all tensed as the attackers moved into the warehouse less than fifty feet away.

Crouched low behind the counter, Sammy moved closer to Bud and whispered he had an idea that might help the cops catch these guys. Bud listened, then smiled. It just might work.

In the back of the tool room, Bud and the crew loaded twelve penny nails into several framing nail guns and hooked them to a large compressor. They rigged the nail guns with duct tape, overriding the safety switches. Sammy adjusted the regulator valve to maximum output pressure. The hoses were only fifty feet long, which would restrict how far they could maneuver. Sammy and Bud took aim with their new weapons.

They looked at each other, then Bud mouthed, “One, two, three . . .”

Bud and Sammy let loose on the unsuspecting assailants. They hit two with the first shots, but the best effect was the noise created by the nails hitting the tin sides of the building. The attackers didn’t know what they were up against. Two of them dashed outside and came under fire from the police. A third was injured bad enough that he dropped his weapon and sprawled out on the floor in pain. Only the leader of the group remained calm. He turned, saw Sammy and Bud with their home rigged weapons and returned fire. Sammy and Bud kept up their assault, but they were no match for the AK-47. Bud was hit in the chest and fell back, bleeding heavily.

Sammy saw his boss fall. It didn’t scare him off. It strengthened his resolve. This attack was tied to Danny’s murder, somehow. Now Bud Yantzy, a man he’d worked with for over twenty years was a victim. He would kill this man or die trying. He leveled the nail gun, took aim, then loosed another barrage of nails. Several twelve penny nails hit the assailant in a close pattern in the forehead, lodging in his skull, penetrating his brain. He died instantly.

Within moments, the remaining gunman lowered his weapon and surrendered.

* * *

Hatch ran back to his car. Only one option left. Climbing into the driver's seat, he started the car and prepared to ram the back of the van, hoping to destroy the launcher. Of course, if he failed, he'd be dead. But the Taurus sat slightly lower than the back of the van, so it was possible that all ramming the van would do was lift up the van's rear end and pin his car underneath. Or the car could crash high enough to block the path of the rockets. Of course, that also might trap him in the Taurus, placing him directly in the path of the missiles. He only had about fifteen seconds to make his move.

He revved the engine several times and put the car in drive. A car pulled away from the curb about half a block away. It was coming in his direction. When the car was just sixty feet away, the driver came into view. It was Vasquez. Hatch waited. When the car was within twenty-five feet, he turned the wheel sharply to the left, gunned the Taurus' engine, and rammed Vasquez in the front driver's side, sending the Toyota careening to the curb. When the Toyota's wheels hit the curb, it nearly flipped onto its side.

The air bag in Hatch's Taurus deployed, stunning him momentarily. He shook his head. The airbag had momentarily knocked the wind out of him. He gathered the air bag and pushed it to the side, then found his Smith and Wesson on the driver's side floor. Grabbing it, he checked to make sure the safety was off and exited his car. He felt a sharp pain in the calf of his right leg, but kept moving towards Vasquez' car, adrenaline keeping the pain in check.

The engineer looked dazed by the collision. But Hatch didn't take any chances. He raised the gun and pointed it directly at Vasquez's head.

When Vasquez looked up and saw Hatch with the gun, he just smiled, as if drugged. He held the cell phone high enough for Hatch to see. He dialed the number to arm the next rocket. All he had to do was hit zero and the next rocket would be on its way into another tank of oil.

Hatch couldn't get the phone away in time. He had decide quickly, but his options were few.

Unaware of the crowd gathering, he yelled at Vasquez, "Drop the phone and keep your hands where I can see them!"

Hatch hoped Vasquez' bleak situation would dissuade him from launching another missile. Vasquez laughed and held the phone higher. Hatch yelled again, "I mean it, Vasquez! I'll shoot!"

Vasquez face twisted into a smile. He yelled back, "Your buddy didn't have the balls and neither do—"

The first shot shattered the driver's side window and struck Vasquez just above the left eye. It didn't penetrate his skull due to losing so much energy piercing the window. The second shot came nearly right on top of the first. With nothing to obstruct its path, the bullet ripped into his skull, killing him instantly.

Hatch kept his gun in place until he was confident the engineer was dead. His arms, now feeling heavy, dropped to his side. He managed to put the safety on and popped the clip out, holding it in his free hand. As he did, two police cars rounded the corner and came to an abrupt stop. The officers leapt from their cars and pointed their weapons at Hatch, who slowly set his weapon and clip on the ground. He laid down on the street waiting for the officers to cuff him. He didn't even feel the heat from the asphalt burn his arms. As they pulled him to his feet, several of the onlookers came up to the officers explaining what happened. They waved the crowd off and half dragged Hatch to one of the cruisers and placed him in the back. The pain in his leg grew to a rhythmic throb. He was pretty sure it was broken.

Several more police cars arrived on the scene. The crowd was juiced with adrenaline. Luckily, the police were able to convince them to head back to their homes.

It took nearly half an hour to clear the street. Three local fire houses were on the scene, working desperately to get the refinery fires under control. Even though five missiles were fired, only a single oil tank was destroyed. Just before the attack, I&C shop personnel had been able to remove the homing devices and toss them into a single tank that was already drained and slated for demolition.

The incendiary grenades used by the Mexicans destroyed the maintenance shop, burning it to the ground.

* * *

From nearly two blocks away, Victoria Garcia had watched the scene unfold through a mini set of binoculars. She was disappointed that Vasquez could only get five of the rockets launched. She was equally dismayed that only one oil tank was destroyed. Something must have gone wrong with the homing devices. *Too bad. I'll have to remember to be more careful in picking my partners next time.*

Victoria got into her red Corvette and drove to the corner a block away from where the van sat, still issuing smoke from the rocket launches. As she turned the corner, she saw Hatch sitting in the back of one of the cruisers. He had single-handedly stopped her plan. She admired his skill and felt bad that Vasquez had killed his friend. Danny wasn't supposed to get hurt, at least not before the raid on the refinery. He certainly wasn't supposed to get killed by her jealous partner. *What a fool to think I would fall in love with him. No matter. There will be other opportunities.*

* * *

Hatch looked up in time to see the red Corvette turn the corner. He saw the unmistakable face of Victoria Garcia as she looked his way. *Touché*. He wondered what amount of hatred could compel someone to carry out such a horrendous act. But then, he knew the power of hate. It was among the greatest of motivators.

Chapter 42

Jimmy Smith didn't notice the ninety-five degree heat in the Emergency Reactor Cooling Room. Sweat oozed from every pore in his body. He pulled out the bag of tools he had stored underneath the massive sixteen-stage, high pressure injection pump. He had about twenty minutes of work before he was ready to complete his part of the plan. His was the most important act of all the attacks taking place around the country at this hour.

But he was distracted. The face of Ingrid Shaw flashed through his mind. In the vision, Ingrid stared in disbelief, her face more a picture of dejection than of fear. Perhaps her heart was breaking before the bullets did their physical damage.

He'd smuggled in the gun, piece by piece, right under the guards' noses. It helped that Ingrid had let him in on a few little known weaknesses in the X-ray equipment. She'd made him swear he would never tell another soul about them, and he hadn't. By the look in her eyes right before Jimmy pulled the trigger, he knew she never understood what she'd done. *Maybe it's better that way. She loved me right to the end.*

He looked around. What had he done? He truly loved her. Their relationship had grown over the past few years, even as he plotted against the United States. He did begin to doubt his teachings, but when he would stray from 'the truth,' his father would talk to him and set him straight. It all became clear when Sheik Al Salil spoke the words of the Holy Book. It would strengthen his resolve for a time. Then the lifestyle he lived would cause him to doubt once again.

When he fell in love with Ingrid, the confusion ran rampant. He even heard his mother praying one evening for Allah to give her strength. Even she was falling prey to the sinful ways of the west.

But young Jimmy Smith, also known by his given name, Ahmed Salil, grew stronger in his faith. Sheik spoke to him just yesterday, providing the needed mental boost to finish the job and find favor in Allah's eyes by striking a blow against the great Satan. *Prove beyond a doubt that your devotion to Allah is greater than any human love.* He'd done that. But why did he feel so empty inside? With this great victory, he should be immersed in overwhelming joy. He was the instrument in Allah's victory today. The words of his father, Sheik Al Salil, rang in his ears. *You will be revered, hailed as a hero, a martyr. Every reward that is described in the Koran will be yours. Rejoice, my son. You have walked proudly into Satan's house and you have unleashed poison into his veins.*

He shook his head to clear his thoughts. No matter how he felt, there was no turning back. He started to loosen the bolts to the metal disc that blocked the end of the polished steel pipe. That pipe penetrated the wall to the containment building and connected directly to the reactor coolant system. The only barrier between the highly radioactive fluid and the Emergency Reactor Cooling Room was a single valve. It was shut now while he loosened the six bolts holding the blocking flange in place.

The muffled sound of an explosion caught his attention. A second later, the ground shook as the concussion from the rocket rippled through the building. He smiled, knowing his father was carrying out his part of the plan. The sound of another alarm rang out for twenty seconds then stopped. A man's voice came over the plant's loudspeakers, "All personnel take cover. Remain out of sight until further notice. All Emergency Response support personnel report to your facilities. This is NOT a drill. I repeat, this is NOT a drill."

At the end of the announcement, the alarm filled the Emergency Reactor Cooling Room. Jimmy Smith, the young engineer whose career seemed to be on the fast track, was now Ahmed Salil, the young jihadist. He took a deep breath and went back to work. After another twenty seconds, the alarm stopped.

A metallic noise startled him. He froze. Fixing his gaze in the direction of the sound, he slowly reached for his pistol. He stared across the room for several seconds. Nothing moved. Only the incessant, shrill noise of a few motors and the flow of water in nearby pipes could be heard. His eyes were wide open, unblinking. He remained perfectly still for nearly five minutes, his muscles aching from the anxiety.

After he was satisfied he was alone, he went back to work on the bolts holding the flange in place. After a full eight minutes of work, he removed the bolts and set them aside. He would need them to reconnect the elbow the mechanics in the fabrication shop were good enough to make for him. They had no idea of the part they played in his plan. He smiled as he thought how he used the system to get exactly what he needed.

It was nearly complete. He picked up the elbow and held it in place with one hand while trying to insert a bolt in the top hole. The elbow was much heavier than he anticipated and it took all his strength to hold it steady. Finally, he got a single bolt in place and get a nut started so that he could release his hold on the pipe. It hung at an awkward angle. Now it would be much easier to finish connecting the elbow to the primary piping.

The other end of the elbow fit perfectly to the other pipe. There were no valves on this one since it was a drain pipe. Connecting the elbow established a flow-path that led directly to the Chequamegon Bay and Lake Superior. Once the reactor core melted and released it's extremely radioactive elements into the primary coolant, the contamination of the bay and lake would take generations to clean up. The largest fresh water supply on earth would be damaged beyond recovery. *Allah be praised!*

* * *

Pat and Evan crouched on the steel grating just outside the door to the Emergency Reactor Cooling Room. They thought about bursting through the door and taking Jimmy by force, but they had no idea where he was in the room. They were also afraid the door might be booby trapped. But there was no other way into or out of the room. Evan believed Jimmy had no intention of leaving this room alive. Bursting through the door was a risk, but it was a risk they had to take.

Based on the drawings Evan recalled seeing, he believed Jimmy was at the blank flange near the center of the room. That would make a surprise attack difficult. The room was filled with piping and steel supports. It was a maze of winding metal. There were also wiring trays and electrical conduit. One thing in their favor was a motor control center just inside the room on the left side of the door. That put the large steel panel between the door and where Jimmy was most likely working.

"Should we wait for reinforcements?" Pat was trying not to think about Diane and her precarious position.

The men heard another explosion followed by a vibration.

"I have a feeling most of the guard force is trying to stop whoever is attacking the site. They don't even realize the real threat is down here. If he's doing what I suspect, we don't have time. He's going to . . ."

Another siren pierced the air from a speaker very close to them. The volume was ear-splitting. After several seconds, the siren stopped. A man's voice came on. "The station has declared a Site Area Emergency. All non-essential station personnel are to assemble at your designated areas. All Emergency response personnel report to your emergency facilities. This is NOT a drill. I repeat, this is NOT a drill."

Pat said, "No time like the present."

The two men stood, took deep breaths, and nodded to each other. Evan ran his card through the reader that controlled access to the room. Nothing happened.

"Shit. He must have disabled the readers."

Pat spotted a red bag on the floor inside an area roped off with yellow and magenta colored rope. A sign hung from the rope read, High Contamination. A crowbar protruded from the red bag. Pat looked at Evan who had spotted the tools at the same time. Evan walked over to the roped off boundary.

"Now's not the time to worry about a little radioactive contamination."

He took the crowbar, wedged it in the narrow gap between the door and the frame and pulled with all his strength. After several seconds, the door latch failed and the door sprang open. The two men held their weapons to their chests, ran through the door, and dove behind the large motor control center. They quickly got to their knees and looked from side to side. They were safe . . . for the moment.

* * *

More smoke rose from the van parked just five hundred yards from the boundary of the Superior Shores Nuclear Power Plant. The seventh rocket slammed into the side of the containment building just north of the turbine building. Small arms fire pierced the vans exterior, but the rocket launcher in the back of the van was unaffected. The guards fired on the van, trying to disable the launcher, but they didn't have the firepower to take it out.

Several guards were injured by small arms fire coming from

various points around the plant. They had to put a stop to the attack or the containment building would soon be breeched. Contaminated air would flow freely from the reactor core, if a meltdown occurred. If the attack continued, their worst nightmares would be realized.

* * *

In the admin building Sally Smith-Jones no longer looked calm, but she didn't appear to be afraid, either. Yusef Hassan still yelled how she and her family had destroyed the lives of his family.

Diane was confused. How could Evan Jones have anything to do with the murder of this man's son? As she listened, it became clear that Hassan wasn't talking about Evan, but some other man.

Then Sally had enough of this raging lunatic. She reached into the sleeve of her blouse and pulled out an eight inch stiletto blade. She lunged at Hassan. As she did, he waved his arm in a defensive move. The narrow tip of the blade caught him in the right shoulder, causing him to fall backwards. She withdrew the knife and lunged again, catching him below the collar bone.

Diane was horrified, then angry that this woman, after taking part in the murder of this man's son, might actually kill him, too. From Evan's desk, she snatched up a large, commercial stapler capable of stapling up to forty pages of paper. She took two steps towards Sally Smith-Jones, then swung the metal stapler, catching the woman in the back of the head.

The woman was dazed, but remained on her feet. She turned towards Diane, the stiletto in her hand. A shot rang out. Sally Smith-Jones fell in a heap at Diane's feet. Yusef Hassan, a smoking .38 revolver in his left hand, stood, still pointing the gun at the fallen woman's head. After a moment, when it was clear that she was dead, he dropped the gun and collapsed on the floor. He began weeping in deep, gasping sobs.

Chapter 43

The noise was unmistakable. At least one person had made it into the Emergency Reactor Cooling Room. But they would be too late. His job was nearly complete. All Ahmed Salil had to do was tighten two more bolts and open the isolation valve. Then the flow of coolant to the Great Lakes couldn't be stopped. But he had to stay focused. His loss of concentration earlier, thinking about Ingrid, had put the mission in jeopardy. He couldn't afford a lapse like that again. Then he heard a voice.

"Jimmy! We know what you're doing! You've got to stop!"

Evan's use of his American name angered Ahmed. He wanted this man to know how much he loathed him. How much he hated that Evan had tried to take over the position his real father still held.

"My name is not Jimmy Smith! My name is Ahmed Salil! You will remember my name after today! The whole world will remember this day!"

Evan's fear rose. In a harsh whisper, he said to Pat, "We have to rush him. He's going to contaminate the lake!"

"Wait a second! Let me see if there's a chance we can get to him."

Pat peaked around the corner of the motor control center and was greeted by a gunshot. It missed by a considerable margin, but the bullet ricocheted off of a steel pipe support and hit the panel next to Evan.

"That was damn close!"

Pat said, "We're not going to be able to reason with him. You go to that side of the electric panel; I'll stay on this side. When I fire a shot, you wait until he comes up to return fire. See if you can get a good shot off."

Evan nodded. He stayed on his hands and knees as he crawled to the edge of the electric panel. Pat waited as Evan moved into position. The steel grating that made up the flooring in this section of the plant bit into his hands and knees as he moved. Pat watched as Evan peered around the corner and across the room, trying to spot his stepson. He looked back at Pat, who nodded that he was ready. Evan nodded back.

Pat raised the M-16 to a firing position. He switched the selector switch to single shot mode. Firing a burst would send bullets bouncing all over the room. Some might come back and hit him or Evan. Now ready, he took a deep breath, nodded at Evan again and quickly leaned around the corner of the large, metal electrical panel. He found his target and pulled the trigger, releasing a single round.

The report was deafening in the enclosed room, even with the noise from machinery and fluid flow in the pipes. Ahmed Salil heard the bullet hit the pipe next to him, then it ricocheted against at least three other objects before coming to rest somewhere in the room. He raised his pistol, took aim in the direction the shot came from and fired. The bullet hit a large, steel panel that housed circuit breakers just inches from Pat.

When Evan saw Ahmed rise slightly to take his shot, he released a volley of three shots. He quickly ducked back behind the circuit breaker panel as two more shots from his stepson rang out. The bullets embedded in the concrete wall behind Pat and Evan.

Pat decided to try to reason with the young man. He signaled to Evan to be ready in case Ahmed became careless and rose from behind the piping.

"Ahmed! There's no escape. You won't leave here alive. Put down your weapon and show yourself. We can end this peacefully now. No one else needs to get hurt."

Salil laughed . "I don't plan to leave here alive! I never planned to leave here alive! Don't you understand? I will become the greatest martyr in history! Before this day is done, I will be in heaven! I will be a hero! My example will be used to raise a greater army against you! You are such fools!"

"Why did you look so sad when you killed your fiancé, then? I saw the pain in your eyes! Didn't she mean anything to you?"

This comment stung. He felt the pain in his chest and his breathing briefly became labored. He remembered her smiling face. Then the vision turned to the face he saw as he shot her, the face that didn't understand what he was doing. He momentarily lost all sense of purpose, until Sheik Al Salil's voice rang out in his head. *You will be a hero in Allah's army. You will be the greatest of Martyrs. Don't lose sight of your mission. The temptations of this country are great, but they are rooted in evil. Remember the words of our leader's Fatwa. They will guide you.*

Ahmed Salil picked up his gun and fired in rapid succession towards Pat's and Evan's position, then he dropped the gun and tightened the last two bolts on the elbow. Another minute and he would open the valve allowing water from the reactor core to pass into Lake Superior. His mission, the culmination of years of planning, was within his grasp.

* * *

As Nancy Brown and Madeline approached Superior Shores, they spoke to the Security Shift Supervisor about the status of their situation. Nancy's face was grim as he told her about the attack. Incoming missiles and small arms fire were continuing inbound on the plant from the west. He gave Nancy the approximate location of the intruders, but couldn't provide a count on the number of assailants.

"The missiles are coming in about thirty to forty seconds apart. And the small arms fire is coming in spurts, not continuously. But it's coming from several locations, so I think there must be at least three or four combatants."

Nancy's jaw was tight as she looked at the map unfolded on her lap. Madeline was driving since she knew the roads around the plant. They were being followed by four other vehicles with Agent Randall Scott and his FBI agents, the Anti-Terror Team, and two Bayfield County Sheriff four wheel drive vehicles. As the plant came into view, a puff of smoke rose from the forested area away from the plant's security fence.

"That must have been a rocket," Nancy said. A trail of smoke headed towards the site, followed by an explosion from the area around the containment building that housed the reactor. "They're trying to breech the containment wall. We're in for a real bad day if they succeed."

Madeline said, "I'm heading west at the next intersection. I think we can come up on them from the rear. Radio Scott and tell him to keep going straight and try to draw their fire so we can get a good spot on their exact locations."

"Roger that."

Nancy radioed Agent Scott, who acknowledged the plan without comment. He'd apparently had a change of heart about being in charge and was now happy to take orders.

Madeline took the corner at nearly fifty, throwing Nancy against the door of the Suburban. *She means business.*

* * *

"Are you sure?" The security shift supervisor couldn't believe what one of his guards had just radioed in. He'd said he'd only seen two assailants. The gun fire was sporadic because they kept moving to different positions and firing bursts, then moving on to the next spot.

"Yes, sir. I can see one perp moving now. I've had eyes on him for the last couple of minutes. When he moves, he looks like he's making a call on a cell phone. Then a missile is fired. I'm certain he's controlling the missiles, sir. The other perp is just firing what appears to be an AK-47."

"I'll be damned. Have the team concentrate their fire on the man with the cell phone. We need to stop the missiles. I want this guy terminated before he blows a hole in containment."

"Yes, sir!"

* * *

Sheik Al Salil moved into his fourth firing position behind a large pine tree. It gave him great cover, but also allowed him a clear view of the containment building where the rockets were blasting away at the reinforced concrete wall. Another two rocket blasts and the wall would be breeched. Taking up his position, he raised the AK-47 and sent a hail of bullets in the direction of the guard force along the plant's perimeter. He leaned the gun against the tree and started to run towards position number one. As he did, he pulled out his cell phone again, dialing as he moved through the wooded area.

As he dialed, he heard his partner, Haji Madu fire another burst from his AK-47. Salil smiled. The young man was a great asset. Madu had gladly taken part in the planning, kidnapping, and execution of Alex Corbin. Then when Yusef Hassan's stupid son, Ali couldn't stomach the beheading and exposed himself on film, Madu had eliminated that weak link as well, placing the body in a public location to distract the local sheriff. All this after he sent the NRC and the federal government off on a wild goose chase at the Erie Shores Nuclear Power Plant with his false claim of a problem at the facility. *Such fools. They believe anything.*

There, the rocket was set. He hit zero and watched as the seventh rocket raced across the sky, striking the building. *Just one more should do it.*

* * *

Nancy caught sight of the man running in the woods as they approached from the west. They left the vehicle at the road and moved in on foot. That there were only two assailants was good news, but they didn't want to assume that count was accurate. They moved as quickly and quietly as they could. When they were within one hundred yards, they saw a man stop and pick up an AK-47. He put the weapon against his shoulder and fired at guard positions in the plant. When the weapon emptied, he removed the spent magazine and replaced it with a fresh one. Methodically, he raised the weapon again and fired a fresh volley at the plant. Salil placed the gun against the tree, preparing to switch positions again.

Something on his right caught his attention. Nancy looked in that direction. Agent Scott and his team approached from the southeast. Salil picked up his AK-47, flipped the switch to full automatic, and fired in that direction. He slung the weapon over his shoulder and started to move away from the advancing force.

Nancy figured this was their best chance. She waved the signal that they should move in quickly. As they did, Salil opened his cell phone again. Realizing he was about to launch another rocket, Nancy dropped to one knee, took aim and fired.

Her team immediately followed suit and a hail storm of bullets struck Sheik Al Salil. As he fell, the cell phone dropped from his hand and landed just out of reach. He pulled himself across the ground towards the phone, straining against the pain that engulfed his body. His fingertips reached the cell. He pulled it to his face, the numbers now a blur as he tried to dial the arming code.

Nancy raised her weapon, preparing to shoot the terrorist again. Out of peripheral vision, she caught movement. She spun and let loose with a volley of shots, but there was no one in view. She turned her attention back to Salil where a member of her team and two deputy sheriffs removed the cell phone from his grip. They searched him and found a knife and a Glock 9mm, fully loaded with the safety off.

Salil bled from the chest and mouth as Anti-Terror Unit members tried to administer first aid. Salil was not cooperating, though he had little strength to resist. His wounds were severe, affecting multiple major organs. Even with all his bodily pain, he wore a smile, believing his son successful in unleashing radioactive contamination into the Great Lakes. *Allah be praised.* His entire body jerked once and he died.

Nancy ordered the team to fan out and search for other assailants. "The guard's supervisor said there were two. Let's find him."

Madeline came up next to her. "Nice shot. Smart decision."

"We couldn't risk trying to capture him. I sure hope they get his kid. We could be standing in the path of a radioactive plume right now and not even know it."

"Well, that's a happy thought."

Nancy flashed her a weak smile.

Just two hundred yards north of Nancy's team, Haji Madu watched as his mentor, Sheik Al Salil, was shot to death. His first impulse was to charge the infidels and try to kill them all. Certainly, there would be heavenly rewards for such bravery. But then, with Salil dead, he could move into a position of authority more quickly. He could become the Imam's right hand man. He would move on to greater battles and rewards.

Madu moved stealthily away from the force of men that would soon pursue him if he didn't move quickly. He remained low to the ground, his AK-47 strapped across his back. It took him only ten minutes to get to his Grand Marquis.

Within an hour he was heading into Northern Minnesota and the safe house Salil had set up. When he arrived, he would make his report to the Imam and await his new orders. He already had several recruits in mind to establish his new cell. *Allah be praised!*

Chapter 44

Pat knew they had little time left to act. The expression on Evan's pale face said it all. They had to move soon if they were to stop the release of massive amounts of radioactivity into the environment. If they failed, it would be a disaster of historic magnitude. The primary source of drinking water for millions of people in both Canada and the United States would be contaminated for generations. The only barrier between the deadly reactor coolant and the Great Lakes was the thin, steel disc of a six inch gate valve. Any second now Ahmed Salil could open the valve and unleash the highly radioactive poison into the greatest of the Great Lakes.

Thinking of a way to surprise Salil, Pat turned to Evan and pointed at the light. He motioned like he was shooting the light with a gun. Then he pointed to other lights. Evan didn't know exactly what Pat had in mind, but he figured Pat wanted him to start shooting out lights. Evan nodded. Starting with the light right over his stepson's head, he took the first shot.

Pat's heart beat hard. He thought about Diane. Was she okay? There was nothing he could do to protect her from her immediate threat, but if he and Evan failed to stop the young madman in the room with them, it wouldn't matter anyway. He put a hand to his chest and felt the spot where a bullet from another madman had nearly pierced his heart. If he had not been wearing a Kevlar vest that early morning just over a year ago, he would have been killed. But the vest had worked and he was here now with another job to do.

He bowed his head. "Dear God, protect her."

It was that simple. No time to elaborate. He hoped God was listening and understood the circumstances.

The shot from Evan's gun startled him. A large fluorescent light above the young terrorist shattered, glass raining down all around him. Several shards found their way into the young man's shirt collar. He dropped his wrench then jumped, trying to get the glass out. His movements only caused the jagged shards to cut into his lower neck and back. He cursed and moved around more. Then he realized his movements only made the glass cut deeper. He stopped moving. Then he laughed. After a few seconds, he laughed louder.

He shouted out, "You fools! You can't stop me! It is Allah's will that you should suffer at my hands!"

He picked up his wrench and went back to tightening the last bolt. Another shot rang out and shattered a second light. Another shot, and a third light went out. There were only three more lights to go. Pat joined in. Within seconds, the room was pitch black.

Pat crawled over to Evan and said, "In ten seconds, fire two shots towards Salil. Start counting now."

On his hands, knees, and stomach, Pat made his way along the walkway, moving towards a spot where he thought he would have a clear shot at the crazed engineer. Sweat dripped down his forehead into his eyes, stinging them, making Pat wipe his face with his shirt sleeve. He kept moving towards the position he'd chosen.

The piercing sound of another alarm filled the room. Machinery noise added to the confusion as Pat tried hard to count the seconds ticking away until Evan would take his best shot. Tension seized his body making it difficult to move, but he forced himself to keep moving down the walkway. The spot he'd chosen, before the lights went out, was on the grating around the outer edge of the room. There was a hand rail that he planned to use to steady the M-16. He hoped it would give him the best opportunity to get off multiple shots. He counted *five, six, seven . . .*

The M-16 hit the handrail and made a loud clang. Pat quickly rolled on his side, hoping to put several feet between him and the point where the gun came in contact with the rail. He heard movement from where Salil was working. He thought he heard several clicks, but no shots rang out.

Evan heard the noise and realized Pat was the source. He was on the count of eight. In a near panic he quickly said "nine, ten" and fired two shots at his stepson as Pat instructed.

The muzzle flash illuminated the entire room for a split second. Salil was in Pat's sights but the metal piping and steel mounts made a shot from this position extremely dangerous. He couldn't wait any longer. He pulled the trigger three times in rapid succession. In the muzzle flashes he saw that Salil had moved to the valve. At least one bullet pinged off a pipe and ricocheted around the room. But he heard Salil yell in pain.

Pat wasn't sure that his shots were fatal. With so much at risk he knew he had to fire again. He took aim into the darkness. As he prepared to pull the trigger a single shot rang out from Salil's pistol.

The flash lit up the room, causing Pat to flinch and lose his aim. Salil was pointing his gun at Evan. He quickly recovered and took aim at the spot where Salil stood and fired three more shots. He heard Salil yell again.

The plant alarm stopped. The room fell into an eerie silence. The acrid scent of cordite filled the room.

Another shot rang out, this time from Evan's gun. Pat heard another groan. Then all he heard was the sound of motors and fluids flowing through pipes. He kept his gun leveled at where Salil had stood, though he couldn't see him in this pitch black room. He wasn't sure if Salil was dead, disabled, or still working to open the valve. He had to move quickly, but cautiously. As he came closer, several battery powered emergency lights came on. Pat was within ten feet of the crazed man. He was slumped over the valve, still trying to open it, even as blood poured from the left side of his chest.

Pat yelled, "Stop!"

Salil didn't even flinch. He kept applying pressure to the valve's hand wheel. In the dim light of the battery powered emergency lights, Pat saw the hand wheel turning ever so slightly.

He yelled again, "Stop, or I'll—"

Pat jumped at the sound of a gunshot from Evan's Glock. Salil's body tensed. As if in slow motion, he slid off the valve and onto the pipe containing the extremely hot primary coolant. Pat heard the sizzle of burning skin. Finally, Salil's body slid to the ground.

Evan yelled to Pat, "Make sure that valve is shut!"

Pat kept his eyes on Salil as he ran to the valve and grabbed for the hand wheel. He yelped in pain as the hot metal wheel burned his hands. Ripping off his shirt, he used it to protect his hands as he grabbed the hand wheel a second time.

He turned it clockwise, all the time reciting, "Righty tighty, righty tighty."

The valve moved only a quarter turn. He felt the disc mate up firmly with the seat. He took a deep breath and put as much pressure on the valve's hand wheel as he could. It didn't budge. Satisfied that the valve was closed tight, Pat took another deep breath and looked down. Salil, smiling, looked up, pointing his gun at Pat's head.

Pat's heart pounded as he thought of Diane and his children. There was no room to run this time. Pipes and supports were everywhere.

Without a word, Salil squeezed the trigger, but nothing happened. The gun didn't make a sound. Salil tried to squeeze the trigger again, but the gun had jammed. His eyes rolled back in his head and his body went slack.

Pat's heart nearly exploded as the tension peaked. Evan appeared next to him, pointing his smoking 9mm at his dead stepson. Evan's hand shook violently. Tears streamed down his face. After several seconds, he let his arm fall to his side.

It was over.

* * *

Pat and Evan made their way to the Radiologically Restricted Area entrance where they had to undergo an extensive check for radioactive contamination. The radiation monitors in the Emergency Reactor Cooling Room indicated that levels were rising, but so far, remained below legal limits. Shutting the valve had prevented highly radioactive fluid from flowing into the room and beyond into Lake Superior.

Operators in the Control Room surmised the reactor core had sustained significant fuel damage, so the plant would remain shut down. It would not be running again anytime soon, but the Chequamegon Bay and Lake Superior were safe.

After a brief cleanup, decontamination, and an extensive survey for any radioactive materials on their clothes or body, Pat and Evan were free to leave the restricted area. Pat's hands were treated for the burns he had sustained while shutting the valve that was the sole barrier between the primary coolant and the lake. Both men were taken to the administration building for questioning. Members from a number of federal agencies, including the FBI, the Anti-terror Unit, and the young NRC resident inspector quizzed them for nearly an hour. There would be more questions, but for now they were free to go. The fact was, they were heroes. They'd been through a traumatic ordeal and needed time to rest.

As Pat left the small conference room where he was questioned, Diane was coming out of a similar room down the hall. She looked pale and exhausted. She stopped in her tracks when she caught sight of him, then started in his direction. The closer she got, the faster her steps became.

He took several steps towards her, afraid she was going to hit him. Then she wrapped her arms around his neck and gave him a bear hug.

"I thought you were dead. No one would tell me anything except that the plant was safe."

Pat held her tight. "I'm so sorry. I put you in danger."

"Shh. You couldn't have known." She paused. "Just hold me."

And he did.

* * *

Evan loaded Diane's suitcase into the back of the Ford Explorer as Pat loaded his own right next to it. They stayed two nights longer than they'd planned, partly because Sheriff Wymer requested it. Pat wasn't sure he could drive around the lake with all his bruises and the slowly healing burns on his hands anyway. But they decided to continue their trip around the lake despite the birth of their new niece, Danielle Alena McKinney. After talking with Joe and Lisa, they all agreed they could finish their planned trip and still be home in plenty of time to enjoy the newest member of the family. Besides, the grandmothers were pretty much taking over the household. As it was, Lisa could hardly get her hands on her daughter.

Evan gave Diane a long hug. He said quietly, "I'm sorry. I had no idea about my wife and stepson. You could have been hurt or worse."

"Like I told Pat, you couldn't have known. They had everyone fooled."

"Thank God you weren't hurt. I would never have been able to live with myself."

They released. She looked Evan in the eyes and said, "You saved countless lives. You had to decide in an instant between your stepson and everyone else. That took courage, but enough about this whole episode. Thank you for letting us stay with you in this beautiful home."

Pat spoke up. "One thing for sure, it wasn't boring."

Evan smiled. But it had a large dose of sadness built in. He'd been thinking over the last two days he might sell the place. He'd always liked Montana and Wyoming. Maybe it was time to move. He had his retirement income and he'd make a great profit from the sale of the house. His parents had already given their blessing after hearing the horrific details of the past week.

Diane climbed in the passenger side of the Explorer. Evan and Pat walked around to the driver's side. Pat put out his hand for a shake. Evan grabbed his hand and pulled him close. Pat winced at the pain from his still sore hands.

Evan said, "Sorry about the hands." He paused then continued, "You sure know how to step in a pile, my friend."

Pat put his free arm around Evan's shoulder. "It's a curse. This time I put Diane in danger. This was supposed to be a relaxing little trip around a quiet lake."

The men released from their embrace. Evan took a deep breath. "You saved my life, man. I can never repay you."

"You already did. You helped stop what could have been the worst terrorist attack this country has ever known. You don't owe anyone anything. If anything, I owe you." Pat paused then said, "You stay in touch and let me know what you plan to do. If you ever want to visit Florida, we have plenty of room."

"I'd like that."

The two men stared at each other for several seconds. Then Pat stuck out his hand again. They shook hands one last time. Pat climbed in behind the wheel. All three of them waived as Pat backed into the turn-around in Evan's drive. They pulled away down the long driveway. Pat lowered his window and waived again until Evan disappeared from the rear-view mirror.

Pat and Diane looked at each other and took a deep breath. For a moment neither knew what to say. It had been an exhausting three days. They were finally on their relaxing trip around the greatest of the Great Lakes.

Chapter 45

The grill was hot. The scent of burgers, hotdogs, and Italian sausage filled the hot, Florida air on Joe and Lisa's covered patio. Joe was in charge of the grill, making sure the cooking was done right. Sean helped, manning the water sprayer so the flames didn't shoot up too high and burn the food.

Danielle Alena McKinney was nearly asleep in her mother's arms. She'd been passed around from the Grandmas to Aunt Diane, to Nancy Brown, even to Pat for a brief time. Joe and Lisa's two week old daughter was exhausted and ready for a nap. Lisa, too, was tired but glowing with pride.

After some prodding from Emma McKinney, Joe told the crowd he and Lisa had set their wedding date. In two more weeks they'd be Mr. and Mrs. Joe McKinney. After a round of cheers, hoots, whistles, and clinking of glasses and beer bottles, the small crowd settled into conversation.

Pat and Diane talked about their upcoming trip to the Magic Kingdom. Lisa apologized for not being able to fulfill their promise to Sean and Anna.

Diane looked at Lisa, holding her sleeping baby girl and said, "I think you've got enough on your plate. Now you've got two babies to take care of." She glanced over towards the grill at Joe.

Lisa smiled. "I think Joseph is going to be a great father. He's already so protective of Danielle and me. Before I got pregnant, he would challenge me to running races and weight-lifting and swimming races. Now he wants me to live in a cushioned bubble. I can't wait to get my strength back. I need to get back into shape. Plus, I want to whip him again at a few of our contests."

Pat and Diane looked at each other, then back to Lisa. Diane said, "Lisa, you look great. Don't rush your recovery. Trust me."

Nancy and Hatch were away from the crowd, comparing notes about the attacks on the power plant and the refinery. They also talked about the five other coordinated attacks that happened simultaneously around the world. The analysis would take months to complete. Nancy figured she'd be busy for years tracking down the perpetrators.

Hatch said, "I still don't get how Victoria Garcia is associated with these Islamic cats. I mean, she's not Muslim or from the Middle East. Apparently, she met up with this Salil dude somehow and formed an alliance."

"We're still trying to figure that one out. But you're right. A big piece of that puzzle is missing."

"So I take it you kinda like this terrorist huntin' stuff."

Nancy smiled at his accent. "You have a way with words. But yeah, I like it. Plus I have a great boss and a great team. So I plan to stick with it, for a while anyway. At least, until a bigger challenge or a better offer comes along."

He wondered what she meant by a better offer, but didn't pursue it. She might be setting some kind of man trap with a statement like that.

"I guess I'll have to visit you in the big city sometime. But in the mean time, how'd you like to visit the swamp?"

Her smile grew. "I'd like that, I think." She paused then added, "I mean I'd visit you anywhere, Mr. Hatcher."

Hatch smiled. All he said was, "Shucks."

His cell phone rang. When he looked at the display, he didn't recognize the number. He looked at Nancy and shrugged. He opened the phone and said, "Yo."

"Ola, Senor Hatch. Do you know who this is?"

"Well, Senorita, I didn't expect to ever hear from you again, not in this lifetime anyway." He limped away from Nancy, who frowned as he turned his back on her. His broken leg was in a walking cast, but it still hurt when he had to move.

He spoke quietly into the phone, "To what do I owe the pleasure?"

"I just wanted to tell you that I'm sorry about your friend Danny. He was a sweet man and didn't deserve to die like that."

"That sure seems hollow considering the number of innocent lives you planned to destroy. I mean, at least four people are dead."

"Yes. Well, they were collateral damage. All I wanted to do was make the men pay . . ."

". . . who killed your brother, Javier."

There was stunned silence on the line. *How did he know?*

"Senorita, ya still there?"

"Si, Senor, I'm here. You've been doing your homework."

"Si, I mean, yeah." He paused. "Ya can't keep killin' people just cause you think they did you wrong. Those dudes who killed your brother, what do they have to do with Texas Star?"

"The old man, the one who hit Javier first, he's a majority owner of the company. His punk boy is a major shareholder, too, all because of his daddy. And you've got a lot of nerve telling me about vengeance, Senor Hatch, after what you did to those two boys who killed your family."

"Touché. I guess I'm not the only one doing homework." *This woman is sharp.* "You're right, Miss Victoria. There's a saying about a pot and a kettle that applies here. I'm just sayin' you can't keep killin'. It'll destroy you. It eats you from the inside"

He took a deep breath, unsure if he should continue talking to her. But he felt some respect for this woman. She could have turned her back on her family and lived her life in fear. Instead, she tracked down the men who destroyed her family. She was just looking for justice of some kind and she knew she wouldn't get it in any court. Then he thought about Danny's apartment sitter, little Alisa Lopez. Was she also collateral damage? She wasn't hurt physically, but Danny's death tore her apart. She was strong willed and had spunk so maybe she would recover and become stronger. Only time would tell. Hatch wouldn't be there to find out. Sadness touched his heart.

As Hatch's thoughts were on Alisa Lopez, Victoria thought about Marianna and Gina, the two girls from the neighborhood by the Texas Star Refinery. She'd seen them right before she drove away from the failed attack. She was happy they were safe and even waved to them from her Corvette as she left the neighborhood. Victoria smiled. She was brought back to reality by the sound of Hatch's voice.

"Miss Victoria, you seem like a real smart lady. But you can't bring your brother back. If I could help you get even I would, but getting' even in your eyes won't settle the score, it just ups the ante. Your enemies see it as you one-upin 'em. So where does it end?"

Victoria was silent for a few moments. She had to admit, Hatch was right. "You make a good point, amigo. In another life, you and I might have made a good team. I'm afraid that isn't to be. I have unfinished business and you can't be a part of it."

"I'm sorry to hear that, Miss Victoria. You are a beautiful woman with brains. That makes you both desirable and dangerous. I hope I'm not on your list."

She smiled. "Not on my bad list. I wish you a long and happy life, Senor Hatch. And I truly am sorry about your friend. Vasquez killed Danny because he was jealous of him. I made the mistake of paying attention to Danny and that hurt Ricardo's pride. That was not part of the plan."

"I wish I could say I forgive you, but I can't."

"Good-bye, Hatch."

"Wait. Before you go, can you tell me how you met Salil?"

"It was a chance meeting. We were both looking for weapons and the dealer introduced us. It was an odd relationship. You know how Muslim men are. But it worked for both of us, at least at the start. He had to try to dominate the planning and I wasn't having any of it. No matter. He won't bother anyone ever again."

"And I hope you won't either, Miss Victoria."

For several seconds, no other words were spoken. Hatch heard the click of the phone disconnecting. He turned back towards Nancy, who was eyeing him closely. He knew he'd have some explaining to do.

He walked back over to Nancy. "Before I tell you, let me grab a couple beers. I need one after that."

Nancy nodded.

Diane and Pat sat reading their son's new journal. He'd only had it for a few weeks and he already had over forty pages written. They were pleased when he proudly showed it to them and explained how much he enjoyed writing in it. Sean actually smiled, which was a rare event. He said he had to get back to helping Uncle Joe with the grill.

"I have to help Uncle Joe because he's going to teach me how to shoot a gun."

With that, Sean ran off to help his uncle. His parents sat and watched him, their jaws hanging open.

After reading for just a few minutes, they turned to each other, not knowing what to say. The journal was exceptionally well written. His handwriting was nearly perfect, the punctuation superior to most high school students.

The pages were filled with thoughts, hopes, prayers, and fears. The emotions of their nearly seven year old son leapt from the pages.

One thing they were happy to see was that he expressed happiness, which was something Sean didn't convey outwardly very often. He always appeared to be analyzing everything and everyone. As they read further, his words softened. Maybe the journal was a good thing. It seemed to provide an outlet for his thoughts and emotions. It wasn't good for him to be so young and have so much conflict bottled up.

Then they got to the most recent entry where he talked about Pat's gun. He wrote about how he thought it was a good idea to have a gun so that you could fight off 'the bad people' who wanted to hurt his family.

> *I have to make sure we're safe. So I have to learn how to use a gun. Uncle Joe says I can't do that until Mom says it's okay. I hope she lets Uncle Joe teach me. I'm afraid it will be too late if I don't learn real soon. I know I can help Dad and Uncle Joe. Anna and Mom and Aunt Lisa and Cousin Danielle and Grandma Emma and Grandma Ann need us to protect them. But if the bad guys ever hurt anyone in my family, I will find them and I will kill them.*

Pat stared at the journal, at a loss for words. Diane gasped, covering her mouth with one hand. She looked up at Joe with a laser-like stare.

Joe turned from the grill towards the small gathering. With a big smile on his face, he yelled, "Burgers are ready!" Then he saw the look on Diane's face and thought, *I'm dead.*

Chapter 46

The Mint wasn't a private club, but the average person on the street didn't know the ritzy, exclusive lounge even existed. It catered to the wealthiest of Houston's young millionaires. Even the "greeters" at the door looked wealthy. They were also the gatekeepers to *The Mint*. They doubled as bouncers, though the need seldom arose.

To get past the gatekeepers you had to look the part and pay the price.

Victoria Garcia strode up to the door and flashed a perfect smile. It was a smile that said, *I belong here; these are my people*. She opened her Louis Vuitton clutch and pulled out a crisp one hundred dollar bill. She handed the bill to the man on the right.

He smiled and pushed her hand back, refusing her offer of a bribe. He tilted his head towards the entrance and said, "Go ahead."

Her smile brightened a bit more. Without saying a word, she headed inside, went right to the bar, and ordered a margarita with Patron tequila. The only lights in this part of the lounge came from fluorescent tubes under the glass shelves holding the vast array of liquor bottles. The bar's surface was a rich, dark mahogany with a highly polished brass edge.

As the bartender made her drink, she searched the lounge, allowing her eyes to adjust to the darkness. Cigar smoke hung in the air. Most of the women wore dresses that were worth the average person's house payment and their shoes worth a car payment or two. The men's Armani suits were perfect even after a day "at the office." She noticed a number of men looking her way, but she wasn't interested in just any man. Just like at Loco Pedro's, she had one specific man in mind.

The majority of the patrons in the club this evening were from Texas Oil, owners of the Texas Star Refinery. The company had just made a "deal in principle" to merge with another oil conglomerate. If approved, the combined company would become the largest oil company in the United States. The drinks were flowing and the smiles were bright. In their heads, the men were counting their million dollar bonuses, and the women were picturing the additions to their diamond jewelry collections and their wardrobes.

The bartender returned with her drink. As she went to put a twenty dollar bill on the counter, the bartender said, “It’s covered.”

Like the doorman, the bartender tilted his head towards the end of the bar. A handsome man of about thirty-five was looking her way, smiling. She raised her glass and smiled. He wasn’t the man she wanted, but maybe he would be useful to her. She walked down to the end of the bar, and flashed a brilliant smile. He swiveled the high, cushioned chair next to his so that she could easily slide in.

Once she was comfortably seated and facing the bar, Victoria placed her clutch on the bar and regarded the man who paid for her first drink of the evening. He was as handsome up close as he was from across the room. He had light hair, perfectly cut and groomed so that every strand was in place. With the limited lighting, she couldn’t tell exactly what color it was, but the color looked consistent, most likely due to hair coloring. He had prominent cheek bones and a smile that was confident, approaching arrogant. She waited, allowing him to make the first move.

He spoke as if he owned the place. For all she knew, he might. “I’ve never seen you in here before. What’s your name?”

“Victoria.”

He tilted his head back slightly at her less than complete answer. “Do you have a last name, Victoria?”

“Yes, but first, you are . . .?”

“Terrence Worthington.” He waited with an expectant grin.

“Garcia. You haven’t seen me in here before because this is the first time I’ve been here. A close friend recommended that I try it. He should be meeting me here soon.”

“Will he mind that we’re talking?

“No, he’s just a friend.”

Terrence gave her that arrogant smile. She smiled back, but she was already beginning to tire of this little game. She had business to tend to and didn’t want this self-important twit to get the wrong idea.

He asked, “What do you think of *The Mint* so far?”

“I like the drinks. They’re priced right, too.”

“I’m glad you’re evening is off to a good start. So what does a beautiful woman like you do for a living?"

"I buy things. Then I sell them."

At her vague answer, he put his hand to his chin, gave it a massage and shot her a skeptical look. "So, what sort of things do you buy and sell?"

She took a sip of her margarita , then set the glass back on the counter. "Well, for one, I buy and sell weapons."

Terence laughed. "You're kidding."

Without a hint of irritation or a change in her expression she said, "No, I'm not. Someone has to and there is excellent money to be made, so that's one of the things I broker."

He stopped laughing when he saw she was serious. He looked away for a second. He appeared nervous about this latest revelation. Victoria took the opportunity to quickly scan the crowd. She still didn't see the man she was most interested in, but she couldn't stand to sit here with Terrence any longer.

She swiveled her chair away from him and stepped down. "Listen, my friend will be here soon. Thanks for the drink." She turned away from Terrence with the perfect hair, and strode confidently across the lounge. She didn't look back to see if he was following her with his eyes, because she couldn't care less.

As Victoria made her way past tables where people talked openly about the coming merger and other topics of less importance, she looked at the faces of the men, hoping to find her person of interest. She stopped at the edge of the seating area to take a sip of her margarita. As she raised her glass, she saw him. He looked directly at her. A cold chill ran through her. A sensation she hadn't felt in years momentarily seized her. Was it fear? Or just a shot of adrenaline? She smiled. It was party time.

* * *

Two hours later, sipping only her second margarita, Victoria listened to the man talk about all his great accomplishments. She paid close attention, as if she hung on his every word. She smiled when he tried to be charming. She laughed at his pitiful, racist jokes. She even touched his hand in a soft and loving way.

While Victoria nursed her drink, Jebediah Walker Marshall, III drank eight tumblers of Macallan Scotch whisky on the rocks. He was beginning to slur his words, though he appeared to still be in control.

It was time to make her move.

"So Jeb, how would you like to see my condo?"

Jeb's smile broadened. Without a word he pushed his chair back and stood. He reached down and placed his hands on the table to keep from stumbling. Victoria pushed her seat back and took him by the arm. "Let me help."

He smiled again, trying to look charming to her. She smiled back, knowing she was in control. The small dose of the date rape drug, GHB that she had slipped into his drink, was working. As long as she could get him to her car without him falling, the evening was going to be grand indeed.

When they got to the entrance to *The Mint*, Jeb stumbled and nearly fell. The greeter who earlier let Victoria in for free grabbed Jeb's arm to help steady him.

He said, "Hey Jeb, take it easy." He looked at Victoria and asked, "Can I get you two a cab?"

"No, that won't be necessary. But could you help me get him to my car? I'll make sure he gets home alright."

The greeter looked at her with an odd expression, then said, "His wife may not like that idea. Are you sure?"

Thinking quickly, she replied, "I'll be bringing him back tomorrow for his car. He'll have to do the explaining to his wife." She flashed a mischievous smile.

It worked. The greeter didn't much care for Jebediah Walker Marshall III anyway. The arrogant bastard regularly cheated on his wife. He didn't care if Jeb caught hell or not, so he helped Victoria load him into her bright red Corvette.

He said, "Nice car."

"Thanks." Then she peeled out of the parking lot.

Jeb was still conscious as Victoria sped along the roads of Houston. As they left the downtown, he asked in a highly slurred voice, "Where do you live?"

Victoria was no longer smiling that bright, happy smile. "You'll see real soon."

As she drove along, Jeb recognized the streets as ones he had driven many times over the years. It gave him a sense of comfort until, in his hazy state of mind, he remembered he was supposed to be going to Victoria's condo.

He said in his slurred voice, "You live in the same part of town as my old man. What a bastard." He paused. His face twisted into an expression that bordered on contempt. He mumbled, "My old man . . ."

"What about your old man?"

He laughed, but it wasn't like he was laughing at a joke. It was filled with sarcasm, even disdain, apparently for his father.

"My old man used to beat me and my brother if we let the family down in any way. Like the time he beat me for losing a wrestling match in junior high. Or the time I threw an interception at the end of a football game."

His speech was so slurred that he nearly spat the words. But Victoria wasn't listening to his whining. She was concentrating on the drive. It was nearly 10:45 P.M. and she wanted to be sure they arrived at their destination before 11:00 P.M.

* * *

When Victoria knocked on the door to the mansion, she wondered if anyone would answer. The hired help was gone for the day. The man and lady of the house usually retired right after the evening news, so they should still be awake. The grounds around the house were lit with all types of accent lighting, but the house looked dark inside. She was afraid the occupants were either already in bed, or were not at home.

Jeb was at her side, though he wasn't standing completely under his own power. Victoria held him up by putting his arm around her shoulder while she grabbed his wrist. She also leaned him against the door jamb while she rang the doorbell and used the large brass knocker.

He asked, "Why are we at my old man's house?"

After several minutes, she was ready to drop him there and give up. Just as she was about to leave Jeb where they stood, the door locks were released and the door swung open.

A woman looked at the couple standing in her doorway. She recognized her son, and gave him a look that said, *Not again*. Then she looked at Victoria with an appraising look.

Victoria spoke first. "I'm sorry, Mrs. Marshall. He must have really had more to drink than I realized."

"And your name is . . .?"

"Victoria Garcia. I met your son earlier this evening at the merger party. I work for Texas Oil at the Lake Jackson office."

Jeb Marshall's mother continued to stare at Victoria, trying to determine if this woman was lying or if she really was an employee. The Marshalls were majority shareholders and her husband had been on the Board of Directors for years, but they knew very few of the company's employees, especially if their title was below Vice President.

Finally, when Victoria was about to say that Jeb was getting heavy, Shirley Marshall said, "Let's get him inside. It's not like he hasn't done this before."

Relieved, Victoria helped Jebediah step over the threshold and into the large entry. Mrs. Marshall got on the opposite side of her son and helped support him as they made their way into the living room.

A cough caught Victoria's attention. An elderly looking man sat in a wheelchair near the fireplace with a blanket across his lap. He coughed again. It sounded like a man who'd smoked all his life and was now paying the price of diseased lungs and perpetual shortness of breath. When he looked up at the trio, his face wrinkled from years in the sun and pale, nearly gray from a lack of oxygen. His thick mustache was nearly white. It was the three inch scar under his left eye that caught Victoria's attention. It was him.

Victoria and Mrs. Marshall helped Jeb to an overstuffed seat. She stood and said, "I left his things in the car. I'll get them and be right back."

Mrs. Marshall said, "You needn't bother, dear. I'm sure you're tired."

"It's no problem at all. It'll just take a second."

She turned and was out the door in a flash. When she returned, she held a brown paper grocery bag in one hand and a pair of polished boots in the other.

Mrs. Marshall said, "Just leave them on the table, dear. We can take care of—"

"Shut up!"

The rebuke was loud and crisp. It stunned the older woman. "I beg your pardon?"

"I said, *Shut up!* And I mean now." The senior Jeb Marshall looked up from his wheelchair, anger in his aged eyes. He coughed loudly and tried to clear his throat enough to scold this insolent, young woman. He coughed again before he could say a word.

Victoria sat down and put on the boots with the hard, pointed tips. She stood and reached into the brown paper bag and pulled out a .40 caliber Glock with a silencer affixed to the end. Mrs. Marshall gasped.

"What is the meaning of this?"

Victoria pointed the pistol at Mrs. Marshall. In a calm, calculated voice, she said, "Your loving, caring husband and your charming, alcoholic son murdered my brother. They beat him with their fists. Then they kicked him with their boots until he was dead. But that's not the worst part. When they were finished, they threw his body in the Rio Grande, like a piece of garbage."

Mrs. Marshall's mouth hung open in horror and disbelief. Whether it was true or not, they were all in grave danger from this angry, but very calm woman.

While Victoria spoke, the elder Jeb Marshall's right eye opened wide, his left eye still just a slit. He was old and his body was failing, but his mind was still sharp. He coughed, then said in a gravelly voice, "So, ya'll just goin' to walk into my house and kill us all?"

Victoria smiled. She liked that the old man was aware of what was happening. "No. I'm just going to kill the two people closest to you."

With her free hand, she grabbed the drunken and drugged Jeb Marshall by the hair and pulled him to the ground. His mother shrieked. His father coughed hard.

Victoria smiled at the man sprawled, helpless, on the carpet. She looked up at the old man, stepped back and kicked his son with the point of her boot, square in the ribs. The thud, coupled with a groan and a stream of air expelled from his lungs, made for a sickening combination of sounds. Mrs. Marshall stood to come to the aid of her son, but Victoria leveled the gun at her head and shouted, "Sit!"

She did, watching her son writhe in pain. She put her hands to her face as tears streamed down her cheeks. The old man slowly reached for the fireplace tools and was about to raise the log poker when Victoria pointed the gun at him and pulled the trigger. The gun made a spit sound as the bullet flew across the room and caught him in the left shoulder. He dropped the poker, yelped in pain, and began to cough anew.

Victoria turned her attention back to the younger man on the floor. She kicked him in the head once, then again, then a third time. She repeated her kicking until his head bled profusely. She gave him one last kick in the ribs.

Young Jeb was still breathing, but his breaths were mixed with the sound of liquid as blood began to fill his throat and lungs. He was dying a slow, painful death. But Victoria was growing weary of how long it was taking him to die. She pointed the gun at his head, then looked up and stared directly at the old man. He was coughing continuously now. She pulled the trigger. The bullet entered young Jeb's skull, killing him instantly. Victoria only wished that there was a cesspool nearby where she could dump the body.

When she looked back at the senior Jeb Marshall, still coughing, she could see losing his son wasn't that much of a loss. But when she leveled the gun at his wife, his one eye showed the complete horror that seized him, causing the old man's whole body to tense. Maybe he thought that she would stop at killing his son. Now he realized that this woman was totally insane.

He suddenly remembered the little voice in the desert. *Javier!*

Victoria saw the recognition in his eyes. Satisfied, she smiled, turned to his wife and said, "I'm very sorry."

She leveled the gun at the senior Jeb Marshall's wife. She looked into the woman's eyes and saw the resignation. In her last moments on earth, she'd been told that her son and husband were cold blooded killers. Did she believe it? Victoria couldn't tell, but she saw that this woman wasn't willing to fight or plead for her life. Maybe she realized her easy life had come at too high a price, the price of another human's blood. Victoria paused for a moment longer, her smile disappearing. Her hand began to shake. The constant coughing from the old man in the wheelchair caused her to tense. She took a deep breath and pulled the trigger, sending a bullet into the woman's heart.

Death was instantaneous.

Victoria turned back to Jebediah Marshall II who was coughing non-stop now. He clutched at his throat, then his chest. His good eye was wide open, staring at the woman who'd just killed his wife. He leaned forward and fell out of his wheelchair. His heart exploded.

Victoria's body went slack, her arms hanging loosely at her side. She took several deep breaths. Then, in a calm, methodical manner, she dropped the gun, removed the boots, and changed into the casual clothes she'd brought in the paper bag. The hate had evaporated, but it left a cavern in her soul. The hunger she'd felt to exact revenge on these murderers was gone. Now that the deed was done, she felt no satisfaction. She took one last look at the dead, thinking she should cry, or laugh, or have some kind of emotion. There was nothing but a void.

* * *

Hatch sat on the front porch swing at his cabin in Moniac, Georgia. The early morning heat already climbing, promising a day where sweat would ooze from one's pores, a day best spent in an air-conditioned room. He'd received a plain, white envelope in the mail with no return address. He looked at the postmark: Del Rio, Texas. He ripped it open and removed the postcard-sized piece of paper. The handwriting was perfect.

You were right. Revenge is not so sweet, but at least the killing is over. I hope you and your friends find peace, Senor Hatch.

Hatch looked out at the marsh and the tall cypress trees draped in Spanish moss. Nancy Brown walked out the front door of his cabin with two longneck beers. She handed one to Hatch and sat next to him on the glider.

She asked, "Who's the card from?"

Without a word, he handed her the note. She read it in silence then leaned her head against his shoulder.

In a sad, quiet voice, he said, "I'm sorry to say it, but she's wrong. As long as humans are livin', the killin' will never be over."

Pete ‘P.J.’ Grondin, born the seventh of twelve children, moved around a number of times when he was young; from Sandusky, Ohio to Bay City, Michigan, then to Maitland and Zellwood, Florida before marrying and returning to Sandusky, OH.

After his service in the US Navy in the Nuclear Power Program serving on the ballistic missile submarine, Pete returned to his hometown of Sandusky, OH where he was elected to the Sandusky City Commission, serving a single term. In addition to writing murder mystery/suspense novels, he works as an application process specialist in the IT department of a major electric utility.

His current novels are *A Lifetime of Vengeance, A Lifetime of Deception, A Lifetime of Exposure, A Lifetime of Terror, and A Lifetime of Betrayal.*

Loconeal Publishing

47686083R00152

Made in the USA
Charleston, SC
15 October 2015